Epps

PRAISE FOR

THE RULE of FOUR

"One part *The Da* ... *e Rose*
and one part *A Sep* ... good
yarn as it is an exce ... hart,
swift, multitextured ... s and informs."
—*San Francisco Chronicle*

"An extremely erudite thriller . . . ingenious . . . The real treat here is the process of discovery." —*New York Times*

"This debut packs all the esoteric information of *The Da Vinci Code* . . . with lovely writing reminiscent of Donna Tartt's *The Secret History* . . . a compulsively readable novel." —*People* (Critic's choice)

"Cerebral, scholarly, exciting, intriguing . . . an Indiana Jones–style hunt for hidden treasure thickly overlaid with Ivy League scholarship." —*Milwaukee Journal Sentinel*

"A masterfully complicated mystery, a powerfully touching romance and a cultural account of the Renaissance, as well as a bittersweet coming-of-age story . . . Riveting, poignant and intensely intimate, *The Rule of Four* is a thinking person's thriller of the highest order." —*BookPage*

"Caldwell and Thomason have created an eager and sympathetic cast. . . . Like Donna Tartt, the authors capture the cloying prettiness of college campuses and the way that beauty can foretell danger. . . . A charming and compulsively readable novel." —*Minneapolis Star Tribune*

THE RULE *of* FOUR

Ian Caldwell

& Dustin Thomason

A DELL BOOK

THE RULE OF FOUR
A Dell Book

PUBLISHING HISTORY
The Dial Press hardcover edition published May 2004
Dell export edition / February 2005

Published by Bantam Dell
A Division of Random House, Inc.
New York, New York

This is a work of fiction. Names, characters, places, and incidents either
are the product of the author's imagination or are used fictitiously. Any
resemblance to actual persons, living or dead, events, or locales is
entirely coincidental.

The "Anonymous Elegy to the Reader" in this novel's epigraph is taken
from Francesco Colonna's *Hypnerotomachia Poliphili*, translated by
Joscelyn Godwin (©1999), and reprinted with grateful acknowledgment
to Thames & Hudson publishers.

Map © 2004 by Jeffrey L. Ward

Image of book © Howard Sokol/Index Stock Imagery
Background cover images courtesy of Leon Battista Alberti and Liane
Lefaivre, editors of *The Hypnerotomachia Poliphili*/The MIT Press
Cover design by Belina Huey and Aenee Kim

Book design by Virginia Norey

Library of Congress Catalog Card Number: 2003070124

ISBN 0-440-29640-4

Printed in the United States of America
Published simultaneously in Canada

www.bantamdell.com

OPM 10 9 8 7

For our parents

Historical Note

The *Hypnerotomachia Poliphili* is one of the most trea-
sured and least understood books of early Western
printing. Scholars continue to debate the identity and
intent of the *Hypnerotomachia*'s mysterious author,
Francesco Colonna. Only in December of 1999, five
hundred years after the original text was printed, and
months after the events depicted in *The Rule of Four*,
did the first complete English translation of the
Hypnerotomachia appear in print.

Gentle reader, hear Poliphilo tell of his dreams,
   Dreams sent by the highest heaven.
You will not waste your labour, nor will listening irk you,
   For this wonderful work abounds in so many things.
If, grave and dour, you despise love-stories,
   Know, I pray, that things are well ordered herein.
You refuse? But at least the style, with its novel language,
   Grave discourse and wisdom, commands attention.
If you refuse this, too, note the geometry,
   The many ancient things expressed in Nilotic signs . . .
Here you will see the perfect palaces of kings,
   The worship of nymphs, fountains and rich banquets.
The guards dance, dressed in motley, and the whole
   Of human life is expressed in dark labyrinths.

—Anonymous Elegy to the Reader,
   Hypnerotomachia Poliphili

Prologue

Like many of us, I think, my father spent the measure of his life piecing together a story he would never understand. That story began almost five centuries before I left for college, and ended long after he died. On a night in November of 1497, two messengers rode on horseback from the shadows of the Vatican to a church named San Lorenzo, outside the city walls of Rome. What happened that night changed their fortunes, and my father believed it might change his own.

I never made much of his beliefs. A son is the promise that time makes to a man, the guarantee every father receives that whatever he holds dear will someday be considered foolish, and that the person he loves best in the world will misunderstand him. But my father, a Renaissance scholar, was never shy about the possibility of rebirth. He told the story of the two messengers so often that I could never forget it, try as I might. He sensed, I see now, that there was a lesson in it, a truth that would finally bind us.

The messengers had been sent to San Lorenzo to deliver a nobleman's letter, which they were warned under pain of death not to open. The letter was sealed four times in dark wax, and purported to contain a secret my father would later spend three decades trying to discover. But darkness had fallen on Rome in those days; her honor had come and gone, and not yet come again. A starry sky was still painted on the ceiling of the Sistine Chapel, and apocalyptic rains had flooded the Tiber River, on whose shores had appeared, old widows claimed, a monster with the body of a woman and the head of an ass. The two greedy horsemen, Rodrigo and Donato, did not heed their master's warning. They heated the wax seals with a candle, then opened the letter to learn its contents. Before leaving for San Lorenzo, they resealed the letter perfectly, copying the nobleman's stamp with such care that the tampering must have been impossible to see. Had their master not been a much wiser man, the two couriers would surely have survived.

For it wasn't the seals that would undo Rodrigo and Donato. It was the heavy black wax in which those seals had been pressed. When they arrived at San Lorenzo, the messengers were met by a mason who knew what was in the wax: an extract from a poisonous herb called deadly nightshade, which, when applied to the eyes, dilates the pupils. Today the compound is used medicinally, but in those days it was used by Italian women as a cosmetic drug, because large pupils were considered a mark of beauty. It was this practice that earned the plant its other name: "beautiful woman," or belladonna. As Rodrigo and

Donato melted and re-melted each seal, then, the smoke from the burning wax took hold. Upon their arrival at San Lorenzo, the mason brought them to a candelabra near the altar. When their pupils failed to contract, he knew what they had done. And though the men struggled to recognize him through their unfocused eyes, the mason did as he'd been told: he took his sword and beheaded them. It was a test of trust, his master said, and the messengers had failed.

What became of Rodrigo and Donato, my father learned in a document he discovered just before he died. The mason covered the men's bodies and drew them from the church, sopping up their blood with cheesecloth and rags. The heads he placed in two saddlebags on either side of his mount; the bodies he slung across the backs of Donato's and Rodrigo's own horses, and hitched them in tow to his own. He found the letter in Donato's pocket, and burned it, for it was a fake, and there was no true recipient. Then, before leaving, he crouched in penitence before the church, horrified by the sin he had committed for his master. In his eyes, the six columns of San Lorenzo formed black teeth from the openings in between, and the simple mason admitted that he trembled when he saw this, for as a child at the widows' knees he had learned how the poet Dante had seen hell, and how the punishment of the greatest sinners was to be chewed forever in the jaws of *lo 'mperador del doloroso regno*.

Maybe old Saint Lawrence stared up from his grave finally, seeing the blood on the poor man's hands, and forgave him. Or maybe there was no forgiveness to be had, and like the saints and martyrs of today, Lawrence was inscrutably silent. Later that night the mason followed his master's orders and brought the bodies of Rodrigo and Donato to a butcher. The fate of their carcasses, it's probably best not to guess. Their parts were tossed into the streets and collected by the dustcarts, I hope, or eaten by dogs before they could find themselves baked into a pie.

But the butcher found another use for the two men's heads. A baker in town, a man with a touch of the devil in him, bought the heads from the butcher and placed them in his own oven as he left for the night. It was a custom in those days for the local widows to borrow the bakers' ovens after dark, while the day's embers were still hot; and when the women arrived, they shrieked and nearly fainted at the sight of what they found.

At first it seems a low fate, to be used as fodder for a trick on old crones. But I imagine a much greater fame came to Donato and Rodrigo in the way they died than ever would've come to them in life. For the widows in every civilization are the keepers of its memory, and the ones who found the heads in the baker's oven surely never forgot. Even when the baker confessed to what he'd done, the widows must've kept telling the story of their discovery to Rome's children, who, for a generation, remembered the tale of the miraculous heads as vividly as they did the monster coughed up by the Tiber floods.

And though the story of the two messengers would eventually be forgotten, a single thing remains beyond doubt. The mason did his job well. Whatever his master's secret was, it never left San Lorenzo. The morning after Donato and Rodrigo were murdered, as the dustcart men heaped filth and innards into their barrows, little notice was taken that two men were dead. The slow progress of beauty into decay into beauty continued, and like the serpent's teeth that Cadmus sowed, the blood of evil watered Roman earth and brought about rebirth. Five hundred years would elapse before anyone discovered the truth. When those five centuries passed, and death found a new pair of messengers, I was finishing my last year of college at Princeton.

Chapter 1

Strange thing, time. It weighs most on those who have it least. Nothing is lighter than being young with the world on your shoulders; it gives you a feeling of possibility so seductive, you know there must be something more important you could be doing than studying for exams.

I can see myself now, the night it all began. I'm lying back on the old red sofa in our dorm room, wrestling with Pavlov and his dogs in my introductory psychology book, wondering why I never fulfilled my science requirement as a freshman like everyone else. A pair of letters sits on the coffee table in front of me, each containing a vision of what I could be doing next year. The night of Good Friday has fallen, cold April in Princeton, New Jersey, and with only a month of college left I'm no different from anyone else in the class of 1999: I'm having trouble getting my mind off the future.

Charlie is sitting on the floor by the cube refrigerator, playing with the Magnetic Shakespeare someone left in our room last week. The Fitzgerald novel he's supposed to be reading for his final paper in English 151w is spread open on the floor with its spine broken, like a butterfly somebody stepped on, and he's forming and re-forming sentences from magnets with Shakespearean words on them. If you ask him why he's not reading Fitzgerald, he'll grunt and say there's no point. As far as he's concerned, literature is just an educated man's shell game, three-card monte for the college crowd: what you see is never what you get. For a science-minded guy like Charlie, that's the height of perversity. He's headed for medical school in the fall, but the rest of us are still hearing about the C-plus he found on his English midterm in March.

Gil glances over at us and smiles. He's been pretending to study for an economics exam, but *Breakfast at Tiffany's* is on, and Gil has a thing for old films, especially ones with Audrey Hepburn. His advice to Charlie was simple: if you don't want to read the book, then rent the movie. They'll never know. He's probably right, but Charlie sees something dishonest in that, and anyway it would prevent him from complaining about what a scam literature is, so instead of Daisy Buchanan we're watching Holly Golightly yet again.

I reach down and rearrange some of Charlie's words until the sentence at the top of the fridge says to fail or not to fail: that is the question. Charlie raises his head to give me a disapproving look. Sitting down, he's almost as tall as I am on the couch. When we stand next to each other he looks like Othello on steroids, a two-hundred-and-fifteen-pound black man who scrapes the ceilings at six-and-a-half feet. By contrast I'm five-foot-seven in shoes. Charlie likes to call us Red Giant and White Dwarf, because a red giant is a star that's unusually large and bright, while a white dwarf is small and dense and dull. I have to remind him that Napoleon was only five-foot-two, even if Paul is right that when you convert French feet to English, the emperor was actually taller.

Paul is the only one of us who isn't in the room now. He disappeared earlier in the day, and hasn't been seen since. Things between him and me have been rocky for the past month, and with all the academic pressure on him lately, he's chosen to do most of his studying at Ivy, the eating club where he and Gil are members. It's his senior thesis he's working on, the paper all Princeton undergrads must write in order to graduate. Charlie, Gil, and I would be doing the same ourselves, except that our departmental deadlines have already come and gone. Charlie identified a new protein interaction in certain neuronal signaling pathways; Gil managed something on the ramifications of a flat tax. I pasted mine together at the last minute between applications and interviews, and I'm sure *Frankenstein* scholarship will forever be the same.

The senior thesis is an institution that almost everyone despises. Alumni talk about their theses wistfully, as if they can't remember anything more enjoyable than writing one-hundred-page research papers while taking classes and choosing their professional futures. In reality, a senior thesis is a miserable, spine-breaking thing to write. It's an introduction to adult life, a sociology professor told Charlie and me once, in that annoying way professors have of lecturing after the lecture is over: it's about shouldering something so big, you can't get out from under it. *It's called responsibility*, he said. *Try it on for size.* Never mind that the only thing he was trying on for size was a pretty thesis advisee named Kim Silverman. It was all about responsibility. I'd have to agree with what Charlie said at the time. If Kim Silverman is the sort of thing adults can't get out from under, then sign me up. Otherwise, I'll take my chances being young.

Paul is the last of us to finish his thesis, and there's no question that his will be the best of the bunch. In fact, his may be the best of our entire graduating class, in the history department or any other. The magic of Paul's intelligence is that he has more patience than anyone I've ever met, and with it he simply wears problems down. To count a hundred million stars, he told me once, at the rate of one per second, sounds like a job that no one could possibly complete in a lifetime. In reality, it would only take three years. The key is focus, a willingness not to be distracted. And that is Paul's gift: an intuition of just how much a person can do slowly.

Maybe that's why everyone has such high expectations for his thesis—they know how many stars he could count in three years, but he's been working on his thesis for almost four. While the average student comes up with a research topic in the fall of senior year and finishes it by the next spring, Paul has been struggling with his since freshman year. Just a few months into our first fall semester, he decided to focus on a rare Renaissance text entitled *Hypnerotomachia Poliphili*, a labyrinthine name I can pronounce only because my father spent most of his career as a Renaissance historian studying it. Three and a half years later, and barely twenty-four hours from his deadline, Paul has enough material to make even the most discriminating graduate programs salivate.

The problem is, he thinks I ought to be enjoying the fanfare too. We worked on the book together for a few months during the winter, and made good progress as a team. Only then did I understand something my mother used to say: that men in our family had a tendency to fall for certain books about as hard as they fell for certain women. The *Hypnerotomachia* may never have had much outward charm, but it has an ugly woman's wiles, the slow addictive tug of inner mystery. When I caught myself slipping into it the same way my father had, I managed to pull myself out and throw in the towel before it could ruin my relationship with a girlfriend who deserved better. Since then, things between Paul and me haven't been the same. A graduate student he knows, Bill Stein, has helped with his research since I begged off. Now, as his thesis deadline approaches, Paul has become strangely guarded. He's usually much more forthcoming about his work, but over the past week he's withdrawn not only from me but from Charlie and Gil too, refusing to speak a word of his research to anyone.

"So, which way are you leaning, Tom?" Gil asks.

Charlie glances up from the fridge. "Yeah," he says, "we're all on tenterhooks."

Gil and I groan. *Tenterhooks* is one of the words Charlie missed on his midterm. He attributed it to *Moby-Dick* instead of Tobias Smollett's *Adventures of Roderick Random* on the grounds that it sounded more like a kind of fishing lure than a word for suspense. Now he won't let it go.

"Get over it," Gil says.

"Name me one doctor who knows what a tenterhook is," Charlie says.

Before either of us can answer, a rustling sound comes from inside the bedroom I share with Paul. Suddenly, standing before us at the door, wearing only boxers and a T-shirt, is Paul himself.

"Just one?" he asks, rubbing his eyes. "Tobias Smollett. He was a surgeon."

Charlie glances back at the magnets. "Figures."

Gil chuckles, but says nothing.

"We thought you went to Ivy," Charlie says, when the pause becomes noticeable.

Paul shakes his head, backtracking into his room to pick up his notebook. His straw-colored hair is pressed flat on one side, and there are pillow creases on his face. "Not enough privacy," he says. "I've been working in my bunk again. Fell asleep."

He's hardly gotten a wink in two nights, maybe more. Paul's advisor, Dr. Vincent Taft, has pressed him to produce more and more documentation every week—and unlike most advisors, who are happy to let seniors hang by the rope of their own expectations, Taft has kept a hand at Paul's back from the start.

"So, what about it, Tom?" Gil asks, filling the silence. "What's your decision?"

I glance up at the table. He's talking about the letters in front of me, which I've been eyeing between each sentence in my book. The first letter is from the University of Chicago, offering me admission to a doctoral program in English. Books are in my blood, the same way medical school is in Charlie's, and a Ph.D. from Chicago would suit me just fine. I did have to scrap for the acceptance letter a little more than I wanted to, partly because my grades at Princeton have been middling, but mainly because I don't know exactly what I want to do with myself, and a good graduate program can smell indecision like a dog can smell fear.

"Take the money," Gil says, never taking his eyes off Audrey Hepburn.

Gil is a banker's son from Manhattan. Princeton has never been a destination for him, just a window seat with a view, a stopover on the way to Wall Street. He is a caricature of himself in that respect, and he manages a smile whenever we give him a hard time about it. He'll be smiling all the way to the bank, we know; even Charlie, who's sure to make a small fortune as a doctor, won't hold a candle to the kind of paychecks Gil will see.

"Don't listen to him," Paul says from the other side of the room. "Follow your heart."

I look up, surprised that he's aware of anything but his thesis.

"Follow the *money*," Gil says, standing up to get a bottle of water from the refrigerator.

"What'd they offer?" Charlie asks, ignoring the magnets for a second.

"Forty-one," Gil guesses, and a few Elizabethan words tumble from the fridge as he closes it. "Bonus of five. Plus options."

Spring semester is job season, and 1999 is a buyer's market. Forty-one thousand dollars a year is roughly double what I expected to be earning with my lowly English degree, but compared to some of the deals I've seen classmates make, you'd think it was barely getting by.

I pick up the letter from Daedalus, an Internet firm in

Austin that claims to have developed the world's most advanced software for streamlining the corporate back office. I know almost nothing about the company, let alone what a back office is, but a friend down the hall suggested I interview with them, and as rumors circulated about high starting salaries at this unknown Texas start-up, I went. Daedalus, following the general trend, didn't care that I knew nothing about them or their business. If I could just solve a few brainteasers at an interview, and seem reasonably articulate and friendly in the process, the job was mine. Thus, in good Caesarian fashion, I could, I did, and it was.

"Close," I say, reading from the letter. "Forty-three thousand a year. Signing bonus of three thousand. Fifteen hundred options."

"And a partridge in a pear tree," Paul adds from across the room. He's the only one acting like it's dirtier to talk about money than it is to touch it. "Vanity of vanities."

Charlie is shifting the magnets again. In a fulminating baritone he imitates the preacher at his church, a tiny black man from Georgia who just finished his degree at the Princeton Theological Seminary. "*Van*ity of *van*ities. *All* is vanity."

"Be honest with yourself, Tom," Paul says impatiently, though he never makes eye contact. "Any company that thinks you deserve a salary like that isn't going to be around for long. You don't even know what they *do*." He returns to his notebook, scribbling away. Like most prophets, he is fated to be ignored.

Gil keeps his focus on the television, but Charlie looks up, hearing the edge in Paul's voice. He rubs a hand along the stubble on his chin, then says, "All right, everybody *stop*. I think it's time to let off some steam."

For the first time, Gil turns away from the movie. He must hear what I hear: the faint emphasis on the word *steam*.

"Right now?" I ask.

Gil looks at his watch, taking to the idea. "We'd be clear for about half an hour," he says, and in a show of support he even turns off the television, letting Audrey fizzle into the tube.

Charlie flips his Fitzgerald shut, mischief stirring. The broken spine springs open in protest, but he tosses the book onto the couch.

"I'm working," Paul objects. "I need to finish this."

He glances at me oddly.

"What?" I ask.

But Paul remains silent.

"What's the problem, girls?" Charlie says impatiently.

"It's still snowing out there," I remind everyone.

The first snowstorm of the year came howling into town today, just when spring seemed perched on the tip of every tree branch. Now there are calls for a foot of accumulation, maybe more. The Easter weekend festivities on campus, which this year include a Good Friday lecture by Paul's thesis advisor, Vincent Taft, have been reorganized. This is hardly the weather for what Charlie has in mind.

"You don't have to meet Curry until 8:30, right?" Gil asks Paul, trying to convince him. "We'll be done by then. You can work more tonight."

Richard Curry, an eccentric former friend of my father's and Taft's, has been a mentor of Paul's since freshman year. He has put Paul in touch with some of the most prominent art historians in the world, and has funded much of Paul's research on the *Hypnerotomachia*.

Paul weighs his notebook in his hand. Just looking at it, the fatigue returns to his eyes.

Charlie senses that he's coming around. "We'll be done by 7:45," he says.

"What are the teams?" Gil asks.

Charlie thinks it over, then says, "Tom's with me."

The game we're about to play is a new spin on an old favorite: a fast-paced match of paintball in a maze of steam tunnels below campus. Down there, rats are more common than lightbulbs, the temperature hits three digits in the dead of winter, and the terrain is so dangerous that even the campus police are forbidden to give chase. Charlie and Gil came up with the idea during an exam period sophomore year, inspired by an old map Gil and Paul found at their eating club, and by a game Gil's father used to play in the tunnels with his friends as seniors.

The newer version gained popularity until nearly a dozen members of Ivy and most of Charlie's friends from his EMT squad were in on it. It seemed to surprise them when Paul became one of the game's best navigators; only the four of us understood it, knowing how often Paul used the tunnels to get to and from Ivy on his own. But gradually Paul's interest in the game waned. It frustrated him that no one else saw the strategic possibilities of it, the tactical ballet. He wasn't there when an errant shot punctured a steam pipe during a big midwinter match; the explosion stripped plastic safety casings off live power lines for ten feet in either direction, and might've cooked two half-drunk juniors, had Charlie not pulled them out of the way. The proctors, Princeton's campus police, caught on,

and within days the dean had rained down a spate of pun-
ishments. In the aftermath, Charlie replaced paint guns
and pellets with something faster but less risky: an old set
of laser-tag guns he picked up at a yard sale. Still, as graduation approaches, the administration has imposed a
zero-tolerance policy on disciplinary infractions. Getting
caught in the tunnels tonight could mean suspension or
worse.

Charlie sidesteps into the bedroom he shares with Gil
and pulls out a large hiking pack, then another, which he
hands to me. Finally he pulls on his hat.

"Jesus, Charlie," Gil says. "We're only going down
there for half an hour. I packed less for spring break."

"Be prepared," Charlie says, hitching the larger of the
two packs over his shoulders. "That's what I say."

"You and the Boy Scouts," I mumble.

"*Eagle* scouts," Charlie says, because he knows I never
made it past tenderfoot.

"You ladies ready?" Gil interrupts, standing by the
door.

Paul breathes deeply, waking himself up, then nods.
From inside his room he grabs his pager and hitches it to
his belt.

At the front of Dod Hall, our dormitory, Charlie and I
part ways with Gil and Paul. We will enter the tunnels at
different locations, and be invisible to each other until
one team finds the other underground.

"I didn't know there was such a thing as a black Boy
Scout," I tell Charlie once he and I are on our own, heading down campus.

The snow is deeper and colder than I expected. I

wrench my ski jacket around me, and force my hands into gloves.

"That's okay," he says. "Before I met you, I didn't know there was such a thing as a white pussy."

The trip down campus passes in a haze. For days, with graduation so near and my own thesis out of the way, the world has seemed like a rush of unnecessary motion—underclassmen hurrying to night seminars, seniors typing their final chapters in sweating computer labs, now snowflakes everywhere in the sky, dancing in circles before they find the ground.

As we walk down campus, my leg begins to ache. For years the scar on my thigh has been predicting bad weather six hours after the bad weather arrives. It's a memento of an old accident, the scar. Not long after my sixteenth birthday I was in a car crash that laid me up in a hospital for most of my sophomore summer. The details are a blur to me now, but the one distinct memory I have of that night is my left femur snapping clean through the muscle of my thigh until one end of it was staring back at me through the skin. I had just enough time to see it before passing out from shock. Both bones in my left forearm broke as well, and three ribs on the same side. According to the paramedics, the bleeding from my artery was stopped just in time for them to save me. By the time they got me out of the wreckage, though, my father, who'd been driving the car, was dead.

The accident changed me, of course: after three surgeries and two months of rehab, and the onset of phantom pains with their six-hour weather delay, I still had metal pins in my bones, a scar up my leg, and a strange hole in my life that only seemed to get bigger the more time wore on. At first there were different clothes—different sizes of pants and shorts until I regained enough weight, then different styles to cover up a skin graft on my thigh. Later I realized that my family had changed too: my mother, who'd retreated into herself, first and most of all, but also my two older sisters, Sarah and Kristen, who spent less and less time at home. Finally it was my friends who changed—or, I guess, finally I was the one who changed them. I'm not sure if I wanted friends who understood me better, or saw me differently, or what exactly, but the old ones, like my old clothes, just didn't fit anymore.

The thing people like to say to victims is that time is a great healer. *The* great healer is what they say, as if time were a doctor. But after six years of thinking on the subject, I have a different impression. Time is the guy at the amusement park who paints shirts with an airbrush. He sprays out the color in a fine mist until it's just lonely particles floating in the air, waiting to be plastered in place. And what comes of it all, the design on the shirt at the end of the day, usually isn't much to see. I suspect that whoever buys that shirt, the one great patron of the everlasting theme park, whoever he is, wakes up in the morning and wonders what he ever saw in it. We're the paint in that analogy, as I tried to explain to Charlie when I mentioned it once. Time is what disperses us.

Maybe the best way to put it is the way Paul did, not long after we met. Even then he was a Renaissance fanatic, eighteen years old and already convinced that civilization had been in a nosedive since the death of Michelangelo.

He'd read all of my father's books on the period, and he introduced himself to me a few days into freshman year after recognizing my middle name in the freshman facebook. I have a peculiar middle name, which for parts of my childhood I carried like an albatross around my neck. My father tried to name me after his favorite composer, a slightly obscure seventeenth-century Italian without whom, he said, there could've been no Haydn, and therefore no Mozart. My mother, on the other hand, refused to have the birth certificate printed the way he wanted, insisting until the moment of my arrival that Arcangelo Corelli Sullivan was a horrible thing to foist on a child, like a three-headed monster of names. She was partial to Thomas, her father's name, and whatever it lacked in imagination it made up for in subtlety.

Thus, as the pangs of labor began, she held a delivery-bed filibuster, as she called it, keeping me out of this world until my father agreed to a compromise. In a moment less of inspiration than of desperation, I became Thomas Corelli Sullivan, and for better or worse, the name stuck. My mother hoped that I could hide my middle name between the other two, like sweeping dust beneath a rug. But my father, who believed there was much in a name, always said that Corelli without Arcangelo was like a Stradivarius without strings. He'd only given in to my mother, he claimed, because the stakes were much higher than she let on. Her filibuster, he used to say with a smile, was staged in the marriage bed, not on the delivery bed. He was the sort of man who thought a pact made in passion was the only good excuse for bad judgment.

I told Paul all of this, several weeks after we met.

"You're right," he said, when I told him my little airbrush metaphor. "Time is no da Vinci." He thought for a moment, then smiled in that gentle way of his. "Not even a Rembrandt. Just a cheap Jackson Pollock."

He seemed to understand me from the beginning.

All three of them did: Paul, Charlie, and Gil.

Chapter 2

Now Charlie and I are standing over a manhole at the foot of Dillon Gym, near the south of campus. The Philadelphia 76ers patch on his knit hat is hanging by a thread, fluttering in the wind. Above us, under the orange eye of a sodium lamp, snowflakes twitch in huge clouds. We are waiting. Charlie is beginning to lose patience because the two sophomores across the street are costing us time.

"Just tell me what we're supposed to do," I say.

A light pulses on his watch and he glances down. "It's 7:07. Proctors change shifts at 7:30. We've got twenty-three minutes."

"You think twenty minutes is enough to catch them?"

"Sure," he says. "If we can figure out where they'll be." Charlie looks back over across the street. "Come *on*, girls."

One of them is mincing through the drifts in a

spring skirt, as if the snow caught her by surprise while she was dressing. The other, a Peruvian girl I know from an intramural competition, wears the trademark orange parka of the swim and dive team.

"I forgot to call Katie," I say, as it dawns on me.

Charlie turns.

"It's her birthday. I was supposed to tell her when I was coming over."

Katie Marchand, a sophomore, has slowly become the kind of girlfriend I didn't deserve to find. Her rising importance in my life is a fact Charlie accepts by reminding himself that sharp women often have terrible taste in men.

"Did you get her something?" he asks.

"Yeah." I make a rectangle with my hands. "A photo from this gallery in—"

He nods. "Then it's okay if you don't call." A grunting sound follows, sort of a half-laugh. "Anyway, she's probably got other things on her mind right now."

"What's that supposed to mean?"

Charlie holds his hand out, catching a snowflake. "First snow of the year. Nude Olympics."

"Jesus. I forgot."

The Nude Olympics is one of Princeton's most beloved traditions. Every year, on the night of the first snowfall, sophomores gather in the courtyard of Holder Hall. Surrounded by dorms crawling with spectators from across campus, they show up in herds, hundreds upon hundreds of them, and with the heroic unconcern of lemmings they take their clothes off and run around wildly. It's a rite that must have arisen in the old days of the college, when Princeton was a men's institution and mass nudity was an expression of the male prerogative, like pissing upright or waging war. But it was when women joined the fray that this cozy little scrum became the must-see event of the academic year. Even the media turn out to record it, with satellite vans and video cameras coming from as far as Philadelphia and New York. Mere thought of the Nude Olympics usually lights a fire under the cold months of college, but this year, with Katie's turn coming around, I'm more interested in keeping the home fires burning.

"You ready?" Charlie asks once the two sophomores have finally passed by.

I shift my foot across the manhole cover, dusting off the snow.

He kneels down and hooks his index fingers into the gaps of the manhole cover. The snow dampens the scrape of steel on asphalt as he drags it back. I look down the road again.

"You first," he says, placing a hand at my back.

"What about the packs?"

"Quit stalling. *Go.*"

I drop to my knees and press my palms on either side of the open hole. A thick heat pours up from below. When I try to lower myself into it, the bulges in my ski jacket fight at the edge of the opening.

"Damn, Tom, the dead move faster. Kick around until your foot finds a step iron. There's a ladder in the wall."

Feeling my shoe snag the top rung, I begin to descend.

"All right," Charlie says. "Take this."

He pushes my pack through the opening, followed by his.

A network of pipes extends into the dark in both directions. Visibility is low, and the air is full of metallic clanks and hisses. This is Princeton's circulatory system, the passageways pushing steam from a distant central boiler to dorms and academic buildings up north. Charlie says the vapor inside the pipes is pressurized at two hundred and fifty pounds per square inch. The smaller cylinders carry high-voltage lines or natural gas. Still, I've never seen any warnings in the tunnels, not a single fluorescent triangle or posting of university policy. The college would like to forget that this place exists. The only message at this entrance, written long ago in black paint, is LASCIATE OGNE SPERANZA, VOI CH'INTRATE. Paul, who has never seemed to fear anything in this place, smiled the first time he saw it. *Abandon all hope*, he said, translating Dante for the rest of us, *ye that enter here.*

Charlie makes his way down, scraping the cover back onto its place after him. As he steps from the bottom rung, he pulls off his hat. Light dances across the beads of sweat on his forehead. The afro he's grown after four months without a haircut barely clears the ceiling. *It's not an afro*, he's been telling us. *It's just a half-fro.*

He takes a few whiffs of the stale air, then produces a container of Vick's VapoRub from his pack. "Put some under your nose. You won't smell anything."

I wave him off. It's a trick he learned as a summer intern with the local medical examiner, a way to avoid smelling the corpses during autopsies. After what happened to my father I've never held the medical profession in particularly high esteem; doctors are drones to me, second opinions with shifting faces. But to see Charlie in a hospital is another thing entirely. He's the strongman of the local ambulance squad, the go-to guy for tough cases, and he'll find a twenty-fifth hour in any day to give people he's never met a fighting chance to beat what he calls the Thief.

Charlie unloads a pair of pin-striped gray laser guns, then the set of Velcro straps with dark plastic domes in the middle. While he keeps fiddling with the packs, I start to unzip my jacket. The collar of my shirt is already sticking to my neck.

"Careful," he says, extending an arm out before I can sling my coat across the largest pipe. "Remember what happened to Gil's old jacket?"

I'd completely forgotten. A steam pipe melted the nylon shell and set the filler on fire. We had to stomp out the flames on the ground.

"We'll leave the coats here and pick them up on the way out," he says, grabbing the jacket from my hand and rolling it up with his in an expandable duffel bag. He suspends it from a ceiling fixture by one of its straps.

"So the rats don't get at it," he says, unloading a few more objects from the pack.

After handing me a flashlight and a two-way hand radio, he pulls out two large water bottles, beading from the heat, and places them in the outer netting of his pack.

"Remember," he says. "If we get split up again, don't head downstream. If you see water running, go against the current. You don't want to end up in a drain or down a chute if the flow increases. This isn't the Ohio, like you got back at home. The water level down here rises *fast*."

This is my punishment for getting lost the last time he and I were teammates. I tug at my shirt for ventilation. "Chuck, the Ohio doesn't go anywhere near Columbus."

He hands me one of the receivers and waits for me to fasten it around my chest, ignoring me.

"So what's the plan?" I ask. "Which way are we going?"

He smiles. "That's where you come in."

"Why?"

Charlie pats my head. "Because you're the sherpa."

He says it as if sherpas are a magical race of midget navigators, like hobbits.

"What do you want me to do?"

"Paul knows the tunnels better than we do. We need a strategy."

I mull it over. "What's the nearest entrance to the tunnels on their side?"

"There's one in back of Clio."

Cliosophic is an old debating society's building. I try to see each position clearly, but the heat is clogging my thoughts. "Which would lead straight down to where we're standing. A straight shot south. Right?"

He thinks it over, wrestling with the geography. "Right," he says.

"And he *never* takes the straight shot."

"Never."

I imagine Paul, always two steps ahead.

"Then that's what he'll do. A straight shot. Beat a path down from Clio and hit us before we're ready."

Charlie considers. "Yeah," he says finally, focusing off into the distance. The edges of his lips begin to form a smile.

"So we'll circle around him," I suggest. "Catch him from behind."

There's a glint in Charlie's eyes. He pats me on the

back hard enough that I nearly fall under the weight of my pack. "Let's go."

We start moving down the corridor, when a hiss comes from the mouth of the two-way radio.

I pull the handset from my belt and press the button.

"Gil?"

Silence.

"*Gil? . . .* I can't hear you. . . ."

But there's no response.

"It's a bug," Charlie says. "They're too far away to send a signal."

I repeat myself into the microphone and wait. "You said these things had a two-mile range," I tell him. "We're not even a mile from them."

"A two-mile range through the *air*," Charlie says. "Through concrete and dirt, not even close."

But the radios are for emergency use. I'm sure it was Gil's voice I heard.

We continue in silence for a hundred yards or so, dodging puddles of sludge and little mounds of scat. Suddenly Charlie grabs the neck of my shirt and pulls me back.

"What the hell?" I snap, almost losing my balance.

He runs the beam of his flashlight across a wooden plank bridging a deep trough in the tunnel. We've both crossed it in previous games.

"What's wrong?"

He gingerly presses a foot down on the board.

"It's fine," Charlie says, visibly relieved. "No water damage."

I wipe my forehead, finding it soaked with sweat.

"Okay," he says. "Let's go."

Charlie walks across the plank in two great strides. It's all I can do to keep my balance before landing safely on the other side.

"Here." Charlie hands me one of the water bottles. "Drink it."

I take a quick drink, then follow him deeper into the tunnels. We're in an undertaker's paradise, the same coffin-like view in every direction, dark walls tapering faintly toward a hazy point of convergence in the darkness.

"Does this *whole* part of the tunnels look like a cata-comb?" I ask. The hand radio seems to be buzzing patches of static between my thoughts.

"Like a what?"

"A catacomb. A tomb."

"Not really. The newer parts are in a huge corrugated pipe," he says, moving his hands in an undulating pattern, like a wave, to suggest the surface. "It's like walking on ribs. Makes you think you were swallowed by a whale. Sort of like . . ."

He snaps his fingers, searching for a comparison. Something biblical. Something Melvillian, from English 151w.

"Like Pinocchio."

Charlie looks back at me, fishing for a laugh.

"It shouldn't be much farther," he says, when he doesn't get one. Turning back, he pats the receiver on his chest. "Don't worry. We'll turn the corner, pop them a few times, and go home."

Just then, the radio crackles again. This time there's no doubt: it's Gil's voice.

Endgame, Charlie.

I stop short. "What does that mean?"

Charlie frowns. He waits for the message to repeat, but there's no other sound.

"I'm not falling for that," he says.

"Falling for what?"

"*Endgame*. It means the game's over."

"No shit, Charlie. Why?"

"Because something's wrong."

"*Wrong?*"

But he raises a finger, silencing me. In the distance I can hear voices.

"That's them," I say.

He lifts his rifle. "Come on."

Charlie's strides quickly get longer, and I have no choice but to follow. Only now, trying to keep up, do I appreciate how expertly he runs through the darkness. It's all I can do to hold him in the ray of my flashlight.

As we near a junction, he stops me. "Don't turn the corner. Kill your flashlight. They'll see us coming."

I wave him on, into the opening. The radio blasts again.

Endgame, Charlie. We're in the north-south corridor under Edwards Hall.

Gil's voice is much clearer now, much closer.

I begin toward the intersection, but Charlie pushes me back. Two flashlight beams jerk in the opposite direction. Squinting in the darkness, I can make out silhouettes. They turn, hearing our approach. One of the beams falls into our sight line.

"Damn!" Charlie barks, shielding his eyes. He points

his rifle blindly toward the light and begins to press at its trigger. I can hear the mechanical bleating of a chest receiver.

"Stop it!" Gil hisses.

"What's the problem?" Charlie calls out as we approach.

Paul is behind Gil, motionless. The two of them are standing in a trickle of light coming through the gaps in a manhole cover overhead.

Gil places a finger over his lips, then points up toward the manhole. I make out two figures standing above us in front of Edwards Hall.

"Bill's trying to call me," Paul says, holding his pager toward the light. He's clearly agitated. "I have to get out of here."

Charlie gives Paul a puzzled look, then gestures for him and Gil to step away from the light.

"He won't move," Gil says under his breath.

Paul is directly beneath the metal lid, staring at the face of his pager as melted snow drips through the holes. There is movement above.

"*You're going to get us caught,*" I whisper.

"He says he can't get reception anywhere else," Gil says.

"Bill's never done this before," Paul whispers back.

I pull at his arm, but he jerks free. When he lights up the silver face of the pager and shows it to us, I see three numbers: 911.

"What's that supposed to mean?" Charlie whispers.

"Bill must've found something," Paul says, losing patience. "I need to find him."

Foot traffic in front of Edwards mashes fresh snow through the manhole. Charlie is getting tense.

"Look," he says, "it's a fluke. You can't get reception down he—"

But he's interrupted by the pager, which begins to beep again. Now the message is a phone number: 116-7718.

"What's that?" Gil asks.

Paul turns the screen upside-down, forming text from the digits: BILL-911.

"I'm getting out of here *now*," Paul says.

Charlie shakes his head. "Not using that manhole. Too many people up there."

"He wants to use the exit at Ivy," Gil says. "I told him it was too far. We can go back to Clio. It's still a couple minutes before the proctors switch."

In the distance, tiny sets of red beads are gathering. Rats are sitting on their haunches, watching.

"What's so important?" I ask Paul.

"We're onto something big—" he begins to say.

But Charlie interrupts. "Clio's our best shot," he agrees. After checking his watch, he starts to walk north. "7:24. We need to get moving."

Chapter 3

The shape of the corridor remains boxy as we keep north, but the walls, which were once concrete, are increasingly of stone. I can hear my father's voice, explaining the etymology of the word *sarcophagus*.

From the Greek meaning "flesh-eating" . . . because Greek coffins were made of limestone, which consumed the entire body—everything but the teeth—within forty days.

Gil's lead has grown to twenty feet. Like Charlie, he moves quickly, accustomed to the landscape. Paul's silhouette blinks in and out of the uneven light. His hair is matted against his forehead, tamped down with sweat, and I remember that he's hardly slept in days.

Thirty yards up, we find Gil waiting for us, his eyes shifting from place to place as he shepherds us toward the exit. He's looking for a backup plan. We're taking too long. I close my eyes, trying to see a map of campus in my thoughts. "Just fifty more feet," Charlie calls to Paul. "A hundred at most."

When we arrive below the manhole near Clio, Gil turns to us.

"I'll pop the lid and look out. Get ready to run back the way we came." He glances down. "I've got 7:29."

He grips the lowest step iron, lifts himself into position, and raises his forearm against the manhole cover. Before applying pressure, he looks over his shoulder and says, "Remember, the proctors can't come down here to get us. All they can do is tell us to come out. Stay down and don't say anyone's name. Got it?"

The three of us nod.

Gil takes a deep breath, shoves his fist upward, and pivots the cover against his elbow. It cracks open half a foot. He takes a quick inventory—then a voice comes from above.

"Don't move! Stay right there!"

I can hear Gil hiss, "*Shit.*"

Grabbing his shirt, Charlie pulls him back, catching him as he loses his footing.

"Go! Over there! Turn your flashlight off!"

I stumble into the darkness, pressing Paul in front of me. I try to remember my way.

Stay to the right. Pipes on the left, stay to the right.

My shoulder glances the wall and tears my shirt. Paul is staggering, exhausted by the heat. We manage twenty paces stumbling over each other before Charlie stops us so Gil can catch up. In the distance a flashlight enters the tunnel through the open manhole. An arm descends after it, followed by a head.

"Come out of there!"

The beam twitches in both directions, sending a triangle of light sharking through the tunnel.

Now a second voice, a woman's.

"This is your last warning!"

I look over at Gil. In the darkness I can see the contours of his head as he shakes it, warning us not to speak.

Paul's breath is wet on the back of my neck. He leans against the wall, beginning to look faint. The woman's voice comes again, deliberately loud as she speaks to her partner.

"Call it in. Post officers at all the manholes."

For a moment the flashlight retracts from the opening. Charlie immediately presses at our backs. We run until we reach a T in the tunnels, then continue past it and veer right around a corner into unfamiliar territory.

"They can't see us here," Gil whispers, out of breath, clicking on his flashlight. Another long tunnel retreats out of sight, toward what I take to be the northwest of campus.

"What now?" Charlie says.

"Back to Dod," Gil suggests.

Paul wipes his forehead. "Can't. They padlocked the exit."

"They'll watch all the main grates," Charlie says.

I begin pacing down the westward tunnel. "Is this the fastest way northwest?"

"Why?"

"Because I think we can get out near Rocky-Mathey. How far is it from here?"

Charlie hands the last of our water to Paul, who drinks it eagerly. "A few hundred yards," he says. "Maybe more."

"Through this tunnel?"

Gil considers for a second, then nods.

"I got nothing better," Charlie says.

The three of them begin to follow me into the dark.

For some distance we continue through the same passageway in silence. Charlie trades flashlights with me once my beam grows too weak, but keeps his focus on Paul, who seems more and more disoriented. When Paul finally stops to lean on a wall, Charlie props him up and helps him on, reminding him not to touch the pipes. With each step, the last drops of water plink in empty bottles. I begin to wonder if I've lost my bearings.

"Guys," Charlie says from behind us, "Paul's fading."

"I just need to sit down," Paul says weakly.

Suddenly Gil directs a flashlight into the distance, bringing a set of metal bars into view. "Damn it."

"Security gate," Charlie says.

"What do we do?"

Gil crouches to look Paul in the eye. "Hey," he says, shaking Paul's shoulders. "Is there a way out of here?"

Paul points at the steam pipe beside the security gate, then makes an unsteady downward swoop with his arm. "Go under."

Scanning the pipe with my flashlight, I see insulation worn away on the pipe's underside, just inches above the floor. Someone has tried this before.

"No way," Charlie says. "Not enough room."

"There's a release latch on the other side," Gil says, pointing to a device by the wall. "Only one of us has to go. Then we can open the gate." He lowers his head to Paul's level again. "You've done this before?"

Paul nods.

"He's dehydrated," Charlie says under his breath. "Does anyone have some water?"

Gil hands a half-empty bottle to Paul, who greedily drinks it down.

"Thanks. Better."

"We should go back," Charlie says.

"No," I say. "I'll do it."

"Take my coat," Gil offers. "For insulation."

I put a hand on the steam pipe. Even through the padding, it's pulsing with heat.

"You won't fit," Charlie says. "Not with the coat."

"I'm okay without it," I tell them.

But when I lower myself to the floor, I realize how tight the opening is. The insulation is scalding. On my stomach, I force myself between the floor and the pipe.

"Exhale and pull yourself through," Gil says.

I inch forward and force myself flat—but when I reach the tightest section, my hands find no grip, only puddles of ooze. Suddenly I'm pinned beneath the pipe.

"Shit," Gil growls, falling to his knees.

"Tom," Charlie says, and I can feel a pair of hands at my feet. "Push off me."

I force my feet off his palms. My chest scrapes hard against the concrete, and one thigh glances the pipe where the insulation is gone. Reflex jerks it away just as I feel the lancing-hot pain.

"You okay?" Charlie asks, when I shimmy through to the other side.

"Turn the latch clockwise," Gil says.

When I do, the security gate unlocks. Gil pushes it open, and Charlie follows, still supporting Paul.

"You sure about this?" Charlie asks, when we advance into the darkness.

I nod. A few steps on, we arrive at a crude *R* painted on a wall. We're approaching Rockefeller, one of the residential colleges. As a freshman, I dated a girl named Lana McKnight who lived there. We spent much of that winter sitting by a lazy fire in her dorm room, back before the flues on campus were shut for good. The things we discussed seem so distant now: Mary Shelley and college Gothic and the Buckeyes. Her mother had taught at Ohio State, like my father. Lana's breasts were shaped like eggplants and her ears were the color of rose petals when we stayed too long by the fire.

Soon I can hear voices coming from overhead. Many of them.

"What's going on?" Gil asks as he draws near the source. The manhole cover is just over his shoulder.

"That's it," I say, coughing. "Our way out."

He looks at me, trying to understand.

In the silence I can hear the voices more clearly— rowdy ones; students, not proctors. Dozens of them, moving around our heads.

Charlie begins to smile. "The Nude Olympics," he says.

It dawns on Gil. "We're right under them."

"There's a manhole in the middle of the courtyard," I remind them, leaning on the stone wall, trying to catch my breath. "All we have to do is pop the lid, join the pack, and disappear."

But from behind me, Paul speaks up in a hoarse voice. "All we have to do is *undress*, join the pack, and disappear."

For a moment there's silence. It's Charlie who starts to unbutton his shirt first.

"Get me *out* of here," he says, choking out a laugh as he pulls it off.

I yank off my jeans; Gil and Paul follow. We begin stuffing our clothes into one of the packs until it's bulging at the seams.

"Can you carry all that?" Charlie asks, offering to take both packs again.

I hesitate. "You know there'll be proctors out there, right?"

But by now Gil is beyond doubt. He begins to climb the rungs.

"Three hundred naked sophomores, Tom. If you can't make it home with that kind of diversion, you *deserve* to be caught."

And with that, he forces open the cover, letting a gust of freezing air cascade into the tunnel. It rejuvenates Paul like a balm.

"Okay, boys," Gil calls down, looking back one more time. "Let's get this meat to market."

My first memory of leaving that tunnel is how bright it suddenly became. Overhead lamps lit the courtyard. Security lights fanned the white earth. Camera flashes pulsed across the sky like fireflies.

Then comes the rush of cold: the howl of the wind, even louder than the feet stomping and the voices roaring. Flakes melt on my skin like dewdrops.

Finally I see it. A wall of arms and legs, spinning around us like an endless snake. Faces pop in and out of view—classmates, football players, women who caught my eye crossing campus—but they fade into the abstraction like clips in a collage. Here and there I see strange outfits—top hats and superhero capes, artwork painted across chests of every description—but it all recedes into the great, rolling animal, the Chinatown dragon, moving to hoots and shouts and flashbulb firecrackers.

"Come on!" Gil shouts.

Paul and I follow, mesmerized. I've forgotten what Holder is like on the night of the first snowfall.

The great conga line swallows us and for a second I'm lost even to myself, pressed tight against bodies in all directions, trying to keep my balance with a pack on my shoulders and snow underfoot. Someone pushes me from behind and I feel the zipper burst. Before I can shut it, our clothes have spilled out the top. In an instant all of them are gone, trampled in the mud. I look around, hoping Charlie's behind me to catch what's left, but he's nowhere to be seen.

"*Breasts and buttocks, buttocks and breasts,*" a young man somewhere is chanting in a cockney accent, as if he were selling flowers on the set of *My Fair Lady*. Across the way I see a fat junior from my lit seminar sneaking into the crowd of sophomores, belly rocking. He's wearing nothing but a sandwich board that reads FREE TEST DRIVE on the front and INQUIRE WITHIN on the back. Finally I spot Charlie. He's already made his way to the other side of the circle, where Will Clay, another member of the EMT squad, is wearing a pith helmet flanked with beer cans. Charlie snags it off the top of his head and the two begin chasing each other through the courtyard until I can't see them anymore.

Laughter fades in and out. In the commotion, I feel a hand grab my forearm.

"Let's go."

Gil yanks me toward the outside of the circle.

"What now?" Paul says.

Gil looks around, spotting proctors at every exit.

"This way," I tell them.

We near one of the dorm entrances and duck into Holder Hall. A drunk sophomore opens the door to her room and stands there, confused, as if we're the ones who are supposed to greet her. She sizes us up, then raises a bottle of Corona in her hand.

"Cheers." She belches, then shuts the door just in time for me to see one of her roommates warming up by the fireplace, wearing nothing but a towel.

"Come on," I say.

They follow me up a flight of stairs, where I bang loudly on one of the doors.

"*What are you doi—*" Gil begins.

But before he can finish, the door opens and I'm greeted by a pair of great green eyes. The lips below them open faintly at the sight of me. Katie is dressed in a tight T-shirt and a pair of weathered jeans; her auburn hair is pulled back into a short ponytail. Before letting us in, she bursts out laughing.

"I *knew* you'd be here," I say, rubbing my hands. When I step in and hug her, the embrace is warm and welcome.

"A birthday suit for my birthday," she says, looking me up and down. Her eyes are glowing. "So this is why you didn't call."

As Katie backs into the room I see Paul fixated on the camera in her hand, a Pentax with a telephoto lens almost as long as her forearm.

"What's that for?" Gil asks when Katie turns to put the camera on a bookshelf.

"Taking shots for the *Prince*," she says. "Maybe they'll print one this time."

This must be why she's not running. Katie has been trying all year to get a photo on the front page of the *Daily Princetonian*, but the seniority system has worked against her. Now she's turned the tables. Only freshmen and sophomores have rooms in Holder, and hers overlooks the entire courtyard.

"Where's Charlie?" she asks.

Gil shrugs, staring down through the window. "Out there playing grab-ass with Will Clay."

Katie returns to me, still smiling. "How long did it take you to plan this?"

I falter.

"Days," Gil improvises, when I can't think of a way to explain that this whole performance wasn't for her. "Maybe a week."

"Impressive," Katie says. "The weathermen didn't know it would start snowing until this morning."

"Hours," Gil revises. "Maybe a day."

Her eyes never leave me. "So let me guess. You need a change of clothes."

"We need three."

Katie retreats to her closet and says, "Must be pretty chilly out there. Looks like the cold was starting to get to you guys."

Paul looks at her as if she can't possibly mean what he thinks. "Is there a phone I could use?" he asks, gathering his wits.

Katie points at a cordless on the desk. I move across the

THE RULE of FOUR   43

room and press up against her, pushing her into the closet. She tries to shake me off, but when I press too hard, both of us fall onto the rows of shoes, high heels in all the wrong places. It takes a second to untangle ourselves, and I stand up expecting moans from Paul and Gil. But their focus is elsewhere. Paul is in the corner, whispering into the phone, while Gil peers out the window. At first I think Gil's looking for Charlie. Then I see the proctor in his line of sight, speaking into his radio as he approaches.

"Hey, Katie," Gil says, "we don't need matching outfits here. Anything works."

"Relax," she says, coming back with handfuls of clothing on hangers. She lays out three pairs of sweatpants, two T-shirts, and a blue dress shirt I've been missing since March. "It's the best I can do on short notice."

We throw ourselves into them. Suddenly, from the entryway downstairs, the hiss of a hand radio cuts the air. The outside door to the building thuds shut.

Paul hangs up the phone. "I have to get to the library."

"You guys go out the back," Katie says, voice quickening. "I'll deal with it."

I take her hand as Gil thanks her for the clothes.

"I'll see you later?" she says to me, conjuring something in her eyes. It's a look that always comes with a smile now, because she can't believe I still fall for it.

Gil groans and drags me out the door by my arm. As we duck out of the building, I can hear Katie's voice calling down to the proctor.

"Officer! Officer! I need your help. . . ."

Gil turns back, eyes trained on her room. When he sees the proctor arrive in the crosshairs of Katie's leaded window, his expression lightens. Before long, as we head into the piercing wind, Holder vanishes behind a curtain of snow. Campus is nearly empty as we descend toward Dod, and any residue of the tunnels' heat seems to radiate away, washed off in tiny beads of snow that roll from my cheeks. Paul walks slightly ahead of us, keeping a more purposeful pace. The entire time, he doesn't speak a word.

Chapter 4

It was through a book that I met Paul. We probably would've met anyway at Firestone Library, or in a study group, or in one of the literature classes we both took freshman year, so maybe there's nothing special about a book. But when you consider that the one in question was five hundred years old, and that it was the same one my father had been studying before he died, the occasion somehow seems more momentous.

The *Hypnerotomachia Poliphili*, which in Latin means "Poliphilo's Struggle for Love in a Dream," was published around 1499 by a Venetian man named Aldus Manutius. The *Hypnerotomachia* is an encyclopedia masquerading as a novel, a dissertation on everything from architecture to zoology, written in a style that even a tortoise would find slow. It is the world's longest book about a man having a dream, and it makes Marcel Proust, who wrote the world's longest book about a man eating a piece of cake, look like Ernest Hemingway. I would venture to guess that Renaissance readers felt the same way. The *Hypnerotomachia* was a dinosaur in its own time. Though Aldus was the greatest printer of his day, the *Hypnerotomachia* is a tangle of plots and characters connected by nothing but its protagonist, an allegorical everyman named Poliphilo. The gist is simple: Poliphilo has a strange dream in which he searches for the woman he loves. But the way it's told is so complicated that even most Renaissance scholars—the same people who read Plotinus while waiting for the bus—consider the *Hypnerotomachia* painfully, tediously difficult.

Most, that is, except my father. He marched through Renaissance historical studies to the beat of his own drum, and when the majority of his colleagues turned their backs on the *Hypnerotomachia*, he squared it in his sights. He'd been converted to the cause by a professor named Dr. McBee, who taught European history at Princeton. McBee, who died the year before I was born, was a mousy man with elephant ears and small teeth who owed all of his success in the world to an effervescent personality and a canny sense of what made history worthwhile. Though he wasn't much to look at, the little man stood tall in the world of the academy. Every year his closing lecture on the death of Michelangelo filled the largest auditorium on campus with spectators and left college men wiping their eyes and reaching for their handkerchiefs. Above all, McBee was a champion of the book that everyone else in his field ignored. He believed there was something peculiar about the *Hypnerotomachia*, possibly something great, and he convinced his students to search for the old book's true meaning.

One of them searched even more avidly than McBee could have hoped. My father was an Ohio bookseller's son, and he arrived on campus the day after his eighteenth birthday, almost fifty years after F. Scott Fitzgerald made it fashionable to be a midwestern boy at Princeton. Much had changed since then. The university was shedding its country club past, and in the spirit of the times, it was falling out of love with tradition. The freshmen of my father's year were the last class required to attend chapel service on Sundays. The year after he left, women arrived on campus for the first time as students. WPRB, the college radio station, ushered them in to the sound of Handel's "Hallelujah Chorus." My father liked to say that the spirit of his youth was best captured in Immanuel Kant's essay "What Is Enlightenment?" Kant, in his mind, was like the Bob Dylan of the 1790s.

That was my father's way: to erase the line in history beyond which everything seems stuffy and arcane. Instead of time-lines and great men, history to him was ideas and books. He followed McBee's advice for two more years at Princeton, and after graduating he followed it all the way back west to the University of Chicago for a Ph.D. on Renaissance Italy. A year of fellowship work in New York ensued, until Ohio State offered him a tenure-track position teaching quattrocento history, and he leapt at the chance to go home. My mother, an accountant whose tastes ran to Shelley and Blake, took up the bookselling business in Columbus after my grandfather retired, and between the two of them I was raised in the fold of bibliophiles, the way some children are raised in religion.

At the age of four I was traveling to book conferences with my mother. By six I knew the difference between parchment and vellum better than I knew a Fleer from a Topps. Before my tenth birthday I had handled some half-dozen copies of the printing world's masterpiece, the Gutenberg Bible. But I can't even remember a time in my life when I didn't know which book was the Bible of our own little faith: the *Hypnerotomachia*.

"It's the last great Renaissance mystery, Thomas," my father would lecture me, the same way McBee must have lectured him. "But no one has come even close to solving it."

He was right: no one had. Of course, it wasn't until decades after the book was published that anyone realized it *needed* solving. That was when a scholar made a strange discovery. When the first letters of every chapter in the *Hypnerotomachia* are strung together, they form an acrostic in Latin: *Poliam Frater Franciscus Columna Peramavit*, which means "Brother Francesco Colonna loved Polia tremendously." Since Polia was the name of the woman Poliphilo searches for, other scholars finally started to ask who the author of the *Hypnerotomachia* really was. The book itself doesn't say, and even Aldus, the printer, never knew. But from that point on, it became common to suppose that the author was an Italian friar named Francesco Colonna. In a small group of professional researchers, particularly those inspired by McBee, it also became common to suppose that the acrostic was only a hint of the secrets that lay within the book. That group's quest was to discover the rest.

My father's claim to fame in all this was a document he found during the summer I turned fifteen. That year—the year before the car accident—he brought me with him on a research trip to a monastery in southern Germany, then later to the Vatican libraries. We were sharing an

Italian studio apartment with two rollaway beds and a prehistoric stereo system, and each morning for five weeks, with the precision of a medieval punishment, he chose a new Corelli masterwork from the compilations he'd brought, then woke me to the sound of violins and harpsichords at exactly half-past seven, reminding me that research waited for no man.

I would rise to find him shaving over the sink, or ironing his shirts, or counting the bills in his wallet, always humming along with the recording. Short as he was, he tended to every inch of his appearance, plucking strands of gray from his thick brown hair the way florists cull limp petals from roses. There was an internal vitality he was trying to preserve, a vivaciousness he thought was diminished by the crow's-feet at the corners of his eyes, by the thinking man's wrinkles across his forehead, and whenever my imagination was dulled by the endless shelves of books where we spent our days, he was always quick to sympathize. At lunchtime we would take to the streets for fresh pastries and gelato; every evening he would bring me into town for sight-seeing. One night in Rome, he led me on a tour of the city's fountains, telling me to toss a lucky penny into each one.

"One for Sarah and Kristen," he said at the Barcaccia. "To help mend their broken hearts."

My sisters had each been in a painful breakup just before we left. My father, who never took much to their boyfriends, considered it a blessing in disguise.

"One for your mother," he said at the Fontana del Tritone. "For putting up with me."

When my father's request for university funding had

fallen through, my mother kept the bookstore open on Sundays to help pay for our trip.

"And one for us," he said at the Quattro Fiumi. "May we find what we're looking for."

What we were looking for, I never really knew—at least, not until we stumbled onto it. All I knew was that my father believed scholarship on the *Hypnerotomachia* had reached a dead end, mainly because everyone was missing the forest for the trees. Thumping his fist on the dinner table, he would insist that the scholars who disagreed with him had their heads in the sand. The book itself was too difficult to understand from within, he said; a better approach was to search for documents that hinted at who the author really was, and why he'd written it.

In reality, my father alienated many people with his narrow vision of the truth. If it hadn't been for the discovery we made that summer, my family might soon have found itself relying entirely on the bookstore for its livelihood. Instead, Lady Fortune smiled on my father, hardly a year before she took his life.

On the third-floor branch of one of the Vatican libraries, in a recessed aisle of bookshelves that even the monkish dusters had not dusted, as we stood back-to-back searching for the clue he'd been pursuing for years, my father found a letter inserted between the pages of a thick family history. Dated two years before the *Hypnerotomachia* was published, it was addressed to a confessor at a local church, and it told the story of a high-ranking Roman scion. His name was Francesco Colonna.

It's difficult to re-create my father's excitement when he saw the name. The wire-frame glasses he wore, which slunk down his nose the longer he read, magnified his

eyes just enough to make them the measure of his curiosity, the first and last thing most people ever remembered
about him. At that moment, as he sized up what he'd
found, all the light in the room seemed to converge inside
those eyes. The letter he held was written in a clumsy
hand, in broken Tuscan, as if by a man who was not accustomed to that language, or to the act of writing. It ram-
bled on and on, sometimes directed at no one in
particular, sometimes directed at God. The author apologized for not writing in Latin or in Greek, which were unknown to him. Then, at last, he apologized for what he
had done.

*Forgive me, Holy Father, for I have killed two men. It was
my own hand that struck the blow, but the design was never
mine. It was Master Francesco Colonna who bid me do it.
Judge us both with mercy.*

The letter claimed that the murders were part of an in-
tricate plan, one that no man as simple as the author himself could have contrived. The two victims were men
Colonna suspected of treachery, and at his direction they
were sent on an unusual mission. They were given a letter
to deliver to a church outside the walls of Rome, where a
third man would be waiting to receive it. Under pain of
death the two men were not to look at the letter, not to
lose it, not to so much as touch it with an ungloved hand.
So began the story of the simple Roman mason who slew
the messengers at San Lorenzo.

■

The discovery my father and I made that summer came to
be known, in academic circles, as the Belladonna Document. My father felt sure it would revive his reputation in

the scholarly community, and within six months he published a small book under that title suggesting the letter's connection to the *Hypnerotomachia*. The book was dedicated to me. In it, he argued that the Francesco Colonna who'd written the *Hypnerotomachia* was not the Venetian monk, as most professors believed, but instead the Roman aristocrat mentioned in our letter. To bolster this claim, he added an appendix including all known records on the lives of both the Venetian monk, whom he called the Pretender, and of the Roman Colonna, so that readers could compare. The appendix alone made believers of both Paul and me.

The details are straightforward. The monastery in Venice where the false Francesco lived was an unthinkable place for a philosopher-author; most of the time, to hear my father tell it, the place was an unholy cocktail of loud music, hard drinking, and lurid sexual escapades. When Pope Clement VII attempted to force restraint on the brethren there, they replied that they would sooner become Lutherans than accept discipline. Even in such an environment, the Pretender's biography reads like a rap sheet. In 1477 he was exiled from the monastery for unnamed violations. Four years later he returned, only to commit a separate crime, for which he was almost defrocked. In 1516 he pled no contest to rape and was banished for life. Undeterred, he returned again, and was exiled again, this time for a scandal involving a jeweler. Mercifully, death took him in 1527. The Venetian Francesco Colonna—accused thief, confessed rapist, lifelong Dominican—was ninety-three years old.

The Roman Francesco, on the other hand, appeared to be a model of every scholarly virtue. According to my father, he was the son of a powerful noble family, who raised him in the best of European society and had him educated by the highest-minded Renaissance intellectuals. Francesco's uncle, Prospero Colonna, was not only a revered patron of the arts and a cardinal of the Church, but such a renowned humanist that he may have been the inspiration for Shakespeare's Prospero in *The Tempest*. These were the sorts of connections, my father argued, that made it possible for a single man to write a book as complex as the *Hypnerotomachia*—and they were certainly the connections that would've ensured its publication by a leading press.

What sealed the matter entirely, to me at least, was the fact that this blue-blooded Francesco had been a member of the Roman Academy, a fraternity of men committed to the pagan ideals of the old Roman Republic, the ideals expressed with such admiration in the *Hypnerotomachia*. That would explain why Colonna identified himself in the secret acrostic as "Fra": the title Brother, which other scholars took as a sign that Colonna was a monk, was also a common greeting at the Academy.

Yet my father's argument, which seemed so lucid to Paul and me, clouded the academic waters. My father hardly lived long enough to brave the teapot tempest he stirred up in the little world of *Hypnerotomachia* scholarship, but it nearly undid him. Almost all of my father's colleagues rejected the work; Vincent Taft went out of his way to defame it. By then, the arguments in favor of the Venetian Colonna had become so entrenched that, when my father failed to address one or two of them in his brief appendix, the whole work was discredited. The idea of connecting two doubtful murders with one of the world's most valuable books, Taft wrote, was "nothing but a sad and sensational bit of self-promotion."

My father, of course, was devastated. To him it was the substance of his career they were rejecting, the fruit of the quest he'd been on since his days with McBee. He never understood the violence of the reaction against his discovery. The only enduring fan of *The Belladonna Document*, as far as I know, was Paul. He read the book so many times that even the dedication stuck in his memory. When he arrived at Princeton and found a Tom Corelli Sullivan listed in the freshman face-book, he recognized my middle name immediately and decided to track me down.

If he expected to meet a younger version of my father, he must have been disappointed. The freshman Paul found, who walked with a faint limp and seemed embarrassed by his middle name, had done the unthinkable: he had renounced the *Hypnerotomachia* and become the prodigal son of a family that made a religion out of reading. The shock waves of the accident were still ringing through my life, but the truth is that even before my father died, I was losing my faith in books. I'd begun to realize that there was an unspoken prejudice among book-learned people, a secret conviction they all seemed to share, that life as we know it is an imperfect vision of reality, and that only art, like a pair of reading glasses, can correct it. The scholars and intellectuals I met at our dinner table always seemed to hold a grudge against the world. They could never quite reconcile themselves to the idea that our lives don't follow the dramatic arc that a good author gives to a great literary character. Only in accidents of pure perfection does the world actually become a stage. And that, they seemed to think, was a shame.

No one ever said it that way, exactly, but when my father's friends and colleagues—all but Vincent Taft—came to see me in the hospital, looking sheepish about the reviews they'd written of his book, mumbling little eulogies for him they'd composed in the waiting room, I began to see the writing on the wall. I noticed it the moment they walked to my bedside: every one of them brought handfuls of books.

"This helped me when *my* father died," said the chairman of the history department, placing Merton's *Seven Storey Mountain* on the food tray beside me.

"I find great comfort in Auden," said the young graduate student writing her dissertation under my father. She left a paperback edition with one corner clipped off to remove the price.

"What you need is a pick-me-up," another man whispered when the others left the room. "Not this bloodless stuff."

I didn't even recognize him. He left a copy of *The Count of Monte Cristo*, which I'd already read, and I could only wonder if he really thought revenge was the best emotion to encourage just then.

None of these people, I realized, could cope with reality any better than I could. My father's death had a nasty finality to it, and it made a mockery of the laws they lived by: that every fact can be reinterpreted, that every ending can be changed. Dickens had rewritten *Great Expectations* so that Pip could be happy. No one could rewrite this.

When I met Paul, then, I was wary. I'd spent the last two years of high school forcing certain changes on myself: whenever I felt the pain in my leg, I would continue to walk; whenever instinct told me to pass by a door without pausing—the door to the gym, or to a new friend's car, or to the house of a girl I was beginning to like—I would make myself stop and knock, and sometimes let myself in. But here, in Paul, I saw what I might have been.

He was small and pale beneath his untended hair, and more of a boy than a man. One of his shoelaces was untied, and he carried a book in his hand as if it were a security blanket. The first time he introduced himself, he quoted the *Hypnerotomachia*. I felt I already knew him better than I wanted to. He'd tracked me down in a coffee shop near campus just as the sun began to set in early September. My first instinct was to ignore him that evening, and avoid him ever after.

What changed all that was something he said just before I begged off for the night.

"Somehow," he said, "I feel like he's *my* father too."

I hadn't told him about the accident yet, but it was exactly the wrong thing to say.

"You don't know anything about him."

"I do. I have copies of all of his work."

"Listen to me—"

"I even found his dissertation. . . ."

"He's not a book. You can't just *read* him."

But it was as if he couldn't hear.

"*The Rome of Raphael*, 1974. *Ficino and the Rebirth of Plato*, 1979. *The Men of Santa Croce*, 1985."

He began counting them on his fingers.

" 'The *Hypnerotomachia Poliphili* and the Hieroglyphics

of Horapollo.' In *Renaissance Quarterly*, June of '87. 'Leonardo's Doctor.' In *Journal of Medical History*, 1989."

Chronological, without a hitch.

" 'The Breeches-Maker.' *Journal of Interdisciplinary History*, 1991."

"You forgot the *BARS* article," I said.

The *Bulletin of the American Renaissance Society*.

"That was in '92."

"It was in '91."

He frowned. " 'Ninety-two was the first year they accepted articles from non-members. It was sophomore year of high school. Remember? That fall."

There was silence. For a second he seemed worried. Not that he was wrong, but that I was.

"Maybe he wrote it in '91," Paul said. "They only *published* it in '92. Is that what you meant?"

I nodded.

"Then it was '91. You were right." He pulled out the book he'd been carrying with him. "And then there's this."

A first edition of *The Belladonna Document*.

He weighed it deferentially. "His best work so far. You were there when he found it? The letter about Colonna?"

"Yes."

"I wish I could've seen it. It must've been amazing."

I looked over his shoulder, out a window on the far wall. The leaves were red. It had started to rain.

"It was," I said.

Paul shook his head. "You're very lucky."

His fingers fanned the pages of my father's book, gently.

"He died two years ago," I said. "We were in a car accident."

"What?"

"He died right after he wrote that."

The window behind him was fogging up at the corners. A man walked by with a newspaper over his head, trying to keep dry.

"Someone hit you?"

"No. My father lost control of the car."

Paul rubbed his finger against the image on the book's dust jacket. A single emblem, a dolphin with an anchor. The symbol of the Aldine Press in Venice.

"I didn't know . . ." he said.

"It's okay."

The silence at that moment was the longest there has ever been between us.

"*My* father died when I was four," he said. "He had a heart attack."

"I'm sorry."

"Thanks."

"What does your mother do?" I asked.

He found a crease in the dust jacket and began to smooth it out between his fingers. "She died a year later."

I tried to tell him something, but all the words I was used to hearing felt wrong in my mouth.

Paul tried to smile. "I'm like Oliver," he continued, forming a bowl with his hands. "*Please, sir, I want some more.*"

I scraped out a laugh, unsure if he wanted one.

"I just wanted you to know what I meant," he said. "About your dad . . ."

"I understand."

"I only said it because—"

Umbrellas bobbed past the bottom of the window like horseshoe crabs in the tide. The murmur in the coffee shop was louder now. Paul began talking, trying to mend things. He told me how, after his parents died, he'd been raised at a parochial school that boarded orphans and runaways. How, after spending most of high school in the company of books, he'd come to college determined to make something better of his life. How he was looking for friends who could talk back. Finally he fell quiet, an embarrassed look on his face, sensing that he'd killed the conversation.

"So what dorm do you live in?" I asked him, knowing how he felt.

"Holder. Same as you."

He pulled out a copy of the freshman face-book and showed me the dog-eared page.

"How long have you been looking for me?" I asked.

"I just found your name."

I looked out the window. A single red umbrella floated past. It paused at the coffee shop window and seemed to hover there before going on.

I turned back to Paul. "Want another cup?"

"Sure. Thanks."

And so it began.

What a strange thing, to build a castle in the air. We made a friendship out of nothing, because nothing was the heart of what we shared. After that night it seemed more and more natural, talking to Paul. Before long I even started to feel the way he did about my father: that maybe we shared him too.

"You know what he used to say?" I asked him one night in his bedroom when we talked about the accident.

"What?"

"The strong take from the weak, but the smart take from the strong."

Paul smiled.

"There was an old Princeton basketball coach who used to say that," I told him. "Freshman year in high school, I tried out for basketball. My dad would pick me up from practice every day, and when I would complain about how much shorter I was than everybody else, he would say, 'It doesn't matter how big they are, Tom. Remember: *The strong take from the weak, but the smart take from the strong.*' Always the same thing." I shook my head. "God, I got sick of that."

"Do you think it's true?"

"That the smart take from the strong?"

"Yeah."

I laughed. "You've never seen me play basketball."

"Well, *I* believe it," he said. "I definitely do."

"You're kidding . . ."

He'd been stuffed in more lockers and browbeaten by more bullies during high school than anyone I'd ever known.

"No. Not at all." He lifted his hands. "We're here, aren't we?"

He placed the faintest emphasis on *we*.

In the silence, I looked at the three books on his desk. Strunk and White, the Bible, *The Belladonna Document*. Princeton was a gift to him. He could forget everything else.

Chapter 5

Paul, Gil, and I continue south from Holder into the belly of campus. To the east, the tall, thin windows of Firestone Library streak the snow with fiery light. At dark the building looks like an ancient furnace, stone walls insulating the outside world from the heat and blush of learning. In a dream once, I visited Firestone in the middle of the night and found it full of insects, thousands of bookworms wearing tiny glasses and sleeping caps, magically feeding themselves by reading stories. They wriggled from page to page, journeying through the words, and as tensions grew and lovers kissed and villains met their ends, the bookworms' tails began to glow, until finally the whole library was a church of candles swaying gently from left to right.

"Bill's waiting for me in there," Paul says, stopping short.

"You want us to come with you?" Gil asks.

Paul shakes his head. "It's okay."

But I hear the catch in his voice.

"I'll come," I say.

"I'll meet you guys back at the room," Gil says. "You'll be back in time for Taft's lecture at nine?"

"Yes," Paul says. "Of course."

Gil waves and turns. Paul and I continue down the path toward Firestone.

Once we're alone, I realize that neither of us knows what to say. Days have passed since our last real conversation. Like brothers who disapprove of each other's wives, we can't even manage small talk without tripping over our differences: he thinks I gave up on the *Hypnerotomachia* to be with Katie; I think he's given up more for the *Hypnerotomachia* than he knows.

"What does Bill want?" I ask as we approach the main entrance.

"I don't know. He wouldn't say."

"Where are we meeting him?"

"In the Rare Books Room."

Where Princeton keeps its copy of the *Hypnerotomachia*.

"I think he found something important."

"Like what?"

"I don't know." Paul hesitates, as if he's looking for the right words. "But the book is even more than we thought. I'm sure of it. Bill and I both feel like we're on the cusp of something big."

It's been weeks since I've caught a glimpse of Bill Stein. Wallowing in the sixth year of a seemingly endless graduate program, Stein has slowly been assembling a dissertation on the technology of Renaissance printing. A jangling skeleton of a man, he aimed at being a professional librarian until larger ambitions got in his way: tenure, professor-ships, advancement—all the fixations that come with wanting to serve books, then gradually wanting books to serve you. Every time I see him outside Firestone he looks like an escaped ghost, a purse of bones drawn up too tight, with the pale eyes and strange curled-red hair of a half Jew, half Irishman. He smells of library mold, of the books everyone else has forgotten, and after talking to him I sometimes have nightmares that the University of Chicago will be inhabited by armies of Bill Steins, grad students who bring to their work a robotic drive I've never had, whose nickel-colored eyes see right through me.

Paul sees it differently. He says that Bill, impressive as he is, has one intellectual flaw: the absence of a living spark. Stein crawls through the library like a spider in an attic, eating up dead books and spinning them into fine thread. What he makes from them is always mechanical and unin-spired, driven by a symmetry he can never change.

"This way?" I ask.

Paul leads me down the corridor. The Rare Books Room stands off in a corner of Firestone, easy to pass without noticing. Inside it, where some of the youngest books are centuries old, the scale of age becomes relative. Upperclassmen in literature seminars are brought here like children on field trips, their pens and pencils confis-cated, their dirty fingers monitored. Librarians can be heard scolding tenure-track professors to look without touching. Emeritus faculty come here to feel young again.

"It should be closed," Paul says, glancing at his digital watch. "Bill must've talked Mrs. Lockhart into keeping it open."

We are in Stein's world now. Mrs. Lockhart, the librarian

time forgot, probably darned socks with Gutenberg's wife in her day. She has smooth white skin draped on a wispy frame made for floating through the stacks. Most of the day she can be found muttering in dead languages to the books around her, a taxidermist whispering to her pets. We pass by without making eye contact, signing a clipboard with a pen chained to her desk.

"He's in there," she says to Paul, recognizing him. To me she gives only a sniff.

Through a narrow connecting area we arrive before a door I've never opened. Paul approaches, knocks twice, and waits for a sound.

"Mrs. Lockhart?" comes the reply in a high, shifting voice.

"It's me," Paul says.

A lock clicks on the other side, and the door opens slowly. Bill Stein appears before us, a half-foot taller than either Paul or me. The first thing I notice is the gunmetal eyes, how bloodshot they are. The first thing they notice is me.

"Tom came with you," he says, scratching at his face. "Okay. Good, fine."

Bill speaks in shades of the obvious, some stopgap between his mouth and mind gone missing. The impression is misleading. After a few minutes of the mundane you see flashes of his aptitude.

"It was a bad day," he says, guiding us in. "A bad week. Not a big deal. I'm fine."

"Why couldn't we talk on the phone?" Paul asks.

Stein's mouth opens, but he doesn't answer. Now he's scratching at something between his front teeth. He unzips his jacket, then turns back to Paul. "Has someone been checking out your books?" he asks.

"What?"

"Because someone's been checking out mine."

"Bill, it happens."

"My William Caxton paper? My Aldus microfilm?"

"Caxton's a major figure," Paul says.

I've never heard of William Caxton in my life.

"The 1877 paper on him?" Bill says. "It's only at the Forrestal Annex. And Aldus's *Letters of Saint Catherine*—" He turns to me. "Not, as generally believed, the first use of italics—" Then back to Paul. "Microfilm last viewed by someone other than you or me in the seventies. Seventy-one, seventy-two. Someone put a hold on it *yesterday*. This isn't happening to you?"

Paul frowns. "Have you talked to Circulation?"

"Circulation? I talked to Rhoda Carter. They know *nothing*."

Rhoda Carter, head librarian of Firestone. Where the book stops.

"I don't know," Paul says, trying not to get Bill more excited. "It's probably nothing. I wouldn't worry about it."

"I don't. I'm not. But here's the thing." Bill works his way around the far edge of the room, where the space between the wall and the table seems too narrow to pass. He slips through without a sound and pats at the pocket of his old leather jacket. "I get these phone calls. Pick up . . . *click*. Pick up . . . *click*. First at my apartment, now at my office." He shakes his head. "Never mind. Down to business. I found something." He glances at Paul nervously. "Maybe what you need, maybe not. I don't know. But I think it'll help you finish."

From inside his jacket he pulls out something roughly the size of a brick, wrapped in layers of cloth. Placing it gently on the table, he begins to unwrap it. It's a quirk of Stein's I've noticed before, that his hands twitch until they have a book between them. The same thing happens now: as he unravels the cloth, his movements become more controlled. Inside the swaddling is a worn volume, hardly more than a hundred pages. It smells of something briny.

"What collection is it from?" I ask, seeing no title on the spine.

"No collection," he says. "New York. An antiquarian shop. I found it."

Paul is silent. Slowly he extends a hand toward the book. The animal-hide binding is crude and cracked, stitched together with leather twine. The pages are hand-cut. A frontier artifact, maybe. A book kept by a pioneer.

"It must be a hundred years old," I say when Stein doesn't offer any details. "A hundred and fifty."

An irritated look crosses Stein's face, as if a dog has just fouled his carpet. "Wrong," he says. "*Wrong.*" It dawns on me that I'm the dog. "*Five* hundred years."

I focus back on the book.

"From Genoa," Bill continues, focusing on Paul. "Smell it."

Paul is silent. He pulls an unsharpened pencil from his pocket, turns it backward, and gently opens the cover using the soft nub of the eraser. Bill has bookmarked a page with a silk ribbon.

"Careful," Stein says, splaying his hands out above the book. His nails are bitten to the quick. "Don't leave marks. I have it on loan." He hesitates. "I have to return it when I'm done."

"Who had this?" Paul asks.

"The Argosy Book Store," Bill repeats. "In New York. It's what you needed, isn't it? We can finish now."

Paul doesn't seem to notice the pronouns changing in Stein's language.

"What is it?" I say more assertively.

"It's the diary of the portmaster from Genoa," Paul says. His voice is quiet, his eyes circling the script on each page.

I'm stunned. "Richard Curry's diary?"

Paul nods. Curry was working on an ancient Genoese manuscript thirty years ago, which he claimed would unlock the *Hypnerotomachia*. Shortly after he told Taft about the book, it was stolen from his apartment. Curry insisted Taft had stolen it. Whatever the truth was, Paul and I had accepted from the beginning that the book was lost to us. We'd gone about our work without it. Now, with Paul pushing to finish his thesis, the diary could be invaluable.

"Richard told me there were references to Francesco Colonna in here," Paul says. "Francesco was waiting for a ship to come into port. The portmaster made daily entries about him and his men. Where they stayed, what they did."

"Take it for a day," Bill says, interrupting. He stands up and moves toward the door. "Make a copy if you need to. A hand copy. Whatever will help finish the work. But I need it back."

Paul's concentration breaks. "You're leaving?"

"I have to go."

"We'll see you at Vincent's lecture?"

"Lecture?" Stein stops. "No. I can't."

It's making me nervous, just watching how twitchy he is.

"I'll be in my office," he continues, wrapping a red tartan scarf around his neck. "Remember, I need it back."

"Sure," Paul says, drawing the little bundle closer to him. "I'll go through it tonight. I can make notes."

"And don't tell Vincent," Stein adds, zipping up his coat. "Just between us."

"I'll have it back for you tomorrow," Paul tells him. "My deadline is midnight."

"Tomorrow, then," Stein says, flicking the scarf behind him and slinking off. His exits always seem dramatic, being so abrupt. In a few lanky strides he's crossed the threshold where Mrs. Lockhart presides, and is gone. The ancient librarian places a wilted palm on a frayed copy of Victor Hugo, stroking the neck of an old boyfriend.

"Mrs. Lockhart," comes Bill's voice, fading from a place we can't see. "Good-bye."

"It's really the diary?" I ask as soon as he's gone.

"Just listen," Paul says.

He refocuses on the little book and begins reading out loud. The translation proceeds haltingly at first, Paul struggling with the Ligurian dialect, the language of Columbus's Genoa, fused with stray French-sounding words. But gradually his pace improves.

"*High seas last night. One ship . . . broken on the shore. Sharks washed up, one very large. French sailors go to the brothels. A Moorish . . . corsair? . . . seen in close waters.*"

He turns several pages, reading at random.

"*Fine day. Maria is recovering. Her urine is improving, the doctor says. Expensive quack! The . . . herbalist . . . says he will treat her for half the price. And twice as quickly!*" Paul pauses, staring at the page. "*Bat dung,*" he continues, "*will cure anything.*"

I interrupt. "What does this have to do with the *Hypnerotomachia*?"

But he keeps shuttling through the pages.

"*A Venetian captain drank too much last night and began boasting. Our weakness at Fornovo. The old defeat at Portofino. The men brought him to the . . . shipyard . . . and strung him from a tall mast. He is still hanging there this morning.*"

Before I can repeat my question, Paul's eyes go wide.

"*The same man from Rome came again last night,*" he reads. "*Dressed more richly than a duke. No one knows his business here. Why has he come? I ask others. Those who know anything will not speak. A ship of his is coming to port, the rumor goes. He has come to see that it arrives safely.*"

I sit forward in my chair. Paul flips the page and continues.

"*What is of such importance that a man like this comes to see it? What cargo? Women, says the drunkard Barbo. Turk slaves, a harem. But I have seen this man, called Master Colonna by his servants, Brother Colonna by his friends: he is a gentleman. And I have seen what is in his eyes. It is not desire. It is fear. He looks like a wolf that has seen a tiger.*"

Paul stops, staring at the words. Curry has repeated the last phrase to him many times. Even I recognize it. *A wolf that has seen a tiger.*

The cover folds shut in Paul's hands, the tough black seed in its husk of cloths. A salty smell has thickened the air.

"Boys," comes a voice from nowhere. "Your time is up."

"Coming, Mrs. Lockhart." Paul starts into motion, pulling the cloths over the book and wrapping it tight.

"What now?" I ask.

"We've got to show this to Richard," he says, putting the little bundle beneath the shirt Katie lent him.

"Tonight?" I say.

As we find our way out, Mrs. Lockhart mumbles, but doesn't look up.

"Richard needs to know Bill found it," Paul says, glancing at his watch.

"Where is he?"

"At the museum. There's an event tonight for museum trustees."

I hesitate. I'd assumed Richard Curry was in town to celebrate the completion of Paul's thesis.

"We're celebrating tomorrow," he says, reading my expression.

The diary peeks out from under his shirt, a wink of black leather in bandages. From above us comes an echoing voice, almost the sound of laughter.

"*Weh! Steck ich in dem Kerker noch? Verfluchtes dumpfes Mauerloch, Wo selbst das liebe Himmelslicht Trüb durch gemalte Scheiben bricht!*"

"Goethe," Paul says to me. "She always closes up with *Faust.*" Holding the door on the way out, he calls back, "Good night, Mrs. Lockhart."

Her voice comes curling through the mouth of the library.

"Yes," she says. "A good night."

Chapter 6

From what I pieced together between my father and Paul, Vincent Taft and Richard Curry met in New York in their twenties, turning up at the same party one night in uptown Manhattan. Taft was a young professor at Columbia, a thinner version of his later self, but with the same fire in his belly and the same bearish disposition. The author of two books in the brief eighteen months since he'd finished his dissertation, he was the critics' darling, a fashionable intellectual making his rounds in the social circles of choice. Curry, on the other hand, who'd been exempted from the draft for a heart murmur, was just beginning his career in the art world. According to Paul, he was cobbling together the right friendships, slowly building a reputation in the fast Manhattan scene.

Their first encounter came late in the party when Taft, who'd grown tipsy, spilled a cocktail on the athletic-looking fellow beside him. It was a typical accident, Paul told me, since Taft was also known as a drunk at the time. At first Curry took little offense—until he realized Taft didn't intend to apologize. Following him to the door, Curry began to demand satisfaction; but Taft, stumbling toward the elevator, ignored him. As the two men descended ten stories it was Taft who did the talking, hurling a barrage of insults at the handsome young man, bellowing, as he staggered toward the street exit, that his victim was "poor, nasty, brutish, and short."

To his imaginable surprise, the young man smiled.

"*Leviathan*," said Curry, who'd written a junior paper on Hobbes while at Princeton. "And you've forgotten *solitary*. 'The life of man is *solitary*, poor, nasty, brutish, and short.' "

"No," replied Taft with a burbling grin, just before collapsing onto a streetlight, "I did not forget it. I simply reserve *solitary* for myself. *Poor, nasty, brutish*, and *short*, however, are all yours."

And with that, Paul said, Curry hailed a cab, ushered Taft into it, and returned to his own apartment where, for the next twelve hours, Taft remained in a deep and crapulent stupor.

The story goes that when he awoke, confused and embarrassed, the two men struck up a clumsy conversation. Curry explained his line of work, as did Taft, and it seemed the awkwardness of the situation might undo the meeting, when, in a moment of inspiration, Curry mentioned the *Hypnerotomachia*, a book he'd studied under a popular Princeton professor named McBee.

I can only imagine Taft's response. Not only had he heard of the mystery surrounding the book, but he must've noticed the spark it created in Curry's eyes. According to my father, the two men began to discuss the circumstances of their lives, quickly realizing what they had in common. Taft despised other academics, finding their work shortsighted and trivial, while Curry saw his workaday colleagues as papery characters, dull and one-dimensional. Both detected an absence of full-bloodedness in others, an absence of purpose. And maybe that explained the lengths to which they went to overcome their differences.

For there *were* differences, and not small ones. Taft was a mercurial creature, hard to know and harder to love. He drank heavily in company, and just as much when he was alone. His intelligence was relentless and wild, a fire even he couldn't control. It swallowed entire books at a sitting, finding flaws in arguments, gaps in evidence, errors in interpretation, in subjects far from his own. Paul said that it wasn't a destructive personality Taft had, but a destructive mind. The fire grew the more he fed it, leaving nothing behind. When it had burned everything in its path, there was only one thing left for it to do. In time, it would turn on itself.

Curry, by contrast, was a creator, not a destroyer—a man of possibilities rather than facts. Borrowing from Michelangelo, he would say that life was like sculpture: a matter of seeing what others couldn't, then chiseling away the rest. To him the old book was just a block of stone waiting to be carved. If no one in five hundred years had understood it, then the time had come for new eyes and fresh hands, and the bones of the past be damned.

For all these differences, then, it wasn't long before Taft and Curry found their common ground. Besides the ancient book, what they shared was a deep investment in abstractions. They believed in the notion of greatness—

greatness of spirit, destiny, grand design. Like twin mirrors placed face-to-face, their reflections doubling back,
they had seen themselves in earnest for the first time, and
a thousand strong. It was the strange but predictable consequence of their friendship that it left them more solitary
than when they began. The rich human backdrop of Taft's
and Curry's worlds—their colleagues and college friends,
their sisters and mothers and former flames—darkened
into an empty stage with a single spotlight. To be sure,
their careers flourished. It wasn't long before Taft was a
historian of great renown, and Curry the proprietor of a
gallery that would make his name.

But then, madness in great ones must not unwatched
go. The two men led a slavish existence. Their only
source of relief came in the form of weekly meetings on
Saturday nights, when they would regroup at one or the
other's apartment, or at an empty diner, and transform the
one interest they had in common into a shared diversion:
the *Hypnerotomachia*.

Winter had come that year when Richard Curry finally
introduced Taft to the one friend of his who'd never fallen
out of touch—the one Curry had met long ago in Professor McBee's class at Princeton, who harbored his own interest in the *Hypnerotomachia*.

Imagining my father in those days is difficult for me.
The man I see is already married, marking the heights of
his three children on the office wall, wondering when his
only son will start to grow, fussing over old books in dead
languages as the world pitches and turns around him. But
that's the man we made him into, my mother and sisters
and I, not the one Richard Curry knew. My father, Patrick
Sullivan, had been Curry's best friend at Princeton. The

two considered themselves the kings of campus, and I imagine they shared the kind of friendship that made it seem that way. My father played a season of junior varsity basketball, every minute of it on the bench, until Curry, as captain of the lightweight football team, recruited him onto the gridiron, where my father acquitted himself better than anyone expected. The two roomed together the following year, sharing almost every meal; as juniors, they even double-dated twin sisters from Vassar named Molly and Martha Roberts. The relationship, which my father once compared to a hallucination in a hall of mirrors, ended the following spring when the sisters wore identical dresses to a dance, and the two men, having drunk too much and having paid attention too little, made separate passes at the twin the other was dating.

I have to believe that my father and Vincent Taft appealed to different sides of Richard Curry's personality. The laid-back, catholic-minded midwestern boy and the fearsome, focused New Yorker were different animals, and they must've sensed it from the first handshake, when my father's palm was swallowed in Taft's meaty butcher's grip.

Of the three of them, it was Taft who had the darkest mind. The parts of the *Hypnerotomachia* that fascinated him were the bloodiest and most arcane. He devised systems of interpretation to understand the meaning of sacrifices in the story—the way animals' necks were cut, the way characters died—to impose meaning onto the violence. He labored over the dimensions of buildings mentioned in the story, manipulating them to find numerological patterns, cross-checking them with astrological tables and calendars from Colonna's time, hoping to find matches. From where he stood, the best approach was to confront the book head-on, match wits with its author, and defeat him. According to my father, Taft had always believed that he would one day outsmart Francesco Colonna. That day, as far as we knew, had never come.

My father's approach could not have been more different. What fascinated him most about the *Hypnerotomachia* was its candid sexual dimension. In the more prudish centuries after its publication, pictures from the book were censored, blacked out, or torn up entirely, the same way many Renaissance nudes were repainted with fig leaves when tastes changed and sensibilities were offended. In the case of Michelangelo, it seems fair to cry foul. But even today, some of the prints from the *Hypnerotomachia* seem a little shocking.

Parades of naked men and women are only the beginning. Poliphilo follows a gaggle of nymphs to a springtime party—and there, hovering in the middle of the festivities, is the enormous penis of the god Priapus, the focal point of the entire picture. Earlier, the mythological queen Leda is caught in the heat of passion with Zeus, who is shown lodged between her thighs in the shape of a swan. The text is even more explicit, describing encounters too bizarre for the woodcuts. When Poliphilo is overcome with physical attraction to the architecture he sees, he admits to having sex with buildings. At least once, he claims the pleasure was mutual.

All of it fascinated my father, whose view of the book understandably shared little with Taft's. Instead of considering it a rigid, mathematical treatise, my father viewed the *Hypnerotomachia* as a tribute to the love of a man for a woman. It was the only work of art he knew that mimicked the beautiful chaos of that emotion. The dreaminess of the story, the unrelenting confusion of its characters, and the desperate wandering of a man in search of love all resonated with him.

As a result, my father—and, at the beginning of his research, Paul—felt that Taft's approach was misguided. *The day you figure out love*, my father told me once, *you'll understand what Colonna meant*. If there was truly anything to be known about it, my father believed it must be found outside the book: in diaries, letters, family documents. He never told me as much, but I think he always suspected that there *was* a great secret locked inside the pages. Against Taft's formulations, though, my father felt it was a secret about love: an affair between Colonna and a woman below his station; a political powder keg; an illegitimate heir; a romance of the kind teenagers imagine before the ugly bride of adulthood comes and snuffs out childish things.

However much his approach differed from Taft's, though, when my father arrived in Manhattan for a research year away from the University of Chicago, he sensed that the two men were making great strides. Curry insisted that his old friend join them in their work, and my father agreed. Like three animals in a single cage, the men struggled to accommodate one another, circling in suspicion until new lines were drawn and new balances struck. Nevertheless, time was their ally in those days, and all three shared faith in the *Hypnerotomachia*. Like a cosmic ombudsman, old Francesco Colonna watched over and guided them, whitewashing dissent with layers of hope. And for a while, at least, the veneer of unity endured.

For more than ten months, Curry, Taft, and my father worked together. Only then did Curry make the discovery that would prove fatal for their partnership. By then he had gravitated out of the galleries and into the auction houses, where the larger stakes of the art world lay; and it was as he prepared his first estate sale that he came across a ragged notebook that had once belonged to a collector of antiquities, recently deceased.

The notebook belonged to the Genoese portmaster, an old man with a crabbed hand who made a habit of re-marking on the state of the weather and his failing health, but who also kept a daily record of all goings-on at the docks in the spring and summer of 1497, including the peculiar events surrounding the arrival of a man named Francesco Colonna.

The portmaster—whom Curry called Genovese, for he never gave his name—gathered the rumors about Colonna circling through the wharf. He made a point of overhearing the conversations Colonna had with his local men, and learned that the wealthy Roman had come to Genoa to oversee the arrival of an important ship, whose cargo only Colonna knew. Genovese began bringing news of incoming ships to Colonna's day lodgings, where he once caught Colonna scribbling notes, which the Roman hid as soon as Genovese entered.

Had it been left at that, the portmaster's diary would've shed little light on the *Hypnerotomachia*. But the portmaster was a curious man, and as he grew impatient waiting for Colonna's ship to arrive, he sensed that the only way to discover the nobleman's intentions was to see Francesco's shipping documents listing the contents of the cargo. Finally he went to ask his brother-in-law, Antonio, a merchant who sometimes trafficked in pirated goods, if a thief might be hired to enter Colonna's lodgings and copy whatever could be found there. Antonio, in exchange for Genovese's help in another shipping scheme, agreed to help.

What Antonio found was that even the most desperate men would refuse the job upon mention of Colonna's name. The only one willing to do it was an illiterate pickpocket. As it happened, though, the pickpocket did his job well. He copied all three documents in Colonna's possession: the first was part of a story, which the portmaster found of no interest and never fully described; the second was a scrap of leather with a complicated diagram drawn on it, which was inscrutable to Genovese; and the third was a peculiar sort of map, consisting of the four cardinal directions, each followed by a set of units, which Genovese struggled in vain to understand. The portmaster was beginning to regret hiring the thief, when an event transpired that quickly made him fear for his life.

Upon his return home at night, Genovese found his wife weeping. She explained that her brother, Antonio, had been poisoned at dinner in his own home, his body discovered by an errand boy. A similar fate had befallen the pickpocket: while drinking at a tavern, the illiterate thief had been stabbed in the thigh by a passing stranger. Almost before the tavern keeper noticed, the man had bled to death, and the stranger had disappeared.

Genovese lived the following days in a sweat, hardly able to perform his duties at the docks. He never returned to Colonna's lodgings, but in his diary he recorded every useful detail of what the thief had found, and he waited nervously for the arrival of Colonna's ship, hoping the nobleman would depart with his cargo. His concerns became so dire that large merchant vessels came and went with hardly a mention. When Francesco's ship finally did come to port, old Genovese could hardly believe his eyes.

Why would a nobleman trouble himself over such a trivial little bark, he wrote, *this grubby runt-duckling of a boat? What could it be carrying that a man of quality would possibly give a dirty damn about?*

And when he learned that it had come around Gibraltar, carrying goods from the north, Genovese was nearly apoplectic. He filled his little book with filthy swears, saying that Colonna was a syphilitic madman, and that only a dunce or a lunatic would believe that anything of value had ever come from a place like Paris.

According to Richard Curry, only two other entries referred to Colonna. In the first, Genovese recorded a

conversation he overheard between Colonna and a
Florentine architect who was the Roman's only regular
visitor. In it, Francesco alluded to a book he was writing,
in which he chronicled the turmoil of recent days.
Genovese, still gripped with fear, made a careful note of it.

The second entry, made three days later, was more
cryptic, but even more reminiscent of the letter I found
with my father. By then, Genovese had convinced himself
that Colonna was truly mad. The Roman refused to let his
men unload the ship in daylight, insisting that the freight
could be moved safely only at dusk. Many of the wooden
cargo cases, the portmaster observed, were light enough
to be carried by a woman or an old man, and he taxed
himself to think of a spice or metal that would be shipped
in this way. Gradually Genovese began to suspect that
Colonna's associates—the architect and a pair of brothers,
also from Florence—were henchmen or mercenaries in
some dark plot. When a rumor seemed to confirm his
fear, he feverishly wrote it down.

*It is said that Antonio and the thief are not this man's first
victims, but that Colonna has had two other men killed at his
whim. I do not know who they are, and have not yet heard
their names spoken, but I am sure it must be about this cargo of
his. They learned of its contents, and he feared their betrayal. I
am convinced of it now: fear is the thing that moves this man.
His eyes betray him, even if his men do not.*

According to my father, Curry made less of the second
entry than of the first, which he believed might be a reference to the writing of the *Hypnerotomachia*. If true, then
the story the thief had discovered among Colonna's belongings, the details of which Genovese never bothered to
record, might have been an early draft of the manuscript.

But Taft, who by then was pursuing the *Hypnero-tomachia* from his own angles, assembling huge catalogs of textual references into a concordance, so that every word of Colonna's could be traced to its origins, failed to see any possible relevance to the chicken-scratch notes the portmaster claimed to see Colonna keeping. Such a ridiculous story, he said, could never shed light on the profound mystery of the great book. He quickly treated the discovery the same way he'd treated every other book he'd read on the subject: as kindling for the fire.

His frustration, I think, was rooted in more than his feelings about the diary. He had seen the balance of power shift against him, the chemistry of his work with Richard Curry decompose as my father lured Curry into new approaches and alternative possibilities.

And so a struggle ensued, a battle of influence, in which my father and Vincent Taft conceived the hatred for each other that would last until the end of my father's life. Taft, feeling that he had nothing to lose, vilified my father's work in an attempt to win Curry back to his side. My father, feeling that Curry was withering under Taft's pressure, responded in kind. In one month, the work of the previous ten was undone. Whatever progress the three men had made together unraveled into separate ownerships, neither Taft nor my father wanting anything to do with what the other had contributed.

Curry, through it all, clung to Genovese's diary. It mystified him, how his friends had let petty grudges compromise their focus. He possessed, in his youth, the same virtue he would later see and admire in Paul: a commitment to truth, and a great impatience with distraction. Of the three men, I think it was Curry who'd fallen hardest for Colonna's book, Curry who wanted most of all to solve it. Maybe because my father and Taft were still university men, they saw something academic in the *Hypnerotomachia*. They knew a scholar's life could be spent in the service of a single book, and it dulled their sense of urgency. Only Richard Curry, the art dealer, maintained his furious pace. He must have sensed his future even then. His life in books was fleeting.

Not one but two events brought matters to a head. The first occurred when my father went back to Columbus to clear his head. Three days before returning to New York he stumbled, quite literally, across a coed from Ohio State. She and her Pi Beta Phi sisters were in the midst of a book drive, soliciting donations from local shops as part of a yearly charity event, and at the door to my grandfather's bookstore their paths crossed before either of them realized it. In a feathery explosion of pages and paperbacks, my mother and father fell to the floor, and the needle of destiny tightened its stitch and shuttled on.

By the time he arrived back in Manhattan, my father was irretrievably lost, thunderstruck by his encounter with the long-haired, azure-eyed sorority girl who called him Tiger and was alluding not to Princeton but to Blake. Even before meeting her, he knew that he'd had enough of Taft. He also knew that Richard Curry had struck out on a path of his own, fixated on the portmaster's diary. Now the call of home nagged. With his father ailing, and with a woman in his one true port, my father returned to Manhattan only to gather his belongings and say goodbye. His years on the East Coast, which had begun so promisingly at Princeton with Richard Curry, were drawing to a close.

When he arrived at their weekly meeting place, though, prepared to deliver the news, my father found himself in the wake of another bombshell. During his absence, Taft and Curry had argued the first night, and fought physically the next. The old football captain proved no match for bear-size Vincent Taft, who took one swing at the younger man and broke his nose. Then, on the evening before my father returned, Curry left his apartment, eyes black and nose bandaged, to have dinner with a woman from his gallery. When he returned to the apartment that night, documents from the auction house, along with all of his *Hypnerotomachia* research, were gone. His most carefully guarded possession, the portmaster's diary, had vanished with them.

Curry was quick with accusations, but Taft denied each one. The police, citing a string of local burglaries, took little interest in the disappearance of a few old books. But my father, arriving in the middle of it all, sided instantly with Curry. Both of them told Taft that they wanted nothing more to do with him; my father then explained that he had a ticket for Columbus in the morning, and that he intended not to return. He and Richard Curry spoke their farewells even as Taft looked silently on.

So ended the formative period in my father's life, the single year that set in motion all the clockwork of his future identity. Thinking back on it, I wonder if it isn't the same for all of us. Adulthood is a glacier encroaching quietly on youth. When it arrives, the stamp of childhood suddenly freezes, capturing us for good in the image of our last act, the pose we struck when the ice of age set in.

The three dimensions of Patrick Sullivan, when the cold began to claim him, were husband, father, and scholar. They defined him until the end.

After the theft of the portmaster's diary, Taft vanished from the story of my father's life, only to resurface as the gadfly of his career, biting from behind the scholar's veil. Curry would not be in touch with my father for more than three years, until the occasion of my parents' wedding. The letter he wrote then was an uneasy thing, dwelling mainly in the shadow of darker days. The first few words offered his congratulations to the bride and groom; everything after was about the *Hypnerotomachia*.

Time passed; worlds diverged. Taft, carried by the momentum of those early years, was offered a permanent fellowship at the prestigious Institute for Advanced Study, where Einstein had worked while living near Princeton. It was an honor my father surely envied, and one that freed Taft from all the obligations of a college professor: other than agreeing to advise Bill Stein and Paul, the old bear never suffered another student or taught another class. Curry took a prominent job at Skinner's Auction House in Boston, and rose on toward professional success. In the Columbus bookshop where my father learned to walk, three new children kept him occupied enough to forget, for a while, that his experience in New York had left a permanent impression. All three men, wedged from each other by pride and circumstance, found surrogates for the *Hypnerotomachia*, ersatz love affairs to stand in for a quest left incomplete. The generational clock ground out another revolution, and time turned friends to strangers. Francesco Colonna, who kept the key that wound the watch, must have thought his secret safe.

Chapter 7

"Which way?" I ask Paul as the library fades behind us.

"Toward the art museum," he says, hunched over to keep the bundle of cloths dry.

To get there we pass Murray-Dodge, a stony blister of a building in the thick of north campus. Inside, a student theater company is performing Tom Stoppard's *Arcadia*, the last play Charlie had to read in English 151w, and the first one he and I will see together. We have tickets to Sunday night's show. Bubbling over the cauldronlike walls of the stage comes the voice of Thomasina, the thirteen-year-old prodigy of the play, who reminded me of Paul the first time I read it.

If you could stop every atom in its position and direction, she is saying, and if your mind could comprehend all the actions thus suspended, then if you were really, really good at algebra you could write the formula for all the future.

Yes, stammers her tutor, who is exhausted by the engine of her mind. *Yes, as far as I know, you are the first person to have thought of this.*

From a distance, the front entrance to the art museum appears to be open, a small miracle on a holiday night. The museum curators are a strange lot, half of them mousy as librarians, the other half moody as artists, and I get the impression most would rather let kindergartners fingerpaint on the Monets than let an undergrad into the museum when it wasn't strictly necessary.

McCormick Hall, home of the art history department, sits slightly in front of the museum proper, the wall of its entrance paneled in glass. As we approach, security guards eye us through the fishbowl. Like one of the avant-garde exhibits Katie took me to see, which I never understood, they have all the trappings of being real, but are perfectly, silently motionless. A sign on the door says MEETING OF PRINCETON ART MUSEUM TRUSTEES. In smaller letters it adds: *Museum Closed to Public.* I hesitate, but Paul barges in.

"Richard," he calls out into the main hall.

A handful of patrons turn to gawk, but no familiar faces. Canvases punctuate the walls of the main floor, windows of color in this dreary white house. Reconstructed Greek vases sit on waist-high pillars in a nearby room.

"Richard," Paul repeats, louder now.

Curry's bald head turns on its long, thick neck. He is tall and wiry, wearing a tailored pinstripe suit with a red tie. When he sees Paul walking toward him, the man's dark eyes are all affection. Curry's wife died more than ten years ago, childless, and he now looks on Paul as his only son.

"Boys," he says warmly, extending his arms, as if we are half our ages. He turns to Paul. "I didn't expect to see you so soon. I thought you wouldn't be done until later. What a nice surprise." His fingers are tickling his cuff links, his eyes full of pleasure. He reaches over to shake Paul's outstretched hand.

"How have you been?"

We both smile. The energy in Curry's voice belies his age, but in other ways the hounds of time are closing in. Since I last saw him, only six months ago, signs of stiffness have crept into his movements, and the faintest hollow has formed behind the flesh of his face. Richard Curry is the owner of a large auction house in New York now, and the trustee of museums much bigger than this one—but according to Paul, after the *Hypnerotomachia* disappeared from his life, the career that replaced it never became more than a sideline, a campaign to forget what came before. No one seemed more surprised by his success, and less impressed by it, than Curry himself.

"Ah," he says now, turning as if to introduce us to someone. "Have you seen the paintings?"

Behind him is a canvas I've never noticed before. Looking around, I realize the art on the walls is not what's usually here.

"These aren't from the university collections," Paul says.

Curry smiles. "No, not at all. Each of the trustees brought something for tonight. We made a bet to see which one of us could put the most paintings on loan to the museum."

Curry, the old football player, still has a residue in his speech of wagers and gambles and gentlemen's bets.

"Who won?" I ask.

"The art museum," he says, deflecting the question. "Princeton profits when we strive."

In the silence that follows, he scans the faces of the patrons who haven't fled the great hall after our interruption.

"I was going to show you this after the trustees' meeting," he says to Paul, "but there's no reason not to do it now."

He gestures for us to follow him, and begins walking toward a room to the left. I glance at Paul, wondering what he means, but Paul seems not to know.

"George Carter, Sr., brought these two . . ." Curry says, showing us the artwork along the way. Two small prints by Dürer sit in frames so old they have the texture of driftwood. "And the Wolgemut on the far side." He points across the floor. "The Philip Murrays brought those two very nice Mannerists."

Curry leads us into a second room, where late-twentieth-century art has been replaced by Impressionist paintings. "The Wilson family brought four: a Bonnat, a small Manet, and two by Toulouse-Lautrec." He gives us time to study them. "The Marquands added this Gauguin."

We travel across the main hall, and in the room of antiquities he says, "Mary Knight brought only one, but it's a very large Roman bust, and she says it may become a permanent donation. Very generous."

"What about yours?" Paul asks.

Curry has brought us in a great circle through the first floor, back to the original room. "This is mine," he says, waving his hand.

"Which one?" Paul asks.

"All of them."

They exchange a look. The main hall contains more than a dozen works.

"Come this way," Curry says to us, returning to a wall of paintings close to where we found him. "These are the ones I want to show you."

He walks us before every canvas on the wall, one at a time, but says nothing.

"What do they have in common?" he asks, after letting us take them in.

I shake my head, but Paul sees it at once.

"The subject. They're all the biblical story of Joseph."

Curry nods. "*Joseph Selling Wheat to the People,*" he begins, pointing to the first. "By Bartholomeus Breenbergh, about 1655. I convinced the Barber Institute to lend it out."

He gives us a moment, then moves to the second painting. "*Joseph and his Brothers,* by Franz Maulbertsch, 1750. Look at the obelisk in the background."

"It reminds me of a print from the *Hypnerotomachia,*" I say.

Curry smiles. "I thought the same thing at first. Unfortunately, there doesn't seem to be a connection."

He walks us toward the third.

"Pontormo," Paul says before Curry can even begin.

"Yes. *Joseph in Egypt.*"

"How did you get this?"

"London wouldn't let it come directly to Princeton. I had to arrange it through the Met."

Curry is about to say something else, when Paul spots the final two paintings in the series. They are a pair of panels, several feet in size, rich with color. The emotion rises in his voice.

"Andrea del Sarto. *Stories of Joseph*. I saw these in Florence."

Richard Curry is silent. He paid for Paul to spend our freshman summer in Italy researching the *Hypnerotomachia*, the only time Paul has ever left the country.

"I have a friend at the Palazzo Pitti," Curry says, folding his hands over his chest. "He has been very good to me. I have them on loan for a month."

Paul stands frozen for a minute, struck silent. His hair is matted to his head, still wet from the snow, but a smile forms on his lips as he turns back to the painting. It occurs to me, finally, after watching his reaction, that the canvases have been mounted in this order for a reason. They form a crescendo of significance only Paul can understand. Curry must have insisted on this arrangement, and the curators must have agreed to it, obliging the trustee who brought more art than all the others combined. The wall in front of us is a gift from Curry to Paul, a silent congratulation on the completion of his thesis.

"Have you read Browning's poem on Andrea del Sarto?" Curry asks, trying to put words to it.

I have, for a literature seminar, but Paul shakes his head.

"You do what many dream of, all their lives," Curry says. *"Dream? Strive to do, and agonize to do, and fail in doing."*

Paul finally turns and puts a hand on Curry's shoulder. It's then that he steps back and takes the bundle of cloths from beneath his shirt.

"What's this?" Curry asks.

"Something Bill just brought me." Paul falters, and I sense he's unsure how Curry will react. He carefully unwraps the book. "I think you should see it."

"My *diary*," Curry says, stunned. He turns it over in his hands. "I can't believe it. . . ."

"I'm going to use it," Paul says. "To finish."

But Curry ignores him; as he looks down at the book, his smile disappears. "Where did it come from?"

"From Bill."

"You said that. Where did he find it?"

Paul hesitates. An edge has entered Curry's voice.

"In a bookstore in New York," I say. "An antiquarian shop."

"Impossible," the man mumbles. "I looked for this book everywhere. Every library, every bookstore, every pawn-shop in New York. All of the major auction houses. It was *gone*. For thirty years, Paul. It was gone."

He turns the pages, carefully scanning them with both his eyes and his hands. "Yes, look. Here's the section I told you about. Colonna is mentioned here"—he advances to another entry, then to another—"and here." Abruptly he looks up. "Bill didn't just stumble onto this tonight. Not the night before your work is due."

"What do you mean?"

"What about the drawing?" Curry demands. "Bill gave you that too?"

"What drawing?"

"The piece of leather." Curry forms dimensions from his thumbs and index fingers, about one foot square. "Tucked into the centerfold of the diary. There was a drawing on it. A blueprint."

"It wasn't there," Paul says.

Curry turns the book in his hands again. His eyes have become cold and distant.

"Richard, I have to return the diary to Bill tomorrow,"

Paul says. "I'll read through it tonight. Maybe it can get me through the final section of the *Hypnerotomachia*."

Curry shakes himself back to the present. "You haven't finished your work?"

Paul's voice fills with anxiety. "The last section isn't like the others."

"But what about the deadline tomorrow?"

When Paul says nothing, Curry runs his hand over the diary's cover, then relinquishes it. "Finish. Don't compromise what you've earned. There's too much at stake."

"I won't. I think I've almost found it. I'm very close."

"If you need anything, just say so. An excavation permit. Surveyors. If it's there, we'll find it."

I glance at Paul, wondering what Curry means.

Paul smiles nervously. "I don't need anything more. I'll find it on my own, now that I have the diary."

"Just don't let it out of your sight. No one has done something like this before. Remember Browning. '*What many dream of, all their lives.*' "

"*Sir,*" comes a voice from behind us.

We turn to find a curator stepping in our direction.

"Mr. Curry, the trustees' meeting is beginning soon. Could we ask you to move to the upstairs deck?"

"We'll talk about this more later," Curry says, reorienting himself. "I don't know how long this meeting will be."

He pats Paul on the arm, shakes my hand, and then walks toward the stairs. When he ascends, we find ourselves alone with the guards.

"I shouldn't have let him see it," Paul says, almost to himself, as we turn toward the door.

He pauses to take in the series of images one more

time, forming a memory he can return to when the museum is closed. Then we find our way back outside.

"Why would Bill lie about where he got the diary?" I ask once we're in the snow again.

"I don't think he would," Paul says.

"Then what was Curry talking about?"

"If he knew more, he would've told us."

"Maybe he didn't want to tell you while I was there."

Paul ignores me. There's a pretense he likes to keep up, that we are equals in Curry's eyes.

"What did he mean when he said he'd help you get excavation permits?" I ask.

Paul looks over his shoulder nervously at a student who has fallen in behind us. "Not here, Tom."

I know better than to push him. After a long silence I say, "Can you tell me why all the paintings had to do with Joseph?"

Paul's expression lightens. "Genesis thirty-seven." He pauses to call it up. *"Now Jacob loved Joseph more than all his children, because he was the son of his old age. And he made him a coat of many colors."*

It takes me a second to understand. The gift of colors. The love of an aging father for his favorite son.

"He's proud of you," I say.

Paul nods. "But I'm not done. The work isn't finished."

"It's not about that," I tell him.

Paul smiles thinly. "Of course it is."

We make our way back to the dorm, and I notice an unpleasant quality to the sky: it's dark, but not perfectly black. The whole roof of it is shot with snow clouds from horizon to horizon, and they are a heavy, luminous gray. There isn't a star to be seen.

At the rear door to Dod, I realize we have no way in. Paul flags down a senior from upstairs, who gives us an odd look before lending us his ID card. A small pad registers its proximity with a beep, then unlocks the door with a sound like a shotgun being shucked. In the basement, two junior women are folding clothes on an open table, wearing T-shirts and tiny boxer shorts in the swelter of the laundry room. It never fails: walking through the laundry room in winter is like entering a desert mirage, air shivering with heat, bodies fantastic. When it's snowing outside, the sight of bare shoulders and legs is better than a shot of whiskey to get the blood pumping again. We're nowhere near Holder, but it feels like we've stumbled onto the waiting room for the Nude Olympics.

I climb to the first floor and head toward the north flank of the building, where our room is the final quad. Paul trails behind me, silent. The closer we get, the more I find myself thinking of the two letters on the coffee table again. Even Bill's discovery isn't enough to distract me. For weeks I've fallen asleep to the thought of what a person could do with forty-three thousand dollars a year. Fitzgerald wrote a short story once about a diamond the size of the Ritz, and in the moments before I doze off, when the proportions of things are in flux, I can imagine buying a ring with that diamond in it, for a woman just on the other side of the dream. Some nights I think of buying enchanted items, the way children do in games they play, like a car that would never crash, or a leg that would always heal. Charlie keeps me honest when I get carried away. He says I ought to buy a collection of very expensive platform shoes, or put a down payment on a house with low ceilings.

"What are they doing?" Paul says, pointing down the hall.

Standing side by side at the end of the corridor are Charlie and Gil. They're looking into the open doorway of our room, where someone is pacing inside. A second glance tells me everything: the campus police are here. Someone must've seen us coming out of the tunnels.

"What's going on?" Paul says, quickening his steps.

I hurry to follow him.

The proctor is sizing up something on our floor. I can hear Charlie and Gil arguing, but can't make out the words. Just as I start to prepare excuses for what we've done, Gil sees us coming and says, "It's okay. Nothing was taken."

"What?"

He points toward the doorway. The room, I see now, is in disarray. Couch cushions are on the floor; books are thrown off shelves. In the bedroom I share with Paul, dresser drawers hang open.

"Oh God . . ." Paul whispers, pushing between Charlie and me.

"Someone broke in," Gil explains.

"Someone *walked* in," Charlie corrects. "The door was unlocked."

I turn to Gil, the last one out. For the past month Paul has asked us to keep the room tight while he finished his thesis. Gil is the only one who forgets.

"Look," he says defensively, pointing at the window across the room. "They came in through there. Not through the door."

A puddle of water has formed beneath a window by the north face of the common room. Its sash is thrown wide, and snow is gathering on the sill, swimming on the back of the wind. There are three huge slashes through the screen.

I step forward into my bedroom with Paul. His eyes are running along the edge of his desk drawers, rising toward the library books mounted on a wall shelf Charlie built him. The books are gone. His head shifts back and forth, searching. His breathing is loud. For an instant we're back in the tunnels; nothing is familiar but the voices.

It doesn't matter, Charlie. That's not how they got in.

It doesn't matter to you, because they didn't take anything of yours.

The proctor is still pacing through the common room.

"Someone must've known . . ." Paul mumbles to himself.

"Look down here," I say, pointing at the lower mattress on the bunk.

Paul turns. The books are safe. Hands shaking, he begins to check the titles.

I pad through my own belongings, finding almost everything untouched. The dust has hardly been disturbed. Someone rifled through my papers, but only a framed reproduction of the *Hypnerotomachia*'s title page, a gift from my father, has been taken off the wall and opened. One corner is bent, but otherwise it's undamaged. I hold it in my hands. Looking around, I spot a single book of mine out of place: the galley proof of *The Belladonna Letter*, before my father decided *The Belladonna Document* had a nicer ring to it.

Gil steps into the foyer between the bedrooms and

calls to us. "They didn't touch anything of Charlie's or mine. What about you guys?"

There's a spot of guilt in his voice, a hopefulness that despite the mess, nothing is gone.

When I look in his direction, I notice what he means. The other bedroom is pristine.

"My stuff's fine," I tell him.

"They didn't find anything," Paul says to me.

Before I can ask what he means, a voice interrupts from the foyer.

"Could I ask you two a few questions?"

The proctor, a woman with leathery skin and curled hair, takes a slow look at us as we appear, snow-soaked, from the corners of the room. The sight of Katie's sweatpants on Paul, and of Katie's synchronized swimming shirt on me, catches her attention. The woman, identified as Lieutenant Williams by the tag on her breast pocket, pulls a steno pad from her coat.

"You two are . . . ?"

"Tom Sullivan," I say. "He's Paul Harris."

"Was anything of yours taken?"

Paul's eyes are still searching his room, ignoring the proctor.

"We don't know," I say.

She glances up. "Have you looked around?"

"We haven't noticed anything missing yet."

"Who was the last person to leave the room tonight?"

"Why?"

Williams clears her throat. "Because we know who left the door unlocked, but not who left the window open."

She lingers over the words *door* and *window*, reminding us of how we brought this on ourselves.

Paul notices the window for the first time. His color fades. "It must've been me. It was so hot in the bedroom, and Tom didn't want the window open. I came out here to work and I must've forgotten to shut it."

"Look," Gil says to the proctor, seeing she's not trying to help, "can we finish this up? I don't think there's anything else to see."

Without waiting for an answer, he forces the window shut and leads Paul to the couch, sitting beside him.

The proctor makes a final scribble in her pad. "Window open, door unlocked. Nothing taken. Anything else?"

We're all silent.

Williams shakes her head. "Burglaries are hard to resolve," she says, as if she's wrestling with our high expectations. "We'll report it to the borough police. Next time, lock up before you leave. You might save yourself some trouble. We'll be in touch if we have any more information."

She trudges toward the exit, boots squeaking at each step. The door swings shut on its own.

I walk over to the window for another look. The melted snow on the floor is perfectly clear.

"They're not going to do a thing," Charlie says, shaking his head.

"It's okay," Gil says. "Nothing was stolen."

Paul is silent, but his eyes are still scanning the room.

I raise the sash, letting the wind rush into the room again. Gil turns to me, annoyed, but I'm staring at the cuts in the screen. They follow the border of the frame on three sides, leaving the material to flap in the wind like a dog door. I look down at the floor again. The only mud is from my shoes.

"Tom," Gil calls back to me, "shut the damned window." Now Paul turns to look as well.

The flap is pushed out, as if someone left through the window. But something's wrong. The proctor never bothered to notice it.

"Come look at this," I say, running my fingers over the fibers of the screen at the edge of each cut. Like the flap, all of the incisions point outward. If someone had cut the screen to get in, the sliced edges would point toward us.

Charlie is already glancing around the room.

"There's no mud either," he says, pointing to the puddle on the floor.

He and Gil exchange a look, which Gil seems to take as an accusation. If the screen was cut from inside, then we're back to the unlocked door.

"That doesn't make sense," Gil says. "If they knew the door was open, they wouldn't leave through the window."

"It doesn't make sense anyway," I tell him. "Once you're inside, you can always leave through the door."

"We should tell the proctors about this," Charlie says, gearing up again. "I can't believe she didn't even look for it."

Paul says nothing, but runs a hand across the diary.

I turn to him. "You still going to Taft's lecture?"

"I guess. It doesn't start for almost an hour."

Charlie is placing books back on the top shelves, where only he can reach. "I'll stop by Stanhope on the way," he says. "To tell the proctors what they missed."

"It was probably a prank," Gil says to no one in particular. "Nude Olympians having some fun."

After a few more minutes of picking up, we all seem to decide that enough is enough. Gil begins changing into a pair of wool trousers, throwing Katie's dress shirt into a bag of dry cleaning. "We could get a bite to eat at Ivy on the way."

Paul nods, leafing through his copy of Braudel's *Mediterranean World in the Age of Philip II*, as if pages might've been stolen. "I need to check on my stuff at the club."

"You guys might want to change," Gil adds, looking us over.

Paul is too preoccupied to hear him, but I know what Gil means, so I return to the bedroom. Ivy isn't the sort of place I'd be caught dead dressed like this. Only Paul, a shadow in his own club, lives by different rules.

What dawns on me as I check my drawers is that nearly all of my clothes are dirty. Rummaging in the far back of my closet, I find a rolled-up pair of khakis and a shirt that's been folded for so long that the folds have become creases, and the creases pleats. I search for my winter jacket, then realize it's still hanging from Charlie's duffel bag in the steam tunnels. Settling for the coat my mother bought me for Christmas, I head into the common room, where Paul is sitting by the window, eyes on the bookshelves, puzzling something out.

"Are you bringing the diary with you?" I ask.

He pats the bundle of rags in his lap and nods.

"Where's Charlie?" I say, looking around.

"Already gone," Gil tells me, guiding us out to the hall. "To see the proctors."

He takes the keys to his Saab and places them inside his coat. Before closing the door behind us, he checks his pockets.

"Room keys . . . car keys . . . ID . . ."

He's so careful, it makes me uneasy. It isn't Gil's way to

concern himself with details. Staring back into the common room, I see my two letters sitting on the table. Then Gil locks the door with the same odd precision, rolling the knob in his palm twice afterward to be sure that it yields nothing. We walk toward his car, and now the silence is heavy. As he revs the engine, proctors shift in the distance, shadows of shadows. We watch them for a second, then Gil jerks the gearshift and brings us gliding into the darkness.

Chapter 8

Past the security kiosk at the north entrance to campus, we turn right onto Nassau Street, Princeton's main drag. At this hour it's lifeless, prowled by two plows and a salt truck that someone has roused from hibernation. Stray boutiques glow in the night, snow gathering below their storefront windows. Talbot's and Micawber Books are closed at this hour, but Pequod Copy and the coffee shops manage a small bustle, filled with seniors rushing to complete their theses in the eleventh hour before departmental deadlines.

"Glad to be done with it?" Gil asks Paul, who has retreated into himself again.

"My thesis?"

Gil looks into the rearview mirror.

"It's not finished yet," Paul says.

"Come on. It's *done*. What do you have left to do?"

Paul's breath frosts the rear window. "Enough," he says.

At the stoplight, we turn onto Washington Road, then toward Prospect Avenue and the eating clubs. Gil knows better than to ask more questions. As we approach Prospect, I know his thoughts are gravitating elsewhere. Saturday night is the Ivy Club's annual ball, and it has been left to him, as club president, to oversee the arrangements. After falling behind while finishing his thesis, he's gotten into the habit of making little trips to Ivy just to convince himself that everything is under control. According to Katie, by the time I arrive to escort her tomorrow night, I'll barely recognize the inside of the club.

We pull up beside the clubhouse, into the space that seems to be reserved for Gil, and when he disengages his key from the ignition a cold silence echoes in the cabin. Friday is the lull in the weekend storm, a chance to sober up between the traditional party nights of Thursday and Saturday. The recent snow has dampened even the hum of voices that usually drifts in the air as juniors and seniors return to campus from dinner.

According to administrators, the eating clubs at Princeton are "an upperclass dining option." The reality is that the eating clubs are basically the only option we have. In the early days of the college, when refectory fires and surly innkeepers forced students to fend for themselves, small groups banded together to take meals under the same roof. Princeton being what it was in those days, the roofs they ate under, and the clubhouses they built to support those roofs, were no mean affair; some of them are nothing short of manors. And to this day the eating club remains Princeton's peculiar institution: a place, like a coed fraternity, where junior and senior members hold parties and eat meals, but do not reside. Almost one hundred and fifty years after the institution first appeared, social life at Princeton is simple to explain. It lies firmly in the hands of the clubs.

Ivy looks grim at this hour. Cloaked in darkness, the sharp points and dark stonework of the building are uninviting. Cottage Club, next door, with its white quoins and round accents, easily outshines it. These two sister clubs, older than the other surviving ten on Prospect Avenue, are Princeton's most exclusive. Their rivalry for the best of each class has endured since 1886.

Gil looks at his watch. "They're not seating for dinner anymore. I'll bring us up some food." He holds the front door open, then guides us up the main stairs.

It's been a while since my last visit here, and the dark oak-paneled walls with their severe-looking portraits always give me pause. To the left is Ivy's dining room, with its long wooden tables and century-old English chairs; to the right is the billiards room, where Parker Hassett is playing a game of pool alone. Parker is Ivy's village idiot, a half-wit from a wealthy family who is just bright enough to realize what a fool some people think he is, and just dumb enough to blame everyone else for it. He plays pool with both hands moving the cue, like a vaudeville actor dancing with a cane. Though he glances over at us when we pass, I ignore him as we mount the stairs, heading for the Officers' Room.

Knocking twice at the door, Gil enters without awaiting a reply. We follow him into the warm light of the room, where Brooks Franklin, Gil's portly vice president, sits at a long mahogany table extending lengthwise just past the door. Atop the table stand a Tiffany lamp and a phone. Around its edge are tucked six chairs.

"I'm glad you showed up when you did," Brooks says to all of us, politely ignoring the fact that Paul is wearing women's clothes. "Parker was telling me his costume plans for tomorrow night, and I was starting to think I might need backup."

I don't know Brooks very well, but ever since we shared an introductory economics class sophomore year, he has related to me as an old friend. I'm guessing that Parker's plans have to do with Saturday's dance, which is traditionally a Princeton-themed costume ball.

"You'll fucking *die*, Gil," Parker says, arriving unannounced from downstairs. Now he has a cigarette in one hand, a glass of wine in the other. "At least *you* have a sense of humor."

He speaks directly to Gil, as if Paul and I are invisible. Down at the table, I can see Brooks shaking his head.

"I've decided to come as JFK," he continues. "And my date's not going to be Jackie. She's going to be Marilyn Monroe."

Parker must see confusion in my expression, because he dashes his cigarette into an ashtray on the table. "Yes, Tom," he says, "Kennedy *graduated* from Harvard. But he went *here* his freshman year."

The latest product of a California wine family that has sent a son to Princeton, and to Ivy, for generations, Parker cleared both of those hurdles thanks only to what Gil, charitably, calls the Hassett family's *momentum*.

Before I can respond, Gil leans forward.

"Look, Parker, I don't have time for this. If you want to

come as Kennedy, that's your business. Just try to show some taste."

Parker, who seemed to expect something better, shoots a sour look at all of us and walks off, wine in hand.

"Brooks," Gil says now, "can you go down and ask Albert if there's any dinner left? We haven't eaten and we're in a rush."

Brooks agrees. He is the perfect vice president: obliging, tireless, loyal. Even when Gil's favors come out sounding like commands, he never seems to be ruffled. Tonight is the only time he has ever looked weary to me, and I wonder if he just finished his thesis.

"Actually," Gil adds, looking up, "I'll bring two of them up here, and eat mine in the dining room. We can talk about the wine order for tomorrow while I eat."

Brooks turns to Paul and me. "Good to see you guys," he says. "Sorry about Parker. I don't know what gets into him sometimes."

"Sometimes?" I say under my breath.

Brooks must hear me, because he smiles before leaving.

"The food should be ready in a few minutes," Gil says. "I'll be downstairs if you guys need me." He focuses on Paul. "We can go to the lecture as soon as you're ready."

For a second after he leaves, I can't escape the feeling that Paul and I are committing some kind of fraud. We're sitting at an antique mahogany table in a nineteenth-century mansion, waiting for someone to bring us our dinners. If I had a nickel for every time this had happened to me since I got to Princeton, I would need another one to rub the two together. Cloister Inn, the club where Charlie and I are members, is a small, simple building with a cozy stone charm. When the floors are polished and the greens are trimmed it's a respectable place to draw a beer or shoot some pool. But in scale and in gravity it is dwarfed by Ivy. Our chef's first priority is quantity, not quality, and unlike our Ivy friends we eat where we please, rather than being seated in the order of our arrival. Half of our chairs are plastic, all of our cutlery is replaceable, and sometimes when the parties we throw are too expensive, or the taps we run are too loose, we find hot dogs in the lunch tray on Fridays. We are like many of the clubs on the street. Ivy has always been the exception.

"Come downstairs with me," Paul says abruptly.

Unsure what he means by it, I follow. We descend past the stained-glass window that runs along the south landing, then down another flight of stairs into the basement of the club. Paul leads me through the hall toward the President's Room. Gil is supposed to have sole access to the room, but when Paul worried about having less and less privacy at his library carrel while trying to finish his thesis, Gil promised him a copy of the key, hoping to lure him back to the club. Paul had found little to recommend Ivy by then, work-obsessed as he was. But the President's Room, large and quiet and accessible to Paul directly through the steam tunnels, was a blessing he couldn't refuse. Others protested that Gil had made a hostel of the club's most exclusive room, but Paul defused all controversy by arriving at the room almost always through the tunnels. It seemed to bother the offended parties less when they didn't have to see him come and go.

As we arrive in front of the door, Paul pops the lock open with his key. Shuffling in behind him, I'm caught by surprise. It's been weeks since I've seen the place. The first thing I remember is how cold it is. Here, in what is effectively the club's cellar, temperatures hover uncomfortably close to freezing. Exclusive or no, the room looks like it's been hit by a hurricane of letters. Books have settled on every surface like mounds of debris: the shelves of Ivy's moldering European and American classics are almost obscured by Paul's reference books, historical journals, nautical maps, and stray blueprint designs.

He closes the door behind us. Beside the desk is a handsome fireplace, and the clutter of papers is so heavy here that some of the titles are bleeding onto the hearth. Still, when Paul scans the room, he seems pleased; everything is as he left it. He walks over and picks up *The Poetry of Michelangelo* from the floor, brushes some paint chips off the cover, and places it carefully on his desk. Finding a long wooden match atop the mantel, he strikes the head and reaches down into the fireplace, where a blue flame breathes life into old newsprint weighted with logs.

"You've done a lot," I tell him, looking at one of the more detailed blueprints unraveled across his desk.

He frowns. "That's nothing. I've made a dozen like that, and they're probably all wrong. I do it when I feel like giving up."

What I'm looking at is a drawing of a building Paul invented. The edifice is stitched together from the ruins of buildings mentioned in the *Hypnerotomachia*: broken arches have been restored; riddled foundations are strong again; columns and capitals, once shattered, now find themselves repaired. There is an entire pile of blueprints beneath it, each one assembled the same way from the odds and ends of Colonna's imagination, each one different. Paul has created a landscape to live in down here, an Italy of his own. On the walls are taped other sketches, some hidden by notes he has affixed over them. In each one the lines are studiously architectural, measured in units I don't understand. A computer could have produced all of them, the proportions are so perfect, the script is so careful. But Paul, who claims to be suspicious of computers, has actually never been able to afford his own, and politely refused Curry's offer to buy him one. Everything here has been drawn by hand.

"What are they supposed to be?" I ask.

"The building Francesco is designing."

I'd almost forgotten Paul's habit of referring to Colonna in the present tense, always using the man's first name.

"What building?"

"Francesco's crypt. The first half of the *Hypnerotomachia* says he's designing it. Remember?"

"Of course. You think it looks like these?" I ask, gesturing at the drawings.

"I don't know. But I'm going to find out."

"How?" Then I remember what Curry said at the museum. "Is that what the surveyors are for? You're going to exhume it?"

"Maybe."

"So you found out why Colonna built it?"

This was the pivotal question we came to, just as our work together ended. The text of the *Hypnerotomachia* alluded mysteriously to a crypt Colonna was constructing, but Paul and I could never agree about its nature. Paul envisioned it as a Renaissance sarcophagus for the Colonna family, possibly intended to rival papal tombs of the kind Michelangelo designed around the same period. Trying harder to connect the crypt to *The Belladonna Document*, I imagined the crypt as a final resting place for Colonna's victims, a theory that went further toward explaining the *Hypnerotomachia*'s great secrecy about the design. The fact that Colonna never fully described the building, or where it could be found, remained the major gap in Paul's work at the moment I left.

Before he can answer my question, a knock comes at the door.

"You moved," Gil says, entering with the club steward.

He stops short, sizing up Paul's room like a man peering into a women's bathroom, sheepish but intrigued. The steward places two settings in cloth napkins on a table, finding patches of space between the books. Between them, they're carrying two plates of Ivy Club china, a pitcher of water, and a basket of bread.

"Warm rustic bread," the steward says, putting the basket down.

"Steak with peppercorns," Gil says, following suit. "Anything else?"

We shake our heads, and Gil takes one last look at the room, then returns back upstairs.

The steward pours water into two glasses. "Would you like something else to drink?"

When we say no, he vanishes too.

Paul serves himself quickly. Watching him eat, I think of the Oliver Twist impression he did the first time we met, the little bowl he made with his hands. Sometimes I wonder if Paul's first memory of childhood is of hunger. At the parochial school where he was raised, he shared the table with six other children, and meals were always first come, first served, until the food ran out. I'm not sure he ever escaped that mentality. One night our freshman year, back when we all took meals together in the dining hall of our residential college, Charlie joked that Paul ate so fast you'd think food was going out of style. Later that night Paul explained why, and none of us joked about it again.

Now Paul extends his arm for a piece of bread, caught up in the joy of eating. The smell of food wrestles with the old mildew stink of books and the smoke of the fire, in a way I might've enjoyed under different circumstances. But here, now, it feels uncomfortable, different memories sewn together. As if he can read my mind, Paul becomes conscious of his reach and looks bashful.

I push the basket toward him. "Eat up," I say, scraping at the food.

Behind us, the fire sputters. Over in the corner is an opening in the wall, the size of a large dumbwaiter: the entrance to the steam tunnels, the one Paul prefers.

"I can't believe you still crawl through that."

He puts down his fork. "It's better than dealing with everyone upstairs."

"It feels like a dungeon down here."

"It didn't bother you before."

I sense an old argument reviving. Paul quickly wipes his mouth with a napkin. "Forget it," he says, putting the diary onto the table between us. "This is what matters now." He taps the cover with two fingers, then pushes the little book toward me. "We have a chance to finish what we started. Richard thinks this could be the key."

I rub at a stain on the desk. "Maybe you should show it to Taft."

Paul gapes at me. "Vincent thinks everything I found with you is worthless. He's been pushing me for progress reports twice a week, just to prove I haven't given up. I'm tired of driving to the Institute every time I need his help, and having him say this is derivative work."

"*Derivative?*"

"And he threatened to tell the department I'm stalling."

"After everything we found?"

"It doesn't matter," he says. "I don't care what Vincent thinks." He taps the diary again. "I want to finish."

"Your deadline is tomorrow."

"We did more together in three months than I did alone in three years. What's one more night?" Under his breath, he adds, "Besides, the deadline isn't what matters."

I'm surprised to hear him say it, but the jab of Taft's rejection is what lingers. Paul must've known it would. I feel more pride in the work I did on the *Hypnerotomachia* than in all the work I did on my own thesis.

"Taft's out of his mind," I tell him. "No one's ever found that much in the book before. Why didn't you request an advisor change?"

Paul's hands begin shredding the bread into little pellets, rolling them between his fingers. "I've been asking myself the same thing," he says, looking away. "Do you know how many times he's bragged to me about ruining the academic career of 'some moron' with his peer reviews or tenure recommendations? He never mentioned your father, but there were others. Remember Professor Macintyre from Classics? Remember his book about Keats's 'Ode on a Grecian Urn'?"

I nod. Taft wrote an article on what he perceived to be the declining quality of scholarship at major universities, using Macintyre's book as a primary example. In three paragraphs Taft identified more factual errors, misattributions, and oversights than two dozen other scholars had found in their own book reviews. Taft's implicit criticism seemed to be aimed at the reviewers, but it was Macintyre who became such a laughingstock that the university pruned him from the departmental ranks at the next tenure review. Taft later admitted that he was just getting even with Macintyre's father, a Renaissance historian who'd given one of Taft's own books a mixed review.

"Vincent told me a story once," Paul continues, voice growing quieter. "About a kid he knew growing up, named Rodge Lang. Kids at school called him Epp. One day a stray dog followed Epp home from school. Epp ran, but the dog kept following him. Epp threw part of his lunch to the dog, but the dog wouldn't leave him alone. Finally he tried to scare the animal off with a stick, but the dog just kept following.

"After a few miles, Epp started to wonder. He led the dog through a briar patch. The dog followed. He threw a rock at the dog, but the dog wouldn't back away. Finally Epp *kicked* the dog. The dog didn't run off. Epp kicked it again, and again. The dog wouldn't move. Epp kicked the dog until it was dead. Then he picked it up and brought it to his favorite tree, and buried it there."

I'm almost too stunned to answer. "What the hell's the moral of *that*?"

"According to Vincent, that's when Epp knew he'd found a loyal dog."

A silence unfolds.

"Was that Taft's idea of a joke?"

Paul shakes his head. "Vincent told me a lot of stories about Epp. They're all like that."

"Jesus. Why?"

"I think they're supposed to be some kind of parable."

"Parables he made up?"

"I don't know." Paul hesitates. "But Rodge Epp Lang also happens to be an anagram. A rearrangement of the letters in 'doppelganger.'"

I feel sick. "Do you think *Taft* did those things?"

"To the dog? Who knows. He might've. But his point was that he and I have the same relationship. I'm the dog."

"So why the hell are you still working with him?"

Paul begins fidgeting with the bread again. "I made a decision. Staying with Vincent was the only way I could finish my thesis. I'm telling you, Tom, I'm convinced this is even bigger than we thought. Francesco's crypt is *this* close. No one has made a find like this in years. And after your father, no one had done more work on the *Hypnerotomachia* than Vincent. I needed him." Paul throws the crust onto his plate. "And he knew it."

Gil arrives in the doorway. "I'm done upstairs," he says, as if we've been waiting for him to finish. "We can go now."

Paul seems glad to end the conversation. Taft's behavior is a reproach to him. I rise and begin to bus my plates.

"Don't worry about those," Gil says, waving me off. "They'll send someone down."

Paul wipes his hands together briskly. Strings of the bread roll up on his palms, and he sloughs them like old skin. We both follow Gil out of the club.

The snow is coming down much harder than before, so thick that I feel I'm watching the world through patches of static. As Gil navigates the Saab westward, approaching the auditorium, I look in the side mirror at Paul, wondering how long he's been keeping all this to himself. We pass between streetlights in the dark, and for short pulses of time I can't see him at all. His face is just a shadow.

The fact is, Paul has always kept secrets from us. For years he hid the truth about his childhood, the details of his parochial school nightmare. Now he's been hiding the truth about his relationship with Taft. Close as he and I are, there's a certain distance now, a feeling that while we have a lot in common, good fences still make good neighbors. Leonardo wrote that a painter should begin every canvas with a wash of black, because all things in nature are dark except where exposed by the light. Most painters do the opposite, starting with a whitewash and adding the shadows last. But Paul, who knows Leonardo so well you'd think the old man slept in our bottom bunk, understands the value of starting with the shadows. The only things people can ever know about you are the ones you let them see.

I might not have grasped this very well, except that an interesting thing happened on campus just a few years before we arrived, which caught both Paul's attention and mine. A twenty-nine-year-old bicycle thief named James Hogue got into Princeton by claiming to be someone he wasn't: an eighteen-year-old ranch hand from Utah. Hogue said he'd taught himself Plato under the stars, and trained himself to run a mile in just over four minutes. When the track team flew him out to campus for a recruiting trip, he said it was the first time he'd slept indoors in a decade. The admissions office was so captivated that it accepted him on the spot. When he deferred for a year, no one gave it a second thought. Hogue said he was tending to his sick mother in Switzerland; in fact, he was serving a term in prison.

What made the hoax so intriguing was that, while roughly half of it was an outrageous lie, the other half was more or less true. Hogue was as good a runner as he let on, and for two years at Princeton he was a star on the track team. He was also a star in the classroom, shouldering a course load you couldn't pay me to take, and getting straight A's to boot. He was even so charming that Ivy tapped him for membership in the spring of his sophomore year. It almost seems a shame that his career ended the way it did. By sheer accident a spectator at a track meet recognized him from a previous life. When word spread, Princeton conducted an investigation and had him arrested in the middle of a science lab. Charges were pressed, and Hogue pled guilty to fraud. Within a matter of months he was in prison again, where he slowly faded back into obscurity.

To me the Hogue story was the news event of that summer; the only thing to rival it was my discovery that *Playboy* had run a Women of the Ivy League issue the previous spring. To Paul, though, it was much more. As someone who always insisted on a varnish of fiction in his own life, pretending he'd eaten well when he hadn't, or pretending not to own a computer because he didn't like using one, Paul could identify with a man who felt bullied by the truth. One of the only advantages of coming from nothing, as James Hogue and Paul both did, is having the freedom to reinvent yourself. In fact, the better I got to know Paul, the more I understood it was less a freedom than a kind of obligation.

Still, seeing what became of Hogue, Paul had to rethink the line between reinventing himself and fooling everyone else. Beginning the day he arrived at Princeton, he walked that line very carefully, keeping secrets rather than telling lies. An old fear returns to me when I consider that. My father, who understood the way the *Hypnerotomachia* had seduced him, once compared the book to an affair with a woman. *It makes you lie,* he said, *even to yourself.* Paul's thesis may be exactly that lie: after four years with Taft, Paul has danced and danced for the book, left his bed and lost sleep for the book, and for all his sweat, the book has given up very little.

Looking back in the mirror again, I can see him watching the snow. There is a blank look in his eyes and his face seems pale. In the distance a traffic light is flashing yellow. My father taught me something else without ever saying a word: never invest yourself in anything so deeply that its failure could cost you your happiness. Paul would sell his last cow for a handful of magical beans. Only now is he beginning to wonder if the beanstalk will grow.

Chapter 9

I think it was my mother who told me that a good friend stands in harm's way for you the second you ask—but a great friend does it without being asked at all. There are so few times in a person's life when a single great friend comes around that it almost seems unnatural when three come around all at once.

The four of us met on a cool night during the fall of our freshman year. Paul and I were already spending much of our time together, and Charlie—who'd introduced himself on the first day of school by barging into Paul's room and offering to help him unpack—was living in a single room down the hall. Thinking nothing could be worse than being alone, Charlie was always on the prowl for new friends.

Paul immediately had misgivings about this wild, imposing character who never stopped pounding at his door with new adventures in mind. Something about Charlie's athletic build seemed to conjure a spell of fear in him, as if he'd been tortured by a bully of that description as a child. For my part, I was surprised that Charlie hadn't gotten tired of us, sedate as we were. Most of that first semester, I was convinced that he would abandon us for companions more like himself. I pegged him for a wealthy minority jock—the kind who had a neurosurgeon mother and an executive father, who eased through a regional prep school with more tutors than trouble, and who arrived at Princeton with nothing particular in mind except to have some fun and graduate in the solid middle of the class.

That all seems funny now. The truth was, Charlie grew up in the heart of Philadelphia, riding with the volunteer ambulance squad through the worst crime districts in the city. He was a middle-class kid from a public school, whose father was a regional sales rep for an East Coast chemical manufacturer, and whose mother taught seventh-grade science. When he applied to college, his parents made it clear that anything beyond in-state tuition was a burden he would shoulder himself. The day Charlie arrived on campus, he'd taken on more student loans, and was more deeply in debt, than the rest of us would be when we graduated. Even Paul, who came from less, had been given a full scholarship because his need was so great.

Maybe that was why, other than Paul during his month of insomnia as thesis deadlines approached, none of us did more and slept less than Charlie. He expected great things for his money, and to justify his sacrifice, he sacrificed even more. It wasn't an easy thing to maintain a sense of identity at a school where only one in fifteen students was black, and only half of those were men. But identity for Charlie never ran along completely conventional lines anyway. He had a world-beating personality and an irresistible sense of purpose, and from the beginning I felt it was his world we were living in, not ours.

Of course, we didn't know all that on the late October night, only six weeks after we first met him, when he came to Paul's door with his most daring plan to date. Since roughly the Civil War, students at Princeton had been in the habit of stealing the clapper from the bell atop Nassau Hall, the oldest building on campus. The original idea was that if the bell couldn't toll the beginning of a new academic year, then the new academic year couldn't begin. Whether anyone actually believed that, I don't know, but I do know that stealing the clapper became a tradition, and that students tried everything from picking locks to scaling walls to do it. After more than a hundred years, the administration got so tired of the stunt, and so worried about a lawsuit, that it finally announced the clapper had been removed. Only, Charlie had information to the contrary. The removal was a hoax, he said; the clapper was intact. And tonight, with our help, he was going to steal it.

I don't need to explain that breaking into a historic landmark with a set of stolen keys and then fleeing from proctors on my bad leg, all in the name of a worthless bell clapper and fifteen minutes of campus fame, didn't strike me as a world-class idea. But the longer Charlie argued his case, the more I saw his point: if juniors and seniors have their research papers and theses, and sophomores choose their majors and eating clubs, then all that's left for freshmen is to take risks or get caught trying. The deans will never be more forgiving, he argued, than they will now. And when Charlie insisted it would take three people—no fewer—he and I decided that the only fair way to resolve things was to take a vote. In a reassuring test of democracy, we held a slim majority over Paul, and Paul, never being one to rock the boat, gave in. We agreed to be lookouts for Charlie, and after planning our course of attack, the three of us assembled what we could in the way of black clothing and set out for Nassau Hall at midnight.

Now, I've said before that the new Tom—the one who survived the terrible car wreck and lived to fight another day—was made of braver, more adventurous stuff than the shrinking violet who was old Tom. But let's be clear. Old or new, Evel Knievel I am not. For an hour after we arrived at Nassau Hall, I stood at my post in a tense sweat, fearing every shadow and twitching at every sound. Then, shortly after one o'clock, it happened. As the first of the eating clubs closed their taprooms for the night, a westward migration began of students and security officers retreating to campus. Charlie had promised that we would be well clear of Nassau Hall by then, but now he was nowhere to be seen.

I turned and hissed at Paul, *"What's taking so long?"*

But there was no response.

Taking a step toward the darkness, I called out again, squinting into the shadows.

"What's he doing up there?"

But when I peered around the corner, there was no sign of Paul. The front door to the building was ajar.

I ran to the entrance. Sticking my head inside, I could make out Paul and Charlie in a distant conversation. *"It's not up there,"* Charlie was saying.

"Hurry up!" I said. *"They're coming."*

Suddenly a voice rose from the darkness behind me. "Campus police! Stop right there!"

I turned in terror. Charlie's voice choked into silence. I must have misheard, because I thought Paul swore.

"Put your hands on your hips," came the voice again.

My mind fogged up. I imagined probation; dean's warnings; expulsion.

"Put your hands on your hips," the voice repeated, louder now.

I obeyed.

For a moment there was silence. I strained to make out the proctor in the darkness, but I could see nothing.

The next sound I heard was his laughter.

"Now shake it, baby. *Dance.*"

The figure who emerged from the shadows was a student. He laughed again and did a tipsy rumba thrust as he approached. He was about halfway between my height and Charlie's, with dark hair that fell over his face. His tailored black blazer covered a starched white shirt with too many buttons undone.

Charlie and Paul crept warily from the building behind me, empty-handed.

The young man walked up to them, smiling. "So it's true?" he said.

"What is?" Charlie growled, glaring at me.

The young man pointed at the bell tower. "The clapper. They really took it out?"

Charlie said nothing, but Paul nodded, still full of adventure.

Our new friend thought for a second. "But you got up there?"

I began to see where this was leading.

"Well, you can't just *leave*," he said.

Mischief danced in his eyes. Charlie was liking him better by the second. Before long I was back at my post, guarding the east door, as all three of them vanished into the building.

When they returned fifteen minutes later, they weren't wearing pants.

"What are you doing?" I said.

They came toward me, arm in arm, doing a little jig in their boxers. Looking up toward the cupola, I could make out six pant legs flapping from the weather vane.

I stammered that we had to get home, but they looked at each other and booed me. The stranger insisted that we go back to one of the eating clubs to celebrate. Time for a few toasts at Ivy, he said, knowing that at this hour on Prospect Avenue, pants would be optional. And Charlie was happy to agree.

As we walked east toward Ivy, then, our new friend told us stories of his own pranks in high school: dyeing the pool red for Valentine's Day; releasing cockroaches in English class when the freshmen were reading Kafka; scandalizing the drama department by inflating a giant penis above the theater roof on opening night of *Titus Andronicus*. You had to be impressed. He, too, as it happened, was a freshman. A graduate of Exeter, he said, by the name of Preston Gilmore Rankin.

"But," he added, as I remember to this day, "call me Gil."

Gil was different from the rest of us, of course. In retrospect, I think he arrived at Princeton so used to the affluence of Exeter that wealth and the distinctions it imposed on life had become invisible to him. The only meaningful yardstick in his eyes was character, and maybe that was why, during our first semester, Gil was drawn immediately to Charlie, and through Charlie, to us. His charm always managed to smooth over the differences, and I couldn't help but feel that to be with Gil was to be in the thick of things.

At meals and parties he always reserved a place for us, and while Paul and Charlie quickly decided that his idea of a social life wasn't exactly like theirs, I found that I enjoyed Gil's company most when we were sitting around a dining table or sidled up at a bar in the Ivy Club taproom, whether with friends or alone. If Paul was at home in a classroom or in a book, and Charlie was at home in an ambulance, then Gil was at home wherever a good conversation was to be had, and the rest of the world be damned. Many of the best nights I remember at Princeton were with him.

Late sophomore spring, the time came for us to choose our eating clubs—and for the clubs to choose us. By then, most of the clubs were using a lottery system to determine selection: candidates added their names to an open list, and the new section of the club was chosen at random. But a few maintained the older system, known as bicker. Bicker resembles rush at a fraternity, in that bicker clubs choose their new members based on merit rather than on chance. And like fraternities, the definitions of merit they use tend not to be the same ones you might find, say, in a dictionary. Charlie and I entered our names in the lottery at Cloister Inn, where our mutual friends seemed to be gathering. Gil, of course, decided to bicker. And Paul, under the influence of Richard Curry, an old Ivy member himself, threw caution to the wind and bickered too.

From the outset, Gil was a shoo-in at Ivy. He satisfied

every possible criterion for admission, from being the son of a club alum, to being a prominent member of the right circles on campus. He was handsome in an effortless way—always stylish, never flashy; dashing yet gentlemanly; bright but not bookish. That his father was a wealthy stockbroker who gave his only son a scandalous allowance did nothing to hurt his chances. It came as no more surprise when he was admitted to Ivy that spring than when he was elected its president a year later.

Paul's acceptance at Ivy was the product of a different logic, I think. It helped that Gil, and more distantly Richard Curry, stood in his corner, making his case in crowds where Paul would never tread. But it wasn't to those connections alone that he owed his success. Paul was also, by that time, acknowledged as one of the academic luminaries of our class. Unlike the bookworms who never ventured from Firestone, he was driven by a curiosity that made him a pleasure to meet and converse with. Upperclassmen at Ivy seemed to find something charming about a sophomore who had no skill with the tired banter of the selection process, but referred to dead authors by their first names, and seemed to know them just that well. It didn't even surprise Paul when they accepted him. When he returned that spring night, soaked with celebratory champagne, I thought he'd found a new home.

For a while, in fact, Charlie and I worried that the club's magnetism would draw the two of them away from us. It didn't help that, by then, Richard Curry had become a prominent influence in Paul's life. The two had met early in our freshman year, when I agreed to have dinner with Curry on a rare trip to New York. The interest the man showed in me after my father's death had always struck me as a strange, selfish thing—I'd never known which of us was the surrogate, the childless father or the fatherless child—so I asked Paul to join us for dinner, hoping to use him as a buffer. It worked better than I intended. The connection was instant: the vision Curry always seemed to have of my personal potential, which he claimed my father shared, was realized all at once in Paul. Paul's interest in the *Hypnerotomachia* resurrected memories of Curry's glory days working on the book with my father and Vincent Taft, and it was only a semester later that he offered to send Paul to Italy for a summer of research. By then, the intensity of the man's support for Paul had begun to worry me.

But if Charlie and I feared that we were losing our two friends, then we were reassured soon enough. At the end of junior year, it was Gil who suggested that the four of us live together as seniors, a decision that meant he was willing to give up living in the President's Room at Ivy to keep us as his roommates on campus. Paul immediately agreed. And so, with a mediocre draw at the housing lottery, we found ourselves in a quad at the north end of Dod. Charlie argued that a fourth-floor room would force us to get more exercise, but convenience and good sense prevailed, and the ground-floor suite, well furnished thanks to Gil, became home for our final year at Princeton.

Now, as Gil, Paul, and I reach the courtyard between the university chapel and the lecture hall, we're greeted by a strange sight. More than a dozen open-air canopies have been set up in the snow, each with a long table of food beneath it. I know immediately what it means; I just can't believe it. The lecture organizers intend to serve refreshments outside.

Like a country carnival just before a hurricane, the tables are completely deserted. The ground beneath the canopies is choppy with mud and tufts of grass. Snow is creeping in from the edges, and in the hectic wind the white tablecloths flutter uneasily, anchored by large dispensers of what will soon be hot chocolate or coffee, and by cold platters of cookies and petits fours in cocoons of plastic wrap. It cuts a peculiar image in the silent courtyard, like a city extinguished in midmotion by a calamity, a makeshift Pompeii.

"You've got to be kidding," Gil says as we park. We get out of the car, and he starts toward the lecture hall, pausing to shake the support poles of the nearest tent. The whole structure trembles. "Wait till Charlie sees this."

On cue, Charlie appears at the door of the lecture hall. For some reason he's preparing to leave.

"Hey, Chuck," I call out as we approach, gesturing at the courtyard. "How do you like all this?"

But Charlie has other things on his mind.

"How was I supposed to get into the auditorium?" he snaps at Gil. "You idiots put some girl at the entrance, and she won't let me through."

Gil holds the door for the rest of us. He understands by "idiots" that Charlie is referring to Ivy. As cochairs of the biggest campus Christian group, three senior women at the club are coordinating the Easter ceremonies.

"Loosen up," Gil says. "They just thought Cottage might try some kind of prank. They're trying to nip it in the bud."

Charlie grabs himself expressively. "Yeah, well, I almost told them to nip *this* in the bud."

"Beautiful," I say, heading for the warmth of the lecture hall. My shoes are already soaked. "Can we go inside?"

At the landing, a sophomore with frosted blond hair and a skier's tan is sitting behind a long table, already shaking her head. When Gil arrives behind us at the top of the stairs, though, everything changes.

The sophomore looks sheepishly at Charlie. "I didn't know you were with Gil . . ." she begins.

From inside I can hear the voice of Professor Henderson from the comparative literature department, introducing Taft to the audience.

"Forget it," Charlie says, walking past the table toward the entrance. The rest of us follow.

The auditorium is filled to capacity. All along the walls and toward the back of the hall by the entrance, those who couldn't find a seat are on their feet. I catch sight of Katie in a back row with another pair of Ivy sophomores, but before I can get her attention, Gil nudges me forward, searching for a place where the four of us can stand. He puts a finger over his lips and points toward the stage. Taft is walking to the podium.

The Good Friday lecture is a tradition with deep roots at Princeton, the first of three Easter celebrations that have become fixtures in the social lives of many students, Christian and non-Christian alike. By legend the events were introduced in the spring of 1758 by Jonathan Edwards, the fiery New England churchman who moonlighted as Princeton's third president. Edwards led the students in a sermon on the night of Good Friday, followed by a religious meal on Saturday evening, and a service at midnight as Easter Sunday began. Somehow these rituals were then transmitted intact down to the present, profiting from that immunity to time and fortune which the university, like an ancient tar pit, confers on everything that unwittingly lumbers into it and dies.

One of those things, as it happened, was Jonathan Edwards himself. Soon after arriving at Princeton, Edwards was given a potent smallpox inoculation, and within three months the old man had died from it. Notwithstanding the fact that he was probably too weak to have invented the ceremonies that have been attributed to him, though, university officials re-create all three of them, year after year, in what is euphemistically called "a modern context."

I suspect Jonathan Edwards was never much for euphemisms or modern contexts. Considering that his most famous metaphor for human life involved a spider dangling above the pit of hell, hung there by a wrathful God, the old man must turn in his grave every spring. The Good Friday sermon is now nothing more than a lecture delivered by a member of the humanities faculty; the only thing mentioned less often than God in the lecture is hell. The original religious meal, which must have been stark and Calvinist in its conception, is now a banquet in the most beautiful of the undergraduate dining halls. And the midnight service, which I'm sure once made the walls tremble, is now a nondenominational celebration of faith, where not even the atheists and agnostics can feel out of place. Maybe for that reason, students of every background attend the

Easter ceremonies, each for a different reason, and all of them depart happily, with their expectations reinforced and their sensitivities respected.

Taft stands at the podium, fat and shaggy as ever. Seeing him, I think of Procrustes, the mythological highwayman who tortured his victims by stretching them on a bed if they were too short, or cutting them down to size if they were too tall. Every time I look at the man I think of how misshapen he is, how his head is too big and his gut is too round, how the fat dangles from his arms as if the flesh were pulled from his bones. Still, there is an operatic quality to the figure he cuts onstage. In his wrinkled white dress shirt and worn tweed coat, he is larger than his own circumstances, a mind bulging at its human seams. Professor Henderson steps toward him, trying to adjust the microphone on his lapel, and Taft remains still, like a crocodile having its teeth cleaned by a bird. This is the giant at the top of Paul's beanstalk. Remembering the story of Epp Lang and the dog, I feel my stomach turn again.

By the time we find a pinch of standing room at the back of the auditorium, Taft has begun, and already it's far from the usual Good Friday drivel. He's delivering a slide show, and over the broad white projection screen comes a series of images, each more terrible than the last. Saints being tortured. Martyrs being slain. Taft is saying that faith is easier to give than life, but harder to take away. He has brought examples to make his point.

"Saint Denis," he says, voice pulsing through the speakers mounted high overhead, "was martyred by decapitation. According to legend, his corpse rose and carried his head away."

Above the lectern is a painting of a blindfolded man

with his head on a block. The executioner is wielding an enormous ax.

"Saint Quentin," he continues, advancing to the next image. "Painted by Jacob Jordaens, 1650. He was stretched on the rack, then flogged. He prayed to God for strength, and survived, but was later put on trial as a sorcerer. He was racked and beaten, and his flesh was pierced with iron wires from the shoulders to the thighs. Iron nails were forced into his fingers, skull, and body. He was ultimately decapitated."

Charlie, failing to see the point of all this, or maybe just unimpressed after the horrors he's seen with the ambulance team, turns to me.

"So what'd Stein want?" he whispers.

Across the screen comes a dark image of a man, naked but for a loincloth, being forced to lie across a metal surface. A fire is being lit below him. "Saint Lawrence," Taft continues, familiar enough with the details not to need cues. "Martyred in 258. Burned alive on a gridiron."

"He found a book Paul needs for his thesis," I say.

Charlie points to the bundle in Paul's hand. "Must be important," he says.

I expect something sharp in the words, a reminder of how Stein cut our game short, but Charlie says them with respect. He and Gil still mispronounce the *Hypnerotomachia*'s title five times out of ten, but Charlie, at least, can identify with how hard Paul has worked, and how much this research means to him.

Taft presses a button behind the lectern again, and an even stranger image appears. A man lies on a wooden tablet, with a hole in the side of his abdomen. A string from within the hole is gradually being turned on a spit by two men on either side of him.

"Saint Erasmus," Taft says, "also known as Elmo. He was tortured by Emperor Diocletian. Though beaten with whips and clubs, he survived. Though rolled in tar and set on fire, he lived. Though thrown into prison, he escaped. He was recaptured and forced to sit in a burning iron chair. Finally he was killed by having his stomach cut open and his intestines wound around a windlass."

Gil turns to me. "This is *definitely* different."

A face in the back row turns to shush us, but seems to think better of it after seeing Charlie.

"The proctors wouldn't even listen to me about the screen," Charlie whispers to Gil, still looking for conversation.

Gil turns back toward the stage, not wanting to resurrect the topic.

"Saint Peter," Taft continues, "by Michelangelo, around 1550. Peter was martyred under Nero, crucified upside-down at his own request. He was too humble to be crucified the same way as Christ."

Onstage, Professor Henderson looks uncomfortable, picking nervously at a spot on her sleeve. Without any thread of argument connecting one slide to the next, Taft's presentation is beginning to seem less like a lecture than like a sadist's peep show. The usual rumble of conversation in the auditorium on Good Fridays has dissolved into titillated silence.

"Hey," Gil says, tapping Paul's sleeve, "does Taft always talk about this stuff?"

Paul nods.

"He's a little off, isn't he?" Charlie whispers.

The two of them, having stayed out of Paul's academic life for so long, are noticing this for the first time.

Paul nods, but says nothing.

"We arrive, then," Taft continues, "at the Renaissance. The home of a man who embraced the language of violence I have been trying to convey. What I wish to share with you tonight is not a story he created by dying, but something of the mysterious story he created while still alive. The man was an aristocrat from Rome named Francesco Colonna. He wrote one of the rarest books ever printed: the *Hypnerotomachia Poliphili*."

Paul's eyes are fixed on Taft, pupils wide in the dark.

"From *Rome*?" I whisper.

Paul looks at me, incredulous. Before he can answer, though, there is an outburst at the entrance behind us. A sharp, violent exchange has erupted between the girl at the door and a large man, as yet obscured. Their voices are spilling through the lecture hall.

To my surprise, when the man emerges into the light, I recognize him at once.

Chapter 10

Against the loud protests of the blonde at the door, Richard Curry enters the auditorium. Dozens of heads in the back of the room turn. Curry scans the audience, then turns toward the stage.

This book, Taft continues in the background, oblivious to the commotion, *is perhaps the greatest remaining mystery of Western printing.*

From all sides, awkward glances size up the intruder. Curry looks disheveled: tie loose, jacket in hand, a dislocated look in his eyes. Paul begins pushing his way through a small crowd of students.

It was published by the most famous press in all of Renaissance Italy, but even the identity of its author remains heavily debated.

"What's that guy doing?" Charlie whispers.

Gil shakes his head. "Isn't that Richard Curry?"

Now Paul is in the back row, trying to get Curry's attention.

It is considered by many to be not only the world's most mis-understood book, but also—perhaps only after the Gutenberg Bible—the world's most valuable.

Paul stands beside the man now. He places a hand on Curry's back, almost cautiously, and whispers something, but the old man shakes his head.

"I am here," Curry says, loudly enough that people in the front row turn to get a glimpse, "to say something of my own."

By now Taft has stopped talking. Every face in the hall is fixed on the stranger. He reaches up and runs his hand over his head. Glaring at Taft, he speaks again.

"The language of violence?" he says, in a shrill, un-familiar voice. "I heard this lecture thirty years ago, Vincent, when you thought *I* was your audience." He turns to the crowd and spreads his arms, addressing them all. "Did he tell you about Saint Lawrence? Saint Quentin? Saint Elmo and the windlass? Hasn't anything changed, Vincent?"

There are murmurs through the audience as people register Curry's scorn. From one corner there is laughter.

"This, my friends," Curry continues, pointing at the stage, "is a hack. A fool and a crook." He turns to focus on Taft. "Even a charlatan can fool the same man twice, Vincent. But you? You prey on the innocent." He places his fingers to his lips and forms a kiss. "Bravissimo, il Fraudolento!" Lifting his arms, he encourages the audi-ence to stand. "An ovation, my friends. Three cheers for Saint Vincent, patron saint of thieves."

Taft meets the intrusion grimly. "Why have you come here, Richard?"

"They know each other?" Charlie whispers.

Paul is trying to distract Curry, telling him to stop, but Curry continues.

"Why have *you* come here, old friend? Is this theater or scholarship? What will you steal this time, now that the portmaster's book is out of your hands?"

At this, Taft lurches forward and booms, "*Stop this. What are you doing?*"

But Curry's voice escapes like a conjured spirit. "Where have you put the piece of leather from the diary, Vincent? Tell me and I'll leave. You can carry on with this farce of yours."

The shadows of the lecture hall creep unpleasantly across Curry's face. Professor Henderson finally shoots to her feet and barks, "Someone get security!"

A proctor is already within arm's reach of Curry when Taft waves him off. His self-possession has returned.

"No," the ogre growls. "Let him go. He will leave of his own accord. Won't you, Richard? Before they have to *arrest* you?"

Curry is unmoved. "Look at us, Vincent. Twenty-five years, and still waging the same war. Tell me where the blueprint is and you won't see me again. That's the only business we have anymore. The rest of this"—Curry sweeps his arms across the lecture hall, encompassing everything—"is worthless."

"Get out, Richard," Taft says.

"You and I tried and failed," Curry continues. "What do the Italians say? *There's no worse thief than a bad book.* Let's be men about it and step aside. Where's the blueprint?"

There are whispers all around. The proctor edges between Curry and Paul—but to my surprise, Curry suddenly lowers his head and begins to move toward the far aisle. The animation in his face disappears.

"You old fool," he says, addressing Taft even with his back toward the stage. "Act on."

Students against the wall push toward the front of the auditorium, keeping their distance. Paul stands rooted to the spot, watching his friend depart.

"Leave, Richard," Taft instructs from the podium. "Don't return."

We all follow Curry's slow progress toward the exit. The sophomore at the door watches with wide, fearful eyes. In a moment he passes across the threshold, into the anteroom, and is gone from sight.

Intense murmuring seizes the lecture hall as soon as he has vanished.

"What the hell was that?" I ask, looking back at the exit.

In our corner, Gil steps over toward Paul.

"Are you okay?"

Paul is fumbling. "I don't understand . . ."

Gil places an arm over his shoulder. "What did you say to him?"

"Nothing," Paul says. "I have to go after him." His hands are shaking, the diary still tucked between them. "I need to talk to him."

Charlie begins to protest, but Paul is too upset to argue. Before any of us can insist otherwise, he turns and heads for the door.

"I'll go with him," I say to Charlie.

He nods. Taft's voice has begun to roll again in the

background, and when I look up at the stage on the way out, the giant seems to be staring directly at me. From her seat, Katie catches my attention. She mouths a question about Paul, but I can't understand what she's saying. Zipping my coat, I head out of the auditorium.

In the courtyard, canopies lurch like skeletons in the dark, dancing on their peg legs. The wind has softened, but the snow continues, thicker than before. Around the corner I hear Paul's voice.

"Are you okay?"

I turn the corner. Not ten feet away is Richard Curry, jacket fluttering in the wind.

"What's wrong?" Paul asks.

"Get back inside," Curry says.

I step forward to hear more, but snow crunches beneath my feet. Curry looks over, and their conversation halts. I expect some spark of recognition in his eyes, but find none. After putting his hand on Paul's shoulder, Curry slowly backs away.

"Richard! Can't we talk somewhere?" Paul calls out.

But the old man distances himself quickly, slipping his arms into his suit jacket. He doesn't answer.

It takes me a second to regain my wits and go to Paul's side. Together we watch Curry disappear into the shadow of the chapel.

"I need to find out where Bill got the diary," he says.

"Right now?"

Paul nods.

"Where is he?"

"Taft's office at the Institute."

I look out across the courtyard. Paul's only transportation is an old Datsun he bought with his stipend from Curry. The Institute is a long way from here.

"Why'd *you* leave the lecture?" he asks.

"I thought you might need some help."

My bottom lip is shivering. Snow is gathering in Paul's hair.

"I'll be okay," he says.

But he's the one without a coat.

"Come on. We can drive out there together."

He looks down at his shoes. "I have to talk to him alone."

"You're sure?"

He nods.

"At least take this," I offer, unzipping the peacoat.

He smiles. "Thanks."

"Call us if you need anything."

Paul puts on the coat and slips the diary under his arm. After a second he begins walking off into the snow.

"You're sure you don't want help?" I shout before he's out of earshot.

He turns back, but only to nod.

Good luck, I say, almost to myself.

And as the cold plunges below the neckline of my shirt, I know there's nothing left to do. When Paul vanishes into the distance, I head back inside.

On my way up to the auditorium I pass by the blonde without a word and find that Charlie and Gil haven't moved from their spot in the rear of the lecture hall. They pay me no attention; Taft has won their interest. His voice is hypnotic.

"Everything okay?" Gil whispers.

I nod, not wanting to get into the details.

"Certain modern interpreters," Taft is saying, "have been content to accept that the book conforms to many conventions of an old Renaissance genre, the bucolic romance. But if the *Hypnerotomachia* is just a conventional love story, then why are only thirty pages devoted to the romance between Poliphilo and Polia? Why do the other three hundred and forty pages form a maze of subplots, strange encounters with mythological figures, dissertations on esoteric subjects? If only one out of every ten words pertains to the romance itself, then how do we explain the other ninety percent of the book?"

Charlie turns to me again. "Do you know all this stuff?"

"Yeah." I've heard the same lecture a dozen times over the dinner table at home.

"In short, it is no mere love story. Poliphilo's 'struggle for love in a dream'—as the Latin title would have it—is much more complex than boy-meets-girl. For five hundred years scholars have exposed the book to the most powerful interpretive tools of their day, and not one of them has found a way out of the labyrinth.

"How difficult is the *Hypnerotomachia*? Consider how its translators have fared. The first French translator condensed the opening sentence, which was originally more than seventy words long, into less than a dozen. Robert Dallington, a contemporary of Shakespeare's who attempted a closer translation, simply despaired. He gave up before he was halfway through. No English translation has been attempted since. Western intellectuals have considered the book a byword for obscurity almost since it was published. Rabelais made fun of it. Castiglione warned Renaissance men not to speak like Poliphilo when wooing women.

"Why, then, is it so difficult to understand? Because it contains not only Latin and Italian, but also Greek, Hebrew, Arabic, Chaldean, and Egyptian hieroglyphics. The author wrote in several of them at once, sometimes interchangeably. When those languages were not enough, he invented words of his own.

"In addition, there are mysteries surrounding the book. To begin with, until very recently no one knew who wrote it. The secret of the author's identity was so closely guarded that not even the great Aldus himself, its publisher, knew who'd composed his most famous work. One of the *Hypnerotomachia*'s editors wrote an introduction to it in which he asks the Muses to reveal the author's name. The Muses refuse. They explain that 'it is better to be cautious, to keep divine things from being devoured by vengeful jealousy.'

"My question to you, then, is this: Why would the author have gone to such trouble if he were writing nothing more than a bucolic romance? Why so many languages? Why two hundred pages on architecture? Why eighteen pages on a temple of Venus, or twelve on an underwater labyrinth? Why fifty on a pyramid? Or another hundred and forty on gems and metals, ballet and music, food and table settings, flora and fauna?

"Perhaps more important, what Roman could have learned so much about so many subjects, mastered so many languages, and convinced the greatest printer in Italy to publish his mysterious book without so much as mentioning his name?

"Above all, what were the 'divine things' alluded to in the introduction, which the Muses refused to divulge? What was the vengeful jealousy they feared these things might inspire?

"The answer is that this is no romance. The author must have intended something else—something that we scholars have as yet failed to understand. But where do we begin searching for it?

"I do not intend to answer that question for you. Instead, I will leave you with a puzzle of your own to muse over. Solve this, and you are one step closer to understanding what the *Hypnerotomachia* means."

With that, Taft triggers the slide machine with a pump of his palm on the remote. Three images appear over the screen, disarming in their stark black and white.

"These are three prints from the *Hypnerotomachia*, depicting a nightmare that Polia suffers late in the story. As she relates, the first shows a child riding a burning chariot into a forest, drawn by two naked women whom he whips

like beasts. Polia looks on from her hiding place in the woods.

"The second print shows the child releasing the women by slicing their red-hot chains with an iron sword. He then thrusts the sword through each of them, and once they are dead, he dismembers them.

"In the final print, the child has torn out the still-beating hearts of the two women from their corpses and fed them to birds of prey. The innards he feeds to eagles. Then, after quartering the bodies, he throws the rest to the dogs, wolves, and lions that have gathered about.

"When Polia awakens from this dream, her nurse explains that the child is Cupid, and that the women were young maidens who offended him by refusing the affections of their suitors. Polia deduces that she has been wrong to rebuff Poliphilo."

Taft pauses, turning his back to the audience in order to contemplate the enormous images that seem to float in the air at his back.

"But what if we suppose that the explicit meaning is not the *real* meaning?" he says, his back still to us, in a disembodied voice that resonates through the microphone on his chest. "What if the nurse's interpretation of the dream is not, in fact, the right one? What if we were to use the punishment inflicted on these women to decipher what their crime truly was?

"Consider a legal punishment for high treason that survived among certain European nations for centuries before and after the *Hypnerotomachia* was written. A criminal convicted of high treason was first *drawn*—meaning that he was tied to the tail of a horse and dragged across the ground through the city. He was brought in this way to the gallows, where he was hanged until he was not fully dead, but only half-dead. At this time he was cut down, and the entrails were sliced from his body and burned before him by the executioner. His heart was removed and displayed to the assembled crowd. The executioner then decapitated the carcass, quartered the remains, and displayed the pieces on pikes in public locations, to serve as a deterrent to future traitors."

Taft returns his focus to the audience as he says this, to see its reaction. Now he circles back toward the slides.

"With this in mind, let us reconsider our pictures. We see that many of the details correspond to the punishment I've just described. The victims are drawn to the location of their deaths—or rather, perhaps a bit ironically, they draw the executioner's chariot themselves. They are dismembered, and their limbs are shown to the assembled crowd, which in this instance consists of wild animals.

"Instead of being hanged, however, the women are slain with a sword. What are we to make of this? One possible explanation is that beheading, either by ax or sword, was a punishment reserved for those of high rank, for whom hanging was deemed too base. Perhaps, then, we may infer that these were ladies of distinction.

"Finally, the animals that appear in the crowd will remind many of you of the three beasts from the opening canto of Dante's 'Inferno,' or the sixth verse of Jeremiah." Taft looks out across the lecture hall.

"I was just about to say that . . ." Gil whispers with a smile.

To my surprise, Charlie hushes him.

"The lion signifies the sin of pride," Taft goes on. "And the wolf represents covetousness. These are the vices of a high traitor—a Satan or a Judas—just as the punishment seems to suggest. But here the *Hypnerotomachia* diverges: Dante's third beast is a leopard, representing lust. Yet Francesco Colonna includes a dog instead of a leopard, suggesting that lust was *not* one of the sins for which the two women are being punished."

Taft pauses, letting the audience chew on this for a moment.

"What we are beginning to read, then," he begins again, "is the vocabulary of cruelty. Despite what many of you may think, it is not a purely barbaric language. Like all of our rituals, it is rich with meaning. You must simply learn to read it. I will therefore offer one additional piece of information, which you may use in interpreting the image—then I will pose a question, and leave the rest to you.

"Your final clue is a fact that many of you probably know, but have overlooked: namely, that we can tell Polia has misidentified the child, simply by noting the weapon the child is carrying. For if the little boy in the nightmare had truly been Cupid, as Polia claims, then his weapon would not have been the sword. It would have been the bow and arrow."

There are murmurs of assent in the crowd, hundreds of students seeing Valentine's Day in an entirely new light.

"Therefore I ask you: who is this child that brandishes a sword, forces women to draw his war chariot through a difficult forest, then slaughters them as if they were guilty of treason?"

He waits, as if preparing to deliver the answer, but instead says, "Solve this, and you will begin to understand the hidden truth of the *Hypnerotomachia*. Perhaps you will also begin to understand the significance not only of death, but of the form death takes when it comes. All of us—we of faith and we who lack it—are too accustomed to the sign of the cross to understand the significance of the crucifix. But religion, Christianity in particular, has always been the story of death in the midst of life, of sacrifices and martyrs. Tonight, of all nights, as we commemorate the sacrifice of the most famous of those martyrs, it is a fact we should be loath to forget."

Removing his glasses, and folding them into his breast pocket, Taft tips his head and says, "I entrust you with this, and place my faith in *you*." With a plodding step back, he adds, "Thank you all, and good night."

Applause erupts from every corner of the hall—at first awkwardly, but soon to a heavy crescendo. Despite the earlier interruption, the audience has been seduced by this strange man, mesmerized by his fusion of intellect and gore.

Taft nods his head and shuffles toward the table by the podium, meaning to sit down, but the applause continues. Some in the audience take to their feet, continuing to clap.

"Thank you," he says again, still standing, hands pressed atop the back of his chair. Even as he speaks, the old smile returns to his features. It's as if he has been watching the audience all along, never the other way around.

Professor Henderson rises and strides toward the lectern, silencing the applause.

"By tradition," she says, "we will be offering refreshments this evening in the courtyard between this auditorium and the chapel. I understand that the maintenance and ground crews have set up a number of space heaters beneath the tables. Please come out to join us."

Turning to Taft, she adds, "That said, let me thank Dr. Taft for such a memorable lecture. You certainly made quite an impression." She smiles, but with a certain restraint.

The audience applauds again, then slowly begins to filter through the exit.

Taft watches it do so, and I in turn watch him. This is one of the few times I have ever seen the man, recluse that he is. Now I finally understand why Paul finds him so magnetic. Even when you know he's making a game of you, it's almost impossible to take your eyes off him.

Slowly Taft begins to hulk across the stage. As the white screen mechanically retracts into a slot in the ceiling, the three slides become a whisper of gray over the blackboards beyond. I can barely make out the wild animals devouring the women's remains, the child floating off into the air.

"You coming?" Charlie asks, lingering behind Gil by the exit.

I hurry after them.

Chapter 11

"You couldn't find Paul?" Charlie asks once I've caught up.

"He didn't want my help."

But when I mention what I overheard outside, Charlie looks at me as if I shouldn't have let him go. Someone stops beside us to greet Gil, and Charlie turns to me.

"Did Paul go after Curry?" he asks.

I shake my head. "Bill Stein."

"Are you guys coming to the reception?" Gil calls out, sensing a quick getaway. "We could use the turnout."

"Sure," I say, and Gil seems pacified. His mind is elsewhere; we're returning to his element.

"We'll have to avoid Jack Parlow and Kelly—they only want to talk about the ball," he says, returning to our sides. "But it shouldn't be bad."

He leads us down the steps into the pale blue

courtyard, where all the tracks Curry and Paul made in the snow have blown over. The tents are brimming with students, and almost immediately I remember how futile it is trying to avoid anyone with Gil around. We march through the snow to a canopy almost beneath the chapel, but he exerts an inescapable social gravity.

First to come is the blond girl from the door.

"Tara, how are you?" Gil says graciously when she arrives beneath the canvas roof. "A lot more excitement than you were expecting, huh?"

Charlie has no interest in her company. To avoid a scene, he concerns himself at the table, where the silver dispensers are warming fresh hot chocolate.

"Tara," Gil says, "you know Tom, don't you?"

She finds a polite way of saying she doesn't.

"Ah, well," Gil says lightly. "Different classes."

It takes me a second to realize he's referring to sophomores and seniors.

"Tom, this is Tara Pierson, a member of the 2001 section," he continues, seeing that Charlie is avoiding us. "Tara, this is my good friend Tom Sullivan."

The introduction serves only to embarrass. No sooner has Gil finished speaking than Tara finds a moment when we can talk out of his sight and points at Charlie.

"I'm *so* sorry about what I said to your friend back there," she begins. "I had no idea who you guys were. . . ."

And on, and on. Her point seems to be that we deserve better treatment than the other nobodies she's never met because Gil and I brush our teeth over the same sink. The longer she talks, the more I wonder how she wasn't laughed out of Ivy. There is a legend—true or not, I don't know—that sophomores like Tara, who have nothing to recommend them but their looks, sometimes find their way into the membership thanks to a special process called "third-floor bicker." They're invited up to the secretive third floor of the club and told that they won't be admitted without some special show of willingness. I can only guess at the exact nature of the deed, and Gil, of course, denies that anything like this process even exists. But I suppose that's the magic of a myth like third-floor bicker: the more unspoken it's left, the more unspeakable it becomes.

Tara must guess what I'm thinking, or maybe she just notices I'm not paying attention anymore, because she finally comes up with some excuse and minces off into the snow. Good riddance, I think, watching her slink over to another tent, hair flopping in the wind.

I spot Katie. She's standing by the outer edge of the tent on the opposite side, tired of talking. The cup of hot chocolate in her hand is still steaming, and her camera is strung around her neck like a charm. It takes me a second to figure out what she's looking at. A few months ago, I would've suspected the worst, searching for the elusive other man in her life, the one who found time for her when I spent nights with the *Hypnerotomachia*. Now I know better. It's just the chapel she's fixed in her sights. It looms like a cliff at the edge of a white sea, a photographer's dream.

There's a curious thing about attraction, something I'm only starting to learn. The first time I met Katie, I thought one look at her would stop traffic. Not everyone agreed with me (Charlie, preferring meatier women, liked Katie's determination more than her looks), but I was smitten. We dressed up for each other—our best clothes, our best manners, our best stories—until I came to the conclusion that it must be my two years of seniority and my friendship with the president of her eating club that lent me what small mystique I had, holding on to such a catch. In those days the idea of touching her hand or smelling her hair was enough to send me sweating to a cold shower. We were each other's trophies, and we spent our days on pedestals.

Since those early weeks I've taken her off the shelf. She's returned the favor. We argue because I keep my room too warm, and because she sleeps with her window open; she chides me for getting seconds of dessert— because someday, she says, even men pay for their petty transgressions. Gil jokes that I've been domesticated, humoring me with the notion that I used to be a wild thing. The fact is, I was made for husbandry. I turn up my thermostat when I'm not cold, and eat dessert when I'm not hungry, because in the shadow of every admonishment from Katie is the hint that she won't tolerate these things in the future, because there will *be* a future. The fantasies I used to have, powered by the electricity of potential between strangers, are weaker things now. I like her best the way she is in this courtyard.

Her eyes are tensed, the sign that a long day is drawing to a close. Her hair is down, and the gusts are playing in the loops of it by her shoulder. It wouldn't bother me just to keep watching from afar, soaking her in. But when I step forward, decreasing our distance, she sees me and gestures to join her.

"What was all that about?" she asks. "Who was that in the lecture?"

"Richard Curry."

"Curry?" She takes my hand and places it in hers. Her bottom lip curls between her teeth. "Is Paul okay?"

"I think so."

Silence creeps in for a moment as we watch the crowd. Men in canvas anoraks are offering their jackets to under-dressed girlfriends. Tara, the blonde from the table, has witched a stranger out of his.

Katie motions back toward the auditorium. "So what'd you think?"

"Of the lecture?"

She nods, beginning to fix her hair in a bun.

"A little gory." The ogre gets no compliments from me.

"But more interesting than usual," she says, extending her cup of hot chocolate. "Hold this?"

She wraps the back of her hair into a knot and strikes it through with two long pins from her pocket. The easy dexterity of her hands, shaping something she can't see, reminds me of the way my mother used to fix my father's ties while standing behind him.

"What's wrong?" she says, reading my expression.

"Nothing. Just thinking about Paul."

"He's going to finish on time?"

The thesis deadline. Even now, she keeps an eye on the *Hypnerotomachia*. Tomorrow night she can lay my old mistress to rest.

"I hope."

Another silence follows, this one less welcome. Just as I try to think of something to change the subject—something about her birthday, about the gift that's waiting for her back at the room—bad luck strikes. It arrives in the form of Charlie. After twenty circuits around the re-freshment table, he has finally decided to join us.

"I came in late," he announces. "Can I get a recap?"

Of all the odd things about Charlie, the oddest is how he can be a fearless gladiator among men, but a blithering clod around women.

"A recap?" Katie says, entertained.

He plunks a petit four into his mouth, then another, scanning the crowd for prospects. "You know. How classes are going. Who's dating who. What you're doing next year. The usual."

Katie smiles. "Classes are fine, Charlie. Tom and I are still dating." She gives him a reproving look. "And I'm only going to be a junior. I'll still be *here* next year."

"Ah," Charlie says, because he has never remembered her age. Producing a cookie from his gallon-size hands, he searches for the right conversational idiom between a sophomore and a senior. "Junior year is probably the hardest," he says, opting for the worst one: advice. "Two junior papers. Prereqs for your major. And long distance with this guy," he says, pointing at me with one hand, feeding with the other. "Not easy." He rolls his tongue through his cheek, savoring the taste of everything he's got in his mouth, ruminating our future besides. "Can't say I'm jealous."

He pauses, giving us time to digest. In a miracle of economy, Charlie has made things worse in less than twenty words.

"Do you wish you'd been able to run tonight?" he says now.

Katie, still hoping for a silver lining, waits for him to explain. More accustomed to the way his mind works, I know better.

"The Nude Olympics," he says, ignoring my signal to change the subject. "Don't you wish you could've run?"

The question is a masterstroke. I can see it coming, but I'm powerless to defend against it. To show his grasp of the fact that Katie is a sophomore, and possibly of the fact that she lives in Holder, Charlie is asking if my girlfriend is upset because she couldn't parade naked in front of the rest of campus tonight. The underlying compliment, I think, is that a woman with Katie's physical assets must be dying to show them off. Charlie seems to have no premonition of the myriad ways this could go wrong.

Katie's face tightens, spotting his train of thought a mile down the tracks. "Why? Should I be?"

"There just aren't a lot of sophomores I know who would pass up the chance," he says. And from his more diplomatic tone, he must sense that he's misstepped.

"What chance would that be?" Katie presses.

I try to help him, searching for euphemisms of drunken nudity, but my mind is a flock of pigeons, fluttering away. All my thoughts are shit and feathers.

"The chance to shed their clothes once in four years?" Charlie fumbles.

Slowly, Katie looks both of us over. Sizing up Charlie's steam-tunnel attire, and my back-of-the-closet outfit, she wastes no words.

"Well, then, I guess we're even. Because there aren't a lot of seniors I know who would pass up the chance to *change* their clothes once in four years."

I fight the impulse to press at the wrinkles in my shirt.

Charlie, reading the leaves, ducks out for another pass at the table. His job here is done.

"You guys are a couple of real charmers," Katie says. "You know that?"

She tries to sound amused, but there's a hint of heaviness she can't hide. She reaches up and runs her fingers through my hair, trying to change things, when an Ivy woman arrives before us, arm in arm with Gil. From the apologetic look on his face, I understand that this is the Kelly he told us to avoid.

"Tom, you know Kelly Danner, don't you?"

Before I can say that I don't, Kelly's face fills with rage. She's focused on something in the far corner of the courtyard.

"Those stupid shits," she curses, throwing her paper cup to the ground. "I knew they would try to pull something like this tonight."

We all turn. There, marching toward us from the direction of the eating clubs, comes a troupe of men in tunics and togas.

Charlie hoots, stepping toward us for a better view.

"Tell them to get out of here," Kelly demands, to no one in particular.

The group comes into focus through the snow. Now it's clear that this is just what Kelly feared: a choreographed stunt. Each toga bears a series of letters across its chest, written in two distinct rows. Though I can't make out the lower row yet, the top one is composed of two letters: "T.I."

T.I. is the common abbreviation for Tiger Inn, the third oldest of the eating clubs, and the only place on campus where the lunatics run the asylum. Rarely does Ivy seem so vulnerable as when T.I. conceives of a new practical joke to try on its venerable sister club. Tonight is the perfect opportunity.

Stray laughter breaks out in the courtyard, but I have to squint to see why. The entire group has disguised itself in long gray beards and wigs. All around us, the closest tents are flooding with students clamoring for a view.

After a brief huddle, the men from T.I. unravel themselves into a long, single line. As they do, I finally make out the second row of words written across each toga. Every man's chest bears a single word, and every word, I see, is a name. The name on the tallest of them, standing in the middle, is Jesus. To his left and right are the twelve apostles, six on each side.

Already the laughter and cheers have grown louder.

Kelly clenches her jaw. I can't tell from Gil's expression whether he's trying to stifle his amusement so as not to offend her, or trying to create the impression that he's entertained by it, when he's not.

The Jesus figure steps forward from the row and raises his arms to silence the audience. Once the courtyard is quiet, he steps back, utters some command, and the entire line breaks into choral formation. Jesus conducts from the side. Producing a pitch pipe from his toga, he blows a single note. The sitting row responds by humming it. The kneeling row joins in with a perfect third. Finally, just as the two rows seem to be losing their breath, the standing apostles contribute a fifth.

The crowd, impressed by the preparation that has gone into this, claps and cheers once more.

"Nice toga!" someone in a nearby tent yells.

Jesus swivels his head, raises an eyebrow in the direction of the sound, and returns to conducting. Finally, raising his

conductor's baton three times in the air with a flick of the
wrist, he throws his arms back theatrically, sweeps them
forward again, and the chorus explodes into song. Their
voices, to the tune of the "Battle Hymn of the Republic,"
carry through the courtyard.

> *We've come to tell the story of the college of the Lord,*
> *But the grapes of wrath fermented in the vintage*
>   *where they're stored,*
> *So excuse us if we're all a little drunk out of our*
>   *gourd.*
> *We saints go marching on.*
>
> *Glory, Glory, we're the fossils*
> *Of all the Nazarene apostles.*
> *If it weren't for Christ we'd be*
> *Just fishermen from Galilee,*
> *So listen to our tale.*
>
> *Now, Jesus was your average ancient Middle*
>   *Eastern male.*
> *He went to public school, but had a special holy grail:*
> *He'd rather burn in hell than go to Harvard or to*
>   *Yale,*
> *So the choice was pretty clear.*
>
> *Glory, Glory, God convinced Him,*
> *Jesus Christ, He went to Princeton.*
> *He made the right decision*
> *When He majored in Religion*
> *And the rest is history.*

So Christ arrived on campus in the fall of year 18,
The Biggest Man on Campus that the world had
    ever seen.
It made the other eating clubs turn jealous Ivy green
When Jesus chose T.I.

Now two apostles from the first row stand and step forward. The first unravels a scroll that reads "Ivy" and the second unravels one that reads "Cottage." After thrusting their noses in the air at one another and prancing self-importantly around Jesus, the song continues.

Chorus: *Glory, Glory, Jesus bickered,*
All the snooty heathens snickered.
Ivy: *We couldn't take a Jew;*
Cottage: *A carpenter won't do;*
Chorus: *So the Lord, He joined T.I.*

Kelly clenches her fists so tightly she almost draws blood.

Now the twelve apostles emerge from the choral formation into a kick line and, with Jesus at the center, lock arms, pump their legs deftly into the air, and conclude:

Jesus, Jesus, He's a fun guy.
Thanks to Him we're all alumni.
There's nothing so divine
As turning water into wine,
His truth is marching on.

With that, all thirteen men turn around and, with choreographed precision, raise the backs of their togas to reveal a message written across their buttocks, one letter per cheek:

HAPPY EASTER FROM THE TIGER INN

A rowdy combination of wild clapping, boisterous cheering, and stray boos ensues. Then, just as the thirteen men are preparing to leave, a loud cracking sound comes from across the courtyard, followed by the crash of glass breaking.

Heads turn in the direction of the noise. On the top story of Dickinson, the history department building, a light flickers on, then off. One of the windowpanes has been shattered. In the darkness, I can see movement.

A T.I. apostle begins to cheer loudly.

"What's going on?" I ask. Squinting, I can make out a person near the broken glass.

"This isn't funny," Kelly growls at Judas, who has drifted within earshot.

He snubs his nose.

"What's he doing?" she demands, pointing at the window.

Judas thinks for a second.

"He's going to piss." He laughs tipsily, then repeats, "He's going to piss out the window."

Kelly storms after the Jesus figure.

"What the hell's going on, Derek?" she says.

The figure in the office appears, then vanishes. From his jerkiness I sense he's drunk. At one moment he seems to be pawing the broken glass, then he disappears.

"I think there's someone else up there," Charlie says.

Suddenly the entire body of the man comes into view. He's backed against the lead panes of the window.

"He's gonna piss," Judas repeats.

From the remaining apostles there arises a sloppy cry of "Jump! Jump!"

Kelly wheels on them. "Shut up, goddamn it! Go get him down!"

Again the man disappears from sight.

"I don't think he's from T.I.," Charlie says with concern. "I think that's some drunk guy from the Nude Olympics."

But the man was wearing clothes. I look into the darkness, trying to make out the shapes. This time, the man doesn't return.

Beside me, the stewed apostles boo.

"Jump!" one of them cries again, but Derek pushes him back and tells him to stay quiet.

"Get the hell out of here," Kelly orders.

"Easy, girl," Derek says, and begins rounding up the stray disciples.

Gil watches all of this with the same inscrutable look of amusement he was wearing when the men first arrived. Glancing at his watch, he says, "Well, looks like we've sucked all the fun out of thi—"

"*Holy shit!*" Charlie cries.

His voice nearly drowns out the echo of the second cracking sound. This time I hear the report clearly. It's a gunshot.

Gil and I turn just in time to see it. The man explodes backward through the glass, and for a matter of seconds he stays frozen in free fall. With a muted thud, his body hits the snow, and the impact sucks all the noise and commotion from the courtyard.

Then there is nothing.

■

The first thing I remember is the sound of Charlie's feet as he dashes toward the body in the snow. Then a large crowd follows, converging around the scene, blocking my view.

"Oh, Jesus," Gil whispers.

Voices in the huddle shout, "Is he okay?" But there's no sign of movement.

Finally I hear Charlie's voice. "I need someone to call an ambulance! Tell them we've got an unconscious man in the courtyard by the chapel!"

Gil pulls his phone from his pocket, but before he can dial, two campus policemen arrive on the scene. One of them presses through the crowd. The other begins directing the spectators back. For a moment I see Charlie crouched over the man, delivering chest compressions—perfect motions, like pistons stroking. How strange it is, suddenly, to see the trade he plies by night.

"We've got an ambulance on the way!"

Faintly, in the distance, I can hear sirens.

My legs begin to shake. I feel the crawling sensation that something dark is passing overhead.

The ambulance arrives. Its rear doors extend open, and two EMTs descend to strap the man into braces and a stretcher. Motion stutters, spectators flickering in and out of view. When the doors swung shut, I can make out the impression where the body landed. The patch of flagstone has an unseemly quality, like a scrape on the flesh of a storybook princess. What I took for mud in the spatter of impact, I begin to see more clearly. Blacks are reds; the dirt is blood. In the office above, there is only darkness.

The ambulance drives off, lights and sirens fading as it shuttles onto Nassau Street. I stare back at the impression. It is misshapen, like a broken snow angel. The wind hisses, and I wrap my arms around my sides. Only when the crowd in the courtyard begins to disperse do I realize that Charlie is gone. He left with the ambulance, and an unpleasant silence has gathered where I expect to hear his voice.

Students are slowly disappearing from the courtyard with hushed voices. "I hope he's okay," Gil says, putting a hand on my shoulder.

For a second I think he means Charlie.

"Let's go home," he says. "I'll give you a ride."

I appreciate the warmth of his hand, but I stand by, just watching. In my mind's eye the man falls again, colliding with the earth. The sequence fragments, and I can hear the crack of glass breaking, then the gunshot.

My stomach begins to turn.

"Come on," Gil says. "Let's get out of here."

And as the wind picks up again, I agree. Katie disappeared somewhere in the shuffle of the ambulance, and a friend of hers standing nearby tells me that she went back to Holder with her roommates. I decide to call her from home.

Gil places a gentle hand between my shoulders, and guides me toward the Saab that sits in the snow near the auditorium entrance. With that unfailing instinct to know what's best, he turns up the heat to a comfortable level, adjusts the volume on an old Sinatra ballad until the wind is a memory, and with a little burst of speed that assures me of our impunity before the elements, heads down campus. Everything behind us fades gradually into the snow.

"Did you see the person who fell?" he asks quietly once we're on our way.

"I couldn't see anything."

"You don't think . . ." Gil shifts forward in his seat.

"Think what?"

"Should we call Paul and make sure he's okay?"

Gil hands me his cell phone, but there's no service.

"I'm sure he's fine," I say, fidgeting with the phone.

We hang in the silence of the cabin for several minutes, trying to drive the possibility out of our minds. Finally Gil forces the conversation elsewhere.

"Tell me about your trip," he says. I'd flown to Columbus earlier in the week to celebrate finishing my thesis. "How was home?"

We manage a patchy conversation, hopping from topic to topic, trying to stay above the current of our thoughts. I tell him the latest news about my older sisters, one a veterinarian, the other applying for a business degree, and Gil asks about my mother, whose birthday he's remembered. He tells me that, despite all the time he devoted to planning the ball, his thesis still managed to get written in those last days before the economics department deadline, when I was gone. Gradually we wonder aloud where Charlie has been accepted to medical school, guessing where he intends to go, since these are matters about which Charlie is modestly silent, even to us.

We bear south, and in the murky night the dormitories hunker on either side. News of what happened at the chapel must be spreading through campus, because no pedestrians are visible, and the only other cars sit silently in lots on the shoulder. The drive down to the parking lot, a half mile beyond Dod, feels almost as long as the slow walk back up. Paul is nowhere to be seen.

Chapter 12

There's an old saw in *Frankenstein* scholarship that the monster is a metaphor for the novel. Mary Shelley, who was nineteen when she began writing the book, encouraged that interpretation by calling it her hideous progeny, a dead thing with a life of its own. Having lost a child at seventeen, and having caused her own mother's death in childbirth, she must have known what she meant by it.

For a time I thought Mary Shelley was all my thesis subject had in common with Paul's: she and the Roman Francesco Colonna (who was only fourteen, some scholars argued, when the *Hypnerotomachia* was written) made a pretty couple, two teenagers wise beyond their years. To me, in those months before I met Katie, Mary and Francesco were time-crossed lovers, equally young in different ages. To Paul, standing nose to nose with the scholars of my father's generation, they were an emblem of youth's power against the obstinate momentum of age.

Oddly enough, it was by arguing that Francesco Colonna was an older man, not a younger one, that Paul made his first headway against the *Hypnerotomachia*. He'd come to Taft freshman year as a bare novice, and the ogre could smell my father's influence on him. Though he claimed to have retired from studying the ancient book, Taft was eager to show Paul the foolishness of my father's theories. Still favoring the notion of a Venetian Colonna, he explained the strongest piece of evidence in favor of the Pretender.

The *Hypnerotomachia* was published in 1499, Taft said, when the Roman Colonna was forty-five years old; that much was unproblematic. But the final page of the actual story, which Colonna composed himself, states that the book was *written* in 1467—when my father's Francesco would have been only fourteen. However unlikely it was that a criminal monk had written the *Hypnerotomachia*, then, it was outright impossible for a teenager to have done it.

And so, like the curmudgeonly king inventing new labors for young Hercules, Taft left it to Paul to shoulder the burden of proof. Until his new protégé could shrug off the problem of Colonna's age, Taft refused to assist any research premised on a Roman author.

It nearly defies explanation, the way Paul refused to buckle under the logic of those facts. He found inspiration not only in Taft's challenge, but in Taft himself: though he rejected the man's rigid interpretation of the *Hypnerotomachia*, he brought the same relentlessness to his sources. Whereas my father had let inspiration and intuition guide him, searching mainly in exotic locales like monasteries and papal libraries, Paul adopted Taft's more thorough approach. No book was too humble, no location too dull. From top to bottom, he began to scour the Princeton library system. And slowly his early conception of books, like a boy's conception of water when he has lived his whole life by a pond, was dethroned by this sudden exposure to the ocean. Paul's book collection, the day he left for college, numbered slightly under six hundred. Princeton's book collection, including more than fifty miles of shelves in Firestone Library alone, numbered well over six million.

The experience daunted Paul at first. The quaint picture my father had painted, of happening across key documents sheerly by accident, was instantly exploded. More painful, I think, was the questioning it forced onto Paul, the introspection and self-doubt that made him wonder if his genius was simply a provincial talent, a dull star in a dark corner of the sky. That upperclassmen in his courses admitted he was far beyond them, and that his professors held him in almost messianic esteem, was nothing to Paul if he couldn't make headway on the *Hypnerotomachia*.

Then, during his summer in Italy, all that changed. Paul discovered the work of Italian scholars, whose texts he was able to wade through thanks to four years of Latin. Digging into the definitive Italian biography of the Venetian Pretender, he learned that some elements of the *Hypnerotomachia* were indebted to a book called *Cornucopiae*, published in 1489. As a detail in the Pretender's life, it seemed unimportant—but Paul, coming at the problem with the Roman Francesco in mind, saw much more in it. No matter when Colonna claimed to have written the book, there was now proof that it was composed after 1489. By then, the Roman Francesco would've been at least thirty-six, not fourteen. And while Paul couldn't imagine why Colonna might lie about the year he wrote the *Hypnerotomachia*, he realized that he'd answered Taft's challenge. For better or worse, he had entered my father's world.

What followed was a period of soaring confidence. Armed with four languages (the fifth, English, being useless except for secondary sources) and with an extensive knowledge of Colonna's life and times, Paul leapt into the text. He gave more and more of each day to the project, taking a stance toward the *Hypnerotomachia* that I found uncomfortably familiar: the pages were a battleground where he and Colonna would match wits, winner take all. Vincent Taft's influence, dormant in the months before his trip, had returned. As Paul's interest slowly took the color of obsession, Taft and Stein became increasingly prominent in his life. If it hadn't been for the intervention of one man, I think we might've lost Paul to them entirely.

That man was Francesco Colonna, and his book was hardly the pushover Paul had hoped. Though Paul flexed his mental muscle, he found that the mountain wouldn't move. As his progress slowed, and the fall of junior year darkened into winter, Paul became irritable, quick with sharp comments and rude mannerisms he could only have learned from Taft. At Ivy, Gil told me, members began to joke about Paul when he sat alone at the dinner table, surrounded by stacks of books, talking to no one. The more I watched his confidence dwindle, the more I understood something my father had said once: the *Hypnerotomachia* is a siren, a fetching song on a distant shore, all claws and clutches in person. You court her at your risk.

And so it went. Spring came; coeds in tank tops tossed Frisbees beneath his window; squirrels and blossoms stooped the tree branches; tennis balls echoed in play; and still Paul sat in his room, alone, shade drawn, door locked, with a message on his whiteboard saying DO NOT DISTURB. All that I loved about the new season, he called a distraction—the smells and sounds, the sense of impatience after a long and bookish winter. I knew that I myself was becoming a distraction to him. Everything he told me started to sound like the weather report from a foreign land. I visited him little.

It took a summer alone to change him. In early September of senior year, after three months on an empty campus, he welcomed us all back and helped us move in. He was suddenly open to interruptions, eager to spend time among friends, less fixated on the past. In the opening months of that semester, he and I enjoyed a renaissance in our friendship better than anything I could've expected. He shrugged off the onlookers at Ivy who hung on his words, waiting for something outrageous; he spent less time with Taft and Stein; he savored meals and enjoyed walks between classes. He could even see the humor in the way garbagemen emptied the Dumpster beneath our window each Tuesday morning at seven o'clock. I thought he was better. More than that: I thought he was reborn.

It was only when Paul came to me in October of senior year, late one night after our last fall midterms, that I understood the other thing our theses had in common: both of our subjects were dead things that refused to stay buried.

"Is there anything that could change your mind about

working on the *Hypnerotomachia*?" Paul asked me that night—and from his tense expression, I knew he'd found something important.

"No," I told him, half because I meant it, but half to get him to tip his hand.

"I think I made a breakthrough over the summer. But I need your help to understand it."

"Tell me," I said.

And however it began for my father, whatever galvanized his curiosity in the *Hypnerotomachia*, this was how it started for me. What Paul said that night gave Colonna's long-dead book new life.

"Vincent introduced me to Steven Gelbman from Brown last year when he saw I was getting frustrated," Paul began. "Gelbman does research with math, cryptography, and religion, all in one. He's an expert at the mathematical analysis of the Torah. Have you heard of this stuff?"

"Sounds like kabala."

"Exactly. You don't just study what the scriptural words say; you study what the *numbers* say. Every letter in the Hebrew alphabet has a number assigned to it. Using the order of the letters, you can look for mathematical patterns.

"Well, I was doubtful at the beginning. Even after sitting through ten hours of lectures on the Sephirothic correspondences, I didn't buy it. It just didn't seem to relate to Colonna. But by the summer I'd finished the secondary sources on the *Hypnerotomachia*, and I started working on the book itself. It was impossible. I would try to force an interpretation onto it, and it would throw everything back in my face. As soon as I thought a few pages were moving in one direction, using a certain structure, making a certain point, suddenly the sentence would end, and in the next one everything would change.

"I spent five weeks just trying to understand the first labyrinth Francesco describes. I studied Vitruvius to understand the architectural terms. I looked up every ancient labyrinth I knew—the Egyptian one at the City of Crocodiles, the ones at Lemnos and Clusium and Crete, half a dozen others. Then I realized there were four different labyrinths in the *Hypnerotomachia*—one in a temple, one in the water, one in a garden, and one underground. As soon as I thought I was beginning to understand one level of complexity, it quadrupled. Poliphilo even gets lost at the beginning of the book and says, *My only recourse was to beg the pity of Cretan Ariadne, who gave the thread to Theseus to escape from the difficult labyrinth*. It's like the book understood what it was doing to me.

"Finally I realized the only thing I knew that *definitely* worked was the acrostic with the first letter of every chapter. So I did what the book told me to do. I begged the pity of Cretan Ariadne, the one person who might be able to solve the maze."

"You went back to Gelbman."

He nodded. "I ate crow. I was desperate. In July, Gelbman let me stay with him in Providence after Vincent insisted I was making progress with the method. He spent the weekend showing me more sophisticated decoding techniques, and that's when things started to pick up."

I remember looking out the window beyond Paul's shoulder as he spoke, sensing that the landscape was changing. We were sitting in our bedroom in Dod, alone on a Friday night; Charlie and Gil were somewhere below our feet, playing paintball in the steam tunnels with a group of friends from Ivy and the EMT squad. The following day I would have a paper to work on, a test to study for. A week later I would meet Katie for the first time. But for that moment, Paul's hold on my attention was complete.

"The most complicated concept he taught me," he continued, "was how to decode a book based on algorithms or ciphers from the text itself. In those cases, the key is built right in. You solve for the cipher, like an equation or a set of instructions, then you use the cipher to unlock the text. The book actually interprets itself."

I smiled. "Sounds like an idea that could bankrupt the English department."

"I was skeptical too," Paul said. "But it turns out there's a long tradition of it. Intellectuals during the Enlightenment used to write entire tracts like that as a game. The texts looked like regular stories, epistolary novels, that kind of thing. But if you knew the right techniques—maybe catching typos that turned out to be intentional, or solving puzzles in the illustrations—you could find the key. Something like 'Use only primes and perfect squares, and letters every tenth word shares; exclude the words of Lord Kinkaid, and any questions from the maid.' You would follow the directions, and there would be a message at the end. Most of the time it was a limerick or a dirty joke. But one of these guys actually wrote his will like that. Whoever could decipher it would inherit his estate."

Paul pulled a single sheet of paper from between the pages of a book. On it was written, in two distinct blocks, the text of a passage written in code, and below it the shorter decoded message. How one became the other, I couldn't see.

"After a while, I started thinking it could work. Maybe the acrostic with the *Hypnerotomachia*'s chapter letters was just a hint. Maybe it was there to tell you what sort of interpretation would work on the rest of the book. A lot of humanists were interested in kabala, and the idea of playing games with language and symbols was popular in the Renaissance. Maybe Francesco had used some kind of cipher for the *Hypnerotomachia*.

"The problem was, I had no idea where to look for the algorithm. I started inventing ciphers of my own, just to see if one might work. I was fighting with it, day after day. I would come across something, spend a week rummaging through the Rare Books Room for an answer—only to find out it didn't make sense, or it was a trap, or a dead end.

"Then, at the end of August, I spent three weeks on a single passage. It's at the point in the story where Poliphilo is examining a set of temple ruins, and he finds a hieroglyphic message carved on an obelisk. *To the divine and always august Julius Caesar, governor of the world* is the opening phrase. I'll never forget it—it almost drove me crazy. The same few pages, day after day. But *that's* when I found it."

He opened a binder on his desk. Inside was a reproduction of every page of the *Hypnerotomachia*. Turning to an appendix he'd created at the end, he showed me a sheet of paper on which he'd clipped the first letter of each chapter into what looked like a ransom note, spelling the famous message about Fra Francesco Colonna. *Poliam Frater Franciscus Columna Peramavit.*

"My starting assumption was simple. The acrostic couldn't just be a parlor trick, a cheap way to identify the author. It had to have a larger purpose: first letters wouldn't just be important for decoding that initial message, they would be important for deciphering the entire book.

"So I tried it. The passage I'd been looking at happens to begin with a special hieroglyph in one of the

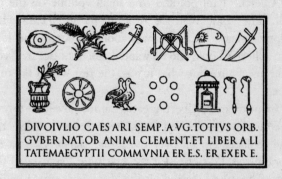

DIVOIVLIO CAES ARI SEMP. A VG.TOTIVS ORB.
GVBER NAT.OB ANIMI CLEMENT.ET LIBER A LI
TATEMAEGYPTII COMMVNIA ER E.S. ER EXER E.

drawings—an eye." He flipped several pages, finally arriving at it.

"Since it was the first symbol in that woodcut, I decided it must be important. The problem was, I couldn't do anything with it. Poliphilo's definition of the symbol—that the eye means God, or divinity—led me nowhere.

"That's when I got lucky. One morning I was doing some work at the student center, and I hadn't slept much, so I decided to buy a soda. Only, the machine kept spitting my dollar back. I was so tired, I couldn't figure out why, until I finally looked down and realized I was putting it in the wrong way. The back side was up. I was just about to turn it over and try again, when I saw it. Right in front of me, on the back of the bill."

"The eye," I said. "Right above the pyramid."

"Exactly. It's part of the great seal. And that's when it hit me. In the Renaissance there was a famous humanist who used the eye as *his* symbol. He even printed it on coins and medals."

He waited, as if I might know the answer.

"Alberti." Paul pointed to a small volume on the far shelf. The spine read *De re aedificatoria*. "*That's* what Colonna meant by it. He was about to borrow an idea from Alberti's book, and he wanted you to notice it. If you could just figure out what it was, the rest would fall into place.

"In his treatise, Alberti creates Latin equivalents for architectural words derived from Greek. Francesco does the same replacement all over the *Hypnerotomachia*—except in one place. I'd noticed it the first time I translated the section, because I started hitting Vitruvian terms I hadn't seen in a long time. But I never thought they were significant.

"The trick, I realized, was that you had to find all the Greek architectural terms in that passage and replace them with their Latin equivalents, the same way they appear in the rest of the text. If you did that, and used the acrostic rule—reading the first letter of each word in a row, the same way you do with the first letter of each chapter—the puzzle unlocks. You find a message in Latin. The only problem is, if you make just one mistake converting the Greek to Latin, the whole message breaks down. Replace *entasi* with *ventris diametrum* instead of just *venter*, and the extra 'D' at the beginning of *diametrum* changes everything."

He flipped to another page, talking faster. "I made mistakes, of course. Luckily, they weren't so big that I couldn't still piece together the Latin. It took me three weeks, right up to the day before you guys came back to campus. But I finally figured it out. You know what it says?" He scratched nervously at something on his face. "It says: *Who cuckolded Moses?*"

He gave a hollow laugh. "I swear to God, I can hear Francesco laughing at me. I feel like the whole book just boiled down to one big joke at my expense. I mean, seriously. *Who cuckolded Moses?*"

"I don't get it."

"In other words, who cheated on Moses?"

"I know what a cuckold is."

"Actually, it doesn't literally say *cuckold*. It says, 'Who gave Moses the horns?' Horns, as early as Artemidorus, are used to suggest cuckoldry. It comes from—"

"But what does that have to do with the *Hypnertomachia*?"

I waited for him to explain, or to say that he'd read the riddle wrong. But when Paul got up and started pacing, I could tell this was more complicated.

"I don't know. I can't figure out how it fits with the rest of the book. But here's the strange thing. I think I may have solved the riddle."

"Someone cuckolded Moses?"

"Well, sort of. At first, I thought it had to be a mistake. Moses is too major a figure in the Old Testament to be associated with infidelity. As far as I knew, he had a wife—a Midianite woman named Zipporah—but she barely appeared in Exodus, and I couldn't find any reference to her cheating on him.

"Then in Numbers 12:1, something unusual happens. Moses' brother and sister speak against him because he marries a Cushite woman. The details are never explained, but some scholars argue that because Cush and Midian are completely different geographical areas, Moses must've had two wives. The name of the Cushite wife never appears in the Bible, but a first-century historian, Flavius Josephus, writes his own account of Moses' life, and claims that the name of the Cushite, or Ethiopian, woman he married was Tharbis."

The details were beginning to overwhelm me. "So *she* cheated on him?"

Paul shook his head. "No. By taking a second wife, Moses cheated on *her*, or on Zipporah, whichever one he married first. The chronology is hard to figure out, but in some usages, cuckold's horns appear on the head of the cheater, not just the cheater's spouse. That must be what the riddle's getting at. The answer is Zipporah or Tharbis."

"So what do you do with that?"

His excitement seemed to dissipate. "That's where I've hit a wall. I tried to use Zipporah and Tharbis as solutions every way I could think of, applying them as ciphers to help crack the rest of the book. But nothing works."

He waited, as if expecting me to contribute something.

"What does Taft think about it?" was all I could think to ask.

"Vincent doesn't know. He thinks I'm wasting my time. As soon as he decided Gelbman's techniques weren't yielding breakthroughs, he told me I should go back to following his lead. More focus on the primary Venetian sources."

"You're not going to tell him about this?"

Paul looked at me as if I misunderstood.

"I'm telling *you*," he said.

"I have no idea."

"Tom, it can't be an accident. Not something this big. This is what your father was looking for. All we have to do is figure it out. I want your help."

"Why?"

Now a curious certainty entered his voice, as if he understood something about the *Hypnerotomachia* that he'd overlooked before. "The book rewards different kinds of thought. Sometimes patience works, attention to detail. But other times it takes instinct and inventiveness. I've read some of your conclusions on *Frankenstein*. They're good. They're original. And you didn't even break a sweat. Just think about it. Think about the riddle. Maybe you'll come up with something else. That's all I'm asking."

There was a simple reason why I rejected Paul's offer that night. In the landscape of my childhood, Colonna's book was a deserted mansion on a hill, a foreboding shadow over any nearby thought. Every unpleasant mystery of my youth seemed to trace its origins to those same unreadable pages: the unaccountable absence of my father from our dinner table so many nights as he labored at his desk; the old arguments he and my mother lapsed into, like saints falling into sin; even the inhospitable oddness of Richard Curry, who fell for Colonna's book worse than any man, and never seemed to recover. I couldn't understand the power the *Hypnerotomachia* exerted over everyone who read it, but in my experience that power always seemed to play out for the worse. Watching Paul struggle for three years, even if it culminated in this breakthrough, had only helped me keep my distance.

If it seems surprising, then, that I changed my mind the next morning, and joined Paul in his work, chalk it up to a dream I had the night after he told me about the riddle. There is a woodcut in the *Hypnerotomachia* that will always stay in the stowage of my early childhood, a print that I bumped into many times after sneaking into my father's office to investigate what he was studying. It's not every day that a boy sees a naked woman reclining under a tree, looking up at him as he returns the favor. And I imagine no one, outside the circle of *Hypnerotomachia* scholars, can say he has ever seen a naked satyr standing at the feet of such a woman, with a horn of a penis extended like a compass needle in her direction. I was twelve when I saw that picture for the first time, all alone in my father's office, and I could suddenly imagine why

he sometimes came to dinner late. Whatever this was, strange and wonderful, beef potluck had nothing on it.

It returned to me that night, the woodcut of my childhood—woman lounging, satyr stalking, member rampant—and I must have done a lot of turning in my bunk, because Paul looked down from his and asked, "You okay, Tom?"

Coming to, I rose and shot through the books on his desk. That penis, that misplaced horn, reminded me of something. There was a connection to be made. Colonna knew what he was talking about. Someone *had* given Moses horns.

I found the answer in Hartt's *History of Renaissance Art*. I'd seen the picture before, but never made anything of it.

"What are these?" I asked Paul, tossing the book up to his bunk, pointing at the page.

He squinted. "Michelangelo's statue of Moses," he said, staring at me as if I'd lost my mind. "What's wrong, Tom?"

Then, before I even had to explain, he stopped short and turned on his bedside light.

"Of course . . ." he whispered. "Oh my God, *of course*."

Sure enough, in the photo I'd shown him, two little nubs stuck out the top of the statue's head, like goatish satyr horns.

Paul jumped down from the bunk, loudly enough that I waited for Gil and Charlie to appear. "You did it," he said, eyes wide. "This *must* be it."

He continued like that for a while, until I started to feel an uncomfortable sense of dislocation, wondering how Colonna could've put the answer to his riddle on a Michelangelo sculpture.

"So why are they there?" I asked finally.

But Paul was already far ahead. He yanked the book off

his bunk and showed me the explanation in the text. "The horns have nothing to do with being a cuckold. The riddle was literal: who gave Moses horns? It's from a mistranslation of the Bible. When Moses comes down from Mount Sinai, Exodus says, his face glows with rays of light. But the Hebrew word for 'rays' can also be translated as 'horns'—*karan* versus *keren*. When Saint Jerome translated the Old Testament into Latin, he thought no one but Christ should glow with rays of light—so he advanced the secondary translation. And that's how Michelangelo carved his Moses. With horns."

In all the excitement, I don't think I even sensed what was happening. The *Hypnerotomachia* had slunk back into my life, ferrying me across a river I never intended to cross. All that stood in our way was figuring out the significance of Saint Jerome, who had applied the Latin word *cornuta* to Moses, thus giving him horns. But for the following week, that was a burden Paul happily took upon himself. Beginning that night, and continuing for some time, I was only a hired gun, his last resort against the *Hypnerotomachia*. I thought it was a position I could keep, a distance I could maintain from the book, letting Paul play the middleman. And so, as he returned to Firestone, white-hot with the possibilities of what we'd found, I went off and made another discovery of my own. Still strutting after my encounter with Francesco Colonna, I can only imagine the impression I made on her.

We met where neither of us belonged, but where both of us felt at home: Ivy. For my part, I'd spent as many weekends there as I had at my own club. For hers, she was already one of Gil's favorites, months before bicker for her sophomore class began, and it was his first thought to introduce us.

"Katie," he said, after getting both of us to the club on the same Saturday night, "this is my roommate, Tom."

I gave a lazy smile, thinking I didn't have to flex much muscle to charm a sophomore.

Then she spoke. And like a fly in a pitcher plant, expecting nectar and finding death, I realized who was hunting who.

"So you're Tom," she said, as if I met the description of a convict from a post office wall. "Charlie told me about you."

The best part about being described to someone by Charlie is that things can only get better from there. Apparently he'd met Katie at Ivy several nights earlier, and when he realized that Gil intended to make the match, he eagerly chipped in with details.

"What did he tell you?" I asked, trying not to look concerned.

She thought for a second, searching for his exact words.

"Something about astronomy. About stars."

"White dwarf," I told her. "It's a science joke."

Katie frowned.

"I don't get it either," I admitted, trying to undo my first impression. "I'm not much for that kind of stuff."

"English major?" she asked, as if she could tell.

I nodded. Gil had told me she was into philosophy.

She eyed me suspiciously. "Who's your favorite author?"

"Impossible question. Who's your favorite philosopher?"

"Camus," she said, even though I meant it rhetorically. "And my favorite author is H. A. Rey."

The words came out like a test. I'd never heard of Rey; he sounded like a modernist, a more obscure T. S. Eliot, an uppercase e. e. cummings.

"He wrote poetry?" I ventured, because I could imagine her reading Frenchmen by firelight.

Katie blinked. Then for the first time since we'd met, she smiled.

"He wrote *Curious George*," she said, and laughed out loud when I tried not to blush.

That was the recipe of our relationship, I think. We gave each other what we never expected to find. In my earliest days at Princeton I had learned never to talk shop with my girlfriends; even poetry will kill romance, Gil had taught me, if you mistake it for conversation. But Katie had learned the same lesson, and neither of us liked it. Freshman year she dated a lacrosse player I'd met in one of my literature seminars. He was smart, taking to Pynchon and DeLillo in a way I never did, but he refused to speak a word about them outside of class. It drove her crazy, the lines he drew through his life, the walls he put up between work and play. In twenty minutes of conversation that night at Ivy, we both saw something we liked, a willingness to have no walls, or maybe just an unwillingness to keep them standing. It pleased Gil that he'd made such a good match. Before long I found myself waiting for the weekends, hoping to run into her between classes, thinking of her before bed, in the shower, in the middle of tests. Within a month, we were dating.

As the senior in our relationship, I imagined for a while that it was my job to apply the wisdom of my experience to everything we did. I made sure we kept to familiar places and friendly crowds, having learned from past girlfriends that familiarity always arrives in the wake of infatuation: two people who think they're in love can find out, when left alone, exactly how little they know about each other. So I insisted on public places—weekends at eating clubs, weeknights at the student center—and agreed to meet at bedrooms and library nooks only when I thought I detected something more in Katie's voice, the come-hither registers I flattered myself I could hear.

As usual, it was Katie who had to straighten me out.

"Come on," she told me one night. "We're going to dinner together."

"Whose club?" I asked.

"A restaurant. Your choice."

We'd been together for less than two weeks; there were still too many parts of her I didn't know. A long dinner alone sounded risky.

"Did you want to ask Karen or Trish to come along?" I asked. Her two roommates in Holder had been fail-safe company. Trish, in particular, who never seemed to eat, dependably talked through any meal.

Katie's back was turned to me. "We could ask Gil to come too," she said.

"Sure." It struck me as an odd combination, but there was safety in numbers.

"What about Charlie?" she asked. "He's always hungry."

Finally I realized she was being sarcastic.

"What's the problem, Tom?" she said, turning back to me. "You're afraid other people will see us alone?"

"No."

"I bore you?"

"Of course not."

"Then what? You think we'll find out we don't know each other very well?"

I hesitated. "Yes."

Katie seemed amazed that I meant it.

"What's my sister's name?" she said finally.

"I don't know."

"Am I religious?"

"I'm not sure."

"Do I steal money from the tip jar at the coffee shop when I'm short on change?"

"Probably."

Katie leaned in, smiling. "There. You survived."

I'd never been with someone who was so confident about getting to know me. She never seemed to doubt the pieces would fit.

"Now let's go to dinner," she said, pulling me by the hand.

We never looked back.

Eight days after my dream about the satyr, Paul came to me with news. "I was right," he said proudly. "Parts of the book are written in cipher."

"How'd you figure it out?"

"*Cornuta*—the word Jerome used to give Moses horns—is the answer Francesco wanted. But most of the normal techniques for using a word as a cipher don't work in the *Hypnerotomachia*. Look . . ."

He showed me a sheet of paper he'd prepared, with two lines of letters running parallel to each other.

a b c d e f g h i j k l m n o p q r s t u v w x y z
C O R N U T A B D E F G H I J K L M P Q S V W X Y Z

"Here's a very basic cipher alphabet," he said. "The top row is what you call the plaintext, the bottom row is the ciphertext. Notice how the ciphertext begins with our keyword, *cornuta*? After that, it's just a regular alphabet, with the letters from *cornuta* removed so they don't get duplicated."

"How does it work?"

Paul picked up a pencil from his desk and began circling letters. "Say you wanted to write 'hello' using this *cornuta* cipher. You would start with the plaintext alphabet on top and find 'H,' then look at its equivalent in ciphertext below it. In this case, 'H' corresponds to 'B.' You do that with the rest of the letters, and 'hello' becomes 'buggj.' "

"That's how Colonna used *cornuta*?"

"No. By the fifteenth and sixteenth centuries, Italian courts had much more sophisticated systems. Alberti, who wrote the architecture treatise I showed you last week, also invented polyalphabetic cryptography. The cipher alphabet changes every few letters. It's much harder."

I point to his sheet of paper. "But Colonna couldn't have used anything like that. It just makes gibberish. The whole book would be full of words like 'buggj.' "

Paul's eyes lit up. "Exactly. Complex encipherment methods don't produce readable text. But the *Hypnerotomachia* is different. Its ciphertext still reads like a book."

"So Colonna used the riddles instead of a cipher."

He nodded. "It's called steganography. Like writing a

message in invisible ink: the idea is that nobody knows it's there. Francesco combined cryptography and steganography. He hid riddles inside a normal-sounding story, where they wouldn't stand out. Then he used the riddles to create deciphering techniques, to make it harder to understand his message. In this case, all you have to do is count the number of letters in *cornuta*, which is seven, then string together every seventh letter in the text. It's not that different from using the first word of every chapter. Just a matter of knowing the right intervals."

"That worked? Every seventh letter in the book?"

Paul shook his head. "Not the whole book. Just a part. And no, it didn't work at first. I kept coming up with nonsense. The problem is figuring out where to start. If you choose every seventh letter beginning with the first one, you get a completely different result than if you choose every seventh letter beginning with the second one. That's where the riddle's answer plays a role again."

He pulled another page from his pile, this one a photocopy of an original page from the *Hypnerotomachia*.

"Right here, in the middle of this chapter, is the word *cornuta*, spelled out in the text of the book itself. If you begin with the 'C' in *cornuta*, and write down every seventh letter for the next three chapters, *that's* how you find Francesco's plaintext. The original was in Latin, but I translated it." He handed me another sheet. "Look."

> *Good reader, this past year has been the most trying I have endured. Separated from my family, I have had only the good of mankind to comfort me, and while traveling the waters I have seen how flawed that good can be. If it is true, what Pico said, that man is pregnant with*

all possibilities, that he is a great miracle, as Hermes Trismegistus claimed, then where is the proof? I am surrounded on one side by the greedy and the ignorant, who hope to profit by following me, and on the other side by the jealous and the falsely pious, who hope to profit by my destruction.

But you, reader, are faithful to what I believe, or you could not have found what I have hidden here. You are not among those who destroy in God's name, for my text is their foe, and they are my enemy. I have traveled broadly in search of a vessel for my secret, a way to preserve it against time. A Roman by birth, I was raised in a city built for all ages. The walls and bridges of the emperors stand after a thousand years, and the words of my ancient countrymen have multiplied, reprinted today by Aldus and his colleagues at their presses. Inspired by these creators of the old world, I have chosen the same vessels: a book and a great work of stones. Together they house what I will give to you, reader, if you can understand my meaning.

To learn what I wish to tell, you must know the world as we have known it, who studied it most of any men in our time. You must prove yourself a lover of wisdom, and of man's potential, so that I will know you are no enemy. For there is an evil abroad, and even we, the princes of our day, do fear it.

Carry on, then, reader. Strive wisely for my meaning. Poliphilo's journey grows harder, as does mine, but I have much more to tell.

I turned the sheet over, looking for more. "Where's the rest of it?"

"That's it," he said. "We have to solve more to get more."

I looked at the page, then up at him in amazement. In the back of my mind, from a corner of unsettled thoughts, came a tapping noise, the sound my father always made when he was excited. His fingers would drum the rhythm of Corelli's Christmas Concerto, twice as fast as any allegro movement, on whatever surface he could find.

"What are you going to do now?" I asked, trying to stay afloat in the present.

But the thought occurred to me anyway, putting the discovery in perspective: Arcangelo Corelli finished his concerto in the early days of classical music, more than one hundred years before Beethoven's Ninth Symphony. Even in Corelli's day, though, Colonna's message had been awaiting its first reader for more than two centuries.

"The same thing you are," Paul said. "We're going to find Francesco's next riddle."

Chapter 13

Every hallway in Dod is empty as Gil and I return to the room, numbed by the long walk north from the parking lot. An airy silence prevails throughout the building. Between the Nude Olympics and the Easter festivities, every soul is accounted for.

I turn on the television for word of what's happened. The local networks carry the Nude Olympics on the late news, after there's been time to edit the footage, and the runners in Holder Courtyard float across the screen in a blur of whites, blinking under the glass like fireflies trapped in a jar.

At last the female news anchor returns to the screen.

"We have breaking news on our top story."

Gil emerges from his bedroom to listen.

"Earlier tonight we reported to you about what may be a related incident at Princeton University. At this hour the accident at Dickinson Hall, which some witnesses describe as a fraternity stunt gone wrong, has taken a tragic turn. Officials at Princeton Medical Center confirm that the man, reportedly a university student, has died. In a prepared statement, Borough Police Chief Daniel Stout repeated that investigators would continue to examine the possibility that, quote, nonaccidental factors had played a role. In the meantime, university administrators are asking students to remain in their rooms, or to travel in groups if they need to be outside tonight."

In the studio, the anchor turns to her cohost. "Clearly a difficult situation, given what we saw earlier at Holder Hall." Returning to the camera, she adds, "We'll be coming back to this story later in the hour."

"He died?" Gil repeats, unable to believe it. "But I thought Charlie . . ." He lets the thought trail off.

"A university student," I say.

Gil looks up at me after a long silence. "Don't think like that, Tom. Charlie would've called."

Against the far wall, the framed picture I bought for Katie sits at an uncomfortable cant. I dial Taft's office, just as Gil returns from his bedroom and hands me a bottle of wine.

"What's this?" I ask.

The phone at the Institute rings over and over. Nothing.

Gil steps toward the makeshift bar he keeps in the corner of the room, grabbing two wineglasses and a corkscrew. "I need to relax."

There's still no answer at Taft's, so I reluctantly put down the receiver. I'm just about to tell Gil how sick I feel, when I glance over and realize that he looks even worse.

"What's wrong?" I ask.

He tops the glasses off. Taking one in his hand, he raises it to me, then takes a sip.

"Have some," he says. "It's good."

"Sure," I say, wondering if he just wants someone to drink with. But the thought of wine is turning my stomach.

He waits, so I nip at my share. The burgundy stings going down, but it has the opposite effect on Gil. The more he's got in him, the better he starts to look.

I tip my glass back. Snow rolls across the pools of light from the post lanterns in the distance. Gil drains his second glass.

"Take it easy, chief," I say, trying to sound nice about it. "You don't want to have a hangover at the ball."

"Yeah, right," he says. "I have to be at the caterer's tomorrow by nine. I should've told them I don't even go to class that early."

It comes out sharp, and Gil seems to catch himself. Picking up the remote from the floor, he says, "Let's see if there's anything else on."

Three different networks are broadcasting from somewhere on campus, but when there doesn't seem to be any new information, Gil gets up and starts a movie.

"*Roman Holiday*," he says, sitting back down. A distant ease comes over his face. Audrey Hepburn again. He puts down the wine.

The longer the movie stays on, the more I find that Gil is right. No matter how heavy my thoughts are, sooner or later I keep coming back to Audrey. I can't get my eyes off her.

After a while, Gil's focus seems to cloud over a little. The wine, I guess. But when he rubs his forehead and focuses a second too long on his hands, I sense there's more to it. Maybe he's thinking of Anna, who broke up with him while I was at home. Thesis deadlines and planning the ball undid them, Charlie told me, but Gil never wanted to talk about it. Anna was a mystery to us from the beginning; he almost never brought her to the room, though at Ivy, I'd heard, they were never apart. She was the first of his girlfriends who couldn't recognize which one of us was picking up the phone, the first who sometimes forgot Paul's name, and she never stopped by the room if she knew Gil wasn't there.

"You know who looks a little like Audrey Hepburn?" Gil asks suddenly, catching me off guard.

"Who?" I say, dialing Taft's office again.

He surprises me. "Katie."

"What made you think of that?"

"I don't know. I was watching you two tonight. You're great together."

He says it as if he's trying to remind himself of something dependable. I want to tell him that Katie and I have had our ups and downs too, that he's not the only one who struggles in a relationship, but it would be the wrong thing to say.

"She's your type, Tom," he goes on. "She's *smart*. I don't even understand what she's saying half the time."

I hang up the phone when there's still no answer. "Where is he?"

"He'll call." Gil takes a long breath, trying to ignore the possibilities. "How long's it been with Katie?"

"Next Wednesday makes four months for us."

Gil shakes his head. He's broken up three times since Katie and I met.

"Do you ever wonder if she's the one?"

It's the first time anyone has asked that question.

"Sometimes. I wish we had more time. I worry about next year."

"You should hear how she talks about you. It's like you've known each other since you were kids."

"What do you mean?"

"I found her at Ivy once, taping a basketball game for you on the TV upstairs. She said it was because you and your dad used to go to the Michigan–Ohio State game together."

I hadn't even asked her to do it. Until we met, she'd never followed basketball.

"You're lucky," he says.

I nod my agreement.

We talk a little more about Katie, then Gil slowly returns to Audrey. His expression lightens, but eventually I can see the old thoughts return. Paul. Anna. The ball. Before long he reaches for the bottle. I'm just about to suggest that he's had enough to drink, when a dragging sound comes from the hallway. The outside door opens, and Charlie stands in the sallow light of the hall. He looks bad. There are blood-colored stains on the cuffs of his clothes.

"You okay?" Gil asks, standing up.

"We've got to talk," Charlie says, with an edge to his voice.

Gil mutes the television.

Charlie goes to the refrigerator and pulls out a bottle of water. He drinks half of it, then pours some over his hands to wet his face. His focus is unsteady. Finally he sits down and says, "The man who fell from Dickinson was Bill Stein."

"Jesus," Gil whispers.

I feel myself go cold. "I don't understand."

Charlie confirms it by the look on his face. "He was in his office in the history department. Someone came in and shot him."

"Who?"

"They don't know."

"What do you mean, they don't know?"

A beat of silence passes. Charlie focuses on me. "What was that pager message about? What did Bill Stein want from Paul?"

"I told you. He wanted to give Paul a book he found. I can't believe this, Charlie."

"He didn't say anything else? Where he was going? Who he was going to see?"

I shake my head. Then, slowly, it returns to me, what I'd mistaken for paranoia: the phone calls Bill had gotten, the books someone else was checking out. A wave of fear descends on me as I tell them.

"Shit," Charlie grumbles. He reaches for the phone.

"What are you doing?" Gil asks.

"The police are going to want to talk to you," Charlie tells me. "Where's Paul?"

"Jesus. I don't know, but we've got to find him. I keep trying Taft's office at the Institute. There's no answer."

Charlie looks at us impatiently.

"He'll be fine," Gil says, and I can hear the wine talking. "Calm down."

"I wasn't talking to you," Charlie snaps.

"Maybe he's at Taft's house," I suggest. "Or Taft's office on campus."

"The cops will find him when they need to," Gil says, face hardening. "We should stay out of this."

Charlie turns. "Two of us are already *in* this."

Gil scoffs. "Give me a break, Charlie. Since when are you in this?"

"Not me, you prick. Tom and Paul. There's more to *us* than just *you*."

"Don't get sanctimonious on me. I'm sick of you butting into everyone else's problems."

Charlie leans forward, lifts the bottle from the table, and throws it in the trash. "You've had enough."

For a second I'm afraid the wine is going to make Gil say something we'll all regret. But after glaring at Charlie, he rises from the couch. "Christ," he says. "I'm going to bed."

I watch him retreat into the bedroom without another word. A second later, the light beneath the door falls dark.

Minutes pass, and they feel like hours. I try the Institute again, but with no luck, so Charlie and I sit in the common room for the duration, neither one speaking. My mind is moving too quickly to make sense of my own thoughts. I stare out the window, and Stein's voice climbs back into my thoughts.

I get these phone calls. Pick up . . . click. *Pick up* . . . click.

Finally Charlie rises. Finding a towel in the closet, he starts to put his bathroom caddy in order. Without a word he heads out the door in his boxer shorts. The men's bathroom is down the hall, and there are half a dozen upperclass women living between it and our quad, but Charlie marches out anyway, towel wrapped around his neck like an oxbow, caddy in hand.

Sitting back on the couch, I reach for today's *Daily Princetonian*. To distract myself, I flip through the pages, searching for a photo credit of Katie's somewhere in the nether corners of the paper, where underclass contributions go to die. I'm always curious about the pictures she takes, the new subjects she chooses, the ones she thinks are too unimportant to mention. After dating someone long enough, you start to imagine she sees everything the same way you do. Katie's photos are a corrective, a glimpse of the world through her eyes.

Before long a sound comes at the door, Charlie returning from the shower. But when a key strikes in the outside lock, I realize it's someone else. The door swings open and it's Paul who enters the room. His face is pale, and his lips are blue from the cold.

"Are you okay?" I ask.

Charlie arrives back just in time. "Where have you *been*?" he demands.

It takes us fifteen minutes to get the details from Paul, given his state. After leaving the lecture, he went to the Institute and searched for Bill Stein in the computer lab there. An hour later, when Stein failed to appear, Paul decided to go back to the dorm. He started the trip in his car, only to have it quit at a stoplight about a mile from campus; then he had to walk back in the snow.

The rest of the night, he says, is a blur. He arrived at the north of campus to find police cars near Bill's office at Dickinson. After asking enough questions, he was driven to the medical center, where someone asked him to identify the body. Taft showed up at the hospital not long after, giving a second identification, but before he and Paul could speak, officers separated them for questioning. The police wanted to know about his relationship with Stein and Taft, about the last time he saw Bill, about where he was at the time of the murder. Paul cooperated in a daze.

When they finally released him, they asked him not to leave campus, and said they'd be in touch. Eventually he made his way toward Dod, but stayed on the outside steps for a while, just wanting to be alone.

Finally, we discuss the conversation we had with Stein in the Rare Books Room, which Paul says the police took down in full. As he talks about Bill, about how agitated Stein was at the library, about the friend he's lost, Paul gives little sign of emotion. He still hasn't recovered from the shock.

"Tom," he says finally, when we're back in our bedroom, "I need a favor."

"Of course," I say. "Name it."

"I need you to come with me."

I hesitate. "Where?"

"The art museum."

He's changing into a dry set of clothes.

"Now? Why?"

Paul rubs at his forehead, working out an ache. "I'll explain on the way."

When we return to the common room, Charlie looks at us like we've lost our minds. "At this hour?" he asks. "The museum's closed."

"I know what I'm doing," Paul says, already making for the hallway.

Charlie gives me a heavy look, but says nothing as I follow Paul out the door.

The art museum sits like an old Mediterranean palace across the courtyard from Dod. From the front, where we entered a few hours earlier, it's just a stumpy modern building with a

Picasso sculpture on the front lawn that looks like a glorified birdbath. When you approach from the side, though, the newer elements give way to older ones, pretty windows in little Romanesque arches, and red roof-tiles that peek out beneath tonight's canopy of snow. Under different circumstances, the view from here would be charming. Under different circumstances, it might be a picture Katie would take.

"What are we doing?" I ask.

Paul is trudging a path before me in his old workman's boots.

"I found what Richard thought was in the diary," he says.

It sounds like the middle of a thought whose beginning he's kept to himself.

"The blueprint?"

He shakes his head. "I'll show you when we get inside."

I'm walking in his footsteps now to keep the snow out of my pant legs. My eyes keep returning to his boots. Paul worked at the museum loading docks our freshman summer, moving incoming and outgoing exhibits onto trucks. The boots were a necessity then, but tonight they leave dirty tracks in the moon-white of the courtyard. He looks like a boy in men's shoes.

We arrive at a door by the west face of the museum. Beside it is a tiny keypad. Paul dials in his docent's password and waits to see if it works. He used to give tours at the art museum, but finally had to take a job in the slide library because the docents weren't paid.

To my surprise, the door opens with a beep and a whisper of a click. I'm so used to the medieval-sounding bolts of the dorm doors, I almost don't hear it. He leads me into a small antechamber, a security room supervised by a guard behind a plate-glass window, and suddenly I feel trapped. After signing a visitation form on a clipboard, though, and pressing our university IDs against the glass, we're cleared to enter the docent's library beyond the next door.

"That's it?" I say, expecting more of a shakedown at this hour.

Paul points to a video camera on the wall, but says nothing.

The docent's library is unimpressive—a few shelves of art history books donated by other guides to help prepare for tours—but Paul continues toward an elevator around the corner. A large sign posted on the sliding metal doors says FACULTY, STAFF, AND SECURITY ONLY. STUDENTS AND DOCENTS NOT PERMITTED WITHOUT ESCORT. The words *students* and *docents* have both been underlined in red.

Paul is looking somewhere else. He pulls a key ring from his pocket and plugs one of them into a slot in the wall. When he turns it to the right, the metal doors slide open.

"Where'd you get that?"

He leads me into the elevator, then presses a button. "My job," he says.

The slide library gives him access to archival rooms in the museum. He is so careful about his work that he has earned almost everyone's trust.

"Where are we going?" I say.

"Up to the image room. Where Vincent keeps some of his slide carousels."

The elevator discharges us on the main floor of the museum. Paul guides me across it, ignoring the paintings he's pointed out to me a dozen times before—the vast

Rubens with its dark-browed Jupiter, the unfinished *Death of Socrates* with the old philosopher reaching for his cup of hemlock. Only when we pass the paintings Curry brought for the trustees' exhibit do Paul's eyes wander.

We reach the door to the slide library, and he produces the keys again. One of them shifts quietly into place, and we enter the darkness.

"Over here," he says, pointing toward an aisle of shelves lined with dusty boxes. Each box contains a slide carousel. Behind another locked door, in a large room I've seen only once, rests much of the university's collection of art slides.

Paul finds the set of boxes he's been searching for, then lifts one from the stack and places it on the shelf before him. A note taped to the side, written in a sloppy hand, says MAPS: ROME. He takes the top off and carries the box to the small open space near the entrance. From another shelf he produces a slide projector, which he plugs into a wall socket near the ground. Finally, with the flick of a switch, a blurry image appears on the opposite wall. Paul adjusts the focus until it sharpens into position.

"Okay," I say. "Now tell me what we're doing here."

"What if Richard was right?" he says. "What if Vincent stole the diary from him thirty years ago?"

"He probably did. What does it matter now?"

Paul brings me up to speed. "Imagine you're in Vincent's position. Richard keeps telling you the diary is the only way to understand the *Hypnerotomachia*. You think he's blowing smoke, just a college kid with an art history degree. Then someone else shows up. Another scholar."

Paul says it with a certain respect. I gather he's referring to my father.

"Suddenly you're the odd man out. Both of them say

the diary is the answer. But you've painted yourself into a corner. You've told Richard the diary is useless, that the portmaster was a charlatan. And more than anything, you hate being wrong. What do you do now?"

Paul is trying to convince me of a possibility I've never had trouble accepting: that Vincent Taft is a thief.

"I get it," I say. "Go on."

"So you somehow steal the diary. But you can't make anything of it, because you've been looking at the *Hypnerotomachia* all wrong. Without the ciphered messages from Francesco, you don't know what to do with the diary. What then?"

"I don't know."

"You're not going to throw it away," he says, ignoring me, "just because you don't understand it."

I nod my agreement.

"So you keep it. Somewhere safe. Maybe the lockbox in your office."

"Or in your house."

"Right. Then, years later, this kid comes along, and he and his friend start making progress on the *Hypnerotomachia*. More than you expected. In fact, more than *you* made in your prime. He starts finding the messages from Francesco."

"You start thinking the diary might be useful after all."

"Exactly."

"And you don't tell the kid about it, because then he would know you stole it."

"*But*," Paul continues, arriving at his point, "say one day someone found it."

"Bill."

Paul nods. "He was always in Vincent's office, at Vincent's house, helping with all the little projects Vincent made him do. And he *knew* what the diary meant. If he'd found it, he wouldn't have just put it back."

"He would've brought it to you."

"Right. And we turned around and showed it to Richard. Then Richard confronted Vincent at the lecture."

I'm skeptical. "But wouldn't Taft have realized it was gone before that?"

"Of course. He *had* to know Bill took it. But what do you think his reaction was when he realized Richard knew about it too? The first thing on his mind would've been to go find Bill."

Now I understand. "You think he went to Stein's office after the lecture."

"Was Vincent at the reception?"

I take it as a rhetorical question until I remember Paul wasn't there; he'd already left to find Stein.

"Not that I saw."

"There's a hallway connecting Dickinson and the auditorium," he says. "Vincent didn't even have to leave the building to get there."

Paul lets it sink in. The possibility drifts through my thoughts clumsily, tethered to a thousand other details. "You really think Taft killed him?" I ask. A strange silhouette forms from the shadows of the room, Epp Lang burying a dog beneath a tree.

Paul stares at the black contours projected on the wall. "I think he's capable of it."

"Out of anger?"

"I don't know." But he already seems to have been through all of the scenarios in his mind. "Listen," he says, "when I was waiting for Bill at the Institute, I started reading the diary more carefully, looking for every mention of Francesco."

He flips it open and inside the front cover is a page of notes he's made on Institute stationery.

"I found the entry where the portmaster records the set of directions the thief copied from Francesco's papers. Genovese says they were written on an empty scrap of paper, and must've formed some kind of nautical route, something about the path Francesco's ship took. The portmaster tried to figure out where the cargo must've come from by working backward from Genoa."

When Paul unfolds the stationery, I can see a pattern of arrows drawn near a compass.

"These are the directions. They're in Latin. They say: *Four south, ten east, two north, six west.* Then they say *De Stadio.*"

"What's *De Stadio*?"

Paul smiles. "I think that's the key. The portmaster took it to his cousin, who told him *De Stadio* was the scale that went with the directions. It can be translated 'Of Stadia,' meaning the directions are measured in stadia."

"I don't get it."

"The stadium is a unit of measurement from the ancient world, based on the length of a footrace in the Greek Olympics. That's where we get our modern word. About six hundred feet is one stadium, so there are between eight and ten stadia in a mile."

"So *four south* means four stadia south."

"Then *ten east*, *two north*, and *six west*. It's all four directions. Does it remind you of something?"

It does: in his final riddle, Colonna referred to what he

called a Rule of Four, a device that would lead readers to his secret crypt. But we gave up on finding it when the text itself failed to produce anything remotely geographical.

"You think that's it? Those four directions?"

Paul nods. "But the portmaster was looking for something on a much bigger scale, a voyage of hundreds and hundreds of miles. If Francesco's directions are in stadia, then the ship couldn't have originated in France or the Netherlands. It must've started its trip about half a mile southeast of Genoa. The portmaster knew that couldn't be right."

I can see Paul's giddiness, thinking he's done the portmaster one better. "You're saying the directions were meant for something else."

He hardly pauses. "*De Stadio* doesn't just have to mean 'Of Stadia.' *De* could also mean 'from.' "

He looks at me expectantly, but the beauty of this new translation is lost on me.

"Maybe the measurements aren't just *of* stadia, or measured in those units," he says. "Maybe they're also taken *from* a stadium. A stadium could be the starting point. *De Stadio* could have a double meaning—you follow the directions *from* a physical stadium building, *in* stadia units."

The map of Rome projected on the wall is coming into focus. The city is littered with ancient arenas. Colonna would've known it better than any city in the world.

"It solves the scale problem the portmaster had," Paul continues. "You can't measure the distance between countries in a few stadia. But you *can* measure the distance across a city that way. Pliny says the circumference of the

Roman city walls in A.D. 75 was about thirteen miles. The entire city was maybe twenty-five or thirty stadia across."

"You think that will lead us to the crypt?" I ask.

"Francesco talks about building where no one can see. He doesn't want anyone to know what's inside it. This may be the only way to find the location."

Months of speculation return to me. We spent many nights wondering why Colonna would build his crypt out in the Roman forests, hidden from his family and friends, but Paul and I never agreed about our conclusions.

"What if the crypt is more than we thought?" he says. "What if the location *is* the secret?"

"Then what's inside it?" I say, reviving the question.

Paul's demeanor changes to frustration. "I don't know, Tom. I still haven't figured it out."

"I'm just saying, don't you think Colonna would've—"

"Told us what was in the crypt? Of course. But the entire second half of the book depends on the last cipher, and I can't solve it. Not alone. So this diary is it. Okay?"

I back off.

"So all we have to do," Paul goes on, "is look at a few of these maps. We start at the major stadium areas—the Coliseum, the Circus Maximus, and so on—and move four stadia south, ten east, two north, and six west. If any of those locations is in what would've been a forest in Colonna's time, we mark it."

"Let's look," I say.

Paul presses the Advance button, shifting through a series of maps made in the fifteenth and sixteenth centuries. They have the quality of architectural caricatures, buildings drawn out of proportion with their surroundings, crowded up against each other until the spaces in between are impossible to judge.

"How are we going to measure distances on those?" I ask.

He answers me by pumping the hand control several more times. After three or four more Renaissance maps, a modern one appears. The city looks more like the one I remember from travel books my father gave me before our trip to the Vatican. The Aurelian Wall on the north, east, and south and the Tiber River on the west create the profile of an old woman's head facing the rest of Italy. The church of San Lorenzo, where Colonna had the two men killed, hovers like a fly just beyond the arch of the old woman's nose.

"This one has the right scale on it," Paul says, pointing to the measurements in the upper-left corner. Eight stadia are marked along a single line, labeled ANCIENT ROMAN MILE.

He walks toward the image on the wall and places his hand beside the scale. From the base of his palm to the tip of his middle finger, he covers the full eight stadia.

"Let's start with the Coliseum." He kneels on the floor and places his hand near a dark oval in the middle of the map, near the old woman's cheek. "Four south," he says, moving a palm-length down, "and ten east." He moves one full hand-length across, then adds half an index finger. "Then two north and six west."

When he finishes, he's pointing to a spot labeled M. CELIUS on the map.

"You think that's where it is?"

"Not there," he says, deflated. Pointing to a dark circle on the map just southwest of his finishing point, he says,

"Right over here is a church. San Stefano Rotondo." He shifts his finger northeast. "This is another one, Santi Quattro Coronati. And here"—he moves the finger southeast—"is Saint John Lateran, where the popes lived until the fourteenth century. If Francesco had built his crypt here, he would've done it within a quarter mile of three different churches. No way."

He begins again. "The Circus Flaminius," he says. "This map is old. I think Gatti placed it closer to here." He moves his finger closer to the river, then repeats the directions.

"Good or bad?" I say, staring at the location, somewhere atop the Palatine Hill.

He frowns. "Bad. This is almost right in the middle of San Teodoro."

"Another church?"

He nods.

"You're sure Colonna wouldn't have built it near a church?"

He looks at me as if I've forgotten the cardinal rule. "Every message says he's terrified of being caught by the zealots. The 'men of God.' How do *you* interpret that?"

Losing patience, he tries two other possibilities—the Circus of Hadrian and the old Circus of Nero, over which the Vatican was built—but in both cases, the rectangle of twenty-two stadia lands him almost in the middle of the Tiber River.

"There's a stadium in every corner of this map," I tell him. "Why don't we think about where the crypt could be, then work backward to see if there's a stadium near it?"

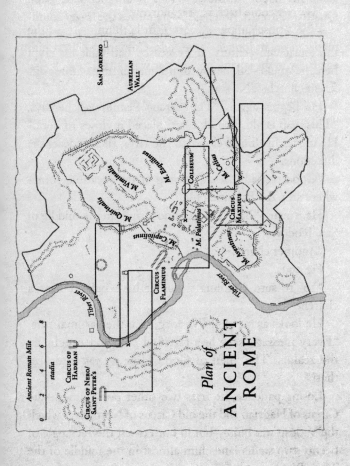

Plan of
ANCIENT ROME

Ancient Roman Mile

0   2   4   6   8
stadia

SAN LORENZO

AURELIAN WALL

M. Esquilinus

M. Viminalis

M. Quirinalis

COLISEUM

M. Caelius

CIRCUS MAXIMUS

M. Capitolinus

M. Palatinus

M. Aventinus

Tiber River

CIRCUS FLAMINIUS

Tiber River

CIRCUS OF HADRIAN

CIRCUS OF NERO/
SAINT PETER'S

He mulls it over. "I'd have to check some of my other atlases at Ivy."

"We can come back here tomorrow."

Paul, whose supply of optimism is thinning, eyes the map a moment longer, then nods. Colonna has beat him again. Even the spying portmaster was outwitted.

"What now?" I ask.

He buttons his coat, turning off the projector. "I want to check Bill's desk in the library downstairs." He returns the slide machine to its shelf, trying to leave everything where he found it.

"Why?"

"To see if anything else from the diary is there. Richard insists there was a blueprint folded inside it."

He opens the door and holds it for me, checking the room before locking it up.

"You have a key for the library?"

He shakes his head. "Bill told me the punch code for the stairwell."

We return into the darkness of the hallway, where Paul leads me down the corridor. Orange security lights wink in the darkness like airplanes crossing at night. We come to a door leading to a stairwell. Below the knob is a box with five numbered buttons. Paul thinks for a second, then begins to punch a short sequence. As the knob unlocks in his hand, both of us freeze. In the silence we can hear something shuffling.

Chapter 14

Go, I mouth, nudging Paul toward the library door.

A plate of security glass forms a small window in the panel, and we peek through it into the darkness of the room.

A shadow is shifting across the top of one of the private tables. The beam of a flashlight hovers across its surface. I can make out a hand reaching into one of the drawers.

"That's Bill's desk," Paul whispers.

His voice carries in the stairwell. The path of the flashlight freezes, then moves in our direction.

I push Paul down below the window.

"Who is that?" I ask.

"I couldn't see."

We wait, listening for footsteps. When we hear them moving away into the distance, I peek into the room again. It's empty.

Paul pushes the door forward. The entire area is

sunk in the long shadows of bookshelves. Moonlight presses at the sheet-glass windows to the north. The drawers of Stein's desk are still open.

"Is there another exit?" I whisper as we approach.

Paul nods and points past a series of ceiling-high shelves.

Suddenly there are footsteps again, shuffling in the direction of the exit, followed by a click. The door latches gently into place.

I move toward the sound.

"What are you doing?" Paul whispers. He signals me back to him, by the desk.

I peer out the security glass into the far stairwell, but I can make out nothing.

Paul is already rummaging through Stein's papers, splaying his penlight over a clutter of notes and letters. He points at a locked drawer that's been pried open. The files in it have been pulled out and scattered over the desk. Edges of paper curl up like untended grass. There seems to be a folder for every professor in the history department.

RECOMMENDATION: CHAIRMAN WORTHINGTON
REC (A–M): BAUM, CARTER, GODFREY, LI
REC (N–Z): NEWMAN, ROSSINI, SACKLER, WORTHINGTON
    (PRE-CHAIR)
REC (OTHER DEPTS): CONNER, DELFOSSE, LUTKE,
    MASON, QUINN
OLD CORRESPONDENCE: HARGRAVE/WILLIAMS, OXFORD
OLD CORRESPONDENCE: APPLETON, HARVARD

It means nothing to me, but Paul is fixed on them. "What's wrong?" I ask.

Paul runs his flashlight across the desktop. "Why does he need all these recommendations?"

Two other files lie open. One is titled REC/CORRESPON-DENCE: TAFT. The other is LEVERAGE/LEADS.

Taft's letter has been pushed into a corner, brushed aside. Paul rolls his shirt cuff over his fingers and yanks the paper into view.

William Stein is a competent young man. He has worked under me for five years, and has mainly been useful in matters administrative and clerical. I am confident that he will do a similar job wherever he goes.

"God," Paul whispers. "Vincent screwed him." He reads it again. "Bill sounds like a secretary."

When Paul unfolds the dog-eared corner of the page, the date is from last month. He picks it up, revealing a handwritten postscript.

Bill: I am writing this for you in spite of everything. You deserve less. Vincent.

"You bastard . . ." Paul whispers. "Bill was trying to get away from you."

He pans the flashlight over the LEVERAGE/LEADS folder. A series of Stein's letter drafts lies on top, worked over in several pens. Lines have been inserted and removed until the text is difficult to follow. As Paul reads them, I can see the penlight begin to quiver in his hand.

Don Hargrave, begins the first letter, *I am pleased to inform you that my research on the* Hypnerotomachia Poliphili *is complete nears completion. My results will be available by the end of April, if not sooner. I assure you they are worth the wait. As I have heard nothing from you and Master Williams since my letter of 17 January, please confirm that the professorship position we discussed remains available. My heart is with Oxford, but I may not be able to fend off other universities once my paper is published and I'm faced with new offers.*

Paul flips to the following page. I can hear him breathing now.

Chairman Appleton, I write to you with good news. My work on the Hypnerotomachia *draws successfully to a close. As promised, The results will cast a shadow over everything else in Renaissance historical studies—or any historical studies—this year or next. Before I publish my results, I want to confirm that the assistant professorship is still available. My heart is with Harvard, but I may not be able to fend off other temptations once my paper is published and I'm faced with new offers.*

Paul reads it a second time, then a third.

"He was going to try to take it from me," he whispers faintly, stepping away from the desk to lean back on the wall.

"How is that possible?"

"Maybe he thought no one would believe it was under-graduate work."

I refocus on the letter. "When did he offer to type up your thesis?"

"Sometime last month."

"He's been meaning to take it for that long?"

Paul glares at me and moves his hand across the desk. "*Obviously.* He's been writing these people since January."

When the letters settle on the desktop, a final sheet of correspondence peeks out from behind the Oxford and Harvard letters. When Paul sees the corner of the sta-tionery, he pulls it out.

Richard, it begins, *I hope this letter finds you well. Perhaps you've had better luck in Italy than you had in New York. If not, then we both know the situation you're in. We also both know Vincent. I think it's fair to say he has plans of his own for anything that comes of this. I therefore have a proposition for you. There's more than enough here to suit both of us, and I've come up with a division of labor I think you'll find fair. Please contact me soon to discuss. Leave me your phone numbers in Florence and Rome as well—the mail over there is unreliable, and I'd prefer to straighten this out ASAP. —B.*

The reply, in a different pen and a different hand, has been written on the bottom of the original letter and sent back. There are two telephone numbers, one preceded by the letter *F*, the other by an *R*. A final note is jotted afterward:

As requested. Call after business hours, my time. What about Paul? —Richard.

Paul is speechless. He rifles through the papers again, but there's nothing else. When I try to console him, he motions me off.

"We should tell the dean," I say finally.

"Tell him what? That we were going through Bill's stuff?"

Suddenly, a bright reflection curves along the opposite wall, followed by colored lights flashing through the sheet-glass windows. A police car has arrived in the front courtyard of the museum, siren mute. Two officers emerge. The red and blue lights go dead just as a second squad car arrives and two more officers follow.

"Someone must've told them we were here," I say.

The note from Curry shakes in Paul's hand. He's standing in place, watching the dark forms hurry toward the main entrance.

"Come on." I yank him toward the bookshelves by the rear exit.

Just then, the front door to the library opens and the beam of a flashlight lances across the room. We duck into a corner. Both officers enter the room.

"*Over there*," the first officer says, gesturing in our direction.

I grab the knob and press the back door open. Paul ducks into the hallway as the first policeman nears. On my haunches, I clamber out and regain my feet. We slide with our backs to the wall, and Paul leads us to the stairs, racing toward the ground floor. When we return to the open space of the main hall, I can see a flashlight skirting a nearby wall.

"Downstairs," Paul says. "There's a service elevator."

We enter the Asian wing of the museum. Sculptures and vases sit behind ghostly walls of glass. Chinese scrolls lie unraveled and mounted beside tomb figures in display cabinets. The room is a murky shade of green.

"This way," Paul urges as the footsteps come closer.

He leads me around a corner, back into a dead end, where the only exit is the large pair of metal doors to the service elevator.

Voices grow louder. I can make out two policemen standing at the foot of the stairs, trying to find their way around in the dark. Suddenly the entire floor is illuminated.

"*We got lights . . .*" comes the voice of a third.

Paul forces his key into the slot on the wall. When the elevator doors part, he pulls me in. A barrage of footsteps follows, moving in our direction.

"*Come on, come on . . .*"

The doors remain open. For a second I think they've cut the power to the elevator. Then, just as the first officer turns the corner, the metal walls slide shut. A hand beats against the doors when the officer catches up, but the sound fades as the cabin begins to move.

"Where are we going?" I ask.

"Out the loading docks," Paul says, trying to catch his breath.

We exit into a holding area of some kind, and Paul forces open the door leading into a huge, cold room. I wait for my eyes to adjust. The garage doors of the loading bays loom before us. The wind outside is so close, it's making the metal panels tremble. I imagine footsteps racing downstairs in our direction, but nothing is audible through the thick door.

Paul rushes over to a switch on the wall. When he turns the knob, an engine stirs and the retractable loading door begins to budge.

"That's enough," I say, once the opening is big enough to admit both of us on our backs.

But Paul shakes his head and the door continues to rise.

"What are you doing?"

The gap between the floor and the bottom of the door increases until it brings the entire vista of south campus into view. For a second I'm stopped short by how beautiful it is, how empty.

Suddenly Paul turns the motor knob in the opposite direction and the door starts to roll shut.

"Go!" he cries.

He darts from the wall toward the open bay, and I fumble, trying to get on my back. Paul is already in front of me. He rolls beneath the door, then pulls me out just before the metal connects with the ground.

I stand up, trying to catch my breath. When I begin moving in the direction of Dod, Paul jerks me back.

"They'll see us from upstairs." He points to the windows on the west side of the building. After scanning the path to our east, he says, "This way."

"Are you okay?" I ask, following.

He bobs his head and we trudge into the night, away from our quad and out of their sight lines. I can feel the wind beneath my coat collar, cooling the sweat on my neck. When I look back, Dod and Brown Hall are almost purely dark, as is every dormitory in the distance. Night has reached all corners of campus. Only the windows at the art museum are shot with light.

We continue east through Prospect Gardens, a botanical wonderland in the heart of campus. The tiny spring plantings are dashed with white, almost invisible underfoot, but the American beech and the cedar of Lebanon stand like guardian angels above them, arms outstretched to shoulder the snow. A police car patrols one of the side streets, and we pick up our pace.

My thoughts are jumpy, my mind working to understand what we've seen. Maybe it was Taft we saw at Stein's desk, rifling through his papers, erasing any connection between them. Maybe he called the police on us. I look over at Paul, wondering if the same thought has crossed his mind, but his expression is blank.

In the distance, the new music department shows signs of life.

"We can go in there for a while," I suggest.

"Where?"

"The practice rooms in the basement. Until we're clear."

Stray notes float in the air as we near. Night-owl musicians come to Woolworth to rehearse in private. Down toward Prospect, another campus police car skids by, splashing slush and rock salt onto the curb. I force myself to walk faster.

Construction on Woolworth has only recently finished, and the building that emerged from the scaffolding is a curious thing, fortresslike from the outside but glassy and fragile-looking from within. Its atrium curves like a river through the music library and classrooms on the ground floor, rising three stories to skylights above. The wind howls jealously around it. Paul unlocks the entrance to the building with his ID card, holding the door as I pass through.

"Which way?" he asks.

I lead him to the nearest staircase. Gil and I have been here twice since the building was opened, both times after drinks on a slow Saturday night. His father's second wife insisted that Gil learn to play something by Duke Ellington, the same way my father insisted that I learn something by Arcangelo Corelli, and between us we have eight years of lessons and almost nothing to show for it. Thumping our bottles on the top of an old baby grand, Gil would bungle "'A' Train," I would butcher "La Follia," and we would pretend to keep a beat that neither of us had ever learned.

Paul and I pad down the basement hallway, to find that only one piano is still at work. Someone in a distant practice room is playing "Rhapsody in Blue." We slip into a small, soundproof studio, and Paul edges behind the upright piano, taking a seat on the stool. He looks at the keys of the piano, mysterious as computer keys to him, and doesn't touch them. The overhead light sputters for a second, then goes dead. It's just as well.

"I can't believe it," he says finally, taking a deep breath.

"Why would they do it?" I ask.

Paul runs his index finger across a key, scratching at the ebony. When he seems not to hear the question, I repeat myself.

"What do you want me to say, Tom?"

"Maybe this is why Stein wanted to help in the first place."

"When? Tonight with the diary?"

"Months ago."

"You mean, when you stopped working on the *Hypnerotomachia*?"

The chronology is a jab, a reminder that Stein's involvement traces ultimately back to me.

"You think this is my fault?"

"No," Paul says quietly. "Of course not."

But the accusation hangs in the air. The map of Rome, like the diary, has reminded me of what I left behind, how much progress we made before I left, how much I enjoyed it. I look at my hands, curled up in my lap. It was my father who said I had lazy hands. Five years of lessons hadn't produced a single presentable Corelli sonata; that's when he started pushing basketball instead.

The strong take from the weak, Thomas, but the smart take from the strong.

"What about the note to Curry?" I say, fixing on the

back of the piano. The wood is unvarnished and raw along the entire side, where the upright is supposed to face a wall. It strikes me as a strange economy, like a professor who doesn't brush the back of his hair because he can't see it in the mirror. My father used to do that. It was a defect of perspective, I always thought—the mistake of someone who could only see the world one way. His students must have noticed it as often as I did. Every time he turned his back on them.

"Richard would never try to take something from me," Paul says, biting at a nail. "We must've missed something."

A hush settles in. The practice room is warm, and when we're both quiet there's no sound at all, besides an occasional hum from down the hall, where Gershwin has been replaced by a Beethoven sonata that rumbles in the distance. It reminds me of sitting through summer storms as a child. The power is out, the house is quiet, and nothing can be heard besides the roll of far-off thunder. My mother is reading to me by candlelight—Bartholomew Cubbins or an illustrated Sherlock Holmes—and the only thing on my mind is how the best stories always seem to be about men in funny hats.

"I think it was Vincent in there," Paul says. "At the police station he lied about his relationship with Bill. He told them Bill was the best graduate student he'd advised in years."

We both know Vincent, Stein's letter said. *It's fair to say he has plans of his own for anything that comes of this.*

"You think Taft wants it for himself?" I ask. "He hasn't tried to publish anything on the *Hypnerotomachia* in years."

"This isn't *about* publishing, Tom."

"What's it about?"

Paul stays quiet for a moment, then says, "You heard what Vincent said tonight. He's never admitted before that Francesco was from Rome." Paul looks down at the pedals of the piano, jutting out from the wooden frame like tiny gold shoes. "He's trying to take this away from me."

"Take what away from you?"

But again Paul hesitates. "Never mind. Forget it."

"What if it was Curry in the museum?" I offer, when he turns away. The letter from Stein to Curry has complicated my vision of the man. It reminds me that he was more taken with the *Hypnerotomachia* than any of them.

"He's not involved, Tom."

"You saw how he acted when you showed him the diary. Curry still thought it was his."

"No. I *know* him, Tom. Okay? You don't."

"What's that supposed to mean?"

"You never trusted Richard. Even when he tried to help you."

"I didn't need his help."

"And you only hate Vincent because of your father."

I turn to him, surprised. "He drove my father to—"

"To what? Run off the road?"

"Drove him to *distraction*. What the hell's wrong with you?"

"He wrote a book review, Tom."

"He ruined his life."

"He ruined his *career*. There's a difference."

"Why are you defending him?"

"I'm not. I'm defending Richard. But Vincent never did anything to you."

I'm just about to dig into Paul, when I see the effect our conversation is having on him. He runs the base of a palm above his cheeks, blotting them. For a second I can only see headlights on the road. A horn is blaring.

"Richard's always been good to me," Paul is saying.

I don't remember my father making a sound. Not once during that drive, not even when we skidded off the road.

"You don't know them," he says. "Either of them."

I'm not sure when the rain began—while we were driving to see my mother at the book show, or on the way to the hospital when I was riding in the ambulance.

"I found this book review once of Vincent's first major work," Paul continues. "A clipping in his house, from the early seventies, back when he was a hotshot at Columbia—before he came to the Institute and his career fell apart. It was glowing, the kind of thing professors dream about. At the end it said, 'Vincent Taft has already begun his next project: a definitive history of the Italian Renaissance. To judge from his existing work, it will be a magnum opus indeed; the sort of rare accomplishment in which the *writing* of history becomes the *making* of history.' I remember that, word for word. I found it spring of sophomore year, before I really knew him. That was the first time I started to understand who he was."

A book review. Like the one he sent my father, just to be sure he'd seen it. *The Belladonna Hoax*, by Vincent Taft.

"He was a star, Tom. You know that. He had more going on upstairs than most of the faculty here combined. But he lost it. He didn't burn out, he just lost it."

The words are gathering momentum, crowding into the air as if a balance can be struck between the silence outside him and the pressure within. I feel like I'm swimming, flailing as the tide pulls me out. Paul begins to talk about Taft and Curry again, and I tell myself they're just characters in another book, men in hats, figments of the blackout imagination. But the more he talks, the more I begin to see them the way he does.

In the aftermath of the debacle surrounding the portmaster's diary, Taft moved from Manhattan into a white clapboard house at the Institute, a mile southwest of the Princeton campus. Maybe it was the solitude that got to him, the absence of colleagues to wrestle with, but within months, rumors of his drinking began to circulate through the academic community. The definitive history he'd planned quietly expired. His passion, his command of his gift, seemed to crumble.

Three years later, on the occasion of his next publication—a thin volume on the role of hieroglyphics in Renaissance art—it became clear that Taft's career had stalled. Seven years after that, when his next article was published in a minor journal, a reviewer called his decline a tragedy. According to Paul, the loss of what Taft had with Curry and my father continued to haunt him. In the twenty-five years that elapsed between his arrival at the Institute and his meeting with Paul, Vincent Taft published only four times, preferring to pass his time writing criticism of other scholars' work, especially my father's. Not once did he recover the fiery genius of his youth.

It was Paul's arrival at his doorstep during the spring of

our freshman year that must've brought the *Hypnero-tomachia* back into his life. Once Taft and Stein began assisting in the thesis work, Paul told me of startling flashes of brilliance in his mentor. Many nights the old bear toiled furiously alongside him, reciting long passages from obscure primary texts when Paul couldn't find them in the library.

"That was the summer Richard funded my trip to Italy," Paul says, rubbing a palm against the edge of the piano stool. "We were so excited. Even Vincent. He and Richard still weren't speaking, but they knew I was onto something. I was starting to figure things out.

"I was staying in a flat Richard owned, the entire top floor of an old Renaissance palace. It was amazing, just gorgeous. There were paintings on the walls, paintings on the ceilings, paintings everywhere. In niches, above staircases. Tintorettos, Carraccis, Peruginos. It was like heaven, Tom. Just breathtaking, it was so beautiful. And he would wake up in the morning and say, all businesslike, 'Paul, I need to get some work done today.' Then we'd get to talking, and half an hour later he would pull off his tie and say, 'To hell with it. Let's take the day off.' We would end up walking through the piazzas and just talking. The two of us, walking and talking for hours.

"That's when he started telling me about his days at Princeton. About Ivy, and all of these adventures he'd had, these crazy things he'd done, these people he'd known. Your father, most of all. It was so alive, so vivid. I mean, it was unlike everything Princeton has ever been to me. I was just completely mesmerized. It was like living a dream, a perfect dream. Richard even called it that. The whole time we were in Italy, he seemed to be walking on clouds. He'd started seeing a sculptor from Venice, and was talking about proposing to her one day. I thought he might even try to reconcile with Vincent after that summer."

"But they never did."

"No. When we got back to the States, everything reverted. He and Vincent never spoke. The woman he'd been seeing broke it off. Richard started coming back to campus, trying to remember the fire he'd had when he and your father studied with McBee. Since then, he's been living more and more in the past. Vincent tried to get me to stay away from him, but this year it's *Vincent* I've been staying away from, trying to avoid the Institute, trying to work at Ivy whenever I could. I didn't want to tell him what we found until I had to.

"That's when Vincent started forcing me to show him my conclusions, asking for weekly progress reports. Maybe he thought it was his only shot at getting the *Hypnerotomachia* back." Paul runs a hand through his hair. "I should've known better. I should've written a B-grade thesis, then gotten the hell out of here. *It is the greatest houses and the tallest trees that the gods bring low with bolts and thunder. For the gods love to thwart whatever is greater than the rest. They do not suffer pride in anyone but themselves.* Herodotus wrote that. I must've read those lines fifty times and never gave them a second thought. It was Vincent who pointed them out to me. He knew what they meant."

"You don't believe that."

"I don't know what I believe anymore. I should've been watching Vincent and Bill more closely. If I hadn't been paying so much attention to myself, I could've seen this coming."

I stare at the light beneath the door. The piano down the hall has fallen silent.

Paul rises and begins moving toward the entrance. "Let's get out of here," he says.

Chapter 15

We hardly speak as we leave Woolworth. Paul walks slightly in front of me, creating enough space for us to keep to ourselves, and in the distance I can make out the tower of the chapel. Police cars squat at its feet like toads beneath an oak, weathering out a storm. Lines of police tape rock in the dying wind. Bill Stein's snow angel must be gone by now, not even a dimple in the white.

We arrive at Dod to find Charlie awake but preparing for bed once again. He's been cleaning up the common room, ordering stray papers and arranging unopened mail into piles, trying to shake off what he saw in the ambulance. After checking his watch, he looks at us disapprovingly but is too tired to make much of it. I stand by and listen as Paul explains what we saw at the museum, knowing that Charlie will insist we call the police. After I explain that we were going through Stein's belongings when we found the letters, though, even Charlie seems to think better of it.

Paul and I retreat into the bedroom and change clothes wordlessly, then go to our separate bunks. As I lie there, recalling the emotion in his voice as he described Curry, something occurs to me that I've never understood before. There was, if only briefly, a quiet perfection to their relationship. Curry had never succeeded in understanding the *Hypnerotomachia*, until Paul came into his life and solved what Curry couldn't, so they could share it together. And Paul had always wanted for so much, until Richard Curry came into his life and showed him what he'd never had, so they could share it together. Like Della and James in the old O. Henry story—James who sold his gold watch to buy Della combs for her hair, and Della who sold her hair to buy James a chain for his watch— their gifts and sacrifices match perfectly. But this time there's a happy twist. The only thing one had to give was all the other needed.

I can't hold it against Paul that he's had this kind of luck. If anyone deserves it, he's the one. Paul never had a family, a face in a picture frame, a voice on the other end of the line. Even after my father died I had all of those things, imperfect as they might be. Yet there's something larger at stake here. The portmaster's diary may prove that my father was right about the *Hypnerotomachia*—that he saw it for what it was, past the dust and the ages, through the forest of dead languages and woodcuts. I disbelieved him, thinking it was ridiculous and vain and shortsighted, the whole idea that there could be anything special about such a tired old book. And all that time, while I accused him of an error of perspective, the only error of perspective was mine.

"Don't do it to yourself, Tom," Paul says unexpectedly from above, so quiet that I barely hear him.

"Do what?"

"Feel sorry for yourself."

"I was thinking about my dad."

"I know. Try to think of something else."

"Like what?"

"I don't know. Like us."

"I don't understand."

"The four of us. Try to be grateful for what you have." He hesitates. "What about next year? Which way are you leaning?"

"I don't know."

"Texas?"

"Maybe. But Katie will still be back here."

His sheets rustle as he repositions himself. "What if I told you I might be in Chicago?"

"What do you mean?"

"For a Ph.D. I got my letter the day after you did."

I'm stunned.

"Where did you think I was going next year?" he asks.

"To work with Pinto at Yale. Why Chicago?"

"Pinto's retiring this year. And Chicago's a better program anyway. Melotti is still there."

Melotti. One of the few other *Hypnerotomachia* scholars I actually remember my father mentioning.

"Besides," Paul adds, "if it was good enough for your dad, then it's good enough for me, right?"

The same idea occurred to me before applying, but

what I'd meant by it was, if my father could get in, then so could I.

"I guess."

"So what do you think?"

"About you going to Chicago?"

He hesitates again. I've missed the point.

"About *us* going to Chicago."

Floorboards creak above us, movement in another world.

"Why didn't you tell me?"

"I didn't know how you'd feel," he says.

"You'd be doing the same program he did."

"As much as I could."

I'm not sure I could take it, being dogged by my father for five more years. I would see him in Paul's shadow even more than I do now.

"Is that your first choice?"

It's a long time before he responds.

"Taft and Melotti are the only two left."

Hypnerotomachia scholars, I realize he means.

"I could always work with a nonspecialist on campus here," he says. "Batali or Todesco."

But writing a *Hypnerotomachia* dissertation for a nonspecialist would be like writing music for the deaf.

"You should go to Chicago," I say, trying to sound like my heart's in it. And maybe it is.

"Does that mean you're going to Texas?"

"I haven't made up my mind."

"You know, it doesn't always have to be about him."

"It's not."

"Well," Paul says, deciding not to press, "I guess we've got the same deadline."

The two envelopes are lying where I left them, side by side on his desk. The desk, it occurs to me, where Paul began to unlock the *Hypnerotomachia*. For a second I imagine my father hovering over it, a guardian angel, guiding Paul toward the truth every night since the beginning. Strange to think I was right here, just a few feet away, asleep almost the whole time.

"Get some rest," Paul says, and I can hear him roll over in his bunk with a long, labored breath. The force of what's happened is returning.

"What are you going to do in the morning?" I ask, wondering if he wants to talk about it.

"I have to ask Richard about those letters," he says.

"Do you want me to come with you?"

"I should go alone."

We don't speak again that night.

Paul falls asleep quickly, to judge from his breathing. I wish I could do the same, but my mind is too crowded for that. I wonder what my father would've thought, knowing we'd found the portmaster's diary after all these years. It might've lightened the loneliness I always supposed he felt, working so long at something that meant so little to so few. I think it would've changed things for him, knowing his son had finally come around.

"Why'd you come late?" I'd asked him one night, after he showed up at halftime during the last basketball game I ever played.

"I'm sorry," he said. "It took me longer than I expected."

He was walking in front of me back to the car, preparing to drive us home. I fixed my eyes on the patch of hair he always forgot to comb, the one he couldn't see in the mirror. It was mid-November, but he'd come to the game in a spring jacket, so absorbed at the office that he'd picked the wrong one from the coatrack.

"What did?" I prodded. "Work?"

Work was the euphemism I used, avoiding the title that was such an embarrassment to me around my friends.

"Not work," he said quietly. "Traffic."

On the way back, he kept the speedometer just two or three miles per hour above the speed limit, the way he always did. The tiny disobedience of it, the way he refused to be bound by rules, but could never really break them, grated on me more and more after getting my driver's permit.

"You played well, I thought," he said, looking over at me in the passenger's seat. "You made both of the foul shots I saw."

"I was oh-for-five in the first half. I told Coach Ames I didn't want to play anymore."

That he didn't pause told me he'd seen it coming.

"You quit? Why?"

"The smart take from the strong," I said, knowing it would be the next thing out of his mouth. "But the tall take from the short."

He seemed to blame himself after that, as if basketball had been the final straw between us. Two weeks later, when I returned from school, the hoop and backboard in our driveway had been taken down and given to a local charity. My mother said she wasn't sure why he'd done it. Because he thought it would make things better, was all she could say.

With that in mind, I try to imagine the greatest gift I

could've given my father. And as sleep descends on me, the answer seems strangely clear: my faith in his idols. That was what he wanted all along—to feel that we were united by something permanent, to know that as long as he and I believed in the same things, we would never be apart. What a job I did, making sure that never happened. The *Hypnerotomachia* was no different from piano lessons and basketball and the way he parted his hair: his mistake. Then, just as he must've known would happen, the moment I lost faith in that book, we were more and more apart, even sitting around the same dinner table. He'd done his best to tie a knot that would never slip, and I managed to untie it.

Hope, Paul said to me once, which whispered from Pandora's box only after all the other plagues and sorrows had escaped, is the best and last of all things. Without it, there is only time. And time pushes at our backs like a centrifuge, forcing us outward and away, until it nudges us into oblivion. That, I think, is the only explanation for what happened to my father and me, just as it happened to Taft and Curry, the same way it will happen to the four of us here in Dod, inseparable as we seem. It's a law of motion, a fact of physics that Charlie could name, no different from the stages of white dwarfs and red giants. Like all things in the universe, we are destined from birth to diverge. Time is simply the yardstick of our separation. If we are particles in a sea of distance, exploded from an original whole, then there is a science to our solitude. We are lonely in proportion to our years.

Chapter 16

The summer after sixth grade, my father sent me to camp, a two-week affair for wayward ex–Boy Scouts, the purpose of which, I realize now, was to get me reinstated among my merit-badge peers. I'd been dekerchiefed the year before for lighting bottle rockets in Willy Carlson's tent, and more specifically for saying I still thought it was funny even after Willy's weak constitution and excitable bladder were explained to me. Time had passed, and, my parents hoped, indiscretions had been forgotten. In the hubbub surrounding twelve-year-old Jake Ferguson, whose pornographic comic book business had turned the morally constipating experience of Scout camp into a lucrative and horizon-broadening enterprise, I was demoted to lesser-evil status. Fourteen days on the south shore of Lake Erie, my parents seemed to think, would bring me back into the fold.

It took less than ninety-six hours to prove them

wrong. Halfway through the first week, a scoutmaster dropped me back at home and drove off in a wordless huff. I'd been dishonorably discharged, this time for teaching campmates an immoral song. A three-page letter from the camp director, heavy with correctional, parole-style adjectives, ranked me among the worst Boy Scout recidivists of greater central Ohio. Unsure what a recidivist was, I told my parents what I'd done.

A troop of Girl Scouts had met us for a day of canoeing, singing a song I knew from my sisters' own dark days of camps and badges: *Make new friends, but keep the old; one is silver, the other is gold.* Having inherited a set of alternative lyrics, I shared them with my fellow men.

> *Make no friends, and kick the old.*
> *All I want is silver and gold.*

Those lines alone were hardly grounds for expulsion, but Willy Carlson, in a brilliant stroke of retribution, gave the oldest camp counselor a kick as he bent over to light a campfire, then blamed the act on my influence, the new lyrics having conjured his foot into the old man's ass. Within hours, the full machinery of Boy Scout justice was in motion, and both of us were packing our bags.

Only two things came out of that experience, other than my permanent retirement from scouting. First, I became good friends with Willy Carlson, whose excitable bladder, it turned out, was nothing but another lie he'd told the scoutmasters to get me kicked out the first time around. You had to like the guy. And second, I got a stern lecture from my mother, the motivation for which I never understood until my Princeton years were almost over. It wasn't the first line of the revised lyrics she objected to, despite the fact that, technically, the kicking of old people was what got me bagged. It was the strange mania of the second line that she read into.

"Why silver and gold?" she said, sitting me down in the small back room of the bookstore, where she kept the overstocks and old filing cabinets.

"What do you mean?" I asked. There was an outdated calendar on the wall from the Columbus Museum of Art, turned to the month of May, showing an Edward Hopper painting of a woman sitting alone in her bed. I couldn't help staring at it.

"Why not bottle rockets?" she asked. "Or campfires?"

"Because those don't work." I remember feeling annoyed; the answers seemed so obvious. "The last word has to rhyme with *old*."

"Listen to me, Tom." My mother placed a hand on my chin and turned my head until I was facing her. Her hair seemed gold in the right light, the same way the woman's did in the Hopper painting. "It's unnatural. A boy your age shouldn't care about silver and gold."

"I *don't*. What does it matter?"

"Because every desire has its proper object."

It sounded like something I'd been told once at Sunday school. "What's that supposed to mean?"

"It means people spend their lives wanting things they shouldn't. The world confuses them into taking their love and aiming it where it doesn't belong." She adjusted the neck on her sundress, then sat beside me. "All it takes to be happy is to love the right things, in the right amounts. Not money. Not books. *People*. Adults who don't understand that never feel fulfilled. I don't want you to turn out like that."

Why it meant so much to her, this correct aiming of my passions, I never understood. I just nodded in a solemn way, promised that I would never sing about precious metals again, and sensed that my mother was pacified.

But precious metals were never the problem. What I realize now is that my mother was waging a bigger war, trying to save me from something worse: becoming my father. My father's fixation on the *Hypnerotomachia* was the essence of misguided passion to her, and she struggled with it until the day he died. She believed, I think, that his love for the book was nothing but a perversion, a crooked deflection, of his love for his wife and family. No amount of force or persuasion could correct it, and I suppose it was when she knew she'd lost the battle to realign my father's life that she brought the fight to me.

How well I kept my promise, I'm afraid to say. The stubbornness of boys in their childish ways must be a prodigy to women, who learn faster than angels how not to misbehave. Throughout my childhood there was a monopoly on mistakes in my house, and I was its Rockefeller. I never imagined the magnitude of the error my mother was warning me against, until I had the misfortune of falling into it. By that time, though, it was Katie, and not my family, who had to suffer for it.

January came, and Colonna's first riddle gave way to another, then a third. Paul knew where to look for them, having detected a pattern in the *Hypnerotomachia*: following a regular cycle, the chapters grew in length from five or ten pages, to twenty, thirty, or even forty. The shorter chapters came in a row, three or four at a time, while the long ones were more solitary. When graphed, the long periods of low intensity were interrupted by sharp upticks in chapter length, creating a visual profile we both came to conceive of as the *Hypnerotomachia*'s pulse. The pattern continued until the first half of the book ended, at which point a strange, muddled sequence began, no chapter exceeding eleven pages.

Paul quickly made sense of it, using our success with Moses and his horns: each spike of long, solitary chapters provided a riddle; the riddle's solution, its cipher, was then applied to the run of short chapters following it, yielding the next part of Colonna's message. The second half of the book, Paul guessed, must be filler, just as the opening chapters of the first half appeared to be: a distraction to maintain the impression of narrative in an otherwise fragmented story.

We divided the labor between us. Paul hunted for riddles in the longer chapters, leaving each one behind for me to solve. The first I tackled was this: *What is the smallest harmony of a great victory?*

"It makes me think of Pythagoras," Katie said when I told her over pound cake and hot chocolate at Small World Coffee. "Everything with Pythagoras was harmonies. Astronomy, virtue, math . . ."

"I think it has to do with warfare," I countered, having spent some time at Firestone looking at Renaissance texts on engineering. Leonardo, in a letter to the Duke of Milan, claimed he could build impenetrable chariots, like

Renaissance tanks, along with portable mortars and great catapults for use in sieges. Philosophy and technology were merging: there was a mathematics to victory, a set of proportions to the perfect war machine. It was only a small step from math into music.

The next morning, Katie woke me at 7:30 to go jogging before her 9:00 class.

"Warfare doesn't make sense," she said, beginning to parse the riddle as only a philosophy major could. "There are two parts to the question: smallest harmony and great victory. Great victory could mean anything. You should focus on the clearer part. Smallest harmony has fewer concrete meanings."

I grumbled as we passed the Dinky train station on our way to the west of campus, envying the stray passengers waiting for the 7:43. Running and thinking were unnatural things to be doing while the sun was still rising, and she knew the fog wouldn't burn off my thoughts until noon. This was just taking advantage, punishing me for not taking Pythagoras seriously.

"So what are you suggesting?" I asked.

She didn't even seem to be breathing hard. "We'll stop at Firestone on our way back around. I'll show you where I think you should look."

It continued like that for two weeks, waking at dawn for calisthenics and brainteasers, telling Katie my half-baked ideas about Colonna so that she would have to slow down to listen, then forcing myself to run faster so that she would have less time to tell me how I was wrong. We were spending the last part of so many evenings with each other, and the earliest part of so many mornings, that I thought it would eventually occur to her, rational as she was, that spending the night at Dod would be more efficient than trekking back and forth to Holder. Every morning, seeing her in spandex and a sweatshirt, I tried to think of a new way to extend the invitation, but Katie always made a point of not understanding. Gil told me that her old boyfriend, the lacrosse player from one of my seminars, had made a game of her from the start, not pushing her for affection on the few occasions when she was drunk, so that she would melt with gratitude when she was sober. The pattern of his manipulation took so long for her to realize that she brought the after-taste of it to her first month with me.

"What should I do?" I asked one night after Katie left, when the frustration was almost too much. I was getting a tiny kiss on the cheek after each morning run, which, all things considered, hardly covered my expenses; and now that I was spending more and more time on the *Hypnero-tomachia*, and getting by on five or six hours of sleep a night, an entirely new sort of debt was accruing. Tantalus and his grapes had nothing on me: when I wanted Katie, all I got was Colonna; when I tried to focus on Colonna, all I could think of was sleep; and when, at last, I tried to sleep, the knock would come at our door, and it would be time for another jog with Katie. The comedy of being chronically late for my own life was lost on me. I was due for something better.

For once, though, Gil and Charlie spoke with one voice: "Be patient," they said. "She's worth it."

And, as usual, they were right. One night in our fifth week together, Katie eclipsed us all. Returning from a philosophy seminar, she stopped by Dod with an idea.

"Listen to this," she said, pulling a copy of Thomas More's *Utopia* from her bag and reading from it.

> *The inhabitants of Utopia have two games rather like chess. The first is a sort of arithmetical contest, in which certain numbers "take" others. The second is a pitched battle between virtues and vices, which illustrates most ingeniously how vices tend to conflict with one another, but to combine against virtues. It shows what ultimately determines the victory of one side or the other.*

She took my hand and placed the book in it, waiting for me to read it again.

I glanced at the back cover. "Written in 1516," I said. "Less than twenty years after the *Hypnerotomachia*." The timing wasn't far off.

"A pitched battle between virtues and vices," she repeated, "showing what determines the victory of one side or the other."

And it began to dawn on me that she might be right.

■

Lana McKnight used to have a rule, back in our dating days. Never mix books and bed. In the spectrum of excitement, sex and thought were on opposite ends, both to be enjoyed, but never at the same time. It amazed me how such a smart girl could suddenly become so ravenously stupid in the dark, flailing around in her leopard-print negligee like some cavewoman I'd thumped with a club, barking things that would've horrified even the pack of wolves that raised her. I never dared to tell Lana that if she moaned less it might mean more, but from the very first night I sensed what a wonderful thing it might be if my mind and my body could be aroused at the same time. I probably should've seen that possibility in Katie from the beginning, after all the mornings we spent exercising both muscles at once. But it was only that night that it happened: as we worked out the implications of her discovery, the last residue of her old lacrosse player finally slipped off the page, erased, leaving us to start again.

What I remember most clearly about that night is that Paul had the grace to sleep at Ivy, and that the lights were on the whole time Katie stayed. We kept them burning while we read Sir Thomas More, trying to understand what game he was referring to, in which great victories were possible when virtues were in harmony. We kept them burning when we found that one of the games More mentioned, called the Philosophers' Game, or Rithmomachia, was precisely the kind Colonna would've favored, the most challenging of any played by medieval or Renaissance men. We kept them burning when she kissed me for saying I thought she was right after all, because Rithmomachia, it turned out, could be won only by creating a harmony of numbers, the most perfect of which produced the rare outcome called a *great victory*. And we kept them burning when she kissed me again for admitting my other ideas must have been wrong, and that I should've listened to her from the beginning. I realized, finally, the misunderstanding that had persisted since the morning of our first jog: while I'd been struggling to stay even with her, she'd been pushing to stay one step ahead. She'd been trying to prove that she wasn't intimidated by seniors, that she deserved to be taken seriously—and it never occurred to her, until tonight, that she'd succeeded.

My mattress was craggy with books by the time we got around to lying down together, hardly even pretending to read anymore. It's probably true that the room was too hot for the sweater she was wearing. And it's probably true that the room would've been too hot for the sweater she was wearing even if the air-conditioning had been on and the snow had been falling the way it did Easter weekend. She was wearing a T-shirt beneath it, and a black bra under that, but it was watching Katie take off that sweater, and seeing the way it left her hair mussed, strands floating in a halo of static electricity, that gave me the feeling Tantalus never quite got to, that a sensational future had finally pressed itself up against a heavy, hopeful present, throwing the switch that completes the circuit of time.

When my turn came around to take clothes off, to share with Katie the wreckage of my left leg, scars and all, I never hesitated; and when she saw them, neither did she. Had we spent those hours in the dark, I would never have made anything of it. But we were never in the dark that night. We rolled, one over another, across Saint Thomas More and the pages of his *Utopia*, into the new positions of our relationship, and the lights were always burning.

The first sign that I'd misunderstood the forces at work in my life came the following week. Paul and I spent much of the next Monday and Tuesday debating the meaning of the newest riddle: *How many arms from your feet to the horizon?*

"I think it has to do with geometry," Paul said.

"Euclid?"

But he shook his head. "Earth measurement. Eratosthenes approximated the earth's circumference by figuring out the different angles of the shadows cast in Syene and Alexandria at noon on the summer solstice. Then he used the angles . . ."

I realized only midway through his explanation that he was using an etymological sense of the word *geometry*—literally, as he'd said, "earth measurement."

"So that, knowing the distance between the two cities, he could triangulate back to the curvature of the earth."

"What does that have to do with the riddle?" I said.

"Francesco's asking for the distance between you and the horizon. Calculate how far it is from any given point in the world to the line where the earth curves over, and you've got an answer. Or just look it up in your physics textbook. It's probably a constant."

He said it as if the answer were a foregone conclusion, but I suspected otherwise.

"Why would Colonna ask for that distance in arms?" I asked.

Paul leaned over and crossed out *arms* on my copy, replacing it with something in Italian. "That should probably be *braccia*," he said. "It's the same word, but *braccia* were Florentine units of measurement. One *braccio* is about the length of an arm."

For the first time, I was sleeping less than he was, the sudden high in my life needling me to keep pressing my luck, to keep mixing my drinks, because this cocktail of Katie and Francesco Colonna seemed to be just what the doctor ordered. I took it as a sign, the fact that my return to the *Hypnerotomachia* had brought a new structure to the world I lived in. Quickly I began to fall into my father's trap, the one my mother tried to warn me about.

Wednesday morning, when I mentioned to Katie that I'd dreamt of my father, she did something that in all our days of jogging she'd never done before: she stopped.

"Tom, I don't want to keep talking about this," she said.

"About what?"

"Paul's thesis. Let's talk about something else."

"I was telling you about my dad."

But I'd grown too used to conversations with Paul, invoking my father's name in any situation and expecting it to deflate all criticism.

"Your dad worked on the book Paul's studying," she said. "It's the same thing."

I mistook the sentiment behind her words for fear: fear that she would be unable to solve another riddle the way she solved the last one, and that my interest in her might fade.

"Fine," I said, thinking I was saving her from that. "Let's talk about something else."

And so a period of many pleasant weeks began, built on a misunderstanding as complete as the one we started with. In the first month we dated, up until the night Katie spent at Dod, she built a façade for me, trying to create something she thought I wanted; and in the second month I returned the favor, avoiding all mention of the *Hypnerotomachia* in front of her, not because its significance had diminished in my life, but because I thought Colonna's riddles made her uneasy.

Had she known the truth, Katie would've been right to worry. The *Hypnerotomachia* was slowly beginning to bully my other thoughts and interests out of focus. The balance I thought I'd struck between Paul's thesis and mine—the waltz between Mary Shelley and Francesco Colonna, which I imagined more vividly the more time I spent with Katie—was devolving into a tug of war, which Colonna gradually won.

Still, before Katie and I knew it, trails had formed in every corner of our shared experience. We ran the same paths each morning; stopped at the same coffee shops before class; and snuck her into my eating club the same ways when my guest passes ran out. Thursday nights we danced with Charlie at Cloister Inn; Saturday nights we shot pool with Gil at Ivy; and Friday nights, when the clubs on Prospect fell quiet, we watched friends perform in Shakespeare comedies or orchestra concerts or a cappella shows across campus. The adventure of our first days together gradually blossomed into something else: a feeling I'd never had with Lana or any of her predecessors, which I can only compare to the sensation of returning home, of joining a balance that needs no adjusting, as if the scales of my life had been waiting for her all along.

The first night Katie noticed I couldn't sleep, she recited a work by her favorite author for me, and I followed Curious George to the ends of the earth, where the weight on my eyelids carried me off. After that, there were many nights I tossed and turned, and Katie found a solution for each of them. Late-night episodes of $M*A*S*H$; long readings from Camus; radio programs she used to listen to at home, now caught on a faint transmission down the coast. We left the windows open sometimes, to hear the rain in late February, or the conversations of drunk freshmen. There was even a rhyming game we invented for empty nights, something Francesco Colonna might not have found as edifying as Rithmomachia, but that we enjoyed just the same.

"There once was a man named Camus," I would say, leading her.

When Katie smiled at night, she was like a Cheshire cat in the dark.

"Who left U. Algiers with the flu," she would respond.

"He had lots of potential."

"But was *not* existential."

"Which made old Jean-Paul Sartre so blue."

But for all the ways Katie had found to make me sleep, the *Hypnerotomachia* still kept me awake more often than not. I'd figured out what the smallest harmony of a great victory was: in Rithmomachia, where the goal is to establish number patterns containing arithmetical, geometric, or musical harmonies, only three sequences produce all three harmonies at once—the requirement for a great victory. The smallest of these, the one Colonna wanted, was the sequence 3-4-6-9.

Paul quickly took the numbers and made a cipher of them. He read the third letter, then the fourth after that, followed by the sixth and ninth, from the appropriate chapters; and within an hour, we had another message from Colonna:

> *I begin my story with a confession. In the keeping of this secret many men have died. Some have perished in the construction of my crypt, which, imagined by Bramante and executed by my Roman brother Terragni, is an unequalled contrivance for its purpose, impervious*

to all things, but above all to water. It has taken many victims, even among the most experienced men. Three have died in the movement of great stones, two in the felling of trees, five in the process of building itself. Others of the dead I do not mention, for they have perished shamefully and will be forgotten.

Here I will convey the nature of the enemy I face, whose rising power lies at the heart of my actions. Reader, you will wonder why I have dated this book 1467, some thirty years before I wrote these words. It was for this reason: in that year the war began which we are still fighting, and which we are now losing. Three years earlier His Holiness, Paul the Second, fired the court abbreviators, making clear his intentions toward my brotherhood. Yet the members of my uncle's generation were powerful men, with much influence, and the expelled brethren flocked to the Accademia Romana, which good Pomponio Leto sustained. Paul saw that our number persisted, and his fury increased. In that year, 1467, he crushed the Academy by force. So that all would know the strength of his determination, he imprisoned Pomponio Leto, and had him accused as a sodomite. Others of our group were tortured. One, at least, would die.

Now we are challenged by an old enemy, suddenly reborn. This new spirit grows in strength, and finds a more powerful voice, so that I have no choice but to construct, with the assistance of friends wiser than I, this device whose secret I disguise here. Even the priest, philosopher though he may be, is not equal to it.

Continue, reader, and I will tell more.

"The court abbreviators were the humanists," Paul explained. "The pope thought humanism bred moral corruption. He didn't even want children to hear the works of the ancient poets. Pope Paul made an example of Leto. For some reason, Francesco took it as a declaration of war."

Colonna's words stayed with me that night, and each night that followed. For the first time, I missed a morning run with Katie, too tired to pull myself from bed. Something told me Paul was wrong about the new riddle—*How many arms from your feet to the horizon?*—and that Eratosthenes and geometry were not the solution. Charlie confirmed that the distance to the horizon would depend on the height of the observer; and even if we could find a single answer and calculate it in *braccia*, I realized, the answer would be enormous, far too big to be useful as a cipher.

"When did Eratosthenes make that calculation?" I asked.

"Around 200 B.C."

That sealed it.

"I think you're wrong," I said. "All the riddles so far have to do with Renaissance knowledge, Renaissance discoveries. He's testing us on what humanists would've known in the 1400s."

"Moses and *cornuta* had to do with linguistics," Paul said, trying on the idea for size. "Correcting faulty translations, like what Valla did with the Donation of Constantine."

"And the Rithmomachia riddle had to do with math," I went on. "So Colonna wouldn't use math again. I think he's choosing a different discipline every time."

It was only when Paul looked so surprised by the

clarity of my thinking that I realized how my role had changed. We were equals now, partners in the enterprise.

The two of us began meeting at Ivy each night, back in those days when he kept the President's Room in better shape, expecting Gil to check up on him at any minute. I ate dinner upstairs with Gil and with Katie, who was only weeks away from beginning the bicker process, then returned downstairs to join Paul and Francesco Colonna. I thought it just as well to leave her alone, hard as she was trying to position herself for admission to the club. Busy with the rituals, she seemed not to make much of my disappearances.

But the night after I missed my third morning run, all of that changed. I was on the cusp of a solution to the riddle, I thought, when by sheer accident she realized how I was spending our hours apart.

"This is for you," she said, letting herself into our room in Dod.

Gil had left the door unlocked again, and Katie no longer knocked when she thought I was alone.

It was a cup of soup she'd brought me from a local deli. She thought I'd been holed up with my thesis this whole time.

"What are you doing?" she asked. "More *Frankenstein*?"

Then she saw the books spread out around me, each with some reference to the Renaissance in the title.

I never thought it was possible, to lie without knowing it. I'd strung her along for weeks on a raft of pretexts—Mary Shelley; insomnia; the pressures we were both facing, which made it hard to spend time together—and eventually it carried me away, drifting from the truth so slowly that the distance each day seemed no greater than the last. She knew I was working on Paul's thesis, I thought; she just didn't want to hear about it. That was the arrangement we'd come to, without ever having to say it.

The conversation that followed was all silences, hashed out in the way she looked at me and I tried to hold her stare. Finally, Katie put the cup of soup on my dresser and buttoned her coat. She looked around the room, as if to remember the details of where things stood, then returned to the door and locked it before letting herself out.

I was going to call her that night—as I knew she expected me to, when she returned to her room alone and waited by the phone, the way her roommates later told me she did—except that something got in the way. Fantastic mistress, that book, flashing leg at all the right times. Just as Katie left, the solution to Colonna's riddle dawned on me; and like a whiff of perfume and an eyeful of cleavage, it made me lose sight of everything else.

The horizon in a *painting* was the solution: the point of convergence in a system of perspective. The riddle wasn't about math; it was about art. It fit the profile of the other puzzles, relying on a discipline peculiar to the Renaissance, developed by the same humanists Colonna seemed to be defending. The measurement we needed was the distance, in *braccia*, between the foreground of the painting, where the characters stood, and the theoretical horizon line, where the earth met the sky. And remembering Colonna's preference for Alberti in architecture, when Paul used *De re aedificatoria* to decipher the first riddle, it was to Alberti I turned first. *On the surface I intend to paint*, Alberti wrote in the treatise I found among Paul's books,

I decide how large I wish the human figures in the foreground of the painting to be. I divide the height of this man into three parts, which will be proportional to the measure commonly called a "braccio"; for, as can be seen from the relationship of his limbs, three "braccia" is just about the average height of a man's body. The proper position for the centric point is no higher from the base line than the height of the man to be represented in the painting. I then draw a line through the centric point, and this line is a limit or boundary for me, which no quantity exceeds. This is why men depicted standing furthest away are a great deal smaller than the nearer ones.

Alberti's centric line, as the accompanying illustrations made clear, was the horizon. According to this system, it was placed at the same height as a man drawn standing in the foreground, who in turn was three *braccia* tall. The solution to the riddle—the number of *braccia* from the man's feet to the horizon—was just that: three.

It took Paul only a half hour to figure out how to apply it. The first letter of every third word in the following chapters, when placed in a row, spelled out the next passage from Colonna.

Now, reader, I will tell you the nature of the composition of this work. With the help of my brethren, I have studied the code-making books of the Arabs, Jews, and ancients. I have learned the practice called gematria from the kabalists, according to which, when it is written in Genesis that Abraham brought 318 servants to help Lot, we see that the number 318 signifies only Abraham's servant Eliezer, for that is the sum of the He-

brew letters of Eliezer's name. I have learned the practices of the Greeks, whose gods spoke in riddles, and whose generals, as the Mythmaker describes in his History, disguised their meanings cunningly, as when Histiaeus tattooed a message on his slave's scalp, so that Aristagoras might shave the man's head and read it.

I will reveal to you now the names of those learned men whose wisdom forged my riddles. Pomponio Leto, master of the Roman Academy, pupil of Valla and old friend of my family's, instructed me in matters of language and translation, where my own eyes and ears did fail me. In the art and harmonies of numbers, I was guided by the Frenchman Jacques Lefèvre d'Etaples, admirer of Roger Bacon and Boethius, who knew all manner of numeration which my own intellect could not illuminate. The great Alberti, who learned his art in turn from the masters Masaccio and Brunelleschi (may their genius never be forgotten), instructed me long ago in the science of horizons and paintings; I praise him now and always. Knowledge of the sacred writing of the descendants of Hermes Thrice-Great, first prophet of Egypt, I owe to the wise Ficino, master of languages and philosophies, who is without equal among the followers of Plato. Finally it is to Andrea Alpago, disciple of the venerable Ibn al-Nafis, that I am indebted for matters yet to be disclosed; and may this contribution be looked upon even more favorably than all the rest, for it is in man's study of himself, wherein all other studies find their origin, that he most closely contemplates perfection.

These, reader, are my wisest friends, who among them have learned what I have not, knowledge that in prior times was foreign to all men. One by one they have *agreed to my single demand: each man, unbeknownst to the others, devised a riddle to which only I and he know the solution, and which only another lover of knowledge could solve. These riddles, in turn, I have placed within my text in fragments, according to a pattern I have told to no man; and the answer alone can produce my true words.*

All this I have done, reader, to protect my secret, but also to transmit it to you, should you find what I have written. Solve but two more riddles, and I will begin to reveal the nature of my crypt.

Katie didn't wake me up the next morning to go running. The rest of that week, in fact, I spoke to her roommates and to her answering machine, but never to Katie herself. Blinded by the progress I was making with Paul, I didn't see how the landscape of my life was eroding. The jogging paths and coffee shops fell away as our distance grew. Katie didn't eat with me at Cloister anymore, but I hardly noticed, because for weeks I rarely ate there myself: Paul and I traveled like rats through the tunnels between Dod and Ivy, avoiding daylight, ignoring the sounds of bicker above our heads, buying coffee and boxed sandwiches at the all-night WaWa off campus so that we could work and eat on our own schedule.

The whole time, Katie was only one floor removed from me, trying not to bite her nails as she moved from clique to clique, searching for the right balance between assertiveness and compliance so that upperclassmen would look on her favorably. That she wouldn't have wanted my interference in her life at that moment was a conclusion I'd come to almost from the beginning, another excuse for spending long days and late nights with Paul. That she might've appreciated some company, a friendly face to return to at night, a companion as her mornings grew darker and colder—that she would've expected my support even more now that she'd come to the first important crossroads in her time at Princeton—was something I was too preoccupied to consider. I never imagined that bicker might've been a trial for her, an experience that tested her tenacity much more than her charm. I was a stranger to her; I never knew what she went through on those Ivy nights.

The club accepted her, Gil told me the following week. He was bracing himself for a long night of breaking the news, good and bad, to each candidate. Parker Hassett had thrown some roadblocks in Katie's way, fixing on her as a special object of his anger, probably because he knew she was one of Gil's favorites; but even Parker came around in the end. The induction ceremony for the new section was the following week, after initiations, and the annual Ivy ball was slated for Easter weekend. Gil listed the events so carefully that I realized he was telling me something. These were my chances to fix things with Katie. This was the calendar of my rehabilitation.

If so, then I was no better a boyfriend than I'd been a Boy Scout. Love, deflected from its proper object, had found a new one. In the weeks that ensued, I saw less and less of Gil, and nothing at all of Katie. I heard a rumor that she had taken an interest in an upperclassman at Ivy, a new version of her old lacrosse player, a man in a yellow hat to my Curious George. But by then Paul had found another riddle, and we'd both started to wonder what secret lay in Colonna's crypt. An old mantra, long dormant, rose up from its slumber and prepared for another season of life.

> *Make no friends, and kick the old.*
> *All I want is silver and gold.*

Chapter 17

I wake in daylight to the sound of a phone. The clock reads half-past nine. Stumbling out of bed, I get to the cordless before it can wake Paul.

"Were you sleeping?" is the first thing Katie says.

"Sort of."

"I can't believe that was Bill Stein."

"Neither can we. What's going on?"

"I'm at the newsroom. Can you come over?"

"Now?"

"You're busy?"

There's something I don't like in her voice, a touch of distance I'm awake just enough to notice.

"Let me jump in the shower. I'll be there in fifteen minutes."

I'm already undressing when she hangs up the phone.

While I get ready, I've got two things on my mind: Stein and Katie. They toggle in my thoughts like someone flicking a switch to check a bulb. In the light I see her, but in the dark I see Dickinson courtyard, canvassed in snow, in the silence after the ambulance has left.

Back at our quad, I throw my clothes on in the common room, trying not to rouse Paul. Searching for my watch, I notice something: the room's even cleaner than when I went to bed. Someone has straightened the rugs and emptied the trash cans. A bad sign. Charlie didn't sleep last night.

Then I catch sight of a message written on the whiteboard.

Tom—

Couldn't sleep. Gone to Ivy for more work. Call when you're up.

—P.

Back in the bedroom, Paul's bunk is empty. Looking at the whiteboard again, I spot the numbers above the text: 2:15. He's been gone all night.

I raise the receiver again, about to dial the President's Room, when I hear the voicemail tone.

Friday, the automated voice says when I punch in the digits. *Eleven fifty-four P.M.*

What follows is the call I missed, the one that must have come while Paul and I were at the museum.

Tom, it's Katie. A pause. *I'm not sure where you are. Maybe you're already on your way over. Karen and Trish want to serve birthday cake now. I told them to wait for you.* Another pause. *I guess I'll see you when you get here.*

The phone is hot in my hand. The black-and-white

photo I bought for her birthday looks dull in its frame, a cheaper thing than it was yesterday. To name a photographer other than Ansel Adams and Mathew Brady, I'd had to ask around. I never learned enough about Katie's pastime to feel confident about her taste. Thinking it over, I decide not to bring the photo with me.

On the walk to the *Prince* office, I keep a brisk pace. Katie meets me at the entrance and leads me toward the darkroom, locking and unlocking doors as we go. She's dressed the same way she was at Holder: in a T-shirt and an old pair of jeans. Her hair is pulled back crookedly, as if she wasn't expecting company, and the neck of her shirt is bent out of shape. I can see a gold necklace crossing her collarbone on one side, and near the thigh of her jeans my eyes linger on a tiny hole where the white of her skin peeks through.

"Tom," she says, pointing to someone at a computer in the corner, "there's someone I want you to meet. This is Sam Felton."

Sam smiles as if she knows me. She's dressed in field hockey–issue sweatpants and a long-sleeve shirt that says IF JOURNALISM WERE EASY, *NEWSWEEK* WOULD DO IT. After reaching for a button on the microrecorder beside her, she pulls the bud of an earphone out of one ear.

"Your date tonight?" she says to Katie, just to make sure she heard right.

Katie says yes, but doesn't add what I expect: *my boyfriend.*

"Sam's working on the Bill Stein story," she says instead.

"Have fun at the ball," Sam tells me, before reaching for the recorder again.

"You're not coming?" Katie asks.

I gather they also know each other from Ivy.

"I doubt it." Sam motions back at the computer, where rows of words scramble across the screen, an ant farm behind the glass. She already reminds me of Charlie in his lab: inspired by how much remains to be done. There will always be more news to write, more theories to prove, more phenomena to observe. The delicious futility of impossible tasks is the catnip of overachievers.

Katie gives a sympathetic look, and Sam returns to transcribing.

"What did you want to talk about?" I ask.

But Katie leads me back to the darkroom.

"It's a little hot in here," she says, opening a door and forcing back a thick set of black curtains. "You might want to take off your coat."

I do, and she hangs it from a hidden hook by the door. I've avoided the inside of this room since I met her, terrified of ruining her film.

Katie walks over to a clothesline strung along one wall. Photographs are clipped to it with clothespins. "It's not supposed to get above seventy-five in here," she says, "or the soup reticulates the negatives."

She might as well be speaking Greek. There's an old rule my sisters taught me: whenever you go on a date with a girl, always meet at a place you know well. French restaurants aren't impressive when you can't read the menu, and highbrow movies backfire when you don't understand the plot. Here, in the darkroom, the possibilities for failure seem spectacular.

"Give me a second," she says, shuttling from one side of the room to the other, quick as a hummingbird. "I'm almost done."

She opens the cover to a small tank, brings the film inside it to a spigot, then places it under running water. I start to feel crowded. The darkroom is small and cluttered, counters overrun with pans and trays, shelves lined with stop bath and fixer. Katie seems to have almost perfect dexterity here. It reminds me of the way she did her hair at the reception, tying it around pins as if she could see what she was doing.

"Should I turn out the lights?" I ask, starting to feel useless.

"Not unless you want to. The negatives have fixed."

So I stand like a scarecrow in the center of the room.

"How's Paul holding up?" she asks.

"Okay."

A respectful silence ensues, and Katie seems to lose the thread of the conversation, attending to another set of photos.

"I stopped by Dod just after 12:30," she begins again. "Charlie said you were with Paul."

There's an unexpected sympathy in her voice.

"It was good of you to stay with him," she says. "This must be terrible for Paul. For everyone."

I want to tell her about Stein's letters, but realize how much explaining it would take. She returns to my side now with a handful of pictures.

"What are these?"

"I developed our film."

"From the movie field?"

She nods.

The movie field is a place Katie brought me to see, an open plot in Princeton Battlefield Park that seems to extend farther and flatter than any stretch of land east of Kansas. A single oak tree stands in the middle of it like a sentinel who won't leave his post, echoing the last gesture of a general who died beneath the tree's branches during the Revolutionary War. Katie first saw the spot in a Walter Matthau movie, and ever since then the tree has been an enchantment for her. It became one in a small string of places she visited over and over again, a rosary of sights that anchored her life the more she returned to them. Within a week of her first night at Dod, she took me to see it, and it was as if the old Mercer Oak were a relative of hers, all three of us making an important first impression. I brought a blanket, a flashlight, and a picnic basket; Katie brought film and a camera.

The pictures are an artifact I don't expect, a small part of us locked in amber. We work through them together, sharing between our hands.

"What do you think?" she says.

Seeing them, I remember how warm the winter was. January's fading light is almost the color of honey, and here we are, both dressed in light sweaters, with coats and hats and gloves nowhere to be seen. The grooves of the tree behind us have the texture of age.

"They're wonderful," I tell her.

Katie smiles awkwardly, still unsure how to take a compliment. I notice stains on her fingertips, the color of newsprint, left by one of the darkroom agents bottled along the wall. Her fingers are long and thin, but with a workmanlike touch, the residue of too much film dipped in too many chemical baths. *This was us*, she's saying, a thousand words at a time. *Remember?*

"I'm sorry," I tell her.

My grip on the pictures loosens, but she reaches for my fingers with her other hand.

"It's not because of my birthday," she says, worried I've missed the point.

I wait.

"Where did you and Paul go after you left Holder last night?"

"To see Bill Stein."

She pauses over the name, but presses on. "About Paul's thesis?"

"It was urgent."

"What about when I stopped by your room just after midnight?"

"The art museum."

"Why?"

I'm uncomfortable with the direction she's taking. "I'm sorry I didn't come over. Paul thought he could find Colonna's crypt, and he needed to look at some of the older maps."

Katie doesn't seem surprised. A hush gathers behind her next words, and I know this is the conclusion she's been building toward.

"I thought you were done with Paul's thesis," she says.

"So did I."

"You can't expect me to watch you do this all over again, Tom. Last time we didn't talk for weeks." She hesitates, not knowing how else to put it. "I deserve better."

A boy's way is to argue, to find a defensible position and hold it, even if it's not heartfelt. I can feel the arguments crowding into my mouth, the little spurs of self-preservation, but Katie stops me.

"Don't," she says. "I want you to think about this."

She doesn't have to spell it out. Our hands part; she leaves the pictures in mine. The hum of the darkroom returns. Like a dog I've kicked, the silence always seems to take her side.

The choice is made, I want to tell her. *I don't need to think this through. It's simple: I love you more than I love the book.*

But to say it now would be the wrong choice. Part of this isn't about answering the question correctly: it's about showing that *I'm* correctible; that twice broken, I can still be fixed. Twelve hours ago I missed her birthday because of the *Hypnerotomachia*. My promises would seem empty right now, even to me.

"Okay," I say.

Katie brings a hand to her mouth and bites at a nail, then catches herself and stops.

"I should work," she says, touching my fingers again. "Let's talk more about this tonight."

I stare at the nub of her nail, wishing I could inspire more confidence.

She pushes me toward the black curtains, handing me my coat, and we return to the main office. "I need to finish the rest of my rolls before the senior photographers take over the darkroom," she says on the way, more for Sam's benefit than for mine. "You're a distraction."

The artifice is wasted. Sam's earphones are still in place; focused on her typing, she doesn't notice me leaving.

At the door, Katie takes her hands away from the small of my back. She seems prepared to speak, but doesn't. Instead, she leans over and gives me a kiss on the cheek, the kind I used to get in our earliest days, as a reward for jogs in the morning. Then she holds the door for me as I leave.

Chapter 18

Love conquers all.

In seventh grade, at a small souvenir stand in New York, I bought a silver bracelet with that inscription for a girl named Jenny Harlow. I thought it was, in one stroke, a portrait of the young man she wanted to date: cosmopolitan, with its Manhattan pedigree; romantic, with its poetic-sounding motto; and classy, with its understated shine. I left the bracelet anonymously in Jenny's locker on Valentine's Day, then waited all day for a response, thinking she was sure to know who'd left it.

Cosmopolitan, romantic, and classy, unfortunately, didn't form a trail of bread crumbs leading directly back to me. An eighth grader named Julius Murphy must've had that combination of virtues in much greater supply than I did, because it was Julius who got a kiss from Jenny Harlow at the end of the day, while I was left with nothing but a dark suspicion that the family vacation to New York had been for naught.

The whole experience, like so much of childhood, was built on misunderstanding. It wouldn't occur to me until much later that the bracelet wasn't made in New York, any more than it was made of silver. But that very Valentine's night, my father explained the particular misinterpretation he found most telling, which was that the poetic-sounding motto wasn't quite as romantic as Julius, Jenny, and I thought.

"You may have gotten the wrong impression from Chaucer," he began, with the smile of paternal wisdom. "There's more to 'love conquers all' than just the Prioress's brooch."

I sensed that this was going to be a lot like the conversation we'd had about babies and storks a few years before: well intentioned, but based on a serious misunderstanding about what I'd been learning in school.

A long explanation followed, about Virgil's tenth eclogue and *omnia vincit amor*, with digressions about Sithonian snows and Ethiopian sheep, all of which mattered a lot less to me than why Jenny Harlow didn't think I was romantic, and why I'd found such a useless way of blowing twelve dollars. If love conquered all, I decided, then love had never met Julius Murphy.

But my father was a wise man in his way, and when he saw he wasn't getting through to me, he opened a book and showed me a picture that made his point for him.

"Agostino Carracci made this engraving, called *Love Conquers All*," he said. "What do you see?"

On the right side of the picture were two naked women.

On the left side, a baby boy was beating up a much larger and more muscular satyr.

"I don't know," I said, unsure which side of the picture I was supposed to be learning from.

"*That*," my father said, pointing to the boy, "is Love."

He let it sink in.

"He's not supposed to be on your side. You fight with him; you try to undo what he does to others. But he's too powerful. No matter how much we suffer, Virgil says, our hardships cannot move him."

I'm not sure I ever completely understood the lesson my father was imparting. I got the simplest bit of it, I think: by trying to make Jenny Harlow fall head over heels for me, I was arm-wrestling Love, which my own cheap bracelet had been telling me was futile. But I sensed, even then, that my father was only using Jenny and Julius as an object lesson. What he really wanted to offer was a piece of wisdom he'd come by the hard way, which he hoped to impress upon me while the stakes of my own failures were still small. My mother had warned me about misguided love, my father's affair with the *Hypnerotomachia* always in the back of her mind; and now my father was offering his counterpoint, riddled in Virgil and Chaucer. He knew exactly how she felt, he was saying; he may even have agreed. But how could he stop it, what power did he have against the force he was fighting, when Love conquered all?

I've never known which of the two of them was right. The world is a Jenny Harlow, I think; we're all just fishermen telling stories about the one that got away. But to this day, I'm not sure how Chaucer's Prioress interpreted Virgil, or how Virgil interpreted love. All that stays with me is the picture my father showed me, the part he never said a word about, where the two naked women are watching Love bully the satyr. I've always wondered why Carracci put two women in that engraving, when he only needed one. Somewhere in that is the moral I took from the story: in the geometry of love, everything is triangular. For every Tom and Jenny, there is a Julius; for every Katie and Tom, there is a Francesco Colonna; and the tongue of desire is forked, kissing two but loving one. Love draws lines between us like an astronomer plotting a constellation from stars, joining points into patterns that have no basis in nature. The butt of every triangle becomes the heart of another, until the roof of reality is a tessellation of love affairs. Taken together, they have the pattern of netting; and behind them, I think, is Love. Love is the only perfect fisherman, the one who casts the broadest net, which no fish can escape. His reward is to sit alone in the tavern of life, forever a boy among men, hoping someday to tell stories about the one that got away.

The rumor was that Katie had found someone else. I'd been replaced by a junior named Donald Morgan, a wiry tower of a man who wore a blazer when a simple dress shirt would do, and who was already priming himself to be Gil's successor as Ivy president. I happened on the new couple one night in late February at Small World Coffee, the same place where I'd met Paul three years earlier, and a cool exchange followed. Donald managed to say only two or three chummy, innocuous things before realizing I wasn't a potential voter in the club elections, at which point he ushered Katie out of the shop and into his old Shelby Cobra on the street.

It was death by papercut, watching him turn the engine three times before it finally roared to life. I couldn't tell whether it was for my benefit or his vanity, the way he idled in his space for another minute until the road was completely empty before pulling out. All I noticed was that Katie never looked at me, not even as they drove away; worse, she seemed to be ignoring me out of anger rather than embarrassment, as if it were my fault, not hers, that we'd come to this. The outrage of it festered until I decided there was nothing else I could do but surrender. Let her have Donald Morgan, I thought. Let her make her bed at Ivy.

Of course, Katie was right. It was my fault. I'd been struggling for weeks with the fourth riddle—*What do a blind beetle, a night-owl, and a twist-beaked eagle share?*—and I sensed that my luck had run dry. Animals in the intellectual world of the Renaissance were tricky subjects. In the same year Carracci made his engraving, *Omnia Vincit Amor*, an Italian professor named Ulisse Aldrovandi published the first of his fourteen volumes on natural history. In one of the most famous examples of his approach to classification, Aldrovandi spent only two pages identifying the various breeds of chickens, then added another three hundred pages on chicken mythology, chicken-related recipes, and even chicken-based cosmetic treatments.

Meanwhile, Pliny the Elder, the ancient world's authority on animals, placed unicorns, basilisks, and manticores on the page directly between rhinos and wolves, and offered his own accounts of how chicken eggs could foretell the sex of a pregnant woman's child. Within ten days of staring at the riddle, I felt like one of the dolphins Pliny described, enchanted by human music but unable to make any of my own. Surely Colonna had something clever in mind with this riddle of his; I was just dumb to its magic.

The first thesis deadline I missed came three days later, when I realized, half-sunk in a pile of Aldrovandi photocopies, that a draft of my final chapter on *Frankenstein* lay unfinished on my desk. My advisor, Dr. Montrose, a sly old English professor, saw my bloodshot look and knew I must be up to something. Never suspecting it was anyone other than Mary Shelley who'd kept me up so many nights, he let the deadline slip. The next one slipped too, and so, very quietly, began the lowest period of my senior year, a stretch of weeks when no one seemed to notice my slow withdrawal from my own life.

I slept through morning classes, and spent afternoon lectures working riddle solutions in my head. More than one night I watched Paul break from his studies early, hardly past eleven, to walk with Charlie to Hoagie Haven for a late-night sandwich. They always asked me to come along, then asked if they could bring me anything back, but I always refused, at first because I took pride in the monastic quality my life had assumed, then later because I saw something derelict in the way they seemed to be ignoring their work. The night Paul went to get ice cream with Gil instead of doing more research on the *Hypnero-tomachia*, I imagined for the first time he wasn't pulling his own weight in our partnership.

"You've lost your focus," I told him. My eyes were getting worse because I had to read in the dark, and it couldn't have come at a worse time.

"I've what?" Paul said, turning around before climbing to his bunk. He thought he'd misheard.

"How many hours are you spending on this a day?"

"I don't know. Maybe eight."

"I've put in ten every day this week. And you're the one going to get ice cream?"

"I was gone for ten minutes, Tom. And I made a lot of progress tonight. What's the problem?"

"It's nearly March. Our deadline is in a month."

He let the pronoun pass. "I'll get an extension."

"Maybe you should work harder."

It was probably the first time anyone had ever spoken those words in Paul's presence. I'd seen him angry only a handful of times, but never like that.

"I *am* working hard. Who do you think you're talking to?"

"I'm close to figuring out the riddle. Where are you?"

"Close?" Paul shook his head. "You're not doing this because you're close. You're doing it because you're *lost*.

That riddle shouldn't be taking you this long. It shouldn't be that hard. You've just lost patience."

I glared at him.

"That's right," he said, as if he'd been waiting to say it for days. "I've almost worked out the *next* riddle, and you're still working on the last one. But I've been trying to stay out of this. We work at our own paces, and you don't even want my help. So fine, do it alone. Just don't try turning this back on me."

We didn't speak again that night.

Had I listened, I might've learned my lesson earlier. Instead, I went out of my way to prove Paul wrong. I began working later and waking earlier, making a habit of rolling my alarm back fifteen minutes each day, hoping he would notice the steady imposition of discipline on the untended quarters of my life. Each day I found a new way to spend more time with Colonna, and each night I tallied my hours like a miser counting coins. Eight on Monday; nine on Tuesday; ten on Wednesday and Thursday; almost twelve on Friday.

What do a blind beetle, a night-owl, and a twist-beaked eagle share? Horned beetles are hung around the necks of infants as a remedy against disease, Pliny wrote; gold beetles make a poisonous honey, and are unable to survive in a locality near Thrace called Cantharolethus; black beetles congregate in dark corners, and are found mostly in baths. But *blind* beetles?

I found more time by not walking out to Cloister for meals: every round trip to Prospect Avenue cost me half an hour, and eating in company, rather than alone, probably cost another half as well. I stopped working in the President's Room at Ivy, both to avoid seeing Paul and to save the minutes I would otherwise have spent in transit. I kept phone calls to a minimum, shaved and showered only as necessary, let Charlie and Gil answer the door, and made a science of the economies I could produce by giving up the humble reliables of my life.

What do a blind beetle, a night-owl, and a twist-beaked eagle share? Of creatures that can fly and are bloodless, Aristotle wrote, some are coleopterous, or sheath-winged, like the beetle; of birds that fly by night, some have crooked talons, such as the night-raven and owl; and in old age the upper beak of the eagle grows gradually longer and more crooked, such that the bird slowly dies of starvation. But what do the three of them *share?*

Katie, I'd decided, was a lost cause. Whatever she'd been to me, she became someone else for Donald Morgan. How I saw so much of them, when I left my room so little, must've had its answer in my thoughts and dreams, where they were constantly making fools of themselves. In corners and alleys, in shadows and clouds, there they were: holding hands and kissing and making sweet talk, all of it for my benefit, flaunting the way a shallow heart is quickly broken but just as quickly fixed. There was a black bra of Katie's that she'd left in my room long ago, which I'd never remembered to return, and it became a sort of trophy to me, a symbol of the part of herself she'd left behind, which Donald couldn't have. I had visions of her standing naked in my bedroom, souvenirs of the day we'd enjoyed our own company so much that she forgot herself around me, forgot that I was someone else, and let her inhibitions go. Every detail of her shape stayed with me, every freckle on her back, every gradation of shadow beneath her breasts. She danced to the music that came over my alarm clock, running one hand through her hair, keeping one hand over the invisible microphone in front of her mouth, and I was the only audience.

What do a blind beetle, a night-owl, and a twist-beaked eagle share? They all fly—but Pliny says that beetles sometimes burrow. They all breathe—but Aristotle says that insects do not inhale. They never learn from their mistakes, for Aristotle says that *many animals have memory . . . but no other creature except man can recall the past at will.* But even men fail to learn from the past. By that yardstick, we are all of us blind beetles and night-owls.

On Thursday, the fourth of March, I reached the high-water mark of my time with the *Hypnerotomachia*. That day I spent fourteen hours rereading sections of six Renaissance natural historians and making twenty-one single-space pages of notes. I went to no classes, ate all three meals at my desk, and slept exactly three and a half hours that night. I hadn't seen *Frankenstein* in weeks. The only other thoughts that had crossed my mind were of Katie, and those just compelled me to make an even greater shambles of my life. The sheer mastery of myself was addictive. Something must've been, because I'd made almost no progress on the riddle.

"Shut the books," Charlie finally said that Friday night, taking a stand. He pulled me by the collar in front of a mirror. "Look at yourself."

"I'm fine—" I began, ignoring the lupine thing that stared back at me, all red eyes and pink nose and scruff.

But Gil stood at Charlie's side. "Tom, you look like hell." He stepped into the bedroom, something he hadn't done in weeks. "Listen, she wants to talk to you. Stop being so stubborn."

"I'm not being stubborn. I've just got other things to do."

Charlie grimaced. "Like what, Paul's thesis?"

I scowled, waiting for Paul to stand up for me. But he just stood there behind them, silent. For more than a week he'd hoped that an answer was just around the bend, that I was making progress against the riddle, just painful progress.

"We're going to the arch sing at Blair," Gil said, meaning the Friday a cappella concert held outdoors.

"All *four* of us," Charlie added.

Gil gently closed the book beside me. "Katie's going to be there. I told her you'd come."

But when I flipped the book back open and said I wasn't going, I remember the look that crossed his face. It was one Gil had never given me before—one he'd always reserved for Parker Hassett and the occasional class clown who didn't know when to stop.

"You're coming," Charlie said, stepping toward me.

But Gil waved him off. "Forget it. Let's just go."

Then I was alone.

It wasn't stubbornness or pride, or even devotion to Colonna, that kept me away from Blair Arch. It was heartache, I think, and defeat. The fact is that I loved Katie, and also, in an odd way, that I loved the *Hypnerotomachia*, and that I'd failed to win either of them. The look on Paul's face as he left meant he knew I'd lost my chance with the riddle, whether I knew it or not; and the look on Gil's face as he left meant he knew I'd done the same with Katie. Staring at a group of woodcuts in the *Hypnerotomachia*—the same ones Taft would use in his lecture a month later, the ones of Cupid driving women into a forest on a burning chariot—I thought of Carracci's engraving. Here I was, being pummeled by the little boy as my two loves looked on. This was what my father meant, the lesson he'd hoped I would learn. *Our hardships cannot move him. Love conquers all.*

The two hardest things to contemplate in life, Richard Curry once told Paul, are failure and age; and those are one and the same. Perfection is the natural consequence of eternity: wait long enough, and anything will realize its potential. Coal becomes diamonds, sand becomes pearls, apes become men. It's simply not given to us, in one lifetime, to see those consummations, and so every failure becomes a reminder of death.

But love lost is a special kind of failure, I think. It's a reminder that some consummations, no matter how devoutly wished for, never come; that some apes will never be men, not in all the world's ages. What's a monkey to think, who with a typewriter and eternity still can't eke out Shakespeare? To hear Katie say that she wanted to make it final, that she and I were finished, would stunt all my sense of possibility. To watch her there, beneath Blair Arch, warming herself in Donald Morgan's arms, would strip the pearls and diamonds from my future.

And then it happened: just as I'd reached the full bloom of self-pity, a knock came at the door. It was followed by a turning of the knob, and the same way it had happened a hundred times before, Katie let herself in. Beneath her coat I could see she was wearing my favorite of her sweaters, the emerald-colored one that matched her eyes.

"You're supposed to be at the arch sing" was the first thing I managed to say, and of all the monkey-written combinations, it was probably the worst.

"So are you," she said, staring me up and down.

I knew how I must look to her. The wolf Charlie had shown me in the mirror was the one Katie saw now.

"Why are you here?" I said, glancing at the door.

"They're not coming." She forced herself back into my focus. "I'm here so you can apologize."

For a second I thought Gil had put her up to this, inventing something about how bad I felt, how I just didn't know what to say. But another glance told me otherwise. She knew I had no intention of saying I was sorry.

"Well?"

"You think this is my fault?" I asked.

"Everyone does."

"What everyone?"

"Do it, Tom. Apologize."

Arguing with her was only making me angrier with myself.

"Fine. I love you. I wish things had worked out. I'm sorry they didn't."

"If you wish things had worked out, why didn't you do anything?"

"Look at me," I told her. The four-day beard, the unkempt hair. "*This* is what I did."

"You did that for the book."

"It's the same thing."

"*I'm* the same as the book?"

"Yes."

She glared at me as if I'd dug myself a hole. But she knew what I was about to say; she'd just never accepted it.

"My father spent his life on the *Hypnerotomachia*," I told her. "I've never felt more excited than when I'm working on it. I lose sleep over it, I don't eat because of it, I have dreams about it." I found myself looking around, searching for words. "I don't know how else to say it. It's like going to the battlefield to see your tree. Being near it makes me feel like everything's right, like I'm not lost anymore." I kept my eyes away from her. "So are you the same as the book to me? Yes. Of course you are. You're the *only* thing that's the same as the book to me."

I made a mistake. I thought I could have you both. I was wrong.

"Why am I here, Tom?"

"To rub it in."

"Why?"

"To make me apologi—"

"Tom." She stopped me with a look. "Why am I here?"

Because you feel the same way I do.

Yes.

Because this was too important to leave it up to me.

Yes.

"What do you want?" I said.

"I want you to stop working on the book."

"That's all?"

"That's *all*? That's all?"

Now, suddenly, emotion.

"I'm supposed to feel sorry for you because you gave up on *us* to act like a slob and live in that book? You ass, I spent four days with my shades down and my door locked.

Karen called my parents. My mom flew down from New Hampshire."

"I'm sor—"

"Shut *up*. It isn't your turn to talk. I went out to the battlefield to see my tree, and I *couldn't*. I couldn't, because now it's *our* tree. I can't listen to music, because every song is something we sang in the car, or in my room, or in here. It takes me an hour to get ready for class, because I feel like I'm dazed half the time. I can't find my socks, I can't find my favorite black bra. Donald's always asking me, 'Honey, what's wrong, Honey, what's wrong?' *Nothing's* wrong, Donald." She pushed her wrists into her cuffs and blotted her eyes.

"That's not wh—" I began again.

But it still wasn't my turn.

"At least with Peter I could understand. We weren't perfect together. He loved lacrosse more than he loved me; I knew that. He wanted to get me in bed, and after that he lost interest." She moved a hand through her hair, trying to push away the bangs that had gotten snarled in tears. "But *you*. I *fought* for you. I waited a month before I let you kiss me the first time. I cried the night after we slept together, because I thought I was going to lose you." She stopped, galled by the thought. "And now I'm losing you to a book. A *book*. At least tell me it's not what I think, Tom. Tell me you've been seeing a senior on the side all this time. Tell me it's because she doesn't do all the stupid things I do, she doesn't dance naked in front of you like some kind of idiot because she thinks you enjoy her singing, or wake you up at 6 A.M. to go running because she wants to make sure, every single morning, that you're still there. Tell me *something*."

She looked up at me, broken in a way that I know ashamed her, and I could only think of one thing. There was a night, not long after the accident, when I accused my mother of not caring for my father. *If you loved him*, I said to her, *you would've supported his work.* The look that crossed her face, which I can't begin to describe, told me there was nothing more shameful in the world than what I had just said.

"I love you," I told Katie, stepping toward her so that she could press her face into my shirt and be invisible for a moment. "I'm so sorry."

And that was the moment, I think, when the tide began to change. My terminal condition, the love affair I thought was in my genes, slowly started to lose its grip on me. The triangle was collapsing. In its place stood a pair of points, a binary star, separated by the smallest possible distance.

A jumble of silences followed, all the things she needed to say but knew she shouldn't have to, all the things I wanted to say but didn't know how to.

"I'll tell Paul," I said, the best and most truthful thing I could, "I'm going to stop working on the book."

Redemption. The realization that I wasn't putting up a fight, that I'd finally figured out what was best for my own happiness, was enough to make Katie do something I think she was saving for much later, after I was back on the wagon for sure. She kissed me. And that moment of contact, like the lightning that gave the monster his second shot at life, created a new beginning.

I didn't see Paul that night; I spent it with Katie and ended up telling him my decision the next day at Dod. He, too, seemed unsurprised. I'd been suffering so much with Colonna that he sensed I might throw in the towel at the first sign of relief. He'd been persuaded by Gil and Charlie that it was the best thing anyway, and somehow he didn't hold it against me. Maybe he guessed I'd be back. Maybe he'd come far enough to think he could finish the riddles alone. Whatever it was, when I finally told him my reasoning—the lesson of Jenny Harlow and Carracci's engraving—he seemed to agree. I could tell from his expression that he knew more about Carracci than I did, but he never once corrected me. Paul, who had more reasons than anyone to believe that some interpretations are better than others, and that the right ones make all the difference, was generous about my spin on things, the same way he'd always been. It was more than his way of showing respect, I think; it was his way of showing friendship.

"It's better to love something that can love you back," he told me.

It was the only thing he needed to say.

What began as Paul's thesis, then, became Paul's thesis once more. At first, it looked as if he might pull it off alone. The fourth riddle, which had taken a whip to me, came to him in three days. I suspect he'd had the idea all along, but kept it from me because he knew I wouldn't take his advice. The answer was in a book called the *Hieroglyphica*, by a man named Horapollo, which turned up in Renaissance Italy in the 1420s, purporting to solve the ages-old problem of interpreting Egyptian hieroglyphics. Horapollo, taken by humanists to be some kind of ancient Egyptian sage, was in fact a fifth-century scholar who wrote in Greek and probably didn't know much more about hieroglyphics than Eskimos know about summer. Some of the symbols in his *Hieroglyphica* involve animals that aren't even Egyptian. Still, amidst the humanist fervor over new knowledge, the text became wildly popular, at least in the small circles where wild popularity and dead languages weren't mutually exclusive.

The night-owl, according to Horapollo, is a symbol of death, *for the night-owl suddenly descends upon the young of the crow in the night, as death comes upon a man suddenly.* An eagle with a twisted beak, Horapollo wrote, signifies an old man dying of hunger, *for when the eagle grows old, he twists his beak and dies of hunger.* The blind beetle, finally, is a glyph that means a man has died from sunstroke, *for a beetle dies when blinded by the sun.* Cryptic as Horapollo's reasoning was, Paul knew immediately that he'd fixed on the right source. And he saw very quickly what the three animals had in common: death. Applying the Latin word for it, *mors,* as his cipher, he produced Colonna's fourth message.

> *You who have come so far are joined by the philosophers of my day, who in your time are perhaps the dust of ages, but who in mine were the giants of mankind. I am soon to put upon you the burden of what remains, for there is much to tell and I grow fearful that my secret is too easily spread. But first, out of deference to your accomplishment, I will offer you the beginnings of my story, so that you will know I have not led you this far in vain.*
>
> *There is a preacher in the land of my brethren who has brought a great pestilence upon the lovers of knowledge. We have battled him with all our wit and influence, but*

this single man raises our countrymen against us. He
thunders in the squares and from the pulpits, and the
common men of all nations take up arms to do us harm.
Just as God, out of jealousy, brought to nothing the tower
in the plain of Shinar, which men built toward the heav-
ens, so He raises His fist against us, who attempt the very
same. I did long ago hope that men wished to be delivered
from ignorance, just as slaves wish to be freed from
bondage. It is a condition unbecoming our dignity, and
contrary to our nature. Yet I find now that the race of men
is a cowardly thing, a perversion like the owl of my rid-
dle, which though it might enjoy sunlight, prefers dark-
ness. You will hear no more of me, reader, upon the
completion of my crypt. To be a prince to such people as
this, is to be a castled kind of beggar. This book will be my
only child; may it live long, and serve you well.

Paul hardly paused to contemplate it; he pushed on to
the fifth and final riddle, which he'd found while I struggled with the fourth: *Where do blood and spirit meet?*

"It's the oldest philosophical question in the book," he
told me, while I puttered around the room, preparing for
a night with Katie.

"What is?"

"The intersection of mind and body, the flesh-spirit
duality. You see it in Augustine, in *contra Manichaeos.* You
see it in modern philosophy. Descartes thought he could
pinpoint the soul somewhere near the pineal gland in the
brain."

He continued that way, paging through a book from
Firestone and sputtering philosophy, while I packed.

"What are you reading?" I asked, pulling my copy of *Paradise Lost* off the shelf to bring with me.

"Galen," Paul said.

"Who?"

"The second father of western medicine, after Hippocrates."

I remembered. Charlie had studied Galen in a history of science class. By Renaissance standards, though, Galen was no spring chick: he died thirteen hundred years before the *Hypnerotomachia* was published.

"Why?" I asked.

"I think the riddle is about anatomy. Francesco must've believed there was an actual organ in the body where blood and spirit met."

Charlie appeared in the doorway with the remains of an apple in his hand. "What are you amateurs talking about?" he said, hearing talk of things medical.

"An organ like this," Paul said, ignoring him. "The *rete mirabile*." He pointed to a diagram in the book. "A network of nerves and vessels at the base of the brain. Galen thought this is where vital spirits turned into animal ones."

"What's wrong with it?" I asked, checking my watch.

"I don't know. It doesn't work as a cipher."

"That's because it doesn't exist in humans," Charlie said.

"What do you mean?"

Charlie looked up and took a last nibble from his apple. "Galen only dissected animals. The *rete mirabile*'s something he found in an ox or a sheep."

Paul's expression faded.

"He also made a meal of cardiac anatomy," Charlie continued.

"There's no septum?" Paul said, as if he knew what Charlie meant.

"There is. There just aren't any pores in it."

"What's a septum?" I asked.

"The wall of tissue between the two sides of the heart." Charlie walked over to Paul's book and flipped through it to find a diagram of the circulatory system. "Galen got it all wrong. He said there were little holes in the septum where blood passed between the chambers."

"There aren't?"

"No," Paul snapped, beginning to sound as if he'd been working on this longer than I thought. "But Mondino made the same mistake about the septum. Vesalius and Servetus figured it out, but not until the mid-1500s. Leonardo followed Galen. Harvey didn't describe the circulatory system until the 1600s. This riddle is from the late 1400s, Charlie. It has to be the *rete mirabile* or the septum. No one knew that air mixed with blood in the lungs."

Charlie chuckled. "No one in the West. The Arabs figured it out two hundred years before your guy wrote his book."

Paul began rifling through his papers. Thinking the matter was settled, I turned to go. "I gotta run. I'll see you guys later."

But just as I moved toward the hallway, Paul found what he'd been looking for: the Latin he'd translated weeks earlier, the text of Colonna's third message.

"The Arab doctor," he said. "Was his name Ibn al-Nafis?"

Charlie nodded. "That's the one."

Paul was all excitement. "Francesco must've gotten the text from Andrea Alpago."

"Who?"

"The man he mentions in the message. *Disciple of the venerable Ibn al-Nafis.*" Before either of us could speak, Paul was talking to himself. "What's Latin for lung? *Pulmo?*"

I made for the door.

"You're not going to wait to see what it says?" he asked, looking up.

"I'm supposed to be at Katie's in ten minutes."

"This'll only take fifteen. Maybe thirty."

I think it occurred to him only at that moment how much things had changed.

"I'll see you guys in the morning," I said.

Charlie, who understood, smiled and wished me luck.

■

It was a signal night for Paul, I think. He realized he'd lost me for good. He also sensed that no matter what Colonna's final message was, it couldn't possibly contain the man's entire secret, when so little had been revealed in the first four parts. The second half of the *Hypnerotomachia*, which we had always assumed was filler, must in reality contain more ciphered text. And whatever consolation Paul took in Charlie's medical knowledge, or in having solved the fifth riddle, it dissipated quickly when he saw Colonna's message and realized that he was right.

I fear for you, reader, as I fear for myself. As you have perceived, it was my intention at the beginning of this text to betray to you my meanings, no matter how deeply I wrapped them in codes. I have wished for you to find what you seek, and have acted as your guide.

Now, however, I find that I have not faith enough in

*my own creation to continue in this manner. Perhaps I
cannot judge the true difficulty of the riddles here contained, even if their creators assure me none but a true
philosopher could solve them. Perhaps these wise men,
too, are jealous of my secret, and have misled me so that
they may steal what is rightfully ours. He is clever indeed, this preacher, with followers in every camp; I fear
he turns my soldiers against me.*

*It is as a defense to you then, reader, that I pursue my
present course. Where you have become accustomed to
finding a riddle within my chapters, you will henceforth
find no riddles at all, and no solutions to lead you. I will
employ only my Rule of Four for the duration of
Poliphilo's journey, but I will offer you no suggestion of
its nature. Only your intellect will guide you now. May
God and genius, friend, shepherd you aright.*

It was confidence alone, I think, that prevented Paul
from sensing his abandonment until many days had
passed. I had left him; Colonna had left him; now he nav-
igated alone. He tried, at first, to reinvolve me in the
process. We had solved so much together that he thought
it would be selfish to let me absent myself in the eleventh
hour. We were so close, he thought; we had so little left
to do.

Then a week passed, and another. I was beginning
again with Katie, relearning her, loving her alone. So
much had happened in the weeks we'd been apart that I
was more than occupied trying to catch up. We alternated
meals at Cloister and at Ivy. She had new friends; we had
new routines. There were family matters of hers I began

to take an interest in. I sensed that once I'd won her trust back completely, she had things she wanted to tell me.

Everything Paul had learned about Colonna's riddles, meanwhile, began to fail him. Like a body of work slowly decaying in function, the *Hypnerotomachia* resisted all his trusted medicines. The Rule of Four was elusive; Colonna had given no indication of its origin. Charlie, the hero of the fifth riddle, stayed up with Paul some nights, worrying about the effect my departure was having. He never asked me to help, knowing what the book had done to me once, but I saw the way he hovered over Paul, like a doctor eyeing a patient he fears is trending badly. A darkness was setting in, a book lover's heartbreak, and Paul was helpless against it. He would suffer, without my help, until Easter weekend.

Chapter 19

On the way back to Dod, I shuffle through Katie's pictures of Princeton Battlefield. In shot after shot I've caught her in midmotion, running toward me, hair streaking behind, mouth half open, her words caught somewhere in the registers of experience beyond the camera's range. The pleasure of imagining her voice in them is the joy of these pictures. In another twelve hours I'll see her at Ivy, escorting her to the ball she's been anticipating almost since we met, and I know what she'll be waiting for me to say. That I've made a choice I can stick to; that I've learned. That I won't be returning to the *Hypnerotomachia*.

When I get back to the room, I expect to find Paul at his desk, but his bunk is still empty, and now the books on his dresser are gone. Taped to the top of the door frame is a note, this one in large red letters.

Tom—

Where are you? Came back looking for you. Figured out 4S-10E-2N-6W! Gone to pick up topo atlas at Fire-stone, then down to McCosh. Vincent says he has the blueprint. 10:15.

—P.

I read the message again, piecing it together. The basement of McCosh Hall is the location of Taft's office on campus. But the last line leaves me cold: *Vincent says he has the blueprint.* I pick up the phone and call the squad house. Charlie's on the line in a matter of seconds.

"What's up, Tom?"

"Paul went to see Taft."

"*What?* I thought he was going to talk to the dean about Stein."

"We need to find him. Can you get someone to cover for y—"

Before I can even finish, a muffled sound interrupts the call, and I hear Charlie talking to someone on the other end.

"When did Paul leave?" he says, returning to the line.

"Ten minutes ago."

"I'm on my way. We'll catch up to him."

Charlie's 1973 Volkswagen Karmann Ghia pulls up in back of Dod more than fifteen minutes later. The old car looks like a metal toad rusted in mid-hop. Before I've even lowered myself into the passenger seat, Charlie's got it in reverse.

"What took you so long?" I ask.

"A reporter showed up at the squad room when I was leaving," he said. "She wanted to talk to me about last night."

"So?"

"Someone at the police department told her what Taft said in his interrogation." We pull onto Elm Drive, where little crests of slush give the asphalt a choppy surface, like ocean water at night. "Didn't you tell me Taft knew Richard Curry a long time ago?"

"Yeah. Why?"

"Because he told the cops he only knew Curry through Paul."

Just as we enter north campus, I spot Paul in the courtyard between the library and the history department, walking toward McCosh.

"Paul!" I call out the window.

"What are you doing?" Charlie snaps at him, pulling up to the curb.

"*I solved it!*" Paul says, surprised to see us. "The whole thing. I just need the blueprint. Tom, you're not going to believe this. It's the most amaz—"

"What? Tell me."

But Charlie isn't hearing any of it. "You're not going to Taft's," he says.

"You don't understand. It's *done*. . . ."

Charlie leans on the car horn, filling the courtyard with noise.

"Listen to me," Charlie interrupts. "Paul, get in the car. We're going home."

"He's right," I say. "You shouldn't have come out here alone."

"I'm going to Vincent's," Paul says quietly, and begins walking in the direction of Taft's office. "I know what I'm doing."

Charlie forces the car into reverse, keeping up with Paul. "You think he's just going to give you what you want?"

"He called me, Charlie. That's what he said he was going to do."

"He admitted he stole it from Curry?" I ask. "Why would he give you the blueprint now?"

"Paul," Charlie says, stopping the car. "He's not giving you anything."

The way he says it, Paul stops.

Charlie lowers his voice and explains what he learned from the reporter. "When the police asked Taft last night if he could think of anyone who might've done something like this to Stein, Taft said he could think of *two* people."

The expression on Paul's face starts to fade, the excitement of his discovery waning.

"The first was Curry," Charlie says. "The second was *you*." He pauses, letting the emphasis stand. "So I don't care what the man told you over the phone. You need to stay away from him."

An old white pickup truck rumbles down the road past us, snow crunching beneath its tires.

"Then help me," Paul says.

"We will." Charlie opens the door. "We'll drive you home."

Paul tightens his coat around him. "Help me by coming with me. After I get the blueprint from Vincent, I don't need him anymore."

Charlie stares. "Are you even *hearing* us?"

But there are sides to this that Charlie doesn't understand. He doesn't know what it means that Taft has been
hiding the blueprint all along.

"I'm *this* close to having it in my hands, Charlie," Paul
says. "All I have to do is stand up for what I've found. And
you're telling me to go home?"

"Look," Charlie begins, "I'm just saying we need to—"

But I interrupt. "Paul, we'll come with you."

"*What?*" Charlie says.

"Come on." I open the passenger door.

Paul turns, not expecting this.

"If he's going with or without us," I say to Charlie under
my breath, leaning back into the car, "then I'm going too."

Paul begins walking toward McCosh as Charlie considers his position.

"Taft can't do anything if there are three of us," I say.
"You know that."

Charlie exhales slowly, sending a cloud of steam into
the air. Finally he makes a space for the car in the snow
and pulls the keys from the ignition.

The walk to Taft's office takes an eternity, pacing up to the
gray edifice in the snow. The room lies in the bowels of
McCosh, where the hallways are so cramped and the
stairs are so steep, we have to descend single file. It's hard
to believe Vincent Taft can breathe in here, let alone
move. Even I get the sensation of being too big for the
place. Charlie must feel like he's trapped.

I look back, just to make sure he's still there. The sight of
him behind us, filling the doorways and covering our backs,
gives me enough confidence to keep moving. I realize now

what I was too bluff to admit before: if Charlie hadn't come with us, I couldn't have gone through with this.

Paul leads us down a final hallway, toward the single room at the end. Because of the weekend and the holiday, every other office is locked up and dark. Only beneath the white door bearing the placard of Taft's name do I see the rich glow of light. The paint on the door is chipped, curling over itself near the edge, where it closes into the jamb. On the bottom of the panel is a faint line of discoloration, the high-water mark of an old flood from the steam tunnels coiled just beneath the basement floor, a stain unpainted since Taft's arrival in the time before time.

Paul raises his hand to knock, when a voice comes from inside. "You're late," Taft growls.

The knob squeaks when Paul turns it. I feel Charlie bump up against my back.

"Go on," he whispers, pushing me forward.

Taft is sitting alone behind a great antique desk, sunken into a leather chair. He has thrown his tweed coat over the back of the chair, and with shirtsleeves rolled up to his forearms, he is proofing manuscript pages with a red pen that looks tiny in his fist.

"Why are *they* here?" he demands.

"Give me the blueprint," Paul says, coming right to the point.

Taft looks at Charlie, then at me. "Sit down," he says, pointing toward a pair of chairs with two thick fingers.

I glance around, trying to ignore him. Wooden bookshelves line the tiny office on all sides, covering the white walls. Trails run through the dust on their surfaces where volumes have been dragged off to be read. There is a path worn in the carpet where Taft walks from the door to his desk.

"*Sit,*" Taft repeats.

Paul is about to refuse, when Charlie nudges him into the chair, wanting to get this over with.

Taft balls a rag in his hand and wipes his mouth with it. "Tom Sullivan," he says, the resemblance finally occurring to him.

I nod, but say nothing. There's an old pillory on the wall above his head, mounted with its jaws open. The only hint of light or color in the room is the red morocco of book bindings and the gold of gilt pages.

"Leave him alone," Paul says, sitting forward. "Where's the blueprint?"

I'm surprised how strong he sounds.

Taft tuts, bringing a cup of tea to his mouth. There's an unpleasant look in his eyes, as if he's waiting for one of us to put up a fight. Finally, he rises from the leather chair, forces the sleeves of his shirt up higher, and plods over to a space in the bookshelves where a safe has been built into the wall. He spins the combination with a hairy hand, then pulls the lever and swings the door on its hinges. Reaching inside, he produces a leather notebook.

"Is that it?" Paul says faintly.

When Taft opens it and hands something to Paul, though, it's only a typed piece of Institute stationery, dated two weeks ago.

"I want you to know where things stand," Taft says. "Read it."

When I see the effect the paper has on Paul, I lean over to read it as well.

Dean Meadows:

Pursuant to our conversation of 12 March regarding Paul Harris, herewith the additional information you requested. As you know, Mr. Harris petitioned for several extensions, and has been highly secretive concerning the content of his work. Only when, at my insistence, he submitted a final progress report last week, did I understand why. Enclosed please find a copy of my upcoming article, "Unveiling the Mystery: Francesco Colonna and the Hypnerotomachia Poliphili," tentatively scheduled for fall publication in Renaissance Quarterly. Also enclosed is a copy of Mr. Harris's progress report, for the purposes of comparison. Please contact me with any further inquiries.

Sincerely,
Dr. Vincent Taft

We're speechless.

The ogre turns to Charlie and me. "I've worked on this for thirty years," he says, a strange evenness in his voice. "Now the results don't even bear my name. You have never been grateful to me, Paul. Not when I introduced you to Steven Gelbman. Not when you received special access to the Rare Books Room. Not even when I granted you multiple extensions on your ineffectual work. Never."

Paul is too stunned to respond.

"I won't have you take this from me," Taft continues. "I've waited too long."

"They have my other progress reports," Paul stutters. "They have Bill's records."

"They've never seen a progress report from you," Taft

says, opening a drawer and pulling out a sheaf of forms. "And they certainly don't have Bill's records."

"They'll know it wasn't yours. You haven't published anything on Francesco in twenty-five years. You don't even work on the *Hypnerotomachia* anymore."

Taft pulls at his beard. "*Renaissance Quarterly* has seen three preliminary drafts of my article. And I've received several calls of congratulation on my lecture last night."

Remembering the dates on Stein's letters, I see the long provenance of this idea, the months of suspicion between Stein and Taft over who would steal Paul's research first.

"But he has his conclusions," I say, when it doesn't seem to dawn on Paul. "He hasn't told anyone."

I expect Taft to react badly, but he seems amused. "Conclusions so soon, Paul?" he says. "To what do we attribute this sudden success?"

He knows about the diary.

"You *let* Bill find it," Paul says.

"You still don't know what he found," I insist.

"And you," Taft says, turning to me, "are as deluded as your father was. If a boy can puzzle out the meaning of that diary, you think *I* can't?"

Paul is dazed, eyes darting around the room.

"My father thought you were a fool," I say.

"Your father died waiting for a Muse to whisper in his ear." He laughs. "Scholarship is rigor, not inspiration. He never listened to me, and he suffered for it."

"He was right about that book. You were wrong."

Hatred dances in Taft's eyes. "I know what he did, boy. You shouldn't be so proud."

I glance over at Paul, not understanding, but he's taken several steps away from the desk, toward the bookshelf.

Taft leans forward. "Can you blame him? Failed, disgraced. The rejection of his book was the coup de grâce."

I turn back, thunderstruck.

"And he did it with his own son in the car," Taft continues. "How pregnant."

"It was an accident. . . ." I say.

Taft smiles, and there are a thousand teeth in it.

I step toward him. Charlie puts a hand against my chest, but I shake it off. Taft slowly rises from his chair.

"*You* did it to him," I say, vaguely aware that I'm shouting. Charlie's hand is on me again, but I pull away, stepping forward until the edge of the desk is knifing into my scar.

Taft turns the corner, bringing himself into reach.

"He's goading you, Tom," Paul says quietly, from across the room.

"He did it to *himself*," Taft says.

And the last thing I remember, before pushing him as hard as I can, is the smile on his face. He falls, the weight of him collapsing onto itself, and there is a thunder I feel in the floorboards. Everything seems to splinter, voices shouting, sights blurring, and Charlie's hands are on me again, yanking me back.

"Come on," he says.

I try to jerk free, but Charlie's grip is stronger.

"Come *on*," he repeats to Paul, who's still staring at Taft on the floor.

But it's too late. Taft staggers to his feet, then lumbers toward me.

"Stay away from him," Charlie says, extending a hand in Taft's direction.

Taft glares at me from across the span of Charlie's arms. Paul is looking around the room, oblivious to them, searching for something. Finally, Taft's senses return and he reaches for the phone.

A stab of fear registers on Charlie's face. "Let's go," he says, stepping back. *"Now."*

Taft punches three numbers, ones Charlie has seen too often to mistake. *"Police,"* he says, staring directly at me. *"Please come immediately. I'm being attacked in my office."*

Charlie is pushing me out the door. "Go," he says.

Just then, Paul darts over to the open safe and pulls out the balance of what remains inside. Then he starts pulling papers and books from the shelves, uprooting bookends, turning over everything in his reach. When he's got a pile of Taft's papers in hand, he backs away and dashes out the door, without so much as a glance at Charlie or me.

We bolt after him. The last thing I hear from the office is the sound of Taft on the phone, announcing our names to the police. His voice carries through the open door, echoing down the hallway.

We dart through the corridor to the dark cellar stairs, when a rush of cold descends from overhead. Two campus police officers have arrived at the foot of the steps on the ground floor above us.

"Stay right there!" one of them calls down the narrow staircase.

We stop short.

"Campus police! Don't move!"

Paul is looking over my shoulder toward the far end of the hall, clutching the papers in his left hand.

"Do what they say," Charlie tells him.

But I know what's caught Paul's eye. There's a janitor's closet down there. Inside is an entrance to the tunnels.

"It's not safe down there," Charlie says under his breath, edging toward Paul to keep him from running. *"They're doing construct—"*

The proctors mistake the movement for flight, and one comes barreling down the stairs, just as Paul makes for the door.

"Stop!" the proctor cries. *"Don't go in there!"*

But Paul is already at the entrance, pulling the wood panel open. He disappears inside.

Charlie doesn't hesitate. Before either of the cops knows it, he's two steps ahead, moving fast toward the door. I hear a thud as he jumps to the tunnel floor, trying to stop Paul. Then his voice, shouting Paul's name, echoes up from below.

"Come out!" the proctor booms, nudging me forward.

The officer leans in and calls again, but only silence follows.

"Call it in—" the first one begins to say, when a thunderous noise comes roaring up from the tunnels, and the boiler room beside us begins to hiss. Immediately I know what's happened: a steam pipe has burst. And now I can hear Charlie screaming.

In an instant, I'm at the threshold of the janitor's closet. The manhole is pure darkness, so I take a wild leap. When I hit the ground, adrenaline is forking through me, live as lightning, and the pain from landing fades before it spreads. I force myself up. Charlie is moaning in the distance, leading me toward him, even as the proctor yells overhead. One of the officers has the sense to realize what's going on.

"We're calling an ambulance," he calls into the tunnel. "Can you hear me?"

I'm moving through a soupy mist. The heat intensifies, but the only thing on my mind is Charlie. For seconds at a time the hiss of the pipe drowns out everything else.

Charlie's groans are clearer now. I push forward, trying to get to him. Finally, at a turn in the pipes, I find him. He's buckled over himself, motionless. His clothes are ragged, and his hair is matted to his head. In the distance, as my eyes adjust, I can see a gaping hole in a barrel-size pipe near the floor.

"Hum," Charlie groans.

I don't understand.

"*Hum* . . ."

I realize he's trying to say my name.

His chest is soaked. The steam hit him right in the gut.

"Can you stand?" I ask, trying to put his arm around my shoulder.

"*Hum* . . ." he mumbles, losing consciousness.

Clenching my teeth, I try lifting him, but it's like trying to move a mountain.

"Come on, Charlie," I plead, jerking him up a little. "Don't fade on me."

But I sense I'm talking to less and less of him. There's more and more dead weight.

"*Help!*" I bark into the distance. "*Please help me!*"

There are gashes in his shirt where the pressure shredded the fabric, soaking him to the skin. I can hardly feel him breathing.

"*Mmm . . .*" he gurgles, trying to curl a finger around my hand.

I grab his shoulders and shake him again. Finally I hear footsteps. A beam of light knifes through the fog and I can see a medic—two of them—rushing toward me.

In a second they're close enough for me to see their faces. But when the beams of their flashlights finally cross Charlie's body, I can hear one of them say, "Oh, Jesus."

"Are you hurt?" the other says to me, padding at my chest with his hands.

I stare back at him, uncomprehending. Then, as I look down at the circle of my stomach lit by his flashlight, I understand. The water sprayed across Charlie's chest wasn't water at all. I'm covered in his blood.

Both of the EMTs are with him now, trying to raise him up. A third medic arrives and tries to move me, but I fight him off, trying to stay at Charlie's side. Slowly I feel myself beginning to slip away. In the heat and the darkness, I'm losing my hold on reality. A pair of hands guides me out of the tunnels, and I see the two officers, with two other policemen behind them now, all watching as the ambulance team drags me above ground.

The last thing I remember is the look on the proctor's face as he stands there, watching me rise from the darkness, bloody from my face to the tips of my fingers. At first he looks relieved, to see me stumble out of the wreckage. Then his expression changes, and the relief disappears from his eyes, as he realizes the blood isn't mine.

Chapter 20

I come to my senses in a bed at Princeton Medical Center several hours after the accident. Paul is sitting beside me, glad to see me awake, and a policeman is standing outside the door. Someone has changed me into a paper gown that crunches like a diaper when I sit up. There is blood beneath my fingernails, dark as dirt, and there's a familiar smell in the air, something I remember from my old hospital past. The smell of sickness mopped over with disinfectant. The smell of medicine.

"Tom?" Paul says.

I prop myself up to face him, but pain shoots through my arm.

"Careful," he says, leaning over. "The doctor says you injured your shoulder."

Now, as I'm becoming more aware, I can feel pain beneath the bandage. "What happened to you down there?"

"It was stupid. I just reacted. I couldn't get back to Charlie once the pipe exploded. All of the steam was coming in my direction. I came back through the nearest exit and the police drove me here."

"Where's Charlie?"

"In the emergency room. They won't let anyone see him."

His voice has gone flat. After rubbing at his eye, he glances out the door. An old woman skids past in a wheelchair, nimble as a kid in a go-cart. The cop watches her, but doesn't smile. There's a little yellow sandwich board on the tile floor that says CAUTION: WET SURFACE.

"Is he okay?" I ask.

Paul keeps his eyes on the door. "I don't know. Will said he was right beside the broken pipe when they found him."

"Will?"

"Will Clay, Charlie's friend." Paul places a hand on the rail of the bed. "He pulled you out."

I try to think back, but all I remember are silhouettes in the tunnels, lit up around the edges by flashlights.

"He and Charlie switched shifts when you guys went looking for me," Paul adds.

There's a great sadness in his voice. He traces this all back to himself.

"Do you want me to call Katie and tell her you're here?" he asks.

I shake my head, wanting to feel more grounded first. "I'll call her later."

The old woman rolls past a second time, and now I spot the cast on her left leg, running from her knee to her toes. Her hair is mussed, and her pants are rolled up above the knee, but there's a twinkle in her eyes, and she gives the officer a defiant smile when she passes by, as if it's a law she's broken, rather than a bone. Charlie told me once that geriatric patients are relieved sometimes to take a little fall, or have a minor illness. Losing a battle reminds them that they're still winning the war. I am struck suddenly by Charlie's absence, by the emptiness where I expect to hear his voice.

"He must've lost a lot of blood," I say.

Paul looks at his hands. In the silence, I can hear wheezing across the partition between my bed and the next. Just then, a doctor enters the room. The officer at the door touches the elbow of her white lab coat, and when she stops, the two of them exchange quiet words.

"Thomas?" she says, coming to the bedside with a clipboard and a frown.

"Yes?"

"I'm Dr. Jansen." She walks to the opposite side of the bed to examine my arm. "How are you feeling?"

"Fine. How's Charlie doing?"

She prods my shoulder a little, just enough to make me squirm. "I don't know. He's been in the ER since he got here."

I'm not clearheaded enough to know what it means that she recognizes Charlie by his first name.

"Will he be okay?"

"It's too early to tell," she says, without looking up.

"When can we see him?" Paul asks.

"One thing at a time," she says, placing a hand between my back and the pillow, then raising me up. "How does this feel?"

"Fine."

"And this?"

She presses two fingers over my collarbone.

"Fine."

The poking continues across my back, elbow, wrist, and head. She tries the stethoscope for good measure, then finally sits back. Doctors are like gamblers, always looking for the right combinations. Patients are like slot machines: twist their arms long enough and you're bound to hit the jackpot.

"You're lucky it wasn't worse," she says. "There's no fracture, but the soft tissue is bruised. You'll feel it when the painkiller wears off. Ice it twice a day for a week, then you'll have to come back so we can take another look."

She has an earthy smell to her, like sweat and soap. I wait for her to pull out a prescription pad, remembering the cabinet of drugs I collected after the car accident, but she doesn't.

"There's someone outside who'd like to talk to you," she tells me instead.

For a second, because she says it so pleasantly, I imagine a friend out in the hall—Gil maybe, returned from the eating clubs, or even my mother, flown in from Ohio. Suddenly, I'm unsure how much time has passed since they dragged me out of the ground.

But a different face appears in the doorway, one I've never seen before. Another woman, but not a doctor, and definitely not my mother. She's heavyset and short, tucked into a round black skirt down to her calves, and opaque black stockings. A white blouse and red suit-jacket give her a maternal air, but my first thought is that she's a university administrator.

The doctor and the woman exchange a look, then switch places, one leaving as the other comes. The black-stockinged woman stops short of the bed and makes a gesture to Paul, beckoning him over. They have a conversation out of earshot—then, unexpectedly, he asks if I'm okay, waits for me to nod, and walks out with another man standing near the door.

"Officer," the woman says, "would you close that behind you?"

To my surprise he nods and shuts the door, leaving us alone.

The woman waddles over to the bedside, pausing to glance at the bed beyond the curtain.

"How are you feeling, Tom?" She sits down in the chair where Paul was, making it disappear. She has squirrelly cheeks. When she talks, they seem full of nuts.

"Not so good," I say warily. I tilt my right side toward her, showing her the bandage.

"Can I get you anything?"

"No, thanks."

"My son was here last month," she says absently, searching for something in her jacket pocket. "Appendectomy."

I'm just about to ask who she is, when she pulls a little leather wallet out of her breast pocket. "Tom, I'm Detective Gwynn. I'd like to talk to you about what happened today."

She unfolds the wallet to show me her badge, then flips it back in her pocket.

"Where's Paul?"

"Speaking with Detective Martin. I'd like to ask you some questions about William Stein. Do you know who he was?"

"He died last night."

"He was killed." She lets a silence punctuate the last word. "Did any of your roommates know him?"

"Paul did. They worked together at the Institute for Advanced Study."

She pulls a steno pad from her jacket pocket. "Do you know Vincent Taft?"

"Sort of," I say, sensing something bigger on the horizon.

"Did you go to his office earlier today?"

Pressure is building in my temples. "Why?"

"Did you get into a fight with him?"

"I wouldn't call it a fight."

She makes a note.

"Were you and your roommate in the museum last night?" she asks, rummaging through a file in her hand.

The question seems to have a thousand outcomes. I think back. Paul covered his hands with his shirt cuffs when he touched Stein's letters. No one could've seen our faces in the dark.

"No."

The detective rolls her lips, the way some women even their lipstick. I can't read her body language. Finally, she produces a sheet of paper from the folder and passes it to me. It's a photocopy of the log-in sheet Paul and I signed for the museum guard. The date and time are stamped beside each entry.

"How did you get into the museum library?"

"Paul had the punch code," I say, giving up. "He got it from Bill Stein."

"Stein's desk was part of our crime scene. What were you looking for?"

"I don't know."

The detective gives me a sympathetic look. "I think your friend Paul," she says, "is getting you into more trouble than you realize."

I wait for her to give it a name, something legal, but she doesn't. Instead she says, "It's your name on this security sheet, isn't it?" She lifts the paper, taking it back. "And you're the one who assaulted Dr. Taft."

"I didn't—"

"Odd, that your friend Charlie was the one who tried to resuscitate William Stein."

"Charlie's a medic . . ."

"But where was Paul Harris?"

For a moment the façade disappears. A curtain rises over her eyes, and the gentle matron is gone.

"You need to start looking out for yourself, Tom."

I can't tell if it's a threat or a caution.

"Your friend Charlie is in the same boat," she says. "If he pulls through this." She waits, letting it sink in. "Just tell me the truth."

"I did."

"Paul Harris left the auditorium before Dr. Taft's lecture was over."

"Yes."

"He knew where Stein's office was."

"They worked together. Yes."

"It was his idea to break into the art museum?"

"He had keys. We didn't break in."

"And it was his idea to go through Stein's desk."

I know better than to keep responding. There are no right answers now.

"He ran from the campus police outside of Dr. Taft's office, Tom. Why would he do that?"

But she wouldn't understand, and doesn't want to. I know where this is heading, but all I can think of is what she said about Charlie.

If he pulls through this.

"He's a straight-A student, Tom. That's his identity here. Then Dr. Taft found out about the plagiarism. Who do you suppose told Taft?"

Brick by brick, as if it's just a matter of building a wall between friends.

"William Stein," she says, knowing I've passed the point of helping her. "Imagine how Paul felt. How angry would he have been?"

Suddenly a knock comes at the door. Before either of us can say a word, it swings open.

"Detective?" says another officer.

"What is it?"

"There's someone out here to talk to you."

"Who?"

He glances down at a card in his hand. "A dean from the college."

The detective remains seated for a second, then rises toward the door.

There's a tight silence after she leaves. After long enough, when she doesn't return, I sit up in bed, looking around for my shirt. I've had enough of hospitals, and I'm well enough to nurse this arm myself. I want to see Charlie; I want to know what they've said to Paul. My jacket is hanging from the coatrack, and I begin to shift my weight gingerly to get out of bed.

Just then, the knob shifts and the door swishes open. Detective Gwynn returns.

"You're free to go," she says abruptly. "The dean's office will be contacting you."

I can only wonder what happened out there. The woman hands me her card and looks at me closely. "But I want you to think about what I said, Tom."

I nod.

There seems to be something more she'd like to add, but she holds her tongue. Without another word, she turns around and leaves.

When the door shuts, another hand reaches in to push it open. I freeze, waiting for the dean to enter. But this time it's a friendly face. Gil has arrived, and he's bearing gifts. In his left hand is exactly what I need right now: a clean change of clothes.

"You okay?" he asks.

"Yeah. What's going on?"

"I got a call from Will Clay. He told me what happened. How's your shoulder?"

"Fine. Did he say anything about Charlie?"

"A little bit."

"Is he okay?"

"Better than when he got here."

There's something to the way Gil says it.

"What's wrong?" I ask.

"Nothing," Gil says finally. "The cops talked to you?"

"Yeah. Paul too. Did you see him out there?"

"He's in the waiting room. Richard Curry's with him."

I fumble out of bed. "He is? Why?"

Gil shrugs, eyeing the hospital food. "Need some help?"

"With what?"

"Getting dressed."

I'm not sure if he's kidding. "I think I can handle it."

He smiles as I struggle to peel off the hospital gown. "Let's check on Charlie," I say, getting used to my own feet again.

But now he hesitates.

"What's wrong?"

An odd look comes over him, embarrassed and angry at the same time.

"He and I got into it pretty deep last night, Tom."

"I know."

"I mean after you and Paul left. I said some things I shouldn't have."

I remember how clean the room was this morning. This is why Charlie didn't sleep.

"It doesn't matter," I say. "Let's go see him."

"He wouldn't want to see me right now."

"Of course he would."

Gil runs a finger beneath his nose, then says, "The doctors don't want him disturbed, anyway. I'll come back later."

He pulls his keys out of his pocket and there's something sad in his eyes. Finally, he puts a hand on the door-knob.

"Give me a call at Ivy if you need anything," he says, and when the door slides open, silent on its hinges, he steps out into the hallway.

The officer is gone, and even the old woman in her wheelchair is nowhere to be seen. Someone has taken the yellow sandwich board away. I wait for Gil to look back, but he doesn't. Before I can say another word, he turns the corner toward the exit and is gone.

Charlie described to me once what epidemics did to human relationships in past centuries, how diseases made men shun the infected and fear the healthy, until parents and children wouldn't sit at the same table with each other, and the whole body politic began to rot. *You don't get sick if you stay to yourself*, I told him, sympathizing with those who took to the hills. Then Charlie looked at me, and in ten words made the best argument in favor of doctors that I've ever heard, which I think applies equally well to friendships. *Maybe not*, he said. *But you don't get well that way either.*

The feeling I got watching Gil leave—the one that made me think of what Charlie said—is the same one I feel as I walk into the waiting room and find Paul sitting by himself: we are each alone in this now, and for the worse. Paul cuts an odd figure there, solitary in a row of white plastic seats, holding his head as he stares at the floor. It's a pose he always strikes when he's deep in thought, leaning over with his fingers wrapped behind the base of his skull, both elbows on his knees. More nights than I can remember, I've woken up to find him sitting at his desk that way, a pen between his fingers, an old lamp casting light over the pages of his notebook.

My first instinct, thinking of that, is to ask him what he found in the diary. Even after everything that's happened, I want to know; I want to help; I want to remind him of an old partnership so that he doesn't feel alone. But seeing him bent over the way he is, fighting with himself over an idea, I know better. I have to remember how he slaved over his thesis after I left, how many mornings he came to breakfast with red eyes, how many nights we brought him cups of black coffee from the WaWa. If someone could count the sacrifices he made for Colonna's book, put a number to them the way a prisoner scratches marks on a wall, they would dwarf what little sweat of mine I've added to the balance. Partnership is what he wanted months ago, when I refused to give it. All I can offer now is my company.

"Hey," I say quietly, walking over to his side.

"Tom . . ." he says, standing.

His eyes are bloodshot.

"You okay?" I ask.

He rubs a sleeve across his face. "Yeah. How about you?"

"I'm okay."

He looks at my arm.

"It'll be fine," I say.

Before I can tell him about Gil, a young doctor with a thin beard steps into the waiting room.

"Is Charlie okay?" Paul asks.

Watching the doctor, I feel a ghost impact, like standing at the tracks as a train hurtles by. He is wearing light green scrubs, the same color as the walls of the hospital where I did my rehabilitation after the accident. A bitter-looking color, like olives mashed with limes. The physical therapist told me to stop looking down, that I would never learn to walk again if I couldn't stop staring at the pins in my leg. Look forward, she said. Always forward. So I stared at the green of the walls.

"His condition is stable," says the man in the scrubs.

Stable, I think. A doctor's word. For two days after they stopped the bleeding in my leg, I was stable. It just meant that I was dying less quickly than before.

"Can we see him?" Paul asks.

"No," the man says. "Charlie is still unconscious."

Paul hesitates, as if unconscious and stable ought to be mutually exclusive. "Is he going to be okay?"

The doctor comes up with a look, something gentle but certain, and says, "I think the worst is over."

Paul smiles faintly at the man, then thanks him. I don't tell Paul what it really means. In the emergency room they are washing their hands and mopping the floors, waiting for the next gurney off the ambulance. The worst is over, for the doctors. For Charlie, it's just begun.

"Thank God," Paul says, almost to himself.

And looking at him now, watching the way relief sets over his face, I realize something. I never believed that Charlie would die from what happened down there. I never believed that he could.

Paul doesn't say much as I check myself out, except to mumble something about the cruelty of what Taft said to me at his office. There's hardly any paperwork to complete, just a form or two to sign, a campus ID to flash, and as I struggle to write my name with my bad hand, I sense that the dean has been here already, smoothing out the wrinkles in advance. I wonder again what she told the detective to get the two of us released.

Then I remember what Gil told me. "Curry was here?"

"He left just before you got out. He didn't look good."

"Why not?"

"He was wearing the same suit he wore last night."

"He knew about Bill?"

"Yeah. It was almost like he thought . . ." Paul lets the thought trail off. "He said, 'We understand each other, son.'"

"What does that mean?"

"I don't know. I think he was forgiving me."

"*Forgiving* you?"

"He told me I shouldn't worry. Everything was going to be okay."

I'm floored. "How could he think you would do that? What did you say?"

"I told him I didn't do it." Paul hesitates. "I didn't know what else to say, so I told him what I found."

"In the diary?"

"It's all I could think of. He seemed so worked up. He said he couldn't sleep, he was so worried."

"Worried about what?"

"About me."

"Look," I tell him, because I'm starting to hear it in his voice, the way Curry has affected him. "He doesn't know what he's talking about."

" 'If I'd known what you were going to do, I would've done things differently.' That's the last thing he said."

I want to lay into Curry, but I have to remind myself that the man who said these things is the closest thing Paul has to a father.

"What did the detective say to you?" he asks, changing the subject.

"She tried to scare me."

"She thought the same thing Richard did?"

"Yes. Did they try to get you to admit to it?"

"The dean came in before they could ask and told me not to answer questions."

"What are you going to do?"

"She said I should find a lawyer."

He says it as if it would be easier to find a basilisk or a unicorn.

"We'll figure something out," I tell him. After I finish

up the discharge paperwork, we head out. There's a police officer stationed near the entrance, who eyes us as we begin walking toward him. A cold wind sets over us the second we step from the building.

We begin the short walk back to campus on our own. The streets are empty, the sky is dimming, and now a bicycle passes by on the sidewalk, carrying a deliveryman from a pizza shop. He leaves a trail of smells behind him, a cloud of yeast and steam, and as the wind picks up again, kicking snow into the air like dust, my stomach rumbles, a reminder that we're back among the living.

"Come with me to the library," Paul says as we approach Nassau Street. "I want to show you something."

He stops at the crosswalk. Beyond a white courtyard is Nassau Hall. I think of pant legs flapping from the cupola, of the clapper that wasn't there.

"Show me what?"

Paul's hands are in his pockets, and he walks with his head down, fighting the wind. We pass through Fitz-Randolph Gate, not looking back. You can walk through the gate into campus as often as you like, the legend goes, but if you walk out of it just once, you will never graduate.

"Vincent told me never to trust friends," Paul says. "He said friends were fickle."

A tour guide leads a small group across our path. They look like carolers. Nathaniel FitzRandolph gave the land to build Nassau Hall, the tour guide says. He is buried where Holder Courtyard now stands.

"I didn't know what to do when that pipe exploded. I didn't realize Charlie only went into the tunnels to find me."

We cross toward East Pyne, heading for the library. In

the distance sit the marble halls of the old debating societies. Whig, James Madison's club, and Cliosophic, Aaron Burr's. The tour guide's voice carries through the air behind us, and I have the growing sensation that I am a visitor here, a tourist, that I have been walking down a tunnel in the dark since the first day I arrived at Princeton, the same way we did through the bowels of Holder Courtyard, surrounded by graves.

"Then I heard you go after him. You didn't care what was down there. You just knew he was hurt."

Paul looks at me for the first time.

"I could hear you calling for help, but I couldn't see anything. I was too scared to move. All I could think was, what kind of friend am I? *I'm* the fickle friend."

"Paul," I say, stopping short. "You don't have to do this."

We're in the courtyard of East Pyne, a building shaped like a cloister, where snow falls through the open quad in the middle. My father has returned to me unexpectedly, like a shadow on the walls, because I realize he walked these paths before I was born, and saw these same buildings. I am walking in his footsteps without even knowing it, because neither of us has made the faintest impression on this place.

Paul turns, seeing me stop, and for a second we are the only living things between these stone walls.

"Yes, I do," he says, turning toward me. "Because when I tell you what I found in the diary, everything else is going to seem small. And everything else *isn't* small."

"Just tell me if it's as big as we hoped."

Because if it is, then at least the shadow my father cast was a long one.

Look forward, the physical therapist says between my ears. *Always forward*. But now, as then, I'm surrounded by walls.

"Yes," Paul says, knowing exactly what I mean. "It is."

There's a spark in his face that brings those three words home, and I am blown back again, struck by the very sensation I'd hoped to find. It's as if my father has pulled through something unthinkable, as if he has come back and been rehabilitated in a single stroke.

I don't know what Paul is about to tell me, but the idea that it could be bigger than I imagined is enough to give me a feeling that's been missing for longer than I knew. It makes me look forward again and actually see something in front of me, something other than a wall. It makes me feel hope.

Chapter 21

On the way to Firestone we pass Carrie Shaw, a junior I recognize from an English class last year, who crosses in front of us and says hi. She and I traded glances across the seminar table for weeks before I met Katie. I wonder how much has changed for her since then. I wonder if she can see how much has changed for me.

"It seems like such an accident that I got sucked into the *Hypnerotomachia*," Paul says as we continue heading east toward the library. "Everything was so indirect, so coincidental. The same way it was for your dad."

"Meeting McBee, you mean."

"And Richard. What if they'd never known each other? What if they'd never taken that class together? What if I'd never picked up your dad's book?"

"We wouldn't be standing here."

He takes it as a throwaway at first, then realizes what I mean. Without Curry and McBee and *The Belladonna Document*, Paul and I would never have met. We would've crossed paths on campus the same way Carrie and I just did, saying hello, wondering where we'd seen each other before, thinking in a distant way what a shame it was that four years had passed and there were still so many unfamiliar faces.

"Sometimes," he says, "I ask myself, why did I have to meet Vincent? Why did I have to meet Bill? Why do I always have to take the long way to get where I'm going?"

"What do you mean?"

"Did you notice how the portmaster's directions don't get straight to the point, either? Four south, ten east, two north, six west. They move in a big circle. You almost end up where you started."

Finally I understand the connection: the wide sweep of circumstance, the way his journey with the *Hypnerotomachia* has wound through time and place, from two friends at Princeton in my father's day, to three men in New York, to a father and son in Italy, and back now to another two friends at Princeton—it all resembles Colonna's strange riddle, the directions that curl back on themselves.

"Don't you think it makes sense that your father is the one that got me started on the *Hypnerotomachia*?" Paul asks.

We arrive at the entrance, and Paul opens the library door for me, as we duck in from the snow. We are in the old heart of campus now, a place made of stones. On summer days, when cars streak by with their windows down and their radios up, and the whole student body wears shorts and T-shirts, buildings like Firestone and the chapel and Nassau Hall seem like caves in a metropolis. But when the temperature drops and the snow falls, no place is more reassuring.

"Last night I started thinking," Paul continues, "Francesco's friends helped him design the riddles, right? Now our friends are helping to *solve* them. You figured out the first one. Katie answered the second one. Charlie knew the last one. Your dad discovered *The Belladonna Document*. Richard found the diary."

We pause at the turnstile, flashing our campus IDs to the guards at the gate. As we wait for the elevator to C-floor, all the way at the bottom, Paul points to a metal plate on the elevator door. There's a symbol engraved on it that I've never noticed before.

"The Aldine Press," I say, recognizing it from my father's old office at home.

Colonna's printer, Aldus Manutius, took his famous dolphin and anchor emblem, one of the most famous in printing history, from the *Hypnerotomachia*.

Paul nods, and I sense this is part of his point. Everywhere he's turned, in this four-year spiral back toward the beginning, he's felt a hand at his back. His whole world, even in the silent details, has been nudging him on, helping him to crack Colonna's book.

The elevator doors open, and we step in.

"Anyway, I was thinking about all that last night," he says, pressing the button for C-floor as we begin our descent. "About how everything seemed to be coming full circle. And it hit me."

A bell dings above our heads, and the doors open onto

the bleakest landscape of the library, dozens of feet underground. The ceiling-high bookshelves of C-floor are so tightly packed that they seem designed to shoulder the weight of the five floors above us. To our left is Microform Services, the dark grotto where professors and grad students huddle in clusters of microfilm machines, squinting at panels of light. Paul begins leading me through the stacks, running his finger along the dusty spines of books as we pass them. I realize he's taking me to his carrel.

"There's a reason everything returns to where it started in this book. Beginnings are the key to the *Hypnerotomachia*. The first letter of every chapter creates the acrostic about Fra Francesco Colonna. The first letters of the architectural terms spell out the first riddle. It's not a coincidence that Francesco made everything come back to beginnings."

In the distance I can see the long rows of green metallic doors, spaced almost as closely as high school lockers. The rooms they guard are no bigger than closets. But hundreds of seniors shut themselves inside for weeks on end to write their theses in peace. Paul's carrel, which I haven't seen in months, sits near the farthest corner.

"Maybe I was just getting tired, but I thought, what if he knew exactly what he was doing? What if you could figure out how to decipher the second half of the book by focusing on something in the very first riddle? Francesco said he didn't leave any solutions, but he didn't say he left no hints. And I had the directions from the portmaster's diary to help me."

We arrive in front of his carrel, and he begins to twist the combination lock on the door. A sheet of black construction paper has been taped to the little rectangular window, making it impossible to see inside.

"I thought the directions had to be about a physical location. How to get from a stadium to a crypt, measured in stadia. Even the portmaster thought the directions were geographical." He shakes his head. "I wasn't thinking like Francesco."

Paul opens the lock and swings the door wide. The little room is filled with books, piles upon piles of them, a tiny version of the President's Room at Ivy. Food wrappers litter the floor. Sheets of paper are taped to the walls, thick as feathers, each one scrawled with a message. *Phineus son of Belus wasn't Phineus king of Salmydessus*, says one. *Check Hesiod: Hesperethousa or Hesperia and Arethousa?* says another. *Buy more crackers*, says a third.

I lift a stack of photocopies from one of the two chairs crammed into the carrel, and try to sit down without knocking anything over.

"So I came back to the riddles," he says. "What was the first riddle about?"

"Moses. The Latin word for horns."

"Right." He turns his back to me to shut the door behind us. "It was about a mistranslation. Philology, historical linguistics. It was about *language*."

He begins searching through a column of books atop the hutch of his desk. Finally he finds what he wants: Hartt's *History of Renaissance Art*.

"Why did we get lucky with the first riddle?" he says.

"Because I had that dream."

"No," he says, finding the page with Michelangelo's sculpture of Moses, the picture that began our partnership. "We got lucky because the riddle was about something verbal, and we were looking for something physical. Francesco didn't care about actual, physical horns; he cared about a word, a mistranslation. We got lucky because that mistranslation eventually manifested itself physically. Michelangelo carved his Moses with horns, and you remembered that. If it hadn't been for the physical manifestation, we would never have found the linguistic answer. But that was the key: the *words*."

"So you looked for a linguistic representation of the directions."

"Exactly. North, south, east, and west aren't *physical* clues. They're *verbal* ones. When I looked at the second half of the book, I knew I was right. The word *stadia* shows up near the beginning of the very first chapter. Look," he says, finding a sheet of paper where he's worked something out.

There are three sentences written on the page: *Gil and Charlie go to the stadium to watch Princeton vs. Harvard. Tom waits as Paul catches up. Katie takes photographs while winsomely smiling and mouthing, I love you, Tom.*

"Winsomely?" I say.

"Doesn't look like much, right? It just sort of rambles, like Poliphilo's story. But plot it out in a grid," he says, turning the piece of paper over. "And you get this:"

```
G i l a n d C h a r l i e g o t o t
h e s t a d i u m t o w a t c h P r
i n c e t o n v s . H a r v a r d .
T o m w a i t s a s P a u l c a t c
h e s u p . K a t i e t a k e s p h
o t o g r a p h s w h i l e w i n s
o m e l y s m i l i n g a n d m o u
t h i n g , I l o v e y o u , T o m
```

I'm waiting for something to jump out at me, but it doesn't.

"That's it?" I ask.

"That's it. Just follow the directions. Four south, ten east, two north, six west. *De Stadio*—'from stadium.' Start with the 's' in 'stadium.' "

I find a pen on his desk and try it out, moving down four, right ten, up two, and left six.

```
G  i  l  a  n  d  C  h  a  r  l  i  e  g  o  t  o  t
h  e  S  t  a  d  i  u  m  t  o  w  a  t  c  h  P  r
i  n  |  e  t  o  n  v  s  .  H  a  r  v  a  r  d  .
T  o  |  w  a  i  T —————————— U  l  c  a  t  c
h  e  |  u  p  .  K  a  t  i  e  t  |  k  e  s  p  h
o  t  O —————————————— L  e  w  i  n  s
o  m  e  l  y  s  m  i  l  i  n  g  a  n  d  m  o  u
t  h  i  n  g  ,  I  l  o  v  e  y  o  u  ,  T  o  m
```

I write down the letters S-O-L-U-T.

"Then repeat the process," he says, "starting with the last letter."

I begin again from T.

```
G  i  l  a  n  d  C  h  a  r  l  i  e  g  o  t  o  t
h  e  S  t  a  d  i  u  m  t  o  w  a  t  c  h  P  r
i  n  |  e  t  o  n  v  s  .  H  a  r  v  a  r  d  .
T  o  |  w  a  i  T —————————— U  l  c  a  t  c
h  e  |  u  p  .  |  a  t  i  e  t  |  k  e  s  p  h
o  t  O —————|—————————— L  e  w  i  N  s
o  m  e  l  y  s  |  i  l  i  n  g  a  n  d  m  |  u
t  h  i  n  g  ,  I —————————————— O  m
```

And there it is, laid out on the page: S-O-L-U-T-I-O-N.

"*That's* the Rule of Four," Paul says. "It's so simple once you understand how Colonna's mind works. Four directions *within* the text. Just repeat it over and over again, then figure out where the word breaks are."

"But it must've taken Colonna months to write."

He nods. "The funny thing is, I'd always noticed there were certain lines in the *Hypnerotomachia* that seemed even more disorganized than others—places where words didn't really fit, where clauses were in strange places, where the weirdest neologisms turned up. It makes sense now. Francesco had to write the text to fit the pattern. It explains why he used so many languages. If the vernacular word didn't fit in the spaces, he would have to try the Latin word, or make one up himself. He even made a bad choice with the pattern. Look."

Paul points to the line where O, L, and N appear.

"See how many cipher letters are on that one line? And there'll be another one once you go six west again. The four-south, two-north pattern doubles back on itself, so every other line in the *Hypnerotomachia*, Francesco had to find text that fit four different letters. But it worked. No one in five hundred years picked up on it."

"But the letters in the book aren't printed that way," I say, wondering how he applied the technique to the actual text. "Letters aren't spaced evenly in a grid. How do you figure out what's exactly north or south?"

He nods. "You can't, because it's hard to say which letter is directly above or below another. I had to work it out mathematically instead of graphically."

It still amazes me, the way he teases simplicity and complexity out of the same idea.

"Take what I wrote, for example. In this case there are"—he counts something—"eighteen letters per line, right? If you work it out, that means 'four south' will always be four lines straight down, which is the same as seventy-two letters to the right of the original starting point. Using the same math, 'two north' will be the same as thirty-six letters to the left. Once you know the length of Francesco's standard line, you can just figure out the math and do everything that way. After a while, you get pretty quick at counting the letters."

In our partnership, it occurs to me, the only thing I ever had that could compare to the speed of Paul's reasoning was my intuition—luck, dreams, chance associations. It hardly seems fair to him that we worked together as equals.

Paul folds the sheet of paper and places it in the trash can. For a second he looks around the carrel, then lifts a stack of books and places it in the crook of my arm, followed by a stack for himself. The painkiller must still be working, because my shoulder doesn't buckle under the heft.

"I'm amazed you figured it out," I tell him. "What did it say?"

"Help me put these back on the shelves first," he answers. "I want to empty this place out."

"Why?"

"Just to be safe."

"From what?"

He half-smiles at me. "Library fines?"

We exit the carrel and Paul guides me toward a long corridor extending far into the darkness. There are bookshelves on either side, branching off into aisles of their own, dead ends begetting dead ends. We are in a corner of the library visited so rarely that the librarians keep the lights off, letting visitors flick the switch on each shelf when they come.

"I couldn't believe it, when I finished," he says. "Even before I was through decoding, I was shaking. It was done. After all this time, *done*."

He stops at one of the rearmost shelves, and I can make out only the silhouette of his face.

"And it was worth it, Tom. I never even saw it coming, what was in the second half of the book. Remember what we saw in Bill's letter?"

"Yes."

"Most of that letter was a lie. You know that work is mine, Tom. The most Bill ever did was translate a few Arabic characters. He made some copies and checked out some books. Everything else I did on my own."

"I know," I say.

Paul covers his mouth with his hand for a second.

"That's not true. Without everything your father and Richard found, and everything the rest of you solved— you, especially—I couldn't have done it. I didn't do it all on my own. The rest of you showed me the way."

Paul invokes my father's name, and Richard Curry's, as if they are a pair of saints, two martyrs from the paintings in Taft's lecture. For a moment I feel like Sancho Panza, listening to Don Quixote. The giants he sees are nothing but windmills, I know, and yet he's the one who sees clearly in the dark, and I'm the one doubting my eyes. Maybe that's been the rub all along, I think: we are animals of imagination. Only a man who sees giants can ever stand upon their shoulders.

"But Bill was right about one thing," Paul says. "The results *will* cast a shadow over everything else in historical studies. For a long time."

He takes the stack of books from my hands, and suddenly I feel weightless. The corridor behind us extends toward a light in the distance, open aisles verging off into space on each side. Even in the darkness, I can see the way Paul smiles.

Chapter 22

We begin making trips back and forth from the carrel, replacing dozens of books, most of them on shelves where they don't belong. Paul only seems to care that they're out of sight.

"Do you remember what was going on in Italy just before the *Hypnerotomachia* was published?" he asks.

"Just what was in the Vatican tour book."

Paul lifts another pile of books into my arms as we walk back into the darkness.

"The intellectual life of Italy during Francesco's day revolves around a single city," he says.

"Rome."

But Paul shakes his head. "Smaller than that. The size of Princeton—the campus, not the town."

I see how enchanted he is by what he's found, how real it's become for him already.

"In that town," he says, "you've got more intellectuals than anyone knows what to do with. Geniuses. Polymaths. Thinkers who are gunning for the big answers to the big questions. Autodidacts who have taught themselves ancient languages no one else knows. Philosophers who are combining religious points from the Bible with ideas from Greek and Roman texts, Egyptian mysticism, Persian manuscripts so old nobody knows how to date them. The absolute cutting edge of humanism. Think of the riddles. University professors playing Rithmomachia. Translators interpreting Horapollo. Anatomists revising Galen."

In my mind's eye the dome of Santa Maria del Fiore comes into focus. My father liked to call it the mother city of modern scholarship. "Florence," I say.

"Right. But that's only the beginning. In every other discipline, you've got the biggest names in Europe. In architecture you've got Brunelleschi, who engineered the largest cathedral dome in a thousand years. In sculpture you've got Ghiberti, who created a set of reliefs so beautiful that they're known as the doors of paradise. And you've got Ghiberti's assistant, who grows up to become the father of modern sculpture—Donatello."

"The painters weren't bad either," I remind him.

Paul smiles. "The single greatest concentration of genius in the history of Western art, all in this little town. Applying new techniques, inventing new theories of perspective, transforming painting from a craft into a science and an art. There must've been three dozen of them, like Alberti, who would've been considered first-class anywhere else in the world. But in this town, they're second-rate. That's because they're competing with the giants. Masaccio. Botticelli. Michelangelo."

As the momentum of his ideas increases, his feet move faster down the dark hallways.

"You want scientists?" he says. "How about Leonardo da Vinci. You want politicians? Machiavelli. Poets? Boccaccio and Dante. And a lot of these guys were contemporaries. On top of it all, you have the Medici, a family so rich it could afford to patronize as many artists and intellectuals as the town could produce.

"All of them, together, in the same small city, at basically the same time. The greatest cultural heroes in all of Western history, crossing each other in the streets, knowing each other on a first-name basis, talking to each other, working together, competing, influencing and pushing each other to go further than they could've gone alone. All in a place where beauty and truth are king, where leading families fight over who can commission the greatest art, who can subsidize the most brilliant thinkers, who can own the biggest library. Imagine that. All of that. It's like a dream. An impossibility."

We return to his carrel and he finally takes a seat.

"Then, in the last few years of the fifteenth century, just before the *Hypnerotomachia* is written, something even more amazing happens. Something that every Renaissance scholar knows about, but that no one has ever connected with the book. Francesco's riddle kept talking about a powerful preacher in the land of his brethren. I just couldn't figure out what the connection could be."

"I thought Luther wasn't until 1517. Colonna was writing in the 1490s."

"Not Luther," he says. "In the late 1400s, a Dominican

monk was sent to Florence to join a monastery called San Marco."

Suddenly it dawns on me. "Savonarola."

The great evangelical preacher, who galvanized Florence at the turn of the century, trying to restore the city's faith at any cost.

"Exactly," Paul says. "Savonarola's a straight arrow—the straightest you'd ever meet. And when he gets to Florence, he begins to preach. He tells people that their behavior is wicked, their culture and art are profane, their government is unjust. He says God looks unkindly on them. He tells them to repent."

I shake my head.

"I know how it sounds," Paul goes on, "but he's *right*. In a way, the Renaissance *is* a godless time. The Church is corrupt. The pope's a political appointee. Prospero Colonna, Francesco's uncle, allegedly dies of gout, and some people think Pope Alexander poisoned him because he came from a rival family. That's the kind of world it is, where people suspect the pope of murder. And that was only the beginning—they suspected him of sadism, incest, you name it.

"Meanwhile, for all of its cutting-edge art and scholarship, Florence is in constant upheaval. Factions fight each other in the streets, prominent families plot against each other to gain power, and even though the city is supposedly a republic, the Medici control everything. Death is common, extortion and coercion are even more common, injustice and inequality are a rule of life. It's a pretty disturbing place, considering all the beautiful things that come out of it.

"So Savonarola arrives in Florence and sees evil wherever he looks. He urges the citizens to clean up their lives, to stop gambling, to start reading the Bible, to help the poor and feed the hungry. At San Marco he begins to gain a following. Even some of the leading humanists admire him. They realize he's well read and conversant about philosophy. Little by little, Savonarola's on the rise."

I stop him. "I thought this was still while the Medici controlled the city."

Paul shakes his head. "Unfortunately for them, their newest heir, Piero, was a fool. He couldn't run the city. The people began to clamor for liberty, a hallowed cry in Florence, and finally the Medici were expelled. Remember the forty-eighth woodcut? The child in the chariot, butchering the two women?"

"The one Taft showed in his lecture."

"Right. That's how Vincent always interpreted it. The punishment was supposed to be for treason. Did he say what he thought it meant?"

"No. He wanted the audience to solve it."

"But he asked about the child in it. Why does he have a sword—something like that?"

I can picture Taft standing beneath the image, his shadow cast onto the screen. "*Why does he make the women pull his chariot through the forest, then kill them that way?*" I say.

"Vincent's theory was that the Cupid figure was supposed to be Piero, the new Medici heir. Piero behaved like a child, so that's how the artist represented him. Because of him, the Medici lost their hold on Florence and were thrown out. So the woodcuts show him retreating through the woods."

"So who are the women?"

"Florence and Italy, Vincent says. By acting like a child, Piero destroyed them both."

"Seems possible."

"It's a decent interpretation," Paul agrees, patting his hand on the underside of his desk, searching for something. "Just not the right one. Vincent refused to accept that the acrostic rule was the key. He would never believe that the first of those images was the important one. He could only see things his way.

"The point is, when the Medici were expelled, the other leading families met to discuss a new government in Florence. The only problem was, no one trusted anyone else. In the end they agreed to let Savonarola take a place of authority. He was the one man everyone knew was incorruptible.

"So Savonarola's popularity grows even more. People begin to take his sermons to heart. Shopkeepers start reading the Bible in their spare time. Gamblers aren't as open about their card games. Drinking and disorder seem to be on the decline. But Savonarola sees that the evils persist. So he steps up his program for civic and spiritual improvement."

Paul reaches even farther beneath his desk. With the sound of tape peeling, he produces a single manila envelope. Inside is a calendar he has drawn up in his own hand. When he flips through the pages, I can see unfamiliar religious holidays marked in red pen—saints' days, feast days—and in black a series of notes I can't make out.

"It's February of 1497," he says, pointing at that month, "two years before the *Hypnerotomachia* is published, and Lent is approaching. Now, the tradition was this: since Lent was a period of fasting and self-denial, the days leading up to it were a period of celebration, a huge festival, so people could enjoy themselves before Lent started. Just like today, that period was called Carnival. Since the forty days of Lent always start on Ash Wednesday, Carnival always culminates the day before—on Fat Tuesday, or Mardi Gras."

Flashes of what he's telling me seem familiar. My father must have told me some of this once, before he gave up on me, or I gave up on him. Or maybe it's just what little I learned in church, before I was old enough to choose how I spent my Sunday mornings.

Paul unearths another diagram. The title reads FLORENCE, 1500.

"Carnival in Florence was a period of huge disorder, drunkenness, debauchery. Gangs of young men would bar street entrances and force people to pay a toll for safe passage. Then they would spend the money on alcohol and gambling."

He points at a large space in the middle of the drawing.

"When they were all completely drunk, they would camp out around fires in the main square and finish the night in a huge brawl, each group throwing stones at the other. Every year people were hurt, even killed.

"Savonarola, of course, is Carnival's most vocal opponent. In his eyes, a challenge has risen against Christianity, leading the people of Florence into temptation. And he recognizes that there's one force, more powerful than the others, contributing to the city's corruption. It teaches men that pagan authorities can rival the Bible, that wisdom and beauty should be worshiped in unchristian things. It leads men to believe that human life is a quest for earthly knowledge and satisfaction, distracting them from the only object that matters: salvation. The force is humanism. And its greatest advocates are the leading intellectuals of the city, the humanists.

"That's when Savonarola comes up with the idea that's probably his greatest legacy to history. He decides that on Shrove Tuesday, the culminating day of Carnival, he will stage a huge event—something that will show the progress and transformation of the city, but at the same time remind the Florentines of their sinfulness. He lets the gangs of young men roam the city, but now he gives them a purpose. He tells them to collect unchristian objects from every neighborhood and bring them back to the main square. He puts all of the objects in a huge pyramid. And on that day, Shrove Tuesday, when the street gangs would usually be sitting around fires and fighting each other with stones, Savonarola has them building another kind of fire." Paul looks at his map, then fixes his eyes on me.

"The bonfire of the vanities," I say.

"Right. The gangs returned with cart after cart. They came back with cards and dice. Chessboards. Eye shadow, rouge pots, perfume, hair nets, jewelry. Carnival masks and costumes. But most importantly, pagan books. Manuscripts by Greek and Roman writers. Classical sculptures and paintings."

Paul returns his drawing to the manila envelope. His voice is somber.

"On Shrove Tuesday, the seventh of February, 1497, the city came out to watch. Records say the pyramid was sixty feet high, two hundred and seventy feet around at its base. And all of it went up in flames.

"The bonfire of the vanities becomes an unforgettable moment in Renaissance history." He pauses, looking past me at the scraps of paper on the wall. They heave faintly when the vent puffs air into the carrel. "Savonarola becomes famous. Before long he's known throughout Italy and beyond. His sermons are printed and read in half a dozen countries. He's admired and hated. Michelangelo was captivated by him. Machiavelli thought he was a fake. But everyone had an opinion, and everyone admitted his power. Everyone."

I see where he's leading me. "Including Francesco Colonna."

"And that's where the *Hypnerotomachia* comes in."

"So it's a manifesto?"

"Of sorts. Francesco couldn't stand Savonarola. To him, Savonarola represented the worst kind of fanaticism, everything that was wrong with Christianity. He was destructive. Vengeful. He refused to let men use the gifts God gave them. Francesco was a humanist, a lover of antiquity. He and his cousins spent their early years studying with the great instructors of ancient prose and poetry. By the time he was thirty, he had amassed one of the most important collections of original manuscripts in Rome.

"Long before the first bonfire, he had been gathering art and books, employing merchants in Florence to buy up what they could and ship it to one of his family estates in Rome. It put a major rift between Francesco and his family, because they believed he was squandering his money on Florentine trinkets. But as Savonarola gained power, Francesco became more resolute: he couldn't bear to think of the pyramid going up in smoke, no matter what the cost to him or his fortune. Marble busts, Botticelli paintings, hundreds of priceless objects. And most of all, the books. The rare, irreplaceable books. He stood at the other end of the intellectual universe from Savonarola. To him, the greatest violence in the world was against art, against knowledge.

"In the summer of 1497, Francesco travels to Florence, to see for himself. And what everyone else admires about Savonarola—his holiness, his ability to think about nothing but salvation—makes Francesco feel the deepest kind of hatred and fear. He sees what Savonarola is capable of doing: destroying the greatest artifacts of the first resurgence in classical learning since the fall of ancient Rome. He sees the death of art, the death of knowledge, the death of the classical spirit. And the death of humanism: the end of the quest to overstep boundaries and exceed limitations, to see the full possibility of thought."

"*That's* what he wrote about in the second half of the book?"

Paul nods again. "Francesco wrote everything into it, all the things he was too scared to come out and say in the first half. He recorded what he saw in Florence, and what he feared. That Savonarola was growing in influence. That he would somehow earn the ear of the French king. That he had admirers throughout Germany and Italy. You can see it increasing, the longer Francesco writes. He became more and more convinced that there were legions of supporters behind Savonarola, in every country of Christendom. *This preacher,* he wrote, *is only the beginning of a new spirit of Christianity. There will be uprisings of fanatical preachers, outbreaks of bonfires throughout Italy.* He says Europe is on the brink of a religious revolution. And with the Reformation approaching, he's *right.* Savonarola won't be around to see it happen, but like you said, when

Luther sets things into motion a few years later, he'll re-member Savonarola as a hero."

"So Colonna saw it all coming."

"Yes. And after seeing Savonarola for himself, Francesco takes a stand. He decides to use his connections to do what very few other people in Rome, or anywhere in the West, could've done about it. Using a small network of trusted friends, he begins to collect even more great works of art and rare manuscripts. He communicates with a huge network of humanists and painters to gather to-gether as many treasures, as many artifacts of human knowledge and achievement, as possible. He bribes ab-bots and librarians, aristocrats and businessmen. Mer-chants travel to cities across the continent for him. They go to the ruins of the Byzantine Empire, where ancient learning is still preserved. They go to infidel lands for Arabic texts. They go to monasteries in Germany, France, and the North. And the whole time, Francesco keeps his identity a secret, protected by his closest friends and hu-manist brothers. Only they know what he intends to do with all of these treasures."

Suddenly I remember the portmaster's diary. Genovese, wondering what could possibly be carried on such a small ship, coming from such an obscure port. Wondering why a nobleman like Francesco Colonna would be so inter-ested in it.

"He finds masterpieces," Paul continues. "Works that no one has seen for hundreds of years. Titles no one knew even existed. Aristotle's *Eudemus*, *Protrepticus*, and *Gryllus*. Greco-Roman imitations by Michelangelo. All forty-two volumes by Hermes Trismegistus, the Egyptian prophet believed to be older than Moses. He finds thirty-eight plays of Sophocles, twelve by Euripides, twenty-three by Aeschylus, all of them considered lost today. In a single German monastery he finds philosophical treatises by Parmenides, Empedocles, and Democritus, all squirreled away for centuries by monks. A scout in the Adriatic discovers works by the ancient painter Apelles—the portrait of Alexander, the Aphrodite Anadyomene, and the line of Protogenes—and Francesco is so excited he tells the scout to buy them even if they might be fakes. A librarian in Constantinople sells him the *Chaldaean Oracles* for a small pig's weight in silver—and Francesco calls it a bargain because the oracles' author, Zoroaster the Persian, is the only known prophet older than Hermes Trismegistus. Seven chapters by Tacitus and a book by Livy appear at the end of Francesco's list as if they're nothing. He almost forgets to mention half a dozen works by Botticelli."

Paul shakes his head, imagining it. "In less than two years, Francesco Colonna assembles one of the greatest libraries of ancient art and literature in the Renaissance world. He brings two seamen into his inner circle to captain his ships and move his cargo. He employs the sons of the trusted members of the Roman Academy to protect caravans traveling roads across Europe. He tests the men he suspects of treachery, recording their every move so he can cover his tracks. Francesco knew he could only trust his secret to a select few, and he was willing to do whatever it took to protect it."

It's hitting me now, the full force of what my father and I stumbled onto: a single loose thread in a web of communication between Colonna and his assistants, a network designed for the sole purpose of protecting the nobleman's secret.

"Maybe Rodrigo and Donato weren't the only ones he tested," I suggest. "Maybe there are more belladonna letters."

"Probably," he says. "And when Francesco was done, he put everything he owned in a place no one would ever think to look. A place where he says his treasures will be safe from his enemies."

I know it even before he says it.

"He petitions the senior members of his family for access to the huge tracts of land they own outside Rome, under the pretext of a profit-making enterprise. But instead of building above ground, in the middle of the forests where his ancestors used to hunt, he designs his crypt. A huge underground vault. Only five of his men ever know its location.

"Then, as 1498 approaches, Francesco makes a crucial decision. In Florence, Savonarola seems to be more popular than ever. He declares that on Shrove Tuesday he will build a bonfire even bigger than the last one. Francesco records part of the speech in the *Hypnerotomachia*. He says all of Italy is at a fever pitch with this new kind of religious madness—and he fears for his treasures. He's spent virtually all of his fortune already, and with Savonarola gaining a foothold in the mind of Western Europe, he senses that goods are becoming harder to move and hide. So he gathers up all that he's collected, places it in the crypt, and seals it off for good."

Slowly it occurs to me that one of the oddest details of the second message finally makes sense. *My crypt*, Colonna wrote, *is an unequalled contrivance for its purpose, impervious to all things, but above all to water.* He waterproofed the vault, knowing that otherwise, locked underground, his treasures would rot.

"He decides that in the days before the bonfire is lit," Paul continues, "he will travel to Florence. He will go to San Marco. And in a final attempt to defend his cause, he will confront Savonarola. By appealing to the man's love of learning, his respect for truth and beauty, Francesco will persuade him to remove the objects of lasting value from the bonfire. He will stop the preacher from destroying what the humanists consider sacred.

"But Francesco is a realist. After hearing Savonarola's sermons, he knows how fiery the man is, how convinced he is that the bonfires are righteous. If Savonarola won't join him, Francesco knows he has only one choice. He must show Florence how barbaric the prophet really is. He will go to the bonfire and remove the objects from the pyramid himself. If Savonarola tries to light the fire anyway, Francesco will be martyred on the pyre, in front of the entire city. He will force Savonarola to become a murderer. Only this, he says, will turn Florence against fanaticism— and with Florence, the rest of Europe."

"He was willing to die for it," I say, half to myself.

"He was willing to *kill* for it," Paul says. "Francesco had five close humanist friends in his confraternity of brothers. One was Terragni, the architect. Two were a pair of real brothers, Matteo and Cesare. The final two were Rodrigo and Donato, and they died for betraying him. He would've done anything to protect what he believed in."

The tiny space of the carrel seems to warp for a second, angles colliding like fragments of time intersecting. I see my father again, writing the manuscript of *The Belladonna*

Document on the old typewriter in his office. He knew exactly what that letter meant; he just didn't know its context. Now Paul has found its place. Though there's a sudden satisfaction to that, there's also a growing sadness I feel as Paul continues his story. The more I hear about Francesco Colonna, the desperate man who couldn't trust even his friends, the more I think of Paul, slaving over the *Hypnerotomachia* the same way Colonna did, on either end of a single thread in time, a writer and a reader. Vincent Taft may have tried to poison Paul against us, telling him that friends were fickle, but the more I see what Paul has done for this book—how he has lived in it for years now, the way I only lived in it for months—the better I understand. It was Francesco Colonna, as much as any living man, who made him doubt.

Chapter 23

"In the months before Francesco leaves for Florence," Paul says, "he takes the one precaution he thinks is foolproof. He decides to write a book. A book that will disclose the location of the crypt, but only to a fellow scholar—not to a layman, and above all, not to the fanatics. He's convinced that no one could solve it except a true lover of knowledge—one who would fear Savonarola as much as Francesco does, and who would never allow the treasures to be burned. And he dreams of a time when humanism will reign again, and the collection will be safe.

"So he finishes the book and asks Terragni to have it delivered anonymously, by courier, to Aldus. By pretending to be its patron, he says he will urge Aldus to keep the book under wraps. He won't identify himself as the author, so that no one will suspect what's in it.

"Then, as Carnival nears, Francesco enlists the

architect and the two brothers, the only three remaining members of his Roman Academy circle, and travels to Florence. They are men of principle, but Francesco understands how difficult their task is, so he insists that every man take an oath to die, if necessary, at the Piazza della Signoria.

"On the night before the bonfire, he asks all three friends to join him for a meal and a prayer. They tell stories of their adventures together, their travels, the things they've done in their lifetimes. That entire evening, though, Francesco says he can see a dark shadow gathering over their heads. He doesn't sleep that night. The next morning, he goes to meet Savonarola.

"From that point forward, all of the text is written by the architect. Francesco says Terragni is the only man he can trust with such a task. Knowing he'll need someone to oversee his interests should anything happen in Florence, he gives Terragni a huge vote of confidence. He gives the architect his final cipher and asks him to add a postscript, coded into the final chapters, to describe what becomes of the friends from the Roman Academy. He gives Terragni the responsibility of supervising the *Hypnerotomachia* after it reaches Aldus, to be sure it makes it into print. Francesco says he has had a vision of his own death, and knows he can't accomplish everything he wants by himself. He takes Terragni with him to record the meeting with Savonarola.

"By then, Savonarola is waiting for them at his cell in the monastery. The meeting was arranged ahead of time, so both sides are prepared. Francesco, trying to be diplomatic, says he admires Savonarola and shares the same goals, the same hatred of sin. He quotes Aristotle on virtue.

"Savonarola counters by quoting Aquinas, almost an identical passage. He asks Francesco why he prefers a pagan source over a Christian one. Francesco praises Aquinas, but says that Aquinas borrowed from Aristotle. Savonarola loses patience. He delivers a line from the Epistle of Paul: *I am going to destroy the wisdom of the wise and bring to nothing the understanding of any who understand. Do you not see how God has shown up human wisdom as folly?*

"Francesco listens with terror. He asks Savonarola why he won't embrace art and scholarship, why he is bent on destroying them. He tells Savonarola that they should be united against sin, that faith is the source of truth and beauty, that they can't be enemies. But Savonarola shakes his head. He says truth and beauty are only *servants* of faith. When they are anything else, pride and profit lead men into sin.

" 'And so,' he says to Francesco, 'I will not be dissuaded. There is more evil in those books and canvases than in all the rest that will be burned. For while playing cards and dice may distract the foolish, your "wisdom" is the temptation of the powerful and the mighty. The greatest families of this city vie to be your patrons. Your philosophers preach to the poets, whose works are widely read. You contaminate the painters with your ideas, and their paintings hang in the palaces of princes, while their frescoes crowd the walls and ceilings of every church. You reach dukes and kings, because they surround themselves with your followers, demanding guidance from the astrologers and engineers who are indebted to you, hiring your scholars to translate their books. No,' he says, 'I will not let pride and profit govern Florence any longer. The truth and beauty you love are false idols, vanities, and they will lead men into wickedness.'

"Francesco is about to leave, knowing his cause will never be reconciled with Savonarola's, but in a last second of anger, he turns and tells Savonarola what he intends to do. 'If you will not accede to my demands,' Francesco says, 'then I will show all the world that you are a madman, not a prophet. I will carry each book and painting from your pyramid until the fire destroys me, so that my blood will be on your hands. And the world will turn against you.'

"He prepares to leave again, when Savonarola says something Francesco never expects. 'My mind cannot be changed,' he says, 'but if you are willing to die for these convictions, then I offer you my respect, and I look on you as a son. Any cause that is true in God's eyes will be reborn, and any martyr who is true to a holy cause will rise from his own ashes and be transported to heaven. I do not wish to see a man of your convictions perish, but the men you represent, who own the objects you intend to save, are moved only by greed and vanity. They will never be reconciled to God's will, except by force. It is sometimes God's design to sacrifice the innocent to test the faithful, and perhaps it is just so now.'

"Francesco is about to contradict him, to argue that knowledge and beauty shouldn't be sacrificed to save corrupt men's souls, when he thinks of his own men, Donato and Rodrigo, and sees the truth of what Savonarola says. He realizes that vanity and avarice are even among the ranks of the humanists, and he understands that there will be no resolution. Savonarola asks him to leave the monastery, because the monks must prepare for the ceremony, and Francesco obeys.

"When he returns to his men with the news, they begin preparing for their final acts. The four men, Francesco and Terragni, Matteo and Cesare, go to the Piazza della Signoria. While Savonarola's assistants prepare the fire, Francesco, Matteo, and Cesare start removing texts and paintings from the pyramid, just as Francesco promised. Terragni stands by, watching and writing. The assistants ask Savonarola if they should stop their preparations, but he says they must continue. As Francesco and the brothers make trip after trip, carrying armfuls of books out of the mound and putting them in a pile at a safe distance, Savonarola tells them the bonfire will be lit. He announces that they will die if they continue. All three men ignore him.

"The entire city, by now, has gathered in the square, waiting to see the fire. The crowd is chanting. The flames begin at the base of the pyramid, and grow. Francesco and the two brothers are still making trips. As the fire gets hotter, they wrap cloths around their mouths to keep from inhaling the smoke. They wear gloves to protect their hands, but the fire burns through them. By the third or fourth trip, their faces are dark with smoke. Their hands and feet are black from rummaging through the fire. The men sense that death is approaching, and at that moment, the architect writes, they realize the glory of martyrdom.

"As their pile grows, Savonarola orders a monk with a wheelbarrow to return the objects to the flames. As soon as the men drop the books and paintings, the monk scoops them up and brings them back. After six or seven trips, everything Francesco has pulled from the fire is already burned. Matteo and Cesare have given up on paintings, because the canvases are destroyed. All three of them stamp at the covers of books with their hands to put out the flames, so the pages won't burn. One of them begins to call out in agony, crying to God.

"By now there's no hope of saving anything. All of the artwork in the pyramid is ruined, most of the books are blackened through. The monk with the wheelbarrow is still pushing everything from their pile back into the fire. Every one of his trips undoes what all three of them do together. Slowly the crowd grows quiet. The whistles and catcalls die out. The people who yelled at Francesco, calling him a fool for trying to save the books, become silent. A few people shout for the men to stop. But the three of them continue their trips, back and forth, throwing their arms into the flames, climbing into the ashes, disappearing for seconds, then reappearing. By now the loudest sound in the square is the roar of the fire. The three men are gasping. They've inhaled too much smoke to scream. Every time they go back to their pile, the architect says, you can make out the red flesh of their hands and feet, where the fire has burned their skin off.

"The first of them collapses into the cinders, facedown. It's Matteo, the youngest. Cesare stops to help, but Francesco drags him away. Matteo doesn't move. The fire crawls over him, and his body sinks into the pyramid. Cesare tries to call out to him, to tell him to stand up, but Matteo doesn't answer. Finally, Cesare stumbles over to the spot where his brother fell. When he's almost standing over Matteo's body, he collapses too. Francesco watches all this from the edge of the bonfire. When he hears Cesare's voice calling for Matteo, then listens to it fade under the fire, he realizes he's alone and falls to his knees. For a second he doesn't move.

"Just as the crowd takes him for dead, he forces himself to his feet. Reaching one last time into the bonfire, he takes two fists of ashes and staggers toward Savonarola. One of Savonarola's assistants blocks his way, but Francesco stops short. He spreads his fingers and lets the ashes fall between them like sand. Then he says, '*Inde ferunt, totidem qui vivere debeat annos, corpore de patrio parvum phoenica renasci.*' It's from Ovid. It means, 'A little phoenix is born anew from the father's body, fated to live the same number of years.' Then he falls at Savonarola's feet and dies.

"Terragni's narrative ends with Colonna's burial. Francesco and the two brothers are given almost imperial funerals by their families and humanist friends. And we know that their martyrdom succeeds. Within weeks, public opinion shifts against Savonarola. Florence is tired of his extremism, his constant doom and gloom. Enemies spread rumors about him, trying to bring about his downfall. Pope Alexander excommunicates him. When Savonarola resists, Alexander declares him guilty of heresy and seditious teaching. He's sentenced to death. On May twenty-third, just three months after Francesco burns to death, Florence sets up a new pyre in the Piazza della Signoria. Right there, on the very spot of the two bonfires, they hang Savonarola and burn his body at the stake."

"What happened to Terragni?" I ask.

"All we know is that he honored his promise to Francesco.

The *Hypnerotomachia* was published by Aldus the following year, 1499."

I rise from my chair, too excited to sit.

"Since then," Paul says, "everyone who's tried to interpret it has been using nineteenth- or twentieth-century tools to pick a fifteenth-century lock." He leans back and exhales. "Until now."

He stops himself, breathless, and falls silent. Footsteps shuffle in the hallway, muffled by the door. I look at him, stunned. Slowly the things of reality, of the true outside, begin to penetrate again, returning Savonarola and Francesco Colonna to a bookshelf in my mind. But there remains an uneasy interaction between the two worlds. I look at Paul, and realize that somehow he has become the crossroads between them, the ligature binding time to itself.

"I can't believe it," I tell him.

My father should be here. My father, and Richard Curry, and McBee. Everyone who ever knew about this book and sacrificed something to solve it. This is a gift for them all.

"Francesco gives directions to the crypt from three different landmarks," Paul says. "It won't be hard to find the location. He even gives the dimensions, and lists everything in it. The only thing that's missing is the blueprint of the lock to the crypt. Terragni designed a special cylinder lock for the entrance. It's so airtight, Francesco says, that it will keep robbers and moisture out for as long as it takes someone to solve his book. He keeps saying he's about to give the blueprint for the lock, and the instructions for opening it, but he always gets distracted, talking about Savonarola. Maybe he told Terragni to include it in the final chapters, but Terragni had so many other things to worry about, he didn't do it."

"And that's what you were looking for at Taft's."

Paul nods. "Richard says there was a blueprint in the portmaster's diary when he found it thirty years ago. I think Vincent kept it when he let Bill find the rest of the diary."

"Did you get it back?"

He shakes his head. "All I got was a handful of Vincent's old handwritten notes."

"So what are you going to do?" I ask.

Paul begins reaching for something else under the desk. "I'm at Vincent's mercy."

"How much have you told him?"

When his hands return to view, they're empty. Losing patience, he moves his chair backward and lowers himself to his knees. "He doesn't know any details about the crypt. Only that it exists."

I notice faint tracks across the floor, ruts that trace quarter-circles back to the metal legs of the desk.

"Last night I started making a map of everything Francesco said about it in the second half of the *Hypnerotomachia*. The location, the dimensions, the landmarks. I knew Vincent might come looking for what I'd found, so I put the map where I used to keep the best work I did in here."

There's a clink of metal against metal, and from the far corner of the desk bottom, Paul produces a screwdriver. The long swatch of tape that secured it to the underside dangles like a weed in his hand. He peels the tape off, then swivels the desk toward us. The front legs slide along the grooves in the tile floor, and suddenly the ventilation duct comes into view. Four screws hold the grille to the wall. The paint has been chipped on all of them.

Paul begins unscrewing the grille. One corner at a time, the vent comes undone. When he reaches into the duct, then removes his hand, he's holding an envelope stuffed with papers. My first instinct is to look out the window of the carrel, to see if anyone's watching us. Now I understand the sheet of black paper that covers it.

Paul opens the envelope. First he pulls out a pair of photographs, each one worn from handling. The first is of Paul and Richard Curry in Italy. They are standing in the middle of the Piazza della Signoria in Florence, directly in front of the Fountain of Neptune. Blurred in the background is a copy of Michelangelo's *David*. Paul is wearing shorts and a backpack; Richard Curry is wearing a suit, but his tie is loose and his collar is unbuttoned. Both of them are smiling.

The second picture is of the four of us, from sophomore year. Paul is kneeling in the middle of the photo, wearing a borrowed tie and holding up a medal. The rest of us are standing around him, with two professors in the background, looking amused. Paul has just won the annual essay contest of the Princeton Francophile Society. We three have shown up as figures from French history to support him. I am Robespierre, Gil is Napoleon, and Charlie, in a huge hoop dress we found at a costume store, is Marie Antoinette.

Paul seems to make nothing of the pictures, placing them gently on the desk as if he's used to seeing them. Now he empties the rest of the envelope. What I mistook for a stack of papers is actually a single large sheet, folded over several times to fit inside.

"This is it," he says, unwrapping it on the surface of the desk.

There, in tiny detail, is a hand-drawn topological map. Elevation lines run in uneven circles, with rough directional markings in a faint grid. Near the middle, written in red, is an angular object shaped like a cross. According to the scale in the corner, it's roughly the size of a dormitory.

"Is that it?" I ask.

He nods.

It's enormous. For a second both of us sit in silence, trying to absorb it.

"What are you going to do with the map?" I ask, now that the carrel is bare.

Paul opens his hand. The four small screws to the ventilation duct roll like seeds in his palm. "Put it somewhere safe."

"Back in the wall?"

"No."

He leans down to screw the face of the duct back in, and looks as if a calm has settled over him. When he rises and begins to pull the sheets of paper from the wall, one after another the messages disappear. Kings and monsters, ancient names, notes he never meant anyone else to see.

"So what are you going to do with it?" I say, still looking at the map.

He crumples the other sheets in his hand. The walls are white again. After sitting down, and folding the map along its creases, he says very evenly, "I'm giving it to you."

"What?"

Paul puts the map into the envelope and hands it to me. He keeps the pictures for himself.

"I promised you'd be the first to know. You deserve to be."

He says it as if he's just keeping his word.

"What do you want *me* to do with it?"

He smiles. "Don't lose it."

"What if Taft comes looking for it?"

"That's the idea. If he does, he'll come looking for me." Paul pauses before speaking again. "And besides, I want you to get used to having it around."

"Why?"

He sits back. "Because I want us to work together. I want us to find Francesco's crypt together."

Finally I understand. "Next year."

He nods. "In Chicago. And Rome."

The vent whirs one last time, whispering through the grille.

"This is yours" is all I can think to say. "Your thesis. You finished it."

"This is so much bigger than a thesis, Tom."

"It's much bigger than a Ph.D. dissertation too."

"Exactly."

Now I hear it in his voice. This is just the beginning.

"I don't want to do this alone," he says.

"What can *I* do?"

He smiles. "Just keep the map for now. Let it burn a hole in your pocket for a while."

It unnerves me, how light the envelope is, the impermanence of what I'm holding. It seems to argue against the reality of all of this, that the wisdom of the *Hypnerotomachia* can sit in the fold of my palm.

"Come on," he says finally, glancing down at his watch. "Let's go home. We need to pick up some things for Charlie."

He takes down the last remnant of his work with one final swoop of his arm. There is no more trace in the carrel of Paul, or of Colonna, or of the long trail of ideas connecting them over five hundred years. The sheet of black paper on the window is gone.

Chapter 24

The last question the recruiter from Daedalus asked during my job interview was a riddle: If a frog falls down a fifty-foot well and has to climb his way out, making three feet of progress every day, but slipping back two feet every night, in how many days will he escape?

Charlie's answer was that he never escapes, because a frog that falls fifty feet doesn't get back up. Paul's answer had something to do with an ancient philosopher who died by walking into a well while staring up at the stars. Gil's answer was that he'd never heard of a frog climbing wells, and what did all this have to do with developing software in Texas, anyway?

The right answer, I think, is that it takes the frog forty-eight days, or two days less than you might expect. The trick is realizing that the frog climbs one foot per day after all is said and done—but on the forty-eighth day, he climbs three feet and reaches the top of the well before he can slide back again.

I don't know what makes me think of that just now. Maybe this is the sort of moment when riddles have an afterglow of their own, a wisdom that illuminates the edges of experience when nothing else can. In a world where half of the villagers always lie and half of them always tell the truth; where the hare never catches the tortoise because the distance between them shrinks by a never-collapsing infinity of halves; where the fox can never be left on the same bank of the river as the hen, or the hen on the same bank as the grain, because with perfect regularity the one will consume the other, and nothing you can do will prevent it: in that world, everything is sensible but the premise. A riddle is a castle built on air, perfectly habitable if you don't look down. The grand impossibility of what Paul has told me—that an ancient rivalry between a monk and a humanist has left a crypt of treasures beneath a forgotten forest—rests on the much more basic impossibility that a book like the *Hypnerotomachia*, written in code, impenetrable, ignored by scholars for five centuries, could exist. It couldn't; yet it's as real to me as I am to myself. And if I accept its existence, then the foundation is set, and the impossible castle can be built. The rest is just mortar and stones.

When the elevator doors open, and the library lobby seems weightless in the wintry light, it feels like we've emerged from a tunnel. Every time I think of that Daedalus riddle, I imagine the frog's surprise when, for the first time, on his last day, three steps forward are not followed by two steps back. There is a suddenness at the top of the well, an unexpected quickening of the journey at its end, that I feel now. The riddle I've known since I was a child—the riddle of the *Hypnerotomachia*—has been solved in less than a day.

We click through the turnstile at the library's front border, and the nip of the wind returns beneath the entrance. Paul presses the door open, and I tighten my coat around me. There is snow everywhere, no stones or walls or shadows, only brilliant tornadoes of white. All around me is Chicago and Texas; graduation; Dod and home. Here I am, suddenly, above ground.

We start south. On the way back to the dorm, a Dumpster has been overturned. Little nests of garbage poke up from mounds of snow, and the squirrels are at them already, pulling out apple cores and near-empty bottles of lotion, passing everything in front of their noses before beginning to eat. They are discriminating little creatures. Experience has taught them that there will always be food here, replenished every day, so everywhere nuts and acorns go unburied. When a vulture-size crow lands on the wheel of the upturned Dumpster, expressing priority, the squirrels just chitter and nibble, ignoring it.

"You know what that crow makes me think of?" Paul says.

I shake my head, and the bird flies off angrily, spreading its wings to a fantastic length, escaping with a single bag of crumbs.

"The eagle that killed Aeschylus by dropping a tortoise on him," Paul says.

I have to glance at him to see that he's serious.

"Aeschylus was bald," he continues. "The eagle was

trying to break the shell open by dropping it on a rock. It couldn't tell the difference."

This reminds me again of the philosopher who fell down the well. Paul's mind is always doing that, tucking the present into the past, making yesterday's bed.

"If you could be anywhere right now," I ask him, "where would it be?"

He looks over at me, amused. "Anywhere?"

I nod.

"In Rome, with a shovel."

A squirrel looks up from a slice of bread he's found, watching us.

Paul turns to me. "What about you? Texas?"

"No."

"Chicago?"

"I don't know."

We pass through the rear courtyard of the art museum, the one separating it from Dod. There are footprints here, back and forth in zigzags.

"You know what Charlie told me?" he says, staring at the marks in the snow.

"What?"

"If you fire a gun, the bullet falls as fast as if you'd dropped it."

This sounds like something I learned in introductory physics.

"You can never outrun gravity," Paul says. "No matter how fast you go, you're still falling like a rock. It makes you wonder if horizontal motion is an illusion. If we move just to convince ourselves we're not falling."

"Where are you going with this?"

"The tortoise shell," he says. "It was part of a prophecy. An oracle said Aeschylus would die of a blow from heaven."

A blow from heaven, I think. God, laughing.

"Aeschylus couldn't escape an oracle," Paul continues. "We can't escape gravity." He weaves his fingers together, a dovetail. "Heaven and earth, speaking in one voice."

His eyes are wide, trying to take in everything, a kid at the zoo.

"You probably say that to all the girls," I tell him.

He smiles. "Sorry. Sensory overload. I'm all over the place. I don't know why."

I do. There's someone else to worry about the crypt now, someone else to worry about the *Hypnerotomachia*. Atlas feels lighter without the world on his shoulders.

"It's like your question," he says, walking backward in front of me as we head toward the room. "If you could be anywhere, where would you be?" He opens his palms, and the truth seems to land in his hands. "Answer: it doesn't matter, because wherever you go, you're still falling."

He smiles when he says it, as if there's nothing depressing about the idea that we're all just in free-fall. The ultimate equality of going anywhere, doing anything, Paul seems to mean, is that being in Dod with me is as good as being in Rome with a shovel. In his own way, I think, in his own words, what he's saying is that he's happy.

He fishes for his key and slips it into the lock. The room is still when we enter. So much action has circled this place since yesterday, break-ins and proctors and police officers, it's unsettling to see it empty and dark.

Paul wanders into the bedroom to put down his coat. Instinctively, I lift the phone and check our voicemail.

Hey, Tom, Gil's voice begins, through a hiss of static. *I'll try to catch up to you guys later but . . . looks like I won't be able to get back to the hospital after all so . . . Charlie for me. . . . Tom . . . black tie. You can borrow . . . need to.*

Black tie. The ball.

By now the second message has begun.

Tom, it's Katie. Just wanted to let you know I'm going to the club to help set up as soon as I'm done here in the darkroom. I think you said you were coming with Gil. A pause. *So I guess we'll talk tonight.*

There's a hesitation before she hangs up, as if she's unsure she put the right emphasis on those last words, the reminder of unfinished business.

"What's going on?" Paul calls from the bedroom.

"I have to get ready," I say quietly, sensing the turn things are taking.

Paul comes out of the room. "For what?"

"The ball."

He doesn't understand. I never told him what Katie and I talked about in the darkroom. What I've seen today, everything he's told me, has turned the world on its ear. But in the silence that follows, I find myself standing where I've stood before. The ancient mistress, forsworn, has returned to tempt me. There is a cycle here which, until this moment, I've been too engrossed to break. Colonna's book flatters me with visions of perfection, an unreality I can inhabit for the tiny price of my mad devotion, my withdrawal from the world. Francesco, having invented this strange bargain, also invented its name: *Hypnerotomachia*, the struggle for love in a dream. If ever there were a time to stay grounded, to resist that struggle and its dream—if ever there were a time to remember a love that has devoted itself madly to *me*, to remember the promise I made to Katie—that time is now.

"What's wrong?" Paul asks.

I don't know how to tell him. I'm not even sure *what* to tell him.

"Here," I say, extending my arm.

But he doesn't move.

"Take the map."

"Why?" At first he only looks puzzled, still too excited to follow.

"I can't do it, Paul. I'm sorry."

His smile fades. "What do you mean?"

"I can't work on this anymore." I place the map in his hand. "It's yours."

"It's ours," he says, wondering what's come over me.

But it isn't. It doesn't belong to us; from the beginning, we have belonged to the book.

"I'm sorry. I can't do it."

Not here; not in Chicago; not in Rome.

"You *did* it," he says. "It's done. All we need is the blueprint for the lock."

The certainty of it, though, is already between us. A look is crawling into his eyes, a drowning look, as if the force that once buoyed him up has suddenly let him down, and all the world is topsy-turvy. We have spent so much time together that I can see it without his even having to say a word: the freedom I feel, my emancipation from a chain of events that began before I was born, is mirrored in reverse with him.

"It's not either/or," he says, gathering himself up. "You could have both if you wanted to."

"I don't think so."

"Your father did."

But he knows my father didn't.

"You don't need my help," I tell him. "You've got what you want."

But I know he doesn't.

A strange silence follows, each of us sensing that the other is right, but that neither of us is wrong. The math of morality falters. He looks as if he wants to plead with me, to make his case one last time, but it's hopeless and he knows it.

Instead, Paul quietly repeats a joke I've heard a thousand times from Gil. He's got no other words for what he's feeling.

"The last man on earth walks into a bar," he murmurs. "What does he say?"

Paul turns his head toward the window, but doesn't offer the punch line. We both know what the last man on earth says. He looks into his beer, lonely and besotted, and says, "Drink, I'd like another bartender."

"I'm sorry," I tell him.

Paul is somewhere else now, though. "I need to find Richard," he mumbles.

"Paul?"

He turns. "What do you want me to say?"

"What do you want from Curry?"

"Remember what I asked you on the way to Firestone?" he says. "What would've happened if I'd never picked up your dad's book? Remember what you answered?"

"I said we never would have met."

A thousand delicate accidents have piled up just so that he and I would meet—so that we could be here, now.

Destiny, from the shambles of five hundred years, has fashioned a castle in the air so that two college boys could be kings. This, he means, is how I treat it.

"When you see Gil," he says, picking up his coat from the floor, "tell him he can have the President's Room back. I don't need it anymore."

Thinking of his car, broken down on a side street by the Institute, I imagine him walking through the snow to find Curry.

"It's not safe to go alone . . ." I begin.

But alone is how he's always gone. He's already walking out the door.

I might have followed him, had the hospital not called a minute later to relay a message from Charlie.

"He's up and talking," the nurse says. "And he's asking for you."

I'm already putting on my hat and gloves.

Halfway to the medical center it stops snowing. For a few blocks there's even a sun visible above the horizon. Clouds everywhere take the shape of table settings—tureens and soup bowls and pitchers, a fork rolling by with a spoon—and I realize how hungry I am. I hope Charlie's doing as well as the nurse said. I hope they're feeding him.

I arrive to find the door to the room blocked by the one person who is more physically intimidating than Charlie: his mother. Mrs. Freeman is explaining to a doctor that after taking the first train from Philadelphia to be here, and listening to a man from the dean's office say that Charlie is dangerously close to suspension, and being a nurse practitioner for seventeen years herself before becoming a science teacher, she is in no mood to have a doctor condescend to her about what's wrong with her son. From the color of his scrubs I recognize him as the man who told Paul and me that Charlie was in stable condition. He of the hospital words and canned smiles. He doesn't seem to realize that the smile hasn't been invented yet that will move this mountain.

Just as I turn in toward Charlie's room, Mrs. Freeman spots me.

"Thomas," she says, shifting her weight.

There is always a sense around Mrs. Freeman that you are watching a geological effect, that if you aren't careful, you'll be crushed. She knows that my mother is raising me alone, so she takes it upon herself to contribute.

"Thomas!" she repeats, the only person who calls me that anymore. "Come over here."

I inch closer.

"What did you get him into?" she says.

"He was trying to—"

She steps forward, trapping me in a shadow. "I warned you about this sort of thing. Didn't I? After that other business on the roof of that building?"

The clapper. "Mrs. Freeman, that was *his* idea—"

"Oh, no. Not that again. My Charlie's no genius, Thomas. He's got to be *led* into temptation."

Mothers. You'd think Charlie couldn't find the wrong side of the tracks if you pushed him off the train. Mrs. Freeman looks at the three of us and sees bad company. Counting my one parent, Paul's none, and Gil's revolving door of steprelations, we don't have as many positive role models among us as Charlie has under one roof. And for some reason, I'm the one with a pitchfork and a tail. If only she knew the truth, I think. Moses had horns too.

"Leave him alone," comes a wheezy voice from inside.

Like the world on its axis, Mrs. Freeman turns.

"Tom tried to get me out of there," Charlie says, weaker now.

A blip of silence follows. Mrs. Freeman looks at me as if to say, Don't you smile, there's nothing smart about getting my boy out of a predicament you got him into. But when Charlie starts to speak again, she tells me to go in and talk to her son before he wears himself out carrying on like that across the room. She has some business with the doctor.

"And, Thomas," she says, before I can get past her, "don't go putting any ideas into that boy's head."

I nod. Mrs. Freeman is the only teacher I've ever known who makes ideas sound like a four-letter word.

Charlie is propped up in a hospital cot with a short metal railing on each side, the kind that isn't high enough to keep a big guy from rolling off the bed on a bad night, but is exactly the right height to let an orderly slip a broomstick between the railings and keep you pinned to the bed forever, a permanent convalescent. I've had more hospital nightmares than Scheherazade had stories, and even time hasn't sponged them all from my memory.

"Visiting hours end in ten minutes," the nurse says without looking at her watch. A kidney-shaped tray is clamped in one of her hands, a duster in the other.

Charlie watches her shuffle out. In a slow, hoarse voice he says, "I think she likes you."

From the neck up he almost looks fine. There's a lick of pink skin jumping out over his collarbone; otherwise he just appears tired. It's his chest where the damage was done. He's wrapped in gauze down to the point where his waist is tucked lightly into the bed, and in places a sweaty pus has seeped to the surface.

"You can stick around to help them change me," Charlie says, drawing my attention back north.

His eyes seem jaundiced. There's a wetness around his nose he would probably wipe if he could.

"How do you feel?" I ask.

"How do I look?"

"Pretty good, considering."

He manages to smile. When he tries to peer down at himself, though, I realize he has no idea how he looks. He is just together enough to know he shouldn't trust his senses.

"Anyone else come to see you?" I ask.

It takes him a while to answer. "Not Gil, if that's what you mean."

"I mean anyone."

"Maybe you missed my mom out there." Charlie smiles, and repeats himself without noticing. "She's easy to miss."

I look out the doorway again. Mrs. Freeman is still talking to the doctor.

"Don't worry," Charlie says, misunderstanding. "He'll come."

But by now the nurse has called everyone who might care that Charlie is conscious again. If Gil isn't here already, he's not coming.

"Hey," Charlie says, changing the subject. "You okay with what happened back there?"

"When?"

"You know. What Taft said."

I try to call up the words. We were at the Institute hours ago. It's probably the last thing he remembers.

"About your dad." Charlie tries to reposition himself and winces.

I stare at the railing, suddenly pinned. Mrs. Freeman has bullied the doctor enough that he finally leads her into a private room to confer. The two of them disappear behind a distant door, and now the hallway is empty.

"Look," Charlie says faintly, "don't let someone like that mess with your head."

This is what Charlie does on death's door. He thinks about my problems.

"I'm glad you're okay," I tell him.

I know he's about to say something smart, when he feels the pressure I'm putting on his hand and keeps it simple.

"Me too."

Charlie smiles at me again, then laughs. "I'll be damned," he says, and shakes his head. His eyes are focused on something beyond me. "I'll be damned," he says again.

He's fading, I think. But when I turn around, Gil is standing in the doorway, a bouquet of flowers in hand.

"I stole these from the ball arrangements," he says hesitantly, as if he's not sure he's welcome here. "You better like them."

"No wine?" Charlie's voice is faint.

Gil gives an awkward smile. "Only the cheap stuff for you." He walks forward and extends a hand to Charlie.

"The nurse told me we've got two minutes," Gil offers. "How are you feeling?"

"Been better," Charlie says. "Been worse."

"I think your mom's here," Gil replies, still searching for a way to begin.

Charlie's starting to drift, but manages another smile. "She's easy to miss."

"You're not going to check out on us tonight, are you?" Gil asks quietly.

"Out of the hospital?" Charlie says, too far away now to know how the question was meant.

"Yeah."

"Maybe," Charlie whispers. "The food in here"—he exhales—"is terrible."

His head falls back onto the pillow just as the leather-faced nurse returns to say our time is up, that Charlie needs his rest.

"Sleep tight, chief," Gil says, putting the bouquet on the nightstand.

Charlie doesn't hear him. He's already breathing through his mouth.

As we leave I look back at him, propped up in his bed, swaddled in bandages and guarded by IVs. It reminds me of comic books I used to read as a kid. The fallen giant that medicine rebuilt. The mysterious patient's recovery that amazed local doctors. Darkness falls on Gotham, but the headlines are all the same. Today a superhero wrestled with a force of nature and lived to complain about the food.

"He's going to be okay?" Gil asks, when we reach the visitors' parking lot. The Saab is sitting alone in the lot, its hood still warm enough to have melted the falling snow.

"I think so."

"His chest looks pretty bad."

I don't know what rehab is like for burn victims, but getting used to your own skin again can't be easy.

"I didn't think you were going to show up," I tell him.

Gil hesitates. "I wish I'd been there with you guys."

"When?"

"All day."

"Is that a joke?"

He turns to me. "No. What's that supposed to mean?"

We stop just short of the car. I realize I'm angry at him, angry at how hard it was for him to find anything to say to Charlie, angry at the way he seemed afraid to visit Charlie this afternoon.

"You were where you wanted to be," I say.

"I came as soon as I heard."

"You weren't with us."

"When?" he asks. "This morning?"

"This whole time."

"Jesus. Tom . . ."

"You know why he's in there?" I say.

"Because he made the wrong decision."

"Because he tried to *help*. He didn't want us going into Taft's office alone. He didn't want Paul to get hurt in the tunnels."

"What do you want, Tom? An apology? Mea culpa. I can't compete with Charlie. That's the way he is. That's the way he's always been."

"That's the way *you* were. You know what Mrs. Freeman said to me in there? The first thing she brought up? Stealing the clapper out of Nassau Hall."

Gil runs his fingers through his hair.

"She blames *me* for that. She always has. You know why?"

"Because she thinks Charlie's a saint."

"Because she can't believe *you're* the kind of person who ever would've done something like that."

He exhales. "So what?"

"You *are* the kind of person who would've done something like that. You *did* do that."

He seems unsure what to say. "Does it occur to you that maybe I'd had half a dozen beers that night before I ran into you guys? Maybe I wasn't thinking straight."

"Or maybe you were different then."

"Yes, Tom. Maybe I was."

Silence falls. The first dimples of snow are forming on the hood of the Saab. Somehow, the words amount to a confession.

"Look," he says, "I'm sorry."

"For what?"

"I should've gone in to see Charlie the first time. When I saw you and Paul."

"Forget it."

"I'm stubborn. I've always been stubborn."

He emphasizes *always*, as if to say, Look, Tom, some things haven't changed.

But everything has changed. In a week, a day, an hour. Charlie, then Paul. Now, suddenly, Gil.

"I don't know," I tell him.

"You don't know what?"

"What you've been doing all this time. Why everything is different. Jesus, I don't even know what you're doing next year."

From his hip pocket Gil produces his key fob and unlocks the doors.

"Let's go," he says. "Before we freeze to death."

We stand in the snow, alone in the hospital parking lot. The sun has nearly slipped off the edge of the sky, introducing darkness, giving everything the texture of ashes.

"Get in," he says. "Let's talk."

Chapter 25

That night I got to know Gil again for the first time, probably also the last. He was almost as charming as I remembered: funny, interested, smart about the things that mattered, smug about the things that didn't. We drove back to the room, Sinatra playing, conversation somehow never faltering, and before I could even ask what I was going to wear to the ball, I opened the door to my bedroom and found a tuxedo waiting for me on a hanger, pressed and spotless, with a note clipped to the plastic garment bag. *Tom—If this doesn't fit, you've shrunk. —G.* In the midst of everything else, he'd found time to bring one of my suits to a rental shop and ask for a tux of matching size.

"My dad thinks I should take some time off," he says, answering my question from before. "Travel for a while. Europe, South America."

It's strange to remember someone you've known

all along. It isn't like returning to the home you grew up in and noticing how it left its shape on you, how the walls you've raised and the doors you've opened since then have all followed the design you saw for the first time there. It's closer to returning home and seeing your mother or sister, who are old enough not to have grown since you last saw them but young enough not to have aged, and realizing for the first time how they look to everyone else, how beautiful they would be if you didn't know them, what your father and brother-in-law saw when they judged them most and knew them least.

"Honestly?" Gil says. "I haven't decided. I'm not sure my dad's one to give advice. The Saab was his idea, and that was a mistake. He was thinking about what he would've wanted at our age. He talks to me like I'm someone else."

Gil was right. He is no longer the freshman who let pants fly above Nassau Hall. He's more careful than that, more circumspect. You would see him and think he was world-wise, self-involved. The natural authority in his speech and his body language is more pronounced now, a quality that Ivy has cultivated. The clothes he wears are quieter by a shade, and his hair, which was always just long enough to be noticed, never seems tousled now. There is a science behind it, because you never notice when it's been cut. He's put on a touch of weight, which makes him handsome in a different way, a hint more staid, and the little affectations he brought from Exeter—the ring he wore on his pinky finger, the stud he wore in his ear—have quietly disappeared.

"I figure I'll wait until the last minute. I'll decide during graduation—something spontaneous, something unexpected. Maybe become an architect. Maybe get back into sailing."

Here he is, changing into his clothes, taking off his wool pants in front of me, not realizing what a perfect stranger I am, a person this version of himself has never met. I realize I'm probably a stranger to myself, that I've never been able to see the person Katie waited for all night last night, the newest model, the up-to-the-minute me. There is a riddle here somewhere, a paradox. Frogs and wells and the curious case of Tom Sullivan, who looked in a mirror and saw the past.

"Man walks into a bar," Gil says, returning to an old standby. "Completely naked. And there's a duck sitting on his head. The bartender says, 'Carl, there's something different about you today.' The duck shakes his head and says, 'Harry, you wouldn't believe it if I told you.'"

I wonder why he chose that joke. Maybe he's been getting at the same point this entire time. We've *all* been talking to him as if he were someone else. The Saab has been our idea of him, and it was our mistake. Gil himself is something unexpected, something spontaneous. An architect, a sailor, a duck.

"You know what I was listening to on the radio the other day?" he asks. "After Anna and I broke up?"

"Sinatra." But I know it's wrong.

"Samba," he tells me. "I was scanning through the stations and WPRB was playing a Latin set. Something instrumental, no voices. Great rhythm. *Amazing* rhythm."

WPRB. The campus radio station that played Handel's *Messiah* when women first arrived at Princeton. I remember Gil on the night I first met him, outside the bell tower at Nassau Hall. He came out of the darkness doing a little rumba thrust, saying, "Now shake it, baby. *Dance*." There has always been music about him, the jazz he's been trying to play on the piano since the day we met. Maybe there's something old about the new after all.

"I don't miss her," he says, trying for the first time to let me in. "She would put this stuff in her hair. Pomade. Her stylist gave it to her. You know how it smells after someone vacuums? Sort of hot and clean?"

"Sure."

"It was like that. She must've blow-dried it until it burned. Every time she would lean her head on me, I would think, you smell like my carpet."

He is everywhere now, free-associating.

"You know who else smelled like that?" he asks.

"Who?"

"Think back. Freshman year."

Hot and clean. The fireplace in Rockefeller comes immediately to mind.

"Lana McKnight," I say.

He nods. "I never knew how you guys stayed together as long as you did. The chemistry was so strange. Charlie and I used to make bets about when you two would break up."

"He told me he *liked* Lana."

"Remember the girl he dated sophomore year?" Gil says, already moving on.

"Charlie?"

"Her name was Sharon, I think?"

"With the different-colored eyes?"

"Now, *she* had great-smelling hair. I remember, she used to sit in our room waiting for Charlie to get back. The whole room would smell like this lotion my mom used to wear. I've never known what it was, but I always loved it."

It occurs to me that Gil has only mentioned stepmothers to me before, never his real mother. The affection gives him away.

"You know why they broke up?" he says.

"Because she dumped him."

Gil shakes his head. "Because he got tired of picking up after her. She would leave things in our room—sweaters, purses, anything—and Charlie would have to bring them back. He didn't realize it was just a move. She was giving him a reason to visit her at night. Charlie just thought she was a slob."

I struggle with my tie, trying to knot it between the fangs of the collar. Good old Charlie. Cleanliness next to godliness.

"She didn't break up with him," Gil continues. "The girls who fall for Charlie never do. He always breaks up with them."

There is a slight suggestion in his voice that this is a fact about Charlie worth bearing in mind, an important character trait, this fault-finding. As if it helps to explain the problems Gil has had with him.

"He's a good guy," Gil says, catching himself.

He seems content to leave it at that. For a second there is no sound in the room but the friction of fabric against fabric as I pull off the black tie and begin again. Gil sits down on his mattress and runs his fingers through his hair. He got into that habit back when his hair was longer. His hands still haven't adapted to the change.

At last I manage a knot, a sort of walnut with wings. I

look in the mirror and decide it's good enough. I slip on my jacket. A perfect fit, even better than my own suit.

Gil is still silent, watching himself in the mirror, as if his image were a painting. Here we are, at the end of his presidency. His Ivy farewell. Tomorrow the club will be run by next year's officers, the members he created at bicker, and Gil will become a ghost in his own house. The best of the Princeton he knew is coming to an end.

"Hey," I say, walking across the foyer into his bedroom. "Try to have a good time tonight."

He doesn't seem to hear me. He places his cell phone on its charger, watching the light pulse. "I wish this wasn't the way things turned out," he says.

"Charlie'll be okay," I tell him.

But he just eyes his jewelry case, the tiny wooden chest where he keeps his valuables, and runs his palm across the top, brushing off the dust. Everything in Charlie's half of the room is old but spotless: a pair of athletic shoes from freshman year sits at the edge of the closet, laces tucked in; last year's pair is still being broken in on weekends. But everything in Gil's half of the room seems unlived-in, new and dusty at the same time. From inside the box he lifts a silver watch, the one he wears on special occasions. Its hands have stopped moving, so he shakes the casing gently, winding it.

"What time you got?" he says.

I show him the face of my watch, and he sets his to match.

Outside, night has risen. Gil takes his key ring in his hand, then the phone from its charger. "My dad's favorite day of college was the Ivy ball his senior year," he says. "He always used to talk about it."

I think of Richard Curry, of the stories he told Paul about Ivy.

He said it was like living a dream, a perfect dream.

Gil places the watch to his ear. He listens to it as if there is something miraculous about the sound, an ocean trapped in a seashell.

"Ready?" he says, pulling the band around his wrist and fastening the metal.

He focuses on me now, checking the cut of the tux.

"Not bad," he says. "I think she'll approve."

"You okay?" I ask.

Gil adjusts his jacket and nods.

"I don't think I'll be telling my kids about tonight. But yeah. I'm fine."

At the door we both take one last look before locking up. With the lights out, the room comes to shadows. When I look out the window at the moon one last time, I see Paul in the reflection of my mind's eye, trudging across campus in his worn winter coat, alone.

Gil looks at his watch and says, "We should be just on time."

Then he and I, in our black suits and black shoes, head out to the Saab in the shoals of the night-colored snow.

A costume ball, Gil had told me. And a costume ball it was. We arrive to find the club magnificent, the center of all attention on Prospect Avenue. Tall berms of snow rise like ramparts along the brick wall that surrounds the club, but the path leading to the front door has been cleared, and the walkway has been covered with a thin layer of black stones. Like rock salt they melt a swath through the ice.

Mirroring the effect are four long cloths draped down the front bays of the clubhouse, each one with a vertical stripe of ivy green flanked by thin pillars of gold.

As Gil parks the Saab in his space, club members and the few other invitees are approaching Ivy ark-style, in twos, each entrance staggered from the next in polite intervals, careful not to intrude on one another. Seniors arrive last, because warm receptions are customary for graduating members, Gil tells me as he shuts off the headlights.

We cross the threshold to find the club bustling. The air is heavy with the heat of bodies, the sweet odor of alcohol and cooked food, the slurring conversations that form and re-form across the floor. Gil's entrance is met with clapping and cheers. Sophomores and juniors stationed across the first floor turn toward the door to welcome him, some crying Gil's name aloud, and it seems for a second that this could still be the night he hoped for, a night like his father had.

"Well," he says to me, ignoring the applause when it continues too long, "this is it."

I look around at the club's transformation. The work Gil has been doing, the errands and planning and conversations with florists and caterers, is suddenly more than just an excuse to leave our room when things aren't well. Everything is different. The armchairs and tables that were once here are gone. In their place, the corners of the front hall have been rounded by quarter-circle tables, all hung with silky cloths in regal dark green and decked in china platters trembling with food. Behind each one, as behind the wet bar to our right, stands an attendant in white gloves. Flower arrangements are everywhere, not a speck of color in any of them: just white lilies and black orchids and varieties I have never seen before. In the storm of tuxedoes and black evening gowns, it's even possible to overlook the brown oak of the walls.

"Sir?" says a waiter dressed in white tie, who has appeared from nowhere bearing a tray of canapés and truffles. "Lamb," he says, pointing at the first, "and white chocolate," pointing at the second.

"Have one," Gil says.

So I do, and all the hunger of the day, the missed meals and hospital food fantasies, all of it instantly returns. When another man circles by with a tray of champagne flutes, I help myself again. The bubbles rise straight to my head, helping to keep my thoughts from drifting back to Paul.

Just then, a musical quartet kicks up from the dining room antechamber, a place where weathered lounge chairs used to stand. A piano and drum set have been tucked into the corner, with enough room for a bass and electric guitar in between. For the time being, it's R&B standards. Later, I know, if Gil has his way, there will be jazz.

"I'll be right back," he says, and suddenly he leaves my side, heading up the stairs. At every step, a member stops him to say something kind, to smile and shake his hand, sometimes to hug him. I see Donald Morgan place a careful hand on Gil's back as he passes, the easy, sincere congratulations of the man who would be king. Junior women already in their drinks look at Gil with foggy eyes, sentimental about the club's loss, *their* loss. He is tonight's hero, I realize, the host and guest of honor both. Everywhere he goes he'll have company. But somehow, without anyone by his side—Brooks or Anna or one of us—he looks alone already.

"Tom!" comes a voice from behind me.

I turn, and the air converges in a single fragrance, the one Gil's mother and Charlie's girlfriend must've worn, because it has the same effect on me. If I imagined that I liked Katie best when I saw her with flaws, with her hair up and her shirt untucked, then I was a fool. Because here she is now, tucked into a black gown, hair down, all collarbones and breasts, and I am undone.

"Wow."

She puts a hand on my lapel and rubs off a flake of dust that turns out to be snow, still lingering in this heat.

"Same to you," she says.

There is something wonderful in her voice, a welcome ease. "Where's Gil?" she asks.

"Upstairs."

She pulls two more flutes of champagne from a passing tray.

"Cheers," she says, giving me one. "So who are you supposed to be?"

I hesitate, unsure what she means.

"Your *costume*. Who'd you come as?"

Now Gil reappears.

"Hey," Katie says. "Long time no see."

Gil sizes the two of us up, then smiles like a proud father. "You both look beautiful."

Katie laughs. "So who are *you* supposed to be?" she asks.

With a flourish, Gil swings back the side of his jacket. Only now do I see what he went upstairs to get. There, hanging between the left flank of his waist and his right hip, is a black leather belt. On the belt is a leather holster, and in the holster is an ivory-handled pistol.

"Aaron Burr," he says. "Class of 1772."

"Flashy," Katie says, watching the pearly butt of the gun.

"What's that?" I blurt.

Gil seems taken aback. "My costume. Burr shot Hamilton in a duel."

He puts an arm at my back and leads me toward the landing between the first and second floors.

"See the lapel pins Jamie Ness is wearing?" He points at a blond senior whose bow tie is embroidered with treble and bass clefs.

On the left lapel I can make out a brown oval; on the right, a black dot.

"That's a football," Gil says, "and that's a hockey puck. He's Hobey Baker, Ivy section of 1914. The only man ever inducted into both the football and hockey halls of fame. Hobey was in a singing group here—that's why Jamie's tie has notes on it."

Now Gil points to a tall senior with bright red hair. "Chris Bentham, right beside Doug: James Madison, class of 1771. You can tell by the shirt buttons. The top one is a Princeton seal—Madison was the first president of the alumni association. And the fourth one is an American flag. . . ."

There is something mechanical in his voice, a tour guide's inflection, as if he's reading a script in his head.

"Just make up a costume," Katie interjects, joining our conversation from the foot of the stairs.

I glance down at her, and the leverage gives me a new appreciation for the way she fits into her dress.

"Oh, listen," Gil says, looking past her, "I've got to go

deal with something. Can you two manage on your own for a second?"

Over by the wet bar, Brooks is pointing to one of the white-gloved attendants, who is leaning heavily against the wall.

"One of the servers is drunk," Gil says.

"No rush," I tell him, noticing how Katie's neck looks impossibly thin from this height, like the stem of a sunflower.

"If you need anything," he says, "just let me know."

Side by side, we begin to descend. The band is playing Duke Ellington, the champagne flutes are clinking, and Katie's lipstick has a high red gloss, the color of a kiss.

"Want to dance?" I say, when I step down from the landing.

Katie smiles and takes me by the hand.

Listen . . . rails a-thrumming . . . on the "A" train.

At the foot of the stairs, Gil's tracks and mine diverge.

Chapter 26

The dance floor is ten degrees hotter than the rest of
the club, couples pressed tight into each other,
merging and turning, an asteroid belt of slow-
dancers, but I instantly feel comfortable. Katie and
I have moved to a lot of music since that first night
we met at Ivy. Each weekend on Prospect Avenue the
clubs hire bands to suit every taste, and in just a few
months we've tried ballroom and Latin and every
style in between. With nine years of tap behind her,
Katie has enough elegance and grace for three or
four dancers, which means that between us we average about as much as the next couple. Still, as her
charity case, I've come a long way. We get bolder the
longer we're at it, succumbing to the champagne. I
manage to dip her once without falling on top of her,
she manages to spin from my good arm once without
dislocating anything, and soon we're dangerous on
the floor.

"I've decided who I am," I tell her, pulling her back toward me.

There's a wonderful contact between us, her cleavage tightening, breasts buoyant.

"Who?" she says.

We're both breathing hard. Tiny drops of sweat are forming at the top of her forehead.

"F. Scott Fitzgerald."

Katie shakes her head and smiles. Her tongue flits in the gap between her teeth. "You can't," she says. "Scott Fitzgerald's not allowed."

We're both talking loudly, our mouths closer and closer to each other's ears in order to hear above the music.

"Why not?" I ask, getting my lips tangled in a few strands of hair. She has a dot of perfume on her neck, the same way she did in the darkroom, and the continuum between there and here—the idea that we really are the same people, just differently dressed—is enough.

"Because he was a member of Cottage," she says, leaning forward. "That's blasphemy."

I smile. "So how long does this keep up?"

"The ball? Until the service starts."

It takes me a second to remember that tomorrow is Easter.

"At midnight?" I ask.

She nods. "Kelly and the others are worried about turnout at the chapel."

Almost on cue, we make another turn on the floor and Kelly Danner passes into view, pointing her index finger at a sophomore in a flashy tux vest, the body language of a witch changing a prince into a toad. All-powerful Kelly Danner, the woman not even Gil trifles with.

"They're making everyone go?" I say, thinking even Kelly would be hard-pressed to manage that.

Katie shakes her head. "They're closing the club and *suggesting* that people go."

There's an edge to her voice when she talks about Kelly, so I decide not to press. Watching the couples around us, I can't help but think about Paul, who always seemed alone here.

Just then, the rhythm of the entire party is thrown off when one final couple arrives at the door, late enough to upstage everyone else. It's Parker Hassett and his date. True to his word, Parker has dyed his hair brown, parted it rigidly down the left side, and donned an inaugural-style tuxedo with white vest and white tie, for a strangely convincing resemblance to John Kennedy. His partner, the always dramatic Veronica Terry, has also come as billed. In a windswept platinum hairdo, candy-apple lipstick, and a dress that billows even without a subway grate to blow it skyward, she is the spitting image of Marilyn Monroe. The costume ball has begun. In a room full of pretenders, these two take the crown.

The reception Parker gets, though, is deadly. Silence falls over the room; from stray corners comes hissing. When Gil, from the landing of the second floor, is the only one able to quiet the crowd, I sense that the honor of arriving last was supposed to have been his, and that Parker has shown up the president at the president's own ball.

At Gil's insistence, the climate in the room slowly cools. Parker makes a quick detour in the direction of the bar, then brings Veronica Terry and his glasses of wine, one in each hand, toward the dance floor. When he approaches, there's a swagger in his step; it never registers in his expression that he is already the least popular person in the room. Once he comes close enough, I realize how he pulls it off. He's traveling in a cloud of cocktail fumes, already drunk.

Katie edges a shade closer to me as he nears, but I make nothing of it until I notice the look that passes between them. Parker gives her a meaningful stare, snide and sexual and assertive all at once, and Katie tugs at my hand, pulling me away from the dance floor.

"What was that all about?" I ask, when we're out of earshot.

The band is playing Marvin Gaye, guitars licking, drums thumping, the leitmotiv of Parker's arrival. John Kennedy is grinding with Marilyn Monroe, the strange spectacle of history humping, and all the other couples have given them a wide berth, the quarantine of social lepers.

Katie looks upset. All the magic of our dancing has evaporated.

"That *prick*," she says.

"What did he do?"

Then, all at once, it comes out: the story I wasn't around to hear; the one she hadn't intended to tell me until later.

"Parker tried to third-floor me at bicker. He said he'd blackball me unless I gave him a lap dance. Now he thinks it's a joke."

We're standing in the middle of the main hall, close enough to the dance floor to see Parker with his hands on Veronica's hips.

"That son of a bitch. What'd you do about it?"

"I told Gil." When she speaks his name, her eyes travel to the stairs, where Gil is making conversation with two juniors.

"That's all?"

I expect her to invoke Donald's name, to remind me where I should've been, but she doesn't.

"Yes" is all she says. "He kicked Parker out of bicker."

I know she means I should let this go, that this wasn't how she wanted me to find out. She's been through enough already. But my temperature is rising.

"I'm going to say something to Parker," I tell her.

Katie looks at me sharply. "No, Tom. Not tonight."

"He can't just act—"

"Look," she says, cutting me off. "Forget about it. We're not going to let him ruin our night together."

"I was only trying to—"

She puts a finger over my lips. "I know. Let's go somewhere else."

She looks around, but there are tuxedos in every direction, conversations and wineglasses and men with silver trays. This is the magic of Ivy. We are never alone.

"Maybe we can use the President's Room," I say.

She nods. "I'll ask Gil."

I notice the trust in her voice when she says his name. Gil's been decent to her, better than decent, possibly without even meaning to. She came to him about Parker, when I was nowhere to be found. He's the first person she thinks of now, for something small. Maybe it's meaningful to her, that they talk over breakfast, even if he almost forgets it. Gil has been a big brother to her, the way he was to me freshman year. Anything good enough for him is good enough for us both.

"No problem," he says to her. "There won't be anyone in there."

So I follow Katie downstairs, watching the shifts in her musculature beneath the gown, the way her legs move, the tightness of her hips.

When the lights go on, I see the room where Paul and I worked so many nights. The place is unchanged, untouched by preparations for the ball, a geography of notes and drawings and books piled into mountain ranges that thread through the room, as tall in places as we are.

"It's not as hot in here," I say, searching for something to tell her. They seem to have turned down the thermostat in the rest of the building to keep the first floor from overheating.

Katie looks around. Paul's notes are taped to the shoulders of the fireplace; his diagrams feather the walls. We are surrounded by Colonna.

"Maybe we shouldn't be in here," she says.

I can't tell if she's worried that we'll intrude on something of Paul's, or that Paul will intrude on something of ours. The longer we stand, sizing up the room, the more I can feel a distance forming between us. This is not the place for what we need.

"Have you ever heard of Schrödinger's cat?" I say finally, because it's the only way I can think to raise what I'm feeling.

"In philosophy?" she says.

"Anywhere."

In my lone physics class, the professor used Schrödinger's cat as an example in wave mechanics, when most of us were too slow for $v = -e^2/r$. An imaginary cat is placed in a locked box with a dose of cyanide, which will be given only if a

Geiger counter is triggered. The catch, I think, is that it's impossible to say whether the cat is living or dead before you actually open the box; until then, probability requires you to say that the box contains equal parts living and dead cat.

"Yes," she says. "What about it?"

"I feel like the cat isn't dead *or* alive right now," I tell her. "It's nothing."

Katie puzzles over what I'm getting at. "You want to open the box," she says at last, sitting on the table.

I nod, propping myself up beside her. The enormous wooden plank accepts us silently. I don't know how to tell her the rest of what I mean: that we, individually, are the scientist on the outside; that we, together, are the cat.

Instead of answering, she takes a finger and runs it behind my right temple, tucking my hair behind my ear as if I've said something charming. Maybe she already knows how to solve my riddle. We are bigger than Schrödinger's box, she's saying. Like any good cat, we have nine lives.

"Does it ever snow like this in Ohio?" she says, consciously changing the subject. Outside, I know, it's begun again, driving down with more power than before, all our winter in this one storm.

"Not in April," I say.

We're side by side on the table, just inches apart. "Not in New Hampshire either," she says. "Not in April, at least."

I accept what she's trying to do, where she's trying to take me. Anywhere but here. I've always wanted to know more about what her life was like at home, what her family did around the dinner table. Upper New England in my imagination is the American Alps, mountains at every turn, Saint Bernards bearing gifts.

"My little sister and I used to do this thing in the snow," she says.

"Mary?"

She nods. "Every year when the pond near our house would freeze over, we would go crack holes in the ice."

"Why?"

She smiles, beautiful. "So the fish could breathe."

Members pass across the top of the stairs, little pockets of heat in motion.

"We would take the ends of broomsticks," she says, "and make holes all the way across the lake. Like punching holes in the top of a jar."

"For fireflies," I say.

She nods and takes my hand. "The ice skaters used to *hate* us."

"My sisters used to take me sledding," I tell her.

Katie's eyes twinkle. She remembers she's got something on me: that she's a big sister, and I'm a little brother.

"There aren't a lot of big hills in Columbus," I continue, "so it was always this one."

"And they would drag you up the hill on the sled."

"Did I tell you this already?"

"That's just what big sisters do."

I can't imagine her pulling a sled up a hill. My sisters were strong as pack dogs.

"Did I ever tell you about Dick Mayfield?" I ask her.

"Who?"

"This guy my sister used to date."

"What about him?"

"Sarah used to kick me off the phone every time Dick would call."

She hears the jab in it. This, too, is what big sisters do.

"I don't think Dick Mayfield had my number." She smiles, folding her fingers into mine.

I can't help thinking of Paul, of the dovetail he made with his hands.

"Dick had my sister's number," I say. "All it took was an old red Camaro with flames traced on the sides."

Katie shakes her head disapprovingly.

"Studly Dick and the Chick Machine," I tell her. "I said that one night when he came over, and my mother made me go to bed without dinner."

Dick Mayfield, conjured from thin air. He called me Tiny Tom. We went riding in the Camaro once, and he told me a secret. *It doesn't matter how small you are. All that matters is the size of the fire in your engine.*

"Mary dated a guy who drove a '64 Mustang," Katie says. "I asked her if they were doing anything in the backseat. She said he was too uptight about messing up the car."

Sex stories sublimated into car stories, a way to talk about everything without talking about anything at all.

"My first girlfriend drove a water-damaged VW," I tell her. "You would lie down on the backseat, and this smell would come up, like sushi. You couldn't do anything back there."

She turns to me. "Your first girlfriend could drive?"

I fumble, realizing what I've given away.

"I was nine," I say, clearing my throat. "She was seventeen."

Katie laughs, and a silence follows. Finally, the moment seems to have come.

"I told Paul," I say to her.

She looks up.

"I'm not working on the book anymore."

For a while she doesn't respond. Her hands rise to her shoulders, rubbing them for warmth. I realize, after so many hints, so much contact, that she hasn't gotten over the temperature of the room.

"Do you want my jacket?" I ask.

She nods. "I'm getting goose bumps."

It's impossible not to look. Her arms are covered with tiny beads. The curves of her breasts are pale, the skin of a porcelain dancer.

"Here," I say, taking off the jacket and placing it across her back.

My right arm passes her far shoulder just for a second, but she reaches up, holding it in limbo. With me half crooked around her, waiting, she leans in. The smell of her perfume returns, carried in the bell of her hair. This, at last, is her answer.

Katie cocks her head, and I reach inside the jacket, into the dark space where it hangs off her shoulders, placing a hand on the far side of her waist. My fingers stick to the rough fabric of her gown, caught by an unexpected friction, and I find that my hold on her is tight and effortless at the same time. A strand of hair falls in front of her face, but she doesn't brush it back. There is a smudge of lipstick just below her lip, so small that it can only be seen from a tiny distance I'm surprised to find I have reached. Then she is too close to focus on anything at all, and there is warmth over my mouth, lips closing in.

Chapter 27

Just as the kiss deepens, I hear the door swing open. I'm about to snap at the intruder, when I see it's Paul standing before us.

"What's going on?" I say, lurching back.

Paul looks around the room, startled. "Vincent was taken back in for questioning," he manages to say. His shock at finding Katie in his room is mirrored by her shock at seeing him here at all.

I hope they're putting it to Taft. "When?"

"An hour ago, two hours. I just spoke to Tim Stone at the Institute."

An uncomfortable hitch follows.

"Did you find Curry?" I ask, wiping the lipstick off my mouth.

But in the pause before he answers, we are silently rehashing our argument about the *Hypnerotomachia*, about the priorities I've set for myself.

"I came here to talk to Gil," he says, cutting the conversation short.

Katie and I watch him edge along the wall toward the desk, gather up some of his old drawings, the ones of the crypt he's been sketching for months, then disappear through the door as quickly as he came. Papers swirl on the floor in the vortex he leaves behind, shifting in a tiny current by the door.

As Katie pushes herself off the table, I think I can read her mind. This book is inescapable. Not all the decisions in the world will make it possible for me to leave it behind. Even here at Ivy, where she thought we could shake it off, the *Hypnerotomachia* is everywhere: on the walls, in the air, breaking in on us when we least expect.

But to my surprise, she's only focused on the facts Paul relayed. "Come on," she says with a burst of energy. "I need to find Sam. If they arrest Taft, she'll have to change the headline."

Upstairs, in the main hall, we find Paul and Gil speaking in a corner. The room seems to have gone quiet at the spectacle of the club recluse making an appearance at such a public event.

"Where is she?" Katie asks, speaking to Sam's date.

I'm too distracted to hear the answer. For two years I've imagined Paul as the butt of every Ivy joke, the curiosity chained up in the cellar. But now seniors stand at attention as if one of the old portraits has come to life. The expression on Paul's face is needful, almost desperate; if he's aware that the whole club is watching him, he gives no sign. I move closer to them, trying to hear, as Paul hands Gil a familiar paper, folded over. The map of Colonna's crypt.

When they both turn to leave, the membership watches as Gil exits the main hall. The seniors understand it first. One by one, on tables and railings and old oak walls, the club officers begin to rap their knuckles. Brooks, the vice president, is first, then Carter Simmons, the club treasurer; and finally, from all sides, comes this knocking, tapping, rumbling of good-bye. Parker, still on the dance floor, begins rapping louder than all the rest, hoping one last time to stand out. But it's too late. Gil's exit, like his entrance when we arrived, takes place in precise time, the science of a dance step to be performed only once. As the noise of the crowd finally dies, I follow them up.

"We're taking Paul to Taft's house," Gil says when I find them in the Officers' Room.

"What?"

"There's something he needs to get. A blueprint."

"You're going *now*?"

"Taft's at the police station," he says, parroting what Paul explained. "Paul needs us to take him."

I can see the cogs turning. He wants to help, the same way Charlie did; he wants to disprove what I said in the hospital parking lot.

Paul says nothing. I can tell from his expression that this was meant to be a trip he and Gil would make alone.

I'm about to explain to Gil that I can't, that he and Paul will have to go without me, when everything becomes more complicated. Katie appears in the doorway.

"What's going on?" she says.

"Nothing," I say. "Let's go back down."

"I couldn't get Sam on the phone," she says, misunderstanding. "She needs to know about Taft. Is it okay if I go to the *Prince* office?"

Gil senses his opportunity. "That's fine. Tom's coming with us to the Institute. We can meet back up at the service."

Katie is about to agree, when the look on my face gives us away.

"Why?" she asks.

Gil simply says, "It's important." For one of the few times in our friendship, his tone suggests the importance he's referring to is much larger than himself.

"Okay," she says warily, reaching out to take my hand in hers. "I'll see you at the chapel."

She's about to add something else, when a huge thud comes from below, followed by an explosion of glass.

Gil hurries for the stairs; we rush down behind him to find a wide puddle of debris. Blood-colored liquid is seeping in all directions, bringing snags of glass with it. Standing at the center of it all, in a perimeter of space everyone else has evacuated, is Parker Hassett, flushed and fuming. He has just thrown the entire wet bar to the ground, shelves, bottles, and all.

"What the hell's going on?" Gil demands of a sophomore watching nearby.

"He just went off. Someone called him a dipso and he went crazy."

Veronica Terry is holding up the ruffled skirts of her white dress, now fringed in pink and spattered with wine. "They've been teasing him all night," she cries.

"For God's sake," Gil demands, "how'd you let him get that drunk?"

She looks at him blankly, expecting pity, getting fury.

Partygoers nearby whisper to each other, holding back satisfied smiles.

Brooks is telling an attendant to raise the bar and re-stock the shelves from the wine cellar, while Donald Morgan, looking newly presidential, tries to calm Parker amidst the hecklers. From the crowd come coos of *Lush!* and *Drunk!* and worse. Laughter at the edges of insult. Parker is across the room from me, cut in half a dozen places by the shrapnel of upturned bottles, standing in a great puddle of mixed drinks like a child, mashing out the lees. When he finally turns on Donald, he is full of rage.

Katie covers her mouth as it unfolds. Parker lunges at Donald, and the two topple over onto the floor, wrestling at first, then hammering each other with fists. Here is the show everyone has been waiting to see, Parker's comeup-pance for a million petty offenses, justice for what he did on the third floor, violence to end two years of mounting ha-tred. A server comes out with a flat-faced mop, creating the spectacle at the fight's edge of a man shoveling liquid. On the hardwood floor the currents of wine and liquor careen past each other, reflecting off the oak walls, and not a drop is absorbed by anything, not mop nor carpet nor even tuxedo, as the two men continue to fight, a great throb of black arms and legs, an insect trying to right itself before drowning.

"Let's go," Gil says, leading us around the brawl that is now someone else's mess.

Paul and I follow him, wordless, sloshing through the wake of bourbon and brandy and wine.

The roads we travel are thin black stitches on a great white gown. The Saab is surefooted, even with Gil leaning on the gas and the wind shrieking around us. On Nassau Street two cars have slammed into each other, lights flashing, drivers shouting, shadows flickering against a pair of tow trucks on the curb. A proctor emerges from the security kiosk at the north of campus, pink in the haze of safety flares, gesturing to us that the entrance is closed—but Paul is already navigating us away from campus, westward. Gil throws the gearshift into third, then fourth, passing roads in streaks.

"Show him the letter," Gil says.

Paul pulls something from inside his coat and hands it back to me in the rear seat.

"What's this?"

The envelope is torn open across the top, but the upper-left corner bears the imprint of the Dean of Students.

"It was in our mailbox tonight," Gil says.

Mr. Harris:

This letter serves to notify you that my office is conducting an investigation into allegations of plagiarism lodged against you by your senior thesis advisor, Dr. Vincent Taft. Due to the nature of the allegations, and their effect on your graduation, a special meeting of the Committee on Discipline will convene next week to consider your case and render a decision. Please contact me to arrange a preliminary meeting and to confirm receipt of this letter.

> *Sincerely,*
> *Marshall Meadows*
> *Associate Dean of Undergraduate Students*

"He knew what he was doing," Paul says, when I've finished reading.

"Who?"

"Vincent. This morning."

"Threatening you with the letter?"

"He knew he had nothing on me. So he started in on your dad."

I can hear it in his voice, the accusation sneaking in. Everything returns to the moment I pushed Taft.

"You're the one who ran," I say under my breath.

Slush sprays the undercarriage of the car as the suspension dances over a pothole.

"I'm the one who called the police too," he says.

"*What?*"

"That's why the police took Vincent in," he says. "I told them I saw Vincent near Dickinson when Bill was shot."

"You lied to them."

I'm waiting for Gil to react, but he keeps his eyes on the road. Staring at the back of Paul's head, I have the strange sensation of looking at myself from behind, of being inside my father's car again.

"Is this it?" Gil says.

The houses before us are fashioned in white clapboard. At Taft's address, all windows are unlit. Just beyond them stands the tree line of the Institute woods, its canopy tinseled in white.

"He's still at the police station," Paul says, almost to himself. "The lights are off."

"Jesus, Paul," I say. "How do even you know the blueprint is here?"

"It's the only other place he could've hidden it."

Gil doesn't even hear us. Shaken by the sight of Taft's house, he lightens pressure on the brakes, letting us roll in neutral, prepared to go back. Just as his foot begins to engage the clutch, though, Paul yanks the door handle and stumbles out onto the curb.

"Damn it." Gil brings the Saab to a halt and gets out. "Paul!"

The wind hisses around the door as he opens it, muffling his words. I can see Paul mouth something to us, pointing at the house. He begins hiking toward it in the snow.

"*Paul* . . ." I get out of the car, trying to keep my voice at a whisper.

A light in the neighboring house comes on, but Paul pays no attention. He paces up to Taft's front porch and puts his ear to the door, gently rapping.

The wind whips through the columns of the façade, licking puffs of snow from the eaves. The window next door goes black. When Paul gets no answer, he tries to turn the knob, but the lock holds fast.

"What do we do?" Gil says, beside him.

Paul knocks again, then pulls a ring of keys from his pocket and cradles one into the slot. Putting a shoulder into the wood, he sweeps the door forward. Hinges squeal.

"We can't do this," I say as I walk toward them, trying for some authority.

But Paul is already inside, scanning the first floor. Without a word, he's deep into the house.

"Vincent?" comes his voice, feeling out the darkness. "Vincent, are you here?"

The words become distant. I hear feet on a staircase, then nothing.

"Where'd he go?" Gil says, moving toward me.

There is an odd odor in here, distant but strong. The wind comes at our backs, snapping our jackets, making the fingers of Gil's hair twist in the updraft. I turn and shut the door behind us. Gil's cell phone begins to ring.

I flip a wall switch, but the room stays dark. My eyes are beginning to adjust. Taft's dining room is in front of me, baroque furniture and dark walls and claw-footed chairs. At the far end is the bottom of a staircase.

Gil's phone rings again. He is behind me, calling out Paul's name. The odor intensifies. Three objects sit in a tangle on the credenza by the staircase. A tattered billfold, a set of keys, a pair of eyeglasses. Suddenly everything comes into focus.

I turn back. "Answer the phone."

By the time he reaches into his pocket, I'm already climbing the stairs.

"Katie . . . ?" I can hear him say.

Everything is overlapping shadows. The staircase seems fractured, like darkness through a prism. Gil's voice rises.

What? Jesus . . .

Then he's racing up the stairs, pushing at my back, barking at me to hurry, telling me what I already know.

Taft's not at the police station. They released him more than an hour ago.

We reach the landing just in time to hear Paul screaming.

Gil is pressing me forward, forcing me up toward the sound. Like the shadow of a wave at the moment before impact, it settles over me that we are too late, that it has already happened. Gil pushes past me, moving down a corridor to the right, and I'm aware of myself in flashes, in the gaps between instincts. My legs are in motion. Time is slowing; the world is cycling in a lower gear.

Oh God, Paul moans. *Help me.*

The walls of the bedroom are shot with moonlight. Paul's voice comes from the bathroom. The smell is here, of fireworks and cap guns, of everything out of place. There is blood on the walls. In the tub is a body. Paul is on his knees, bent over the porcelain rim.

Taft is dead.

Gil stumbles out of the room, but my eyes trip over the sight. Taft lies on his back in the basin, his gut flattened on top of him. There is a gunshot in his chest, and another between his eyes, with a well of blood still seeping across his forehead. When Paul extends a trembling arm, I feel the sudden urge to laugh. The sensation comes, then fades. I feel sleepy, almost drunk.

Gil is calling the police. *An emergency*, he says. *On Olden Street. At the Institute.*

His voice is loud against the silence. Paul mumbles the house number, and Gil echoes it into the phone.

Hurry.

Suddenly Paul raises himself from the floor. "We need to get out of here."

"What?"

My senses are returning. I put a hand on Paul's shoulder, but he darts into the bedroom, looking everywhere— the space beneath the bed, the crack between the doors of Taft's closet, odd slats in tall bookshelves.

Ian Caldwell & Dustin Thomason

"It's not here . . ." he says. Then he turns, struck by something else. "The *map*," he blurts. "Where's my map?"

Gil looks at me as if this is it, the sign that Paul has lost touch.

"In the lockbox at Ivy," he says, taking Paul by the arm. "Where we put it."

But Paul shakes him off and begins toward the stairs on his own. In the far distance there comes the sound of sirens.

"We can't leave," I call out.

Gil glances at me, but follows him. The sirens are closer now—blocks away, but rising. Outside, through the window, the hills are the color of metal. In a church somewhere, it is Easter.

"I lied to the police about Vincent," Paul cries back. "I can't be here when they find him."

I follow them out the front door, pushing toward the Saab. Gil fires the engine, flooding it with gas, and the car roars in neutral, loud enough to bring on the lights in the house next door. Throwing the gearshift into first, he guns the engine again. When the tires catch asphalt, the car rockets into motion. Just as Gil turns onto an adjoining road, the first patrol car arrives at the opposite end of the street. We watch as it comes to a stop in front of Taft's house.

"Where are we going?" Gil says, glancing at Paul in the rearview mirror.

"Ivy," he says.

Chapter 28

The club is silent when we arrive. Someone has piled rags on the floor of the main hall to sop up the alcohol Parker spilled, but puddles of booze still glisten. Curtains and tablecloths are stained. Nowhere is the staff to be found. Kelly Danner seems to have emptied the club of every last soul.

The carpet on the stairway to the second floor is damp underfoot, where partygoers have trudged alcohol up on the bottoms of their shoes. At the entrance to the Officers' Room, Gil closes the door and flicks on the overhead lamp. The remains of the broken wet bar are pushed up into a corner. A fire has been left to die in the fireplace, but the embers are still raw, spitting up stray flames and red heat.

Seeing the phone on the table, I think of the number I couldn't remember when Gil's cell phone went dead, and it comes to me suddenly, what all of this is. A failure of memory; a miscommunication. The line connecting Richard Curry to Paul has filled with static, and somehow Curry's message was lost. Yet Curry had made his demands clear.

Tell me where the blueprint is, Vincent, he said at the Good Friday lecture, *and you won't see me again. That's the only business we have anymore.* But Taft refused.

Gil produces a key and opens the mahogany lockbox. "Here," he says to Paul, pulling out the map.

I can see Curry again, advancing toward Paul in the courtyard, then backing away toward the chapel, toward Dickinson Hall and Bill Stein's office.

"Jesus," Gil says, "how are we going to deal with this?"

"Call the police," I tell him. "Curry could come for Paul."

"No," Paul says. "He won't hurt me."

But Gil meant something else: dealing with what we've done, fleeing Taft's house. "*Curry* killed Taft?" he says.

I lock the door. "And he killed Stein."

The room suddenly feels airtight. The wreckage of the wet bar, brought up from downstairs, gives the place a sweet, rotten odor.

Gil stands at the head of the table, speechless.

"He won't hurt me," Paul repeats.

But I remember the letter we found in Stein's desk. *I have a proposition for you. There's more than enough here to suit both of us.* Followed by Curry's reply, which I'd misunderstood until now: *What about Paul?*

"He will," I say.

"You're wrong, Tom," Paul snaps.

But I'm seeing more and more clearly where this all leads.

"You showed Curry the diary when we went to the exhibit," I tell him. "He knew Taft had stolen it."

"Yes, but—"

"Stein even *told* him they were going to steal your thesis. Curry wanted to get it before they did."

"Tom—"

"Then, at the hospital, you told him everything you'd found. You even told him you were looking for the blueprint."

I reach for the phone, but Paul places a hand down on the receiver, holding it in place.

"Stop, Tom," he says. "Listen to me."

"He *killed* them."

Now it's Paul who leans in, looking heartbroken, to say something Gil and I don't expect.

"*Yes.* That's what I'm telling you. Will you just listen? That's what he meant at the hospital. Remember? Just before you came into the waiting room? *We understand each other, son.* He told me he couldn't sleep because he was worried about me."

"So?"

Paul's voice trembles. "Then he said, *If I'd known what you were going to do, I would've done things differently.* Richard thought I *knew* he'd killed Bill. He meant he would've done it differently if he'd known I was going to leave Vincent's lecture early. That way the police wouldn't have come looking for me."

Gil begins pacing. On the far side of the room, a log breaks in the fireplace.

"Remember the poem he mentioned at the exhibit?"

"Browning. 'Andrea del Sarto.'"

"How did it go?"

" 'You do what many dream of, all their lives,' " I tell him. " 'Dream? Strive to do, and agonize to do, and fail in doing.' "

"Why would he choose that poem?"

"Because it went with the del Sarto painting."

Paul bangs his hand on the table. "No. Because we solved what he and your father and Vincent never solved. What Richard dreamed of doing, all his life. What he strove, and agonized, and failed in doing."

A frustration has come over him that I haven't seen since we worked together, when he seemed to expect that we could act as a single organism, think a single thought. *It shouldn't be taking you that long. It shouldn't be that hard.* We are riddling again, puzzling meaning from a man he thinks we ought to know equally. I have never understood Colonna, or Curry, well enough for Paul.

"I don't understand," Gil says, seeing that something has come between us, something outside his experience.

"The paintings," Paul says, still to me, trying to make me see. "The stories of Joseph. I even told you what they meant. We just didn't know what Richard was getting at. *Now Jacob loved Joseph more than all his children, because he was the son of his old age. And he made him a coat of many colors.*"

He waits for me to give some signal, to tell him I understand, but I can't.

"It's a gift," he says finally. "Richard thinks he's giving me a gift."

"A *gift*?" Gil asks. "Have you lost your mind? What gift?"

"*This,*" Paul says, extending his arms, encompassing everything. "What he did to Bill. What he did to Vincent.

He stopped them from taking it away from me. He's giving me what I found in the *Hypnerotomachia*."

There is an awful equanimity when he says it, fear and pride and sadness circling around a quiet certainty.

"Vincent stole it from him thirty years ago," Paul says. "Richard wouldn't let the same thing happen to me."

"Curry lied to Stein," I tell him, unwilling to let him be fooled by a man trading on an orphan's weakness. "He lied to Taft. He's doing the same thing to you."

But Paul is past the point of doubting. Beneath the horror and disbelief in his voice is something approaching gratitude. Here we are, in another room of borrowed paintings, another exhibit in the museum of fatherhood Curry built for the son he never had, and the gestures have become so grand that the motives are unimportant. It's a final wedge. It reminds me, suddenly, that Paul and I are not brothers. That we believe in different things.

Gil begins to speak, coming between us to bring this discussion back to earth, when a shuffling sound comes from outside. All three of us turn.

"What the hell was that?" Gil says.

Then Curry's voice comes.

"*Paul,*" he murmurs, from just on the other side of the door.

We all freeze.

"Richard," Paul says, coming to. And before Gil or I can stop him, he reaches for the lock.

"Get away from there!" Gil says.

But Paul has already unfastened the door, and a hand on the other side has turned the knob.

There, standing in the threshold, wearing the same

black suit from last night, is Richard Curry. He is wild-eyed, startled. There is something in his hand.

"I need to speak to Paul alone," he says in a hoarse voice.

Paul sees what we must all see: the mist of blood near the collar of his dress shirt.

"Get out of here!" Gil barks.

"What have you done?" Paul says.

Curry stares at him, then raises an arm, holding something in an outstretched hand.

Gil eases forward into the hallway. "Get out," he repeats.

Curry ignores him. "I have it, Paul. The blueprint. Take it."

"You're not going near him," Gil says, voice shaking. "We're calling the police."

My eyes are trained on the dark sheaf in Curry's hand. I step into the hall beside Gil so that we're both in front of Paul. Just as Gil reaches for his cell phone, though, Curry catches us off guard. In a single movement he lunges between us, pushing Paul back into the Officers' Room, and slams the door. Before Gil and I can move, the lock clicks into place.

Gil pounds on the wood with his fist. "Open it!" he screams as he pushes me back and forces his shoulder into the door. The thick wood panel gives nothing. We back up and give two blows together, until the lock seems to bow. Each time, I hear sounds on the other side.

"One more," Gil yells.

On the third push, the metal lock snaps out of its joint, and the door flies open with the sound of a single gunshot.

We catapult into the room to see Curry and Paul at opposite ends of the fireplace. Curry's hand is still out-stretched. Gil charges toward them, striking Curry at full speed, knocking him onto the floor by the hearth. Curry's head scrapes the metal grille off its mark, making sparks fly and embers suddenly pulse with color.

"Richard," Paul says, running toward him.

Paul pulls Curry from the hearth and props him against the wet bar. The gash in the man's head is pouring blood into his eyes as he struggles to orient himself. Only now do I see the blueprint in Paul's hand.

"Are you okay?" Paul says, shaking Curry's shoulders. "He needs an ambulance!"

But Gil is focused. "The police will take care of him."

It's then that I feel the great rush of heat. The back of Curry's jacket has caught fire. Now the wet bar has burst into flame.

"Get back!" Gil barks.

But I'm frozen in place. The fire is rising toward the ceiling, across the curtains pressed against the wall. Accelerated by the alcohol, the blaze is moving with speed, swallowing up everything around it.

"Tom!" Gil barks. "Get them away from there! I'm going for an extinguisher!"

With Paul's help, Curry is pushing himself to his feet. Suddenly, the man shoves Paul off and staggers into the hallway, pulling off his jacket.

"Richard," Paul pleads, following.

Gil races back through the door and begins hosing the curtains with the extinguisher. But the fire is growing too quickly to be put out. Smoke rolls from the doorway along the ceiling.

Finally we retreat toward the door, forced out by the

heat and smoke. I cover my mouth with my hand, feeling my lungs tighten. When I turn toward the stairs, I can make out Paul and Curry struggling through a thick cloud of black smoke, their voices rising.

I cry out Paul's name, but the bottles in the wet bar begin to explode, drowning out my voice. Gil is hit by the first wave of shards. I pull him out of the way, listening for a response from Paul.

Then, through the smoke, I hear it. "Go, Tom! Get out!"

The walls are sprayed with tiny reflections of fire. A bottleneck comes pitching into the air over the stairs; it hangs above us, spraying flames, then tumbles to the first floor.

For a second there is nothing. Then the glass lands in the pile of soaking rags, finding the whiskey and brandy and gin, and the floor flashes to life. From below come popping sounds, wood combusting, fire spreading. The front door is already blocked. Gil is bellowing into his cell phone, calling for help. The fire is rising toward the second floor. My mind seems lit with sparks, a white light when I close my eyes. I am floating, buoyed by the heat. Everything seems so slow, so heavy. Ceiling plaster crashes to the ground. The dance floor is shimmering like a mirage.

"How do we get out?" I shout.

"The service stairway," Gil says. "Upstairs."

"Paul!" I yell.

But there's no answer. I inch toward the stairs, and now their voices have disappeared. Paul and Curry are gone.

"Paul!" I bellow.

The blaze has swallowed up the Officers' Room and begins moving toward us. I feel a strange numbness in my thigh. Gil turns to me, pointing. My pant leg is torn open. Blood is running down the tuxedo fabric, black on black. He pulls off his jacket and ties it around the gash. The tunnel of fire seems to close in around us, urging us up the stairs. The air is almost black.

Gil pushes me up toward the third floor. At the top, nothing is visible, only grades of shadow. A band of light glows beneath a door at the end of the hall. We move forward. The fire has come to the foot of the stairs, but seems to remain at bay.

Then I hear it. A high, collapsing moan, coming from inside the room.

The sound freezes us momentarily. Then Gil lunges forward and opens the door. When he does, the sensation of drunkenness from the ball returns to me. Bodily warmth, like the tingle of flight. Katie's touch on me, Katie's breath on me, Katie's lips on me.

Richard Curry stands arguing with Paul behind a long table at the far end of the room. There's an empty bottle in his hand. His head lolls on his shoulders, pouring blood. There is nothing but the smell of alcohol here, the remnants of a bottle poured over the table, a cabinet in the wall opened to reveal another stash of liquor, an old Ivy president's secret. The room is as long as the building's breadth, framed in silver by the moonlight. Shelves of books line the walls, with leather spines deep into the darkness beyond Curry's head. On the north-facing wall there are two windows. Puddles glisten everywhere.

"Paul!" Gil yells. "He's blocking the service stairs, behind you."

Paul turns to look, but Curry's eyes are fixed on Gil and me. I'm paralyzed by the sight of him. The ridges of his face are so drawn that gravity seems to be pulling at him, dragging him down.

"*Richard,*" Paul says firmly, as if to a child, "*we all have to get out.*"

"Move away," Gil shouts, stepping forward.

But as he does, Curry smashes the bottle on a table and lunges, swiping Gil's arm with the jagged bottleneck. Blood runs between Gil's fingers in black ribbons. He staggers back, watching the blood pour onto his arm. Seeing this, Paul sags against the wall.

"Here," I call out, yanking the handkerchief from my pocket.

Gil moves slowly. When he pulls a hand away to take the cloth, I see how deep the cut is. Blood runs over the furrow as soon as the pressure is gone.

"Go!" I say, pulling him to the windows. "Jump out! The bushes will break your fall."

But he is frozen, staring at the bottleneck in Curry's hands. Now the door to the library is quaking, hot air building on the other side. Tendrils of smoke are starting to stream in from beneath the door, and I can feel my eyes watering, my chest getting heavy.

"*Paul,*" I cry through the smoke. "*You have to get out!*"

"Richard," Paul yells. "Come on!"

"*Let him go!*" I bellow at Curry—but now the fire is roaring to be let in. From beyond comes a terrible ripping sound, wood tearing under its own weight.

Suddenly Gil collapses onto the wall beside me. I rush to the window and open it, propping him against the frame, struggling to keep him upright.

"Help Paul . . ." Gil mumbles, the last thing he says to me before the life begins to fade from his eyes.

A frigid wind strikes through the room, kicking up snow from the bushes below. As gently as I can, I lift him into position. He looks angelic in the light, effortless even now. Staring down at the bloody handkerchief, clinging to his arm out of nothing but its own weight, I begin to feel everything dissolve around me. With one last look, I let go. In an instant, Gil is gone.

"*Tom,*" comes Paul's voice, so distant now that it seems to come from a cloud of smoke. "*Go.*"

I turn to see Paul struggling in Curry's arms, trying to pull him toward the window, but the old man is much stronger. He won't be moved. Curry shoves Paul toward the service stairs instead.

"*Jump!*" I hear below me, voices pouring up through the open window. "*Jump down!*"

Firefighters, spotting me inside.

But I turn back. "Paul!" I yell. "Come on!"

"*Go, Tom,*" I can hear him say, one last time. "*Please.*"

The words become distant too quickly, as if Curry has carried him down into the haze. The two of them are retreating into the ancient bonfires, wrestling like angels through the lifetimes of men.

"*Down*" is the final word I hear from inside the room, spoken in Curry's voice. "*Down.*"

And again, from outside: "*Hurry! Jump!*"

"*Paul,*" I scream, backing up toward the ledge of the window as the flames begin to corner me. Hot smoke presses like a fist against my chest. Across the room, the door to the service stairs swings shut. There is no one to be seen. I let myself fall.

Those are the last things I remember before the slush of snow engulfs me. Then there is only an explosion, like a sudden dawn at midnight. A gas pipe, bringing the entire building to its feet. And the soot begins to fall.

In the silence, I am shouting. To the firemen. To Gil. To anyone who will listen. I have seen it, I am shouting: Richard Curry, opening the entrance to the service stairs, pulling Paul away.

Listen to me.

And at first, they do. Two firemen, hearing me, approach the building. A medic is beside me, trying to understand. *What stairs?* he asks. *Where do they come out?*

The tunnels, I tell him. *They come out near the tunnels.*

Then the smoke clears, and the hoses make sense of the club's face, and everything begins to change. There is less searching, less listening. There is nothing left, they are saying, in the slowness of their steps. There is no one inside this.

Paul is alive, I shout. *I saw him.*

But every second is a strike against him. Every minute is a fistful of sand. By the way Gil is looking at me now, I realize how much has changed.

"I'm okay," he says to the medic tending to his arm. He wipes a wet cheek, then points to me. "Help my friend."

The moon hangs over us like a watchful eye, and as I sit there, staring past the silent men who hose down the shattered clubhouse, I imagine Paul's voice. *Somehow*, he says, far away, staring at me over coffee, *I feel like he's my father too.* Over the black curtain of the sky I can see his face, so full of certainty that I believe him even now.

So what do you think? he is asking me.

About you going to Chicago?
About us *going to Chicago.*

Where we were taken that night, what questions were asked of us, I don't remember. The fire kept burning in front of me, and Paul's voice hummed in my ears, as though he might still rise from the flames. I saw a thousand faces before that sunrise, bearing messages of hope: friends roused from their rooms by the fire; professors awakened in their beds by the sound of sirens; the chapel service itself stopped in mid-reading by the spectacle of it all. And they gathered around us like a traveling treasury, each face a coin, as if it had been declared on high that we ought to suffer our losses by counting what remained. Maybe I knew then that it was a rich, rich poverty we were entering. What dark comedy the gods favored, who made this. My brother Paul, sacrificed on Easter. The tortoise shell of irony, dropped heavy on our heads.

That night the three of us survived, together, out of necessity. We met in the hospital, Gil and Charlie and I, bedfellows again. None of us spoke. Charlie fingered the crucifix around his neck, Gil slept, and I stared at the walls. Without news about Paul, we all invested ourselves in the myth of his survival, the myth of his resurrection. I should have known better than to believe there was anything indivisible about a friendship, any more than there was about a family. And yet the myth of it sustained me then. Then, and ever after.

Myth, I say. And never hope.

For the box of hope lay empty.

Chapter 29

Time, like a doctor, washed its hands of us. Before Charlie was even out of the hospital, we had become old news. Classmates stared at us as if we were out of context, fugitive memories with an aura of former significance.

Within a week, the cloud of violence over Princeton had burned off. Students began to walk across campus after dark again, first in groups, then alone. Unable to sleep, I would wander off to the WaWa in the middle of the night, only to find it full of people. Richard Curry lived on in their conversations. So did Paul. But gradually the names I knew disappeared, replaced by exams and varsity lacrosse games and the yearly spring talk, a senior who'd slept with her thesis advisor, the final episode of a favorite television show. Even the headlines I read while waiting in line at the register, the ones that kept my mind off being alone when everyone else seemed to be with friends, suggested that the world had moved forward without us. On the seventeenth day after Easter, the front page of the *Princeton Packet* announced that a plan for an underground parking lot in town had been nixed. Only at the bottom of page two was it reported that a wealthy alumnus had donated two million dollars toward the rebuilding of Ivy.

Charlie was out of his hospital bed in five days, but spent another two weeks in rehab. Doctors suggested cosmetic surgery on his chest, where patches of his skin had become thick and gristly, but Charlie refused. I visited him at the medical center every day but one. Charlie wanted me to bring him potato chips from the WaWa, books for his classes, scores from every Sixers game. He always gave me a reason to come back.

More than once he made a point of showing me his burns. At first I thought it was to prove something to himself, that he didn't feel disfigured, that he was much stronger than what had happened to him. Later I sensed that the opposite was true. He wanted to make sure I knew he *had* been changed by this. He seemed to fear that he'd stopped being a part of my life and Gil's at the moment he ran into the steam tunnels after Paul. We were getting along without him, mending our losses alone. He knew we'd begun to feel like strangers in our own skins, and he wanted us to know that he was in the same position, that we were all still in this together.

It surprised me that Gil visited him as much as he did. I was there for a few of the visits, and there was the same awkwardness every time. Both of them felt guilty in a way that was intensified by seeing the other. However irrational, Charlie felt that he'd abandoned us by not being at Ivy. At times, he even saw Paul's blood on his own hands, weighing Paul's death as the price of his own weakness. Gil seemed to feel that he himself had abandoned us long ago, in a way that was harder to express. That Charlie could feel so guilty, having done so much, only made Gil feel worse.

One night before he went to bed, Gil apologized to me. He said he wished he'd done things differently. We deserved better. From that night on, I never found him watching old movies. He took his meals at restaurants that seemed farther and farther from campus. Every time I invited him to lunch at my club, he found a reason not to come. It took four or five rejections for me to understand that it wasn't the company he objected to; it was the thought of seeing Ivy on the way there. When Charlie got out of the hospital, he and I were together breakfast, lunch, and dinner. More and more, Gil ate and drank alone.

Slowly our lives fell out of scrutiny. If we felt like pariahs at first, when everyone grew tired of hearing about us, then we felt like ghosts afterward, when everyone began to forget. The university's memorial service for Paul was held in the chapel, but could've fit in a small classroom for the tiny crowd it drew, hardly as many students as professors, and most of those just members of the EMT squad or of Ivy, showing up out of compassion for Charlie or Gil. The only faculty member who approached me after the service was Professor LaRoque, the woman who first sent Paul to see Taft—and even she seemed interested only in the *Hypnerotomachia*, in Paul's discovery rather than in Paul himself. I told her nothing, and made a point of doing the same every time the *Hypnerotomachia* came up after that. I thought it was the least I could do, not giv-

ing away to strangers the secret Paul had worked so hard
to keep between friends.

What briefly caused a resurgence of interest was the
discovery, a week after the headline about the underground parking lot, that Richard Curry had liquidated his
assets just before leaving New York for Princeton. He had
placed the money in a private trust, along with the resid-
ual properties of his auction house. When banks refused
to reveal the terms of the trust, Ivy asserted a right to the
money, as compensation for its damages. Only when the
club's board decided that not a stone of the new building
would be bought with Curry's money did the flap subside.
Meanwhile, papers flocked to the news that Richard
Curry had left all of his money to an unnamed trustee,
and a few even suggested what I already believed—that
the money was meant for Paul.

Knowing nothing of Paul's thesis, though, the greater
public could make little sense of Curry's intentions, so
they dug into his friendship with Taft until the two men
became a farce, an explanation for all evil that was no explanation at all. Taft's home at the Institute became a
ghost house. New Institute Fellows refused to live there,
and townie teenagers dared each other to break in.

The only benefit of the new climate, the one of fantastic theories and sensational headlines, was that it soon became impossible to suggest that Gil and Charlie and I had
done anything wrong at all. We weren't flamboyant
enough to play a role in what had happened, bizarre as
everyone thought it was, not when the local news could
fill its coverage with pictures of Rasputin Taft and the lunatic Curry who killed him. The police and the university

both acknowledged that they had no intention of pursuing any action against us, and I suppose it made a difference to our parents that we would graduate without disgrace. None of it mattered much to Gil, since that sort of thing never did, and I couldn't get around to giving much of a damn myself.

Still, I think it took a load off Charlie's mind. He lived increasingly in the shadow of what had happened. Gil called it a persecution complex, the way he expected misfortune at every turn, but I think Charlie had simply convinced himself that he could've saved Paul. Whatever it was, there was going to be a reckoning for his failures—if not at Princeton, then in the future. It wasn't so much persecution Charlie feared; it was judgment.

The only hint of pleasure in my final days of college came from Katie. At first she brought food to Gil and me, while Charlie was still in the hospital. In the wake of the fire, she and other Ivy sophomores had begun a co-op, buying their own food and making their own meals. Afraid that we weren't eating, she always cooked for three. Later, she would take me on walks, insisting that the sun had restorative powers, that there were traces of lithium in cosmic rays you could only catch at dawn. She even took pictures of us, as if she saw something in those days worth remembering. The photographer in her was convinced that the solution lay somehow in the right exposure to light.

Without Ivy in her life, Katie seemed even closer to what I wanted her to be, and even less like the side of Gil I never understood. Her spirits were always up, and her hair was always down. The night before graduation, she invited me back to her room after a movie, claiming she wanted me to say good-bye to her roommates. I knew she meant something else, but that night I told her I couldn't do it. There would be too many pictures of the certainties she carried with her, family and old friends and the dog at the foot of her bed in New Hampshire. A final night in a room surrounded by all her fixed stars would only remind me of how much my own life was in flux.

We watched in those final weeks as the investigation into the fire at Ivy drew to a close. At last, on the Friday before commencement, as though the announcement had been timed to give closure to the academic year, the local authorities acknowledged that Richard Curry, "in a way coincident with firsthand accounts, precipitated a fire within the Ivy Club, causing the death of both men inside the building." In support of this, they advanced two shards of a human jaw, which matched Curry's dental records. The explosion of the gas main had left little else.

Yet the investigation remained open and nothing specific was ever said of Paul. I knew why. Just three days after the explosion, an investigator had confessed to Gil that they held out hope of Paul's survival: the remains they'd found were merely scraps, and what few of them were identifiable were Curry's. For the following days, then, we waited hopefully for Paul's return. But when he never did return, never staggered from the woods or turned up in a familiar place, having forgotten himself for a time, the investigators seemed to realize it was better to be silent than to ply us with false hope.

Graduation came warm and green, without a whisper of wind, as though such a thing as Easter weekend could never have been. There was even a butterfly in the air, fluttering like a displaced emblem, as I sat in the yard of Nassau Hall, surrounded by classmates in our robes and tassels, waiting to be pronounced. Up there, in the tower, I imagined a bell tolling silently without a clapper: Paul, celebrating our fortune, just behind the creases of the world.

There were phantoms everywhere in that daylight. Women in evening gowns, from the Ivy ball, dancing in the sky like nativity angels, announcing a new season. Nude Olympians streaking in the courtyards, unashamed of their nakedness, in a specter of the season just past. The salutatorian quipped in Latin, jokes I didn't understand, and for an instant I imagined that it was Taft up there who addressed us; Taft, and behind him Francesco Colonna, and behind them a chorus of wizened philosophers who all delivered a solemn refrain, like drunken apostles singing the "Battle Hymn of the Republic."

The three of us returned to the room one last time after the ceremony. Charlie was heading back to Philadelphia for a summer of ambulance work before medical school in the fall. He had chosen the University of Pennsylvania, he told us finally, after wavering for so long. He wanted to stay near home. Gil was collecting the knickknacks from his bedroom with a touch of eagerness I half expected. He confessed to having a ticket out of New York that evening. Going to Europe for a while, he said. To Italy, of all places. He needed some time to figure things out.

We collected our last day's mail together, Charlie and I,

once Gil was gone. Inside the box were four small envelopes, identical in size. They contained registration slips
for the alumni directory, one to each of us. I placed mine
in my pocket, and took Paul's, as well, realizing he hadn't
been stricken from our class list. I wondered for a moment
if they'd drawn up a diploma for him, too, which now sat
somewhere uncollected. But on the fourth envelope, the
one addressed to Gil, his name had been crossed off, and
mine had been written in his hand. I opened it and read.
The form had been completed, with an address penned
out for a hotel in Italy. *Dear Tom,* it said, across the inside
lip of the envelope. *I left Paul's here for you. I thought you
would want it. Tell Charlie I'm sorry for leaving in a rush. I
know you understand. If in Italy, please call. —G.*

I hugged Charlie before we parted. A week later, he
called me at home to ask if I planned to attend our class
reunion the following year. It was the sort of pretext only
Charlie would invent for a phone call, and we spoke for
several hours. Finally, he asked if I would give him Gil's
address in Italy. He said he'd found a postcard Gil would
enjoy, which he tried to describe to me. I realized, under-
neath what he was saying, that Gil hadn't given him a for-
warding address. Things between them had never really
recovered.

I wasn't in Italy, that summer or afterward. Gil and I
met three times in the four years that followed, each time
at a class reunion. There was less and less to be said between us. The facts of his life gradually assembled with
the graceful preordination of words in a litany. He returned to Manhattan after all; like his father, he became a
banker. Unlike me, he seemed to age well. At twenty-six,
he announced his engagement to a beautiful woman one

year our junior, who reminded me of a star from an old movie. Seeing them together, I could no longer deny the pattern to Gil's life.

Charlie and I kept up much better. To be honest, he wouldn't let me go. He holds the distinction in my life of being the hardest-working friend I've ever had, the one who refuses to let a friendship fail just because the distance grows and the memories fade. In the first year of medical school, he married a woman who reminded me of his mother. Their first child, a daughter, was named after her. Their second child, a son, was named after me. A bachelor myself, I can judge Charlie as a father honestly, without worrying how I fare in comparison. The only way to do it justice is to say that Charlie is an even better father than friend. In the way he cares for his children there is a hint of the natural protectiveness, the world-beating energy, the enormous gratitude for the privilege of life, that he always showed at Princeton. Today he is a pediatrician, God's own doctor. His wife says that on certain weekends he still runs with the ambulance. I hope someday, as he still believes, Charlie Freeman will come before heaven at the hour of judgment. I've never known a better man.

What became of me, I'm hard-pressed to say. After graduation I returned to Columbus. Except for a single trip to New Hampshire, I spent all three months of my summer at home. Whether it was because my mother understood my loss even better than I did, or because she couldn't help feeling glad that Princeton was behind me—behind *us*—she opened up. We talked; she joked. We ate together, just the two of us. We sat on the old sledding hill, the one my sisters used to pull me up, and she told me what she'd been doing with herself. There were plans to open a second bookstore, this one in Cleveland. She explained the business model, the way she'd been running the ledgers, the possibility of selling the house now that it was going to be empty. I understood only the most important part, which was that she'd finally started moving on.

For me, though, the problem wasn't moving on. It was understanding. As the years have passed, the other uncertainties of my life have seemed to clarify themselves in a way my father's life never did. I can imagine what Richard Curry was thinking on that Easter weekend: that Paul was in the same position Curry himself had once been in, that it would be unbearable to let his orphan son become another Bill Stein or Vincent Taft, or even Richard Curry. My father's old friend believed in the gift of a clean slate, a blank check on an unlimited trust; it just took us too long to understand him. Even Paul, in the days when I still hoped for his survival, gave me reason to think he'd simply left us all behind, escaping through the tunnels without ever returning; the dean had left him with little hope of graduation, and I had left him with no hope of Chicago. When I'd asked him where he wanted to be, he'd told me honestly: in Rome, with a shovel. But I never reached the age when I could ask my father those sorts of questions, even if, in retrospect, he was probably the sort of man to give them an honest answer.

I suppose, then, looking back on it, that the only way I can explain why I became an English major after having lost my faith in books—why I had such a sense of possibility working on Colonna's book after rejecting my father's love of it—is that I was looking for those pieces I thought my father must have left me, the ones that could piece him back together. For as long as I knew Paul, for the duration of our research on the *Hypnerotomachia*, the answer almost seemed to be in my grasp. For as long as we worked together, there was always hope I might eventually understand.

When that hope fled, I honored my contract and became a software analyst. The job I got by solving a riddle, I took because I'd failed to solve another. Time in Texas passed more quickly than I can account for. The heat of summer there reminded me of nothing I'd known before, so I stayed. Katie and I wrote almost weekly during her last two years at Princeton, letters I began to wait for in the mail, even as they became less frequent. The last time I saw her was during a trip to New York to celebrate my twenty-sixth birthday. By the end of it, I think even Charlie could sense that time had come between Katie and me. As we walked through Prospect Park in the autumn sun, near the Brooklyn gallery where Katie worked, I began to understand that the things we once cherished had remained behind us at Princeton, and that the future had failed to replace them with a vision of things yet to come. Katie, I knew, had been hoping to begin something new that weekend, to chart a new course by a new set of stars. But the possibility of rebirth, which had buoyed my father for so long, and preserved his faith in his son, was an article of faith I'd slowly come to doubt. After that weekend, I began to fall out of Katie's life entirely. Shortly afterward, she called me at work for the last time. She knew the problem lay on my end of things, that mine were the letters that had become shorter and more distant. Her voice brought back an ache I hadn't expected.

She told me I wouldn't be hearing from her again until I figured out for myself where we stood. Finally, she gave me her number at a new gallery, and told me to call when things were different.

Things were never different. Not for me, anyway. It wasn't long before my mother's new bookstore prospered, and she called me back to run the one in Columbus. I told her it was too difficult to leave Texas, now that I had roots. My sisters visited me, and Charlie with his family once, each leaving with advice on how I could get myself out of this slump, how I could get past this, whatever it was. The truth is, I've just been watching things change around me. The faces are younger every year, but I see the same formulations in all of them, reissued like money, new priests in old denominations. I remember that in the economics class I took with Brooks, we were taught that a single dollar, circulated long enough, could buy everything in the world—as if commerce were a candle that could never burn itself out. But I see that same dollar now in every exchange. The goods it buys, I no longer need. Most days, they hardly seem like goods at all.

It was Paul who weathered time's passage the best. He always remained at my side, twenty-two and brilliant, like an incorruptible Dorian Gray. I believe it was when my engagement to an assistant professor at the University of Texas began to collapse—a woman who reminded me, I see now, of my father and mother and Katie all at once—that I took to calling Charlie every week, and thinking of Paul more and more. I wonder if he wasn't right to go out as he did. Striving. Young. While we, like Richard Curry, suffered the depredations of age, the disappointments of a promising youth. Death is the only escape from time, it seems to me now. Maybe Paul knew he was beating it all along: past, present, and any distinction in between. Even now, he seems to be leading me toward the most important conclusions of my life. I still consider him my closest friend.

Chapter 30

Maybe, then, I'd made my decision before I ever received this package in the mail. Maybe the package was only the accelerant, like the alcohol Parker spilled on the club floor that night. Not even thirty, and I feel like an old man. The eve of our fifth reunion, and fifty years seem to have gone by.

Imagine, Paul said to me once, that the present is simply a reflection of the future. Imagine that we spend our whole lives staring into a mirror with the future at our backs, seeing it only in the reflection of what is here and now. Some of us would begin to believe that we could see tomorrow better by turning around to look at it directly. But those who did, without even realizing it, would've lost the key to the perspective they once had. For the one thing they would never be able to see in it was themselves. By turning their backs on the mirror, they would become the one element of the future their eyes could never find.

At the time, I thought Paul was parroting wisdom he'd gotten from Taft, which Taft had stolen from some Greek philosopher, the idea that we spend our lives backing into the future. What I couldn't see, because I was turned the wrong way, was that Paul meant it for me, about me. For years I've been determined to get on with my life by doggedly hunting down the future. It was what everyone told me I should do, to forget the past, to look forward, and in the end I did it better than anyone might've expected. When I arrived, though, I began to imagine that I knew exactly what my father felt, that I could identify with the way things seemed to turn against him with no explanation.

The fact is, I don't know the first thing about it. I turn around now, toward the present, and find that I've had nothing like the disappointments he experienced. In a business I knew nothing about, which never captured my heart, I've done well for myself. My superiors marvel that, after being the last man out of the office for five years, I have never taken a single day off. Not knowing any better, they mistake it for devotion.

Seeing that now, and comparing it to the way my father never did anything he didn't love, I come to a certain understanding. I don't know him any better than I ever did, but I know something about the position I've taken all these years, turning to stare at the future. It's a blind way to face life, a stance that lets the world pass you by, just as you think you're coming to grips with it.

Tonight, long after leaving the office, I quit my job in Texas. I watched the sun go down over Austin, realizing it had never once snowed in all my time here, not in April, not even in midwinter. I've almost forgotten what it feels like to crawl into a bed so cold, you wished there was someone else in it. Texas is so hot, it helps you believe you're better off sleeping alone.

The package was waiting at my house when I came back from work today. A little brown mailing tube propped against my door, so unexpectedly light, I thought it might be empty. There was nothing on the outside but my house number and postal code, no return address, only a handwritten routing number in the left corner. I remembered a poster Charlie said he was sending me, an Eakins painting of a lone rower on the Schuylkill River. He'd been trying to convince me to move closer to Philadelphia, trying to convince me that it was the right city for a man like me. His son should see more of his godfather, he said. Charlie thought I was slipping away.

So I cracked the tube open, saving it for after the regular mail, the credit card offers and sweepstakes notifications and nothing that resembled a letter from Katie. In the glow of the television, the barrel seemed hollow, no poster from Charlie, no message. Only when I stuck my finger inside did I feel something thin curled around the circumference. One side of it felt glossy, the other side ragged. I pulled it out less gently than I should have, considering what it was.

Bottled inside the little package was an oil painting. I rolled it open, wondering for a second if Charlie had outdone himself and bought me an original. But when I saw the image on the canvas, I knew better. The style was much older than nineteenth-century American, much older than any century American. The subject was religious. It was European, from the first true age of painting.

It is difficult to explain the feeling of holding the past

in your hands. The smell of that canvas was stronger and more complex than anything in Texas, where even wine and money are young. There was a trace of the same smell at Princeton, possibly at Ivy, certainly in the oldest rooms of Nassau Hall. But the odor was much more concentrated here, in this tiny cylinder, the smell of age, hardy and thick.

The canvas was dark with grime, but slowly I made out the subject. In the background stood the statuary of ancient Egypt, obelisks and hieroglyphs and unfamiliar monuments. In the foreground was a single man, to whom others had come in submission. Seeing a hint of pigment, I looked more closely. The man's robe was painted with a brighter palette than the rest of the scene. In the dusty desert, it was radiant. This man before me, I hadn't thought of in years. It was Joseph, now a great official in Egypt, rewarded by the pharaoh for interpreting dreams. Joseph, revealing himself to his brothers who came to buy grain, the very brothers who left him for dead so many years before. Joseph, restored to his coat of many colors.

On the bases of the statuary had been painted three inscriptions. The first read: CRESCEBAT AUTEM COTIDIE FAMES IN OMNI TERRA APERUITQUE IOSEPH UNIVERSA HORREA. *There was famine all over the world. Then Joseph opened the granaries.* Then: FESTINAVITQUE QUIA COMMOTA FUERANT VISCERA EIUS SUPER FRATRE SUO ET ERUMPEBANT LACRIMAE ET INTROIENS CUBICULUM FLEVIT. *Joseph hurried out; so strong was the affection he felt for his brother that he wanted to cry.* On the base of the third statue was simply a printed signature. SANDRO DI MARIANO—better known by the nickname his older brother gave him: "little barrel,"

THE RULE of FOUR   443

or Botticelli. By the date below his name, the canvas was over five hundred years old.

I stared at it, this relic that only one other pair of hands had touched since the day it was sealed below ground. Beautiful in a way that no humanist could resist, with its pagan statuary that Savonarola could never abide. Here it was, nearly destroyed by age, but somehow still intact, still vibrant beneath the soot. Alive, after all this time.

I laid it on the table when my hands became too unsteady to hold it, and I reached into the tube again, looking for something I'd missed. A letter, a note, even just a symbol. But it was empty. The handwriting on the outside, spelling out my address with such care. But nothing else. Only postmarks and a routing code in the corner.

Then that routing code caught my eye: 39-055-210185-GEN4519. There was a pattern to it, like the logic of a riddle. It formed an exchange, a phone number overseas.

At the dark end of a bookshelf I found a volume someone had given me for Christmas years ago, an almanac, with its catalogs of temperatures and dates and zip codes, suddenly useful. Toward the back was a list of foreign prefixes.

39, the country code for Italy.

055, the area code for Florence.

I stared at the rest of the numbers, beginning to feel the return of my pulse, the old drumming in my ears. 21 01 85, a local phone number. GEN4519, possibly a room number, an extension. He was at a hotel, in an apartment.

There was famine all over the world. Then Joseph opened the granaries.

I looked back at the painting, then over at the mailing tube.

GEN4519.

Joseph hurried out; so strong was the affection he felt for his brother that he wanted to cry.

GEN4519. GEN45:19.

In the home I'd made, it was easier to find an almanac than a Bible. I had to rummage through old boxes in my attic before coming across the Bible that Charlie claimed to have left behind accidentally after his last visit. He thought he might be able to share his faith with me, the certainties that came with it. Indefatigable Charlie, hopeful to the end.

I have it now, in front of me. Genesis 45:19 comes at the conclusion of the story Botticelli painted. After revealing himself to his brothers, Joseph becomes a gift-giver, just like his father before him. After all he has suffered, he says he will take his brothers back, they who now starve in Canaan, and let them share in the bounty of his Egypt. And I, who have made the mistake most of my life of trying to leave my father behind me, of thinking I could move forward by keeping him in the past, I understand perfectly.

Get your father and come, the verse says. *Never mind about your property, for the best of all Egypt will be yours.*

I pick up the phone.

Get your father and come, I think, wondering how he understood, even when I didn't.

I put the phone back down and reach for my daybook, to copy the number before anything can happen to it. In those lonely pages, the new H of Paul Harris and the old M of Katie Marchand are the only two entries on the spread. It feels unnatural to add a name now, but I am fighting the sensation that all I have is this set of digits on the mailing tube, a single chance that could be erased by the simplest mistake, an opportunity that could bleed into nothing beneath a single drop of water.

There is sweat on my hands as I lift the receiver again, hardly aware of the time that has passed as I sat here, trying to think of the words to put to this. Out the bay window of my bedroom, in the glittering Texas night, I can see nothing but the sky.

Never mind about your property, for the best of all Egypt will be yours.

I refresh the dial tone and start pushing the buttons on the keypad. A number I never thought my fingers would form, a voice I never thought I'd hear again. There is a distant buzz, the ringing of a telephone in another time zone. Then, after the fourth ring, a voice.

You've reached Katie Marchand at Hudson Gallery, Manhattan. Please leave a message.

Then a beep.

"Katie," I say, into the hum of silence, "this is Tom. It's almost midnight here. Texas time."

The hush of the other end is haunting. It might have overwhelmed me, if I didn't know exactly what I wanted to say.

"I'm leaving Austin tomorrow morning. I'll be gone for a while; I'm not sure how long."

There is a photo of the two of us in a small frame on my desk. We're slightly off-center, both holding one side of the camera and pointing it toward ourselves. The campus chapel is behind us, stony and still, Princeton whispering in the background even now.

"When I get back from Florence," I tell her, the

sophomore in my picture, my accidental gift, just before the machine in New York cuts off, "I want to see you."

Then I place the receiver back in its cradle and stare out the window again. There will be bags to pack, travel agents to call, new pictures to take. Even as I begin to realize the magnitude of what I'm doing, a thought occurs to me. Somewhere in the city of rebirth, Paul is lifting himself out of bed, staring out his window, and waiting. There are pigeons cooing on rooftops, cathedral bells tolling from towers in the distance. We are sitting here, continents apart, the same way we always did: at the edges of our mattresses, together. On the ceilings where I am going there will be saints and gods and flights of angels. Everywhere I walk there will be reminders of all that time can't touch. My heart is a bird in a cage, ruffling its wings with the ache of expectation. In Italy, the sun is rising.

Authors' Note

The identity of the *Hypnerotomachia*'s author has remained uncertain for over five hundred years. In the absence of definitive proof favoring the Roman Francesco Colonna or his Venetian namesake, scholars have continued to grapple with the strange acrostic, "Poliam Frater Franciscus Columna Peramavit," sometimes citing it as evidence of the author's mysterious intent.

Girolamo Savonarola (1452–1498) was both respected and reviled by the citizens of Florence during his brief tenure as the city's religious leader. Though to some he remains a symbol of spiritual reform against the excesses of his time, to others he is known only as the destroyer of countless paintings, sculptures, and manuscripts in the bonfires for which he is best remembered.

As of the publication of *The Rule of Four*, no connection has been made between the *Hypnerotomachia* and Savonarola.

Richard Curry amends Browning's poem "Andrea del Sarto" to suit his needs, and Tom, remembering Curry's usage, does the same. Browning's original line is: "*I* do what many dream of, all their lives" (emphasis added). Tom and Paul sometimes refer to scholarly books, including those by Braudel and Hartt, by shorthand titles; and Paul, in his enthusiastic overview of Florence's history, indicates that Florentine artists and intellectuals spanning several centuries were living "at the same time." Tom takes the liberty of shortening the official name of Princeton Battlefield State Park to Princeton Battlefield Park, of attributing "Take the 'A' Train" to Duke Ellington instead of Billy Strayhorn, and of suggesting, in his first meeting with Katie, that the name of poet E.E. Cummings was intended to appear in lowercase, when Cummings himself (in this respect, at least) probably preferred conventional capitalization.

The authors take responsibility for other inventions and simplifications. The Nude Olympics traditionally began at midnight—not at sunset, as *The Rule of Four* suggests. Jonathan Edwards was indeed Princeton's third president, and died as described in this novel, but he did not initiate the Easter ceremonies described here, which are fully invented. Though the eating clubs on Prospect throw many formal events each year, the particular Ivy ball Tom attends is fictional. And the floor plan of the Ivy Club, like those of a few other locations mentioned, has been changed to suit the needs of the story.

Finally, time itself has taken a toll on some of the Princeton fixtures so familiar to Tom and his friends. Katie's sophomore class was the last to run naked in Holder Courtyard on the night of the first snowfall (though it did so in January, not in April): the university outlawed the Nude Olympics just before Tom's graduation in 1999. And Katie's beloved tree, the Mercer Oak that once stood in Princeton Battlefield State Park, collapsed on March 3, 2000, of natural causes. It can still be seen in the Walter Matthau movie *I.Q.*

In nearly all other respects, we have tried to remain as faithful as possible to the history of the Italian Renaissance and of Princeton. We are deeply indebted to those two great settings of the mind.

I.C. and D.T.

Acknowledgments

We owe many thanks. *The Rule of Four* was nearly six years in the making, and for two young men in their twenties it felt like a lifetime.

First to Jennifer Joel—überagent, friend, muse—who believed in us long before anyone else did; and to Susan Kamil, who loved us as her own, and toiled over the manuscript as feverishly as Tom and Paul would have.

Many thanks to the others without whom this wouldn't have been possible: Kate Elton, Margo Lipschultz, Nick Ellison, Alyssa Sheinmel, Barb Burg, Theresa Zoro, Pam Bernstein, Abby Koons, and Jennifer Cayea.

Ian would like to begin by thanking Jonathan Tze. The idea for Paul's thesis, from which much of this book sprang, is half his. At Princeton, thanks also go to Anthony Grafton, who suggested a research paper on the *Hypnerotomachia*; to Michael Sugrue, whose enthusiasm and encouragement were never in short supply; and, especially, to David Thurn, whose wisdom and friendship made all the difference. At Thomas Jefferson High School for Science and Technology, Mary O'Brien and Bettie Stegall gave literature and creative writing a voice in the wilderness. Joshua "Ned" Gunsher was an inspiration for Tom's clapper misadventure, and also helped to map out the Ivy Club of fact, before we reimagined it in fiction. For fifteen years, Davin Quinn's writerly companionship has been a comfort and a guiding light; with

Robert McInturff, Stewart Young, and Karen Palm, he formed part of the model for a book about friendship. Above all, my mother and father, my sister, Rachel, and my fiancée, Meredith, kept faith when hope seemed lost, not only these past six years, but every time I seemed to be a hopeless case. Their love makes even the joy of writing seem small.

For their editorial guidance and great friendship, Dusty would first like to thank Samuel Baum, Jose Llana, and Sam Shaw. Thanks go, too, to those who were there in as many different ways as there are names: Sabah Ashraf, Andy and Karen Barnett, Noel Bejarano, Marjorie Braman, Scott Brown, Sonesh Chainani, Dhruv Chopra, Elena DeCoste, Joe Geraci, Victor and Phyllis Grann, Katy Heiden, Stan Horowitz, the Joel family, David Kanuth, Clint Kisker, Richard Kromka, John Lester, Jon Locker, Tobias Nanda, Nathaniel Pastor, Mike Personick, Joe and Spencer Rascoff, Jeff Sahrbeck, Jessica Salins, Joanna Sletten, Nick Simonds, Jon Stein, Emily Stone, Larry Wasserman, and Adam Wolfsdorf. To my family, Hyacinth and Maxwell Rubin, Bob and Marge Thomason, Lois Rubin, and all the Thomasons, Blounts, Katzes, Cavanaghs, and Nassers, thank you for your unending support. Most of all, my love to James and Marcia Thomason, and Janet Thomason and Ron Feldman, for whom no words could be enough, and to Heather Jackie, for whom four letters are enough: BTPT.

Finally, we would both like to thank Olivier Delfosse, friend and photographer, who, for better or worse, came closer than anyone to being the third author of *The Rule of Four*.

About the Authors

IAN CALDWELL was Phi Beta Kappa in history at Princeton University. He lives in Newport News, Virginia. DUSTIN THOMASON won the Hoopes Prize at Harvard University. He lives in New York City. They began writing *The Rule of Four* after graduating in 1998. The two have been best friends since they were eight years old.